TWO RIP-ROARIN' WESTERNS BY T.V. OLSEN, WINNER OF THE GOLDEN SPUR AWARD! A $7.98 VALUE FOR ONLY $4.99!

McGIVERN

McGivern pivoted to face the oncoming Apaches. The light was bad, and he was shooting at a moving target. The .45 bucked against his palm, and he knew he'd missed as the Indian, untouched, released his shaft.

It made a close and hateful whir, struck an outcrop two feet from his head. For a split second McGivern saw that the arrow had been deflected at an angle—before it ripped sidelong through his hair and scalp.

This was the beginning of the showdown, the fight that would determine whether men like himself or gunrunners like Belden would be the law of the West.

THE HARD MEN

"Give me the rope," Soderstrom said.

Rafe's withered face altered with comprehension. "But, God, Mr. Soderstrom! This is plain-out murder. You'll get strung up yourself for it."

For answer Soderstrom jerked the noose tight around Sears's neck and tossed the free end of the rope up and over the cottonwood limb. He leaned on the rope and Sears began to gag and choke.

Soderstrom turned his head and saw that Rafe's face was dead white, and that he had his six-gun out and loosely pointed. Deliberately Soderstrom turned his back and gave the rope more pressure....

T.V.OLSEN

McGIVERN
&
THE HARD MEN

LEISURE BOOKS ◨ NEW YORK CITY

A LEISURE BOOK®

May 1994

Published by special arrangement with Golden West
Literary Agency.

Dorchester Publishing Co., Inc.
276 Fifth Avenue
New York, NY 10001

Printed in the United States of America.

McGIVERN

1

THE DOUHERTY WAGON lay on its side, blackened ribs already partly submerged in the loose sand whipped along by hot air currents from upcanyon. A dozen yards beyond lay the charred body of the stagecoach. McGivern swung down from his line-backed dun, walked stiff-legged to the coach, and stared at it for a measureless time. He turned away, squinted eyes scanning the ground. He hadn't supposed he'd find anything. The detail from Fort Laughlin had scoured the canyon thoroughly, and the wind would by now have obliterated all sign of the massacre. Even a trained scout would find nothing.

The high cliffs of red sandstone that walled the gorge caught the sunglare, shimmered part of it skyward in transparent waves, and reflected the rest, angrily beating it against McGivern's body. Mechanically he shucked off his coat—fine black broadcloth, splotched now with white alkali muddied by sweat stains—and fastened it behind his saddle.

He remained by his horse, one arm slung across the saddle swell, aware at last of the crushing exhaustion of these long hours of rocking in the saddle at a deadly pace with the contained thoughts of a madman. *So this is how it ends*, he thought detachedly. *Nothing*. Nothing but the mute token of the charred coach, a broadcloth wedding suit—a now-limp, now-grimy symbol of plans that would never materialize—and his tired mind trying to pull nightmare fragments of memory into some kind of meaning. . . .

Yesterday he had risen as usual in the bachelor's quarters behind his freight yard at Silver City. Only this morning was different . . . his last one in these lonely rooms. Today Ann was arriving on the noon stage. The new house he'd built on the edge of town was furnished and ready. The town hall had been engaged for the afternoon ceremony, with Parson Negley, circuit preacher, officiating, and all of McGivern's friends—teamsters, miners, and their families—turning out for a shivaree.

McGivern had bathed and shaved with extra care, put on his new suit and stepped out to his office. There he collided with the white-haired agent from the telegraph office. The old man was out of breath; wordlessly he handed McGivern the yellow sheet of paper that sent him on a dead run for the stables, throwing his hull on his best saddle mount and kicking the animal savagely into motion before he was securely in leather.

It was a mistake. No wedding joke could be this cruel, so it had to be a mistake. That was the frenzied conviction that kept churning in his mind through the long hours that followed, as he drove his exhausted sorrel along the western trail from Silver City. And knowing all the while, in the back of his mind, that Colonel Dudley C. Cahill, commandant at Fort Laughlin, didn't make that kind of mistake.

By late afternoon he'd reached the fort. The orderly had ushered him into the C. O.'s office, and Cahill had given him the whole story.

A band of young Chiricahua bucks, fired by two rebellious war chiefs, had broken off San Carlos Reservation a month ago and drifted south, cutting a two-hundred-mile swath of lightning raids, striking at widely isolated points. The route leading to Fort Laughlin from the east fell inside that swath. Within a single week, two stages on the Butterfield Overland line had been attacked—the teams driven off, the coaches overturned and burned, and the bodies of drivers and passengers riddled with arrows.

With this grim precedent as a warning, the stage which had rolled out for Fort Laughlin two days ago had joined forces with an Army paymaster's wagon heading in the same direction. The Douherty paywagon had been accompanied by a detail of ten mounted troopers, which should have been enough to discourage an attack. Yet when they entered Creagh Canyon, where the road wended between towering walls, the Apaches had struck.

"Yesterday," Colonel Cahill had told McGivern, "when the stage and the payroll detail were six hours overdue at the fort, I sent out a patrol under Lieutenant Kearny, accompanied by an ambulance wagon. When they returned this morning, it was with a wagonful of—bodies. There were no survivors. The troopers . . . the stage passengers . . . all . . ."

One of the bodies was that of a woman, still clutching a torn reticule. In it the colonel had found a letter from Tom McGivern of Silver City, addressed to Miss Ann Fulverton of Nealtown, Ohio. The colonel had at once dispatched a telegram to McGivern, whom he knew.

McGivern's memories after that were confused. There had been the brutal, necessary job of identification. He had seen the ugly aftermath of massacre before, but never in this personal, shocking manner. A quick lance thrust had killed Ann; he was thankful only for the swiftness of her death.

The next morning he threw his saddle on a borrowed Army mount and headed east for Creagh Canyon to view the scene for himself, with a vague hope that he could turn up something; he had no idea what.

Nor did he have any idea now, leaning on the dun's sweat-frothed flank in the oppressive heat, staring at the wrecks of stage and paywagon and the blank floor

7

of the canyon. Mostly the impulse that brought him here had been a need to move, to try to outride the crazy grief that left him numb and wondering.

A hot breath of wind launched stinging sand against his face, arousing him. He turned to mount and begin the long ride back to the fort. As he started to swing his left foot to stirrup, his toe struck something covered by an inch of earth. He stooped and brushed away the loose sand, down to a gleam of metal. He tugged and the object lifted easily.

A rifle. A shiny new '73 Winchester repeater. The Army didn't supply its men with such guns. It might have belonged to a stage passenger ... or else, the Apaches. . . .Swift anger touched McGivern as he turned the rifle in his hands. If the Chiricahuas had been armed with new Winchesters, it was little wonder they'd dared to attack a large party of whites.

The anger was biting and welcome, scouring into his apathy and grief. He shoved the rifle into his empty saddle boot, swung astride the dun and turned its head for Fort Laughlin. He was erect in the saddle now, his face set stonily.

2

COLONEL DUDLEY C. CAHILL signed the last of a batch of quartermaster's requisitions, threw down his pen with a grunt of relief, and called to his secretary-orderly. The corporal stepped in from the outer office, took the bundle of papers from the colonel's desk, tapped them neatly into alignment, and hesitated.

"Well, Haney?"

"McGivern just rode through the stockade gate. . . .I guess he's back, sir," the corporal ended feebly.

"Astute observation," the colonel said dryly. "Suppose you spend more time with your filing, less looking out the window. McGivern will be over directly. Show him in."

"Yes, sir." His sallow face flushed, the corporal retreated to the outer office.

The colonel sighed, stretched his arms, shoved back his swivel chair and walked to the window to stare across the parade grounds drowsing in the quiet of deepening dusk. A pair of troopers were gossiping apathetically on the sutler's porch. A hot breath of wind brushed up a spume of dust and passed on through the window to stir the colonel's thin white hair. He was a fleshy, dour-faced man with a cold cigar clamped in his bulldog jaws, a man who had spent most of his fifty-five years in the service, all of the sixteen since the end of the Civil War in the Army of the West.

A trickle of sweat coasted down his ribs beneath his faded blue blouse, and he cursed around his cigar. Damn this country. A man never stopped sweating. He smiled thinly, then. Arizona grew on a man—the same way Hell would, he supposed; yet he liked the land and its people—even the savage Apache foe he'd engaged so often. He liked it all, except for the scum who were a part of neither side, who plied their intrigues between Indian and white, stirring up every dormant tension . . . the territorial politicians, the treaty breakers . . . and the lower echelons of scum, the whiskey-and-gun runners.

God wither all their seed, the colonel thought wearily, feeling the deep-rutted futility of his position. He was Army, a mere link in a vast hierarchy of command. In his way, he felt the same boredom as the corporal. At times he wished he were a free agent who could smash the scum he had to protect, though it meant a continuation of their hate-mongering plots.

A free agent like Tom McGivern.

The colonel felt a twinge of guilt, thinking of the plan that had rooted in his mind after McGivern had left the fort yesterday. A man like McGivern would want revenge. The colonel meant to give that urge direction. Indirectly he would be taking advantage of McGivern's deep grief, better healed and forgotten as soon as possible. But the stakes were large, involving many lives.

He saw McGivern leave the stables now and slant across the parade grounds toward his office, drag-footed with weariness. Pity touched the colonel; he hoped wryly that he could keep the justification he had given himself topmost in his mind during the next fifteen minutes.

He walked back to his desk, sat, and leaned his elbows on the desk, steepling his fingers and staring morosely through them at the door. "Colonel Cahill is expecting you, Mr. McGivern," he heard the corporal say. McGivern tramped in, closed the inner office door, toed a chair out of the corner, swung it around facing the colonel's desk, and slacked into it. He leaned a rifle he was carrying against the desk. The colonel watched him a moment in silence, remembering what he knew of this man.

For six years, Tom McGivern had been Chief of Scouts at this fort. Before that, he had worked cows, bossed Texas trail herds until the railroad hand ended the drover days; then he prospected for gold around Tombstone, once performing the incredible feat of living alone for three months in hostile Apache country, matching his desertcraft against the wily Chiricahuas and Mescaleros while he panned and dug for gold, sometimes almost under their noses. Later he'd used this knowledge against them when he'd guided the troops that had rounded up roving bands of hostiles and reservation breakaways. To cap it, McGivern had once lived for a year with the Apaches at San Carlos, learning their language, and hashing over old exploits with the very warriors he had fought.

Three years ago he had taken the accumulated savings of his prospecting and Army pay and had bought a thriving freight business in Silver City. The colonel had heard little of him since then—until yesterday, when he'd found a letter on the body of an Apache-murdered woman . . . a girl who had come hundreds of miles to marry Tom McGivern. It was old friendship that had prompted the colonel to instant dispatch of a telegram to McGivern.

Looking at him now, the colonel saw a tall and rawhide-spare man, heavy through the chest and shoulders, his Indian-dark hair streaked with gray under a dust-colored Stetson, his white linen shirt patched with sweat and dust. McGivern's lean, leathery face was composed and sober, with brown-to-amber eyes weather-tracked at the outer corners by the slight squint of a man perpetually watchful. It was a face which—Indian-like—showing nothing. But the colonel

11

remembered that letter to Ann Fulverton, the careful, painful scrawl of a shy and lonely man. Even with his friends McGivern had always been reserved, but with her he had held back nothing.

Knowing it makes my job that much worse, the colonel thought, but he drew a deep breath and plunged, speaking quietly:

"Hate the 'Paches, Mac?"

McGivern was brooding at the floor, his long legs outstretched, his arms folded. The colonel wondered if he'd heard. Then McGivern looked up. "Hate a whole tribe, Dud? After living with them, knowing the best of them, knowing how they've been put upon by us whites?"

"Not even after—"

McGivern's head swung up angrily. "You know as well as me where the blame goes."

The colonel exhaled slowly, nodded. "Approximately." Here was a man. McGivern hadn't lost his cool perspective, even in his stunned grief.

McGivern reached down and picked up the Winchester repeater, hefting it in his big fist. "I found this in Creagh Canyon. Your men missed it. This is what I mean, Dud. Your Army regulation rifle is the .45-.70 Springfield. A good gun within its limits. Steel-barreled, deadly up to six hundred yards. But a single-shot." McGivern laid the Winchester on the desk, tapping it with his forefinger. "The War Department should have learned something from the Little Big Horn. Custer's men all had single-shot Springfields.... About five hundred of the Sioux had Winchester repeaters like this one. Lever action is so smooth you get off all fifteen loads in as many seconds."

McGivern's chair creaked as he let his bulk ease back again, his words slapping at the colonel like padded clubs. "Since we got to rob, cheat, push the Indian into fighting back, you'd think we'd at least arm the cavalry so they could make a decent show. And maybe...."

"Yes," the colonel said softly. "Maybe your girl would be alive. And those troopers. And a lot of people we'll

12

never know. But the question remains: exactly where do you set the blame?"

McGivern shrugged stonily. "You can't pinpoint it. These Winchesters are used everywhere by civilians. The Indians can pick them up from greasy-thumbed traders, massacred wagon trains, murdered settlers. . . ."

The colonel stood, circled the desk with his hands folded behind his back. "Maybe we *can* pinpoint this last atrocity, Mac."

McGivern looked up with a flicker of interest. He said nothing, just waited.

The colonel swung to face him. "From time to time there've been survivors of this late series of raids. They all agreed on one thing: this bunch—numbering between thirty and forty 'Paches—were all armed with repeating rifles."

"All?" McGivern echoed, alert now. "They didn't pick up that many rifles at random."

"Something else: the payroll chest was gone from the Douherty wagon. Why? White man's money means nothing to hostiles."

McGivern leaned forward with a scowl, lacing his hands around his knee. "You think they staged this last raid just to get the Army payroll?"

"To pay off the white men who supplied them with the guns. We," he laid an official emphasis on the word, "believe that someone has turned gun-running into big business."

McGivern was silent for a time. Then: "Tell me all you know about this band, Dud."

The colonel walked back to his desk, sank into his chair with a sigh. "Not much, I'm afraid. They're all younger bucks who grew up on the reservation and never tasted the warpath. Of course they were champing at the bit. It didn't take much for Maco and Nachito to strike the spark that made them break."

"Your patrols haven't run down anything?"

The colonel's lips twisted around the cigar. "Ever try chasing an eddy of dust? It flurries up, but the desert swallows it. We've found nothing. This bunch if well-

13

led." He eyed McGivern with a faint irony. "Maco's an old friend of yours, isn't he?"

McGivern shrugged. The enmity between the Apache war chief and the ex-scout went back a long way, to a time when McGivern had guided the troops that had rounded up Maco and some other hostile hot-bloods and returned them to the reservation. Soon Maco had broken out, and in retaliation had gone out of his way to kill McGivern's best friend, a prospecting partner. McGivern had offered his services free to the troops that had brought Maco to bay a second time. Coming to Fort Laughlin to capitulate, Maco had suddenly, in wild fury, attacked McGivern with a knife, and had been thrown in the post guardhouse for a month.

"This Nachito, though . . . I never heard of him."

"He's a bad one," the colonel said flatly. "Can't tell you much, except in years he's not much past twenty—but already a war chief with four years of experience as Geronimo's lieutenant behind him. That was in Sonora. I expect he came north to get a band of his own. Maco is crazy blind with hatred for all white-eyes, and Nachito must have played on that to get the weight of Maco's prestige among the San Carlos Apaches behind him. This Nachito is clever and dangerous—as you may find out."

McGivern's eyes veiled. "You think so?"

"It's in your mind to trace those gunrunners through the 'Paches, isn't it? You have my blessing. Unofficially, of course."

McGivern didn't reply, but his jaw had hardened. He came slowly to his feet. Watching him, the colonel knew another pang of regret. *Revenge is all he's got now,* he thought. *God forgive me if it destroys him.*

"Mac, you're dead on your feet. Go to my quarters and get some sleep. Make your plans later."

McGivern said tonelessly, "Not much to plan, Dud. When's the funeral?"

"It'll be a mass burial, early tomorrow," the colonel said awkwardly. "If you like—"

"No," McGivern said in the same toneless way. "The

post cemetary will be all right.I'll stay for the burial, then start back to Silver City. I want to wrap up my affairs—first."

The colonel stood at the window, watching McGivern's high, lean figure trudge toward officers' row. It would be a long and danger-geared trail for the ex-scout . . . yet McGivern was the man to take the wild land out there in his two hands and wring what he wanted out of it.

3

THREE MONTHS LATER McGivern rode into Saguaro, a ranch-center village two hundred miles west of San Carlos. He was thinned past gauntness now, worn to lean rawhide. He wore his old scout clothes—age-rusty cavalry pants with the yellow stripe down the outseam, a discolored buckskin jacket, and knee-length Apache moccasins with the stiff, upcurling toe. A curl-brimmed smoke-smudged hat that was pulled almost eyebrow level, and a two weeks' growth of neglected black beard, along with the alkali and dried sweat that stained his clothes, gave him a scrubby, raffish appearance. A holstered Colt, buckled over the jacket, sagged at his hip. The Winchester he'd found at the canyon massacre was in the saddle boot under his knee. His untiring quest had long since become ingrained into a cold, watchful pattern on his face.

He knew these things in a detached way, without caring. Jogging now through the residential end of Saguaro, a side street lined with flowered lawns, picket fences, and summer-smoldering rows of poplar, he was concerned only with a silent conviction that the search would end here.

Late afternoon shadows like gaunt fingers rippled

16

over horse and rider as they turned into the main street. In addition to its saloons and several stores, Saguaro boasted a feed company, a livery stable, a freighting yard, blacksmith and gun shops, and a couple of eating places. Shade trees of oak, ash and sycamore marched along the business district, relieving the usual drab and weathered monotony of a small range town.

McGivern's shuttling glance found and stopped on an aging frame building with the nearly weathered away legend ROOMS across its upper front. He turned in at the tie rail, dismounted, and tied his horse. He uncinched his blanket and saddlebags, lifted them to his shoulder, skirted the rail and tramped onto the narrow porch.

Two men loafed in chairs back-tilted against the building, their booted feet propped on a railing between the porch columns. McGivern halted. The bigger man glanced up at him, smiled disarmingly, and lowered his feet. The other man stared at McGivern without moving. He was young, lath-narrow, with a pinched face. His banjo eyes were reckless and hungry, waiting for trouble, wanting it.

"I don't like stepping over your legs, friend," McGivern said quietly.

"Walk around," the narrow man said, shifting a straw he was chewing to the corner of his thin lips. "There's a whole street to walk in."

"Maybe you better start walking," McGivern said.

The man came swiftly to his feet, hooking a thumb in his gunbelt. He flicked the straw back and forth with his tongue. "You're mouthy, mister. We don't like mouthy strangers."

McGivern felt his muscles pull up with the tension of a week on the trail, of months of obsessive purpose. *Tough, cocky gunslick*, he thought, and then, warningly: *Don't let him rawhide you; you can't afford a fight now.*

He glanced at the big man who was quietly watching this, a faint smile on his lips. He was a great-shouldered fellow with an imperial Roman profile crowned by a

17

tight cluster of golden curls. His eyes were gray and watchful, tolerant eyes that seemed to reserve judgment, with an amused and cynical twinkle in them.

"You know him?" McGivern asked the big man, nodding at the feisty one.

"Guilty," the big man said. He chuckled.

"You know better," McGivern went on thinly. "If the cub wants to cut my sign, tell him to cut it right."

The narrow youth began coldly, "Listen, you out-at-the-pants drifter—"

"Cinch up, Pride," the big man said sharply. "If you want to play with mud pies, there's a whole streetful of ingredients. Step away." Pride did not move; a slow flush darkened his face. "I said step away!"

Pride met McGivern's stare for a long hot moment, then moved back against the wall. McGivern walked by them without a backward glance, shouldered open and stepped through the double doors of the hotel. The lobby was not really cool, but it seemed so after the glaring street. McGivern paused inside, breathing deeply the aroma of frying steaks he could hear crackling in the kitchen. His belly knotted with hunger. He walked on to the desk and asked the young clerk for a room.

"And how long will you be staying, sir?"

"No telling." McGivern signed the register. "What time you serve supper?"

"Oh . . . in fifteen minutes. That'll be two dollars in advance. Room one-oh-four."

McGivern paid, received his key, and tramped up the staircase. He halted in the shadowy corridor at the head of the stairs as the lobby doors creaked open. He watched the two men from the porch come in and cross the lobby. The big man halted by the desk and spoke quietly to the clerk, who turned the register book around. The big man scanned it.

The ghost of a smile touched McGivern's lips. He pivoted on moccasined feet and faded down the corridor to his room.

* * *

"Thomas McGivern, Silver City," the big man read aloud from the register. "Mean anything to you, Charlie?"

The clerk yawned. "Sorry, Reggie; never laid eyes on him."

The big man nodded, turned, and walked back to the doorway, trailed by his companion. They stepped out onto the walk.

"How about you?"

"What?"

"Ever see him before?"

Pride scratched his head, scowling. "Naw. Heard that name somewheres . . . McGivern."

Reggie cuffed his battered hat back on his golden curls, frowning at McGivern's horse at the rail. "That's a McClellan saddle. And he was wearing cavalry pants. Doesn't walk or sit his horse like a soldier-boy; still. . . ."

"It could be trouble," Pride put in, his black eyes dancing hotly. "Want me to brace him?"

"No, you fool!" Reggie said sharply. "You'll tip our hand sure. . . ."

"Not if he's dead," Pride said gently.

Reggie gave him a contemptuous glance. "Don't bet on it. This one can handle himself."

"Why'd he back down?"

Reggie shook his head pityingly. "Fella, you never learn. This one's poison. I smell it. Have to feel him out careful, learn why he's here. Strangers with Army gear don't ride in every day, even every month. If his business isn't with us, no point in drawing his attention."

"So what do we do?" Pride ask querulously.

Reggie pulled his lower lip. "I'll see Belden, talk it over. You stay and watch the hotel. If he comes out, follow him. But don't start anything. Hear me, Pride?"

"Sure, sure," Pride said softly.

McGivern unlocked his door and entered. The room was a hot little cubbyhole stale with sealed-off air, furnished with a washstand, a battered dresser and an iron bedstead. He lowered his saddle and gear onto the bed, skirted it to reach the window. He wrestled the

19

warped sash up a couple of inches, letting the hot dusty air of the street wash through the room.

Voices drifted from the sidewalk below, then broke off. McGivern saw the big man move from under the porch awning and angle downstreet, walking fast. He turned into the freight office. McGivern moved back from the window, again smiling faintly. Five minutes in Saguaro, and he'd drawn lightning. He had no wish to keep his identify secret. Deliberately whetting their curiosity might provoke a giveaway move from the enemy, and he was steeled for the risk involved.

His smile faded as he stepped to the washstand, peeling off his jacket and calico shirt. It wasn't enough to be privately certain; he needed proof. For all he knew, he might have to fight the whole town. They couldn't be sure why he was here. While they were unsure, his life would probably not be imperiled. All the same, he decided warily that he'd watch his back if they had more like Pride on their payroll.

He poured water into the cracked basin and sponged off his lanky upper body. He toweled himself slowly, frowning out the window, unconsciously rubbing the long pale scar across his shoulder and upper back where Maco's knife had made its slashing try four years ago. He needed information about the town and its people; he would, he thought wryly, need to know whom he could trust, with no more than shrewd guess-work to go on.

Till now it had been a matter of dogged patience, of ferreting out and tracking down leads. Yet it had consumed time, precious time. Weeks, months of it.

At first he'd thought his best prospects would lay with the Apaches. He knew them and they knew him. After leaving the fort he'd headed back to Silver City and sold out his freighting outfit to one of his competitors. That part of his life was a closed chapter. He had built a position of civic responsibility, given up a life free as the wind because he'd cared for a woman more. Though the reason for that self-denial was gone, in his thoughts the old life was almost as tasteless.

The sale completed, he'd packed his meager belongings and headed north for San Carlos. But he'd found Apache friends with whom he'd drunk and joked strangely reticent, and he knew the tribal grapevine had gone ahead and the tribal ranks had closed against him. He was only another, *pinda-likoye* now, a hated enemy who wanted to learn matters which would hurt their brothers.

At first stymied, McGivern had realized finally that the solution was so close he'd missed it. Those rifles could only have reached this remote territory by wagon freighters—a business which he knew inside and out. He had written letters, enlisted the help of teamsters and freighter friends.

He'd learned that four hundred Winchesters and forty thousand rounds of .44-.40 ammunition had been shipped from New York by steamer to New Orleans, where they were held in the warehouse of a Frank Belden. This Belden had a brother, George, in Saguaro, Arizona, to whom he freighted supplies overland at cut rates which had enabled George Belden to monopolize the choicest freight contracts in the territory, with the mines, the Army, Indian traders, and cattle towns. And Saguaro, where George Belden made his headquarters, was only a hundred miles from San Carlos Reservation.

Four hundred rifles. Forty thousand shells. That was a lot of death in the wrong hands, McGivern thought soberly as he set out his soap and razor. Colonel Cahill had been right. This was a big thing, touching the lives of every Apache and white in the territory. At least a part of that shipment had already gone into the hands of Maco and Nachito and their band, and their successful maraudings had sent a wave of restiveness throughout Apacheland. Even at this late date, a new full-scale uprising could be in the offing.

How much of the gun shipment had already passed into Apache hands? This was the question that kept turning in McGivern's mind. Probably the arms were being shipped from New Orleans in gradual amounts, mixed with other freight to avert suspicion. If so, there was still a possibility of catching the gunrunners red-handed, and on this assumption McGivern must set his plans.

He shaved carefully, shrugged into a fairly clean shirt from his warbag, locked his room and went downstairs. He ate supper in the almost empty dining room, lingered over coffee and a cigar, then stood and went leisurely out through the lobby to the front porch.

Dusk was closing down over Saguaro, squares of oily light beginning to fill the windows. McGivern halted on the porch to relight his dead cigar, slowly turning out of a slight wind to face the row of lounging chairs. A single narrow figure slouched there; the matchlight washed against Pride's glinting eyes as he hunched forward a little, letting his feisty stare hit McGivern's.

McGivern snapped the match in his fingers and dropped it. He stepped off the porch and untied his horse. He led it downstreet to the livery stable and left orders for its feed and care with the hostler. Upstreet again, he turned in at the Belle Fourche Casino opposite the hotel. He paused by the swing doors to look back, and saw Pride stand and start across the street. *He'll be watching me tonight,* McGivern thought unconcernedly, and pushed on through the swing doors.

The Belle Fourche was good-sized for a small town. The wide, vaulted front room was overhung with a curling strata of cigar smoke and the smell of stale whisky. The long mahogany bar was well-crowded for a week night. At the back of the room was a wide archway spanned by beaded black curtains, and from beyond these came the rattle of roulette wheels and the murmurs of card players.

McGivern was about to move on to the bar when the broad shape of a woman pushed through the beaded curtains from the gambling room. She halted, hand still raised from parting the curtains, then waddled forward to meet him. "For God's sake—Tom McGivern!"

McGivern couldn't stop his own broad grin, stiff and unaccustomed as it felt. "Ma. Ma Gates."

Ma Gates never changed, McGivern thought, meeting her handclasp. She looked much as she had thirteen years ago when he, a callow, timid boy just off his first trail drive, had seen her in a bawdy house in Abilene. She wasn't fat, despite her thick girth balanced by her unusual height. There were a few more lines, maybe, around the shrewd, pale eyes—eyes wise and tired from viewing three generations of seamy frontier life, from the keelboat days of the Natchez Trace to the raw young Arizona mining towns, and the lines reminded McGivern that she must be past sixty now. Her full, high-necked black gown and lofty forehead under the red-dyed billow of her hair gave her an impressive look, like a kind of tribal sachem, which befitted the living legend she'd become throughout the West.

"For God's sake," Ma said again, still holding his hand as she glanced around. "There's a table, Mac; let's sit down. What's happened to you?"

They sat at a corner table, and Ma Gates signaled the bartender for a bottle of the house's best. "Nothing much," McGivern answered. "Still drifting." He noted that Pride had already bellied to the bar, glowering at him in the backbar mirror.

Ma leaned her thick arms on the table, facing him, her hard, shrewd eyes narrowed. "Don't lie to me, fella. You've changed. You always was a lad who seen a lot, but it never really got to you before."

McGivern's jaw hardened. He was about to speak when the bartender came with a tray bearing a bottle and two glasses. He poured their drinks and left.

"Forget it," Ma said then, brusquely. "Was curious, that's all. Always fancied you. You was never one of them sugar-mouthed hypocrites who sneaked into a cathouse the back way and otherwise crossed the street to avoid an honest chippie."

McGivern had to grin. "There was never any fooling you, Ma." He looked down at his glass, hardly believing his good luck at finding Ma Gates in Saguaro. She knew more about any place and its people than did the lifelong residents. McGivern hadn't seen her since the city fathers had hustled her and her girls out of Silver City three years ago. Always close-mouthed and no easy mark, she'd open up to one of the few people she fancied.

He glanced around at the Casino and its furnishings. "You're doing all right, it seems. But where's the old line?"

Ma chuckled. "I still hire girls. But only to sing, shill at the tables, talk with the lonesome drinkers. The West is gotten filled up, Mac, settled down. The towns've got banks, schools, churches, and citizens who are solid as all hell. Folks get pious soon as they can afford to be."

McGivern smiled. "And you too?"

Ma Gates shrugged. "Why not? I got to live. At that, even the Belle Fourche is only just tolerated since I took over. Lot of the community pillars remember Ma Gates from the old days." A glint of unpleasant humor touched her eyes. "I could point out a lot of dirty wash on *their* back lines, was I minded."

McGivern laughed. "I'll bet you could, too." He leaned forward. "Look, I wonder if you know—"

"Hell, I know you now."

The harsh voice cut into McGivern's quiet speech, and he looked up. Pride Bloom was coming from the bar toward their table, weaving a little. With a corner of his mind, McGivern had taken note of the three fast whiskies Pride had downed—enough to crowd the gunman to rashness.

Pride halted by their table, glaring down at him, "I 'member," he said. "McGivern. You was scout for Fort Laughlin. You got a friend of mine, Jack Hurdy, sent to the Federal pen."

"Have your drink, Mac," Ma said, not even glancing at Pride. "It's out of my private bottle."

McGivern lifted his glass, let the fiery liquor coast down his throat. It warmed his belly, set his nerves

24

tingling. *All right,* he thought resignedly, *it had to come.*

Pride was left flat-footed and ignored. He glared foolishly. "You listen damnit."

"I knew Mescal Jack," McGivern said steadily. "He was whisky-running to the 'Paches, and I caught him. Sneaking, yellow-backed half-breed. You say he's your friend?"

"Stan' up, you," Pride snarled.

"Look, you snot-nosed troublerouser," Ma began.

"Shut up, Fatty. I'm tellin' Buckskin, here, to stand up."

In dead silence McGivern scraped back his chair and came to his feet.

4

IN BUILD THEY WERE evenly matched. McGivern, usually heavier, had sloughed every ounce of excess weight in these last months, had pared down to sheer bone and muscle. Pride looked ganglier, almost awkward in his movements, but McGivern had noted on the hotel porch earlier that the man could move with a catlike grace if he chose. Nor did he believe that Pride was as drunk as he appeared; his eyes gleamed warily, unglazed. His elbow-rolled sleeves showed wiry, knotted forearms.

Ma stood now, backing from the table; at the same time Pride moved in, feinting at McGivern's midriff with his left hand, then throwing a straight arm at his face. It was a fast, neat combination; McGivern barely turned his head in time, then rolled back a pace with the blow so that Pride's fist glanced lightly off his cheekbone and spent its momentum in the lunge he couldn't stop. As he stumbled against the ex-scout, McGivern lifted his shoulder against Pride's chin with an impact that clicked his jaws together. McGivern whipped his right hand up and down, chopping the edge of his rock-hard lower palm against Pride's neck. He jerked Pride's gun from its holster and tossed it to a

26

bystander, then caught Pride by the neck and threw him roughly away. Pride was flung on his back across the table, which skittered away under his weight, crashing him to the floor.

McGivern stepped to the chair he'd just vacated and put his hands on its back, waiting. Pride came up on his hands and knees, shaking his head like a ringy bull. He came upright suddenly, legs driving against the floor, diving low at McGivern before he was fully on his feet. McGivern dropped the chair on its side and kicked it, shooting it in front of Pride's legs, which plunged between the rungs and tripped him. His face plowed against the splintery floor.

A riffle of laughter came from the tense bystanders, and McGivern guessed that more than one of them had been mauled by this bully-boy. But McGivern had received his own maulings at the hands of Apache bucks in reservation games, warriors trained from youth to every trick of rough-and-tumble wrestling. Twice he could have followed through and battered Pride senseless; cold patience checked him.

Pride climbed to his feet, slowly this time, drawing the back of his hand across his bleeding mouth and nose. He rushed, and McGivern met him with a savage impact, bringing up the heel of his hand in a vicious clout to Pride's chin. The gunman's head snapped back, but not before he'd wrapped his arm about McGivern's neck in a crude headlock. McGivern kept his body bent, away from the lift of knee or boot which Pride tried to bring up. His face mashed against Pride's rank-smelling shirt, he concentrated on throwing wicked, jolting punches to Pride's middle. The gunnie's ability to absorb punishment, yet hang doggedly to his hold, was impressive. He groaned with each pummeling blow, unable to crush McGivern's corded neck muscles with his armhold, but he wouldn't let go.

McGivern knew with a growing baffled anger that to free himself he'd have to reverse the headlock with a counterlock on Pride. He worked to wedge his hand in

27

from behind through the choking circle of Pride's arm, then brought it up at the back of the man's neck. He had his grip now—a half nelson that brought him behind Pride. Then he twisted savagely, breaking the necklock and whipping his free hand under Pride's opposite arm. He clamped both hands at the back of Pride's neck in a deadly full nelson with which he might easily break the man's neck.

Their struggling had carried them almost against the bar, which the customers had vacated for a wide space. The fighters were facing the bar now, and McGivern relentlessly bent Pride's head downward till his face almost touched his knees. Then he suddenly released Pride with a vicious shove. Pride stumbled once, bringing his head up to catch his balance, and the edge of the bar caught him full in the face with a sickening sound. His knees folded; he sagged against the bar and then toppled on his back, his bleeding face turned up.

McGivern stood above him, breathing gustily. The flurry of talk lifted excitedly around him, and as swiftly hushed when the batwing doors creaked open. The big blond man he'd seen earlier with Pride stood there. He advanced into the room, watching McGivern curiously. Halting by Pride, he prodded the motionless form with a speculative toe, then turned his sleepy gaze back on McGivern.

"Get Pride out of here, Reggie," Ma Gates said sharply. "And tell Belden he'll be gettin' a bill for damages . . . Call it moral damage," she added with vindictive satisfaction.

"All right," Reggie said without glancing at her. He smiled with no censure at McGivern. "I know he bought that, but I think you broke his nose."

"I meant to," McGivern said gently.

Reggie's eyes narrowed; his grin stayed neutral. "Don't get snakey, friend. No sweat of mine." On the floor, Pride groaned. Reggie bent and hauled him effortlessly to his feet, saying, "Come on, you damned fool."

He started toward the door, supporting Pride, and halted there as a man came in, confronting them. "What happened, Harlan?"

Reggie jerked his head over his shoulder at McGivern, said curtly, "Ask him," and pushed on past, the swing doors closing behind him.

The newcomer was McGivern's age. His stocky body was clad in a spotless white shirt and black trousers stuffed in high-polished jackboots. A flat-crowned black Stetson rode his sandy hair without crease or flourish. A sheriff's star shone on his neatly-buttoned black vest. His long face had a no-nonsense, businesslike set that went with his suit, but somehow McGivern wasn't impressed.

He surveyed McGivern coldly. "Did you hit him?"

"As hard as I could."

Ma chuckled. The sheriff looked at her, the distaste deepening in his face. "I've warned you about trouble, Mrs. Gates."

"Come off your high horse with me, Pauly-boy," Ma said dryly.

The sheriff flushed as though her words, her tone, had touched a raw nerve. "I'm trying to do my duty," he said stiffly. "You make it difficult."

"Duty's a high-soundin' word," Ma said imperturbably, "but that ain't what makes you tick, sonny. It used to be booze, now it's Belden."

Somebody laughed. The sheriff swung his glare at the man, then at McGivern. "We don't need your kind in Saguaro, saddle bum."

"You want to move me?" McGivern asked softly.

The sheriff dropped his hand to his gun, but that was all. There was a general hoot of laughter from the crowd. His face burning, the lawman turned on his heel and walked out.

Ma touched McGivern's arm. "Let's sit, Mac. Where was we?"

McGivern righted their table and chairs, and when they were seated he said: "We were talking about people. Like your sheriff."

29

Ma snorted disgustedly. "Paul Hornbeck. He was the town drunk before George Belden decided he needed a sheriff who'd burp every time George swallowed. He took Paul out of the gutter, dressed him up, paid for his campaign, and bullied and barbecued a majority of the voters in his favor. Nobody wants trouble with Belden. Paul took it serious, straightened up, quit the bottle, settled down to work. That means lettin' Belden's bullies, like Pride Bloom, raise all hell, while soft-pedaling complaints anyone has about George Belden and his business ethics. Paul ain't bad, just gutless. Feel kind of sorry for the pompous ninny. . . ."

"This Belden. He the power in Saguaro?"

Ma eyed him thoughtfully. "Paul maybe gave you some good advice, Mac."

"About moving on?"

"You beat up Belden's testiest bully. Belden owns the freight company, half the stores, the hotel, the stable, two of the three saloons. I've kept the Belle Fourche going only because I know how to give better entertainment than any of his places, though he's had his barkeeps cut liquor prices, even operate at a loss, to try and break me." Ma's wise old eyes narrowed. "Belden's a new kind of crook, Mac; he operates behind the sanction of the respectable element. The banker, the merchants, the town council, all know Saguaro is dependent on his business enterprises, and they'll close their eyes to a lot. Like when a rival freight yard tries to start, only to have their teamsters shot up, their wagons burned—by 'unknown' riders. Like when Belden's tough nuts insult their wives and daughters on the streets—"

"The big fellow," McGivern interrupted. "Reggie. Who's he?"

"Reggie Harlan. Sort of a right-hand trouble-shooter for Belden. Does all the legwork. His front is managin' Belden's Chain Anchor spread—ten miles west of town. It used to be a fine ranch till Belden came to Saguaro two years ago and bought it. Rumor has it he was one of that New York Tweed Ring. He talks and acts Eastern, an' he's got plenty of crooked political and business savvy. Anyways, he's made the Chain Anchor over into a general headquarters for all his activities. It's a big spread, with no one around for miles to get in his way. He runs a few cattle for a blind, but there's not an honest puncher on the place. His whole crew of tough nuts and hired guns hang out there, with Reggie Harlan to keep 'em in line."

"You figure I'm in trouble with this crowd already?" McGivern murmured.

Ma Gates grinned shrewdly. "Depends," she said, "on why you're here. You was settled down in Silver City with a payin' freight business, last I seen you. Your stomping days were over. But here you are, a ragtag-an'-bobtail drifter miles from home. You'd be here for a reason—and the reason just might concern George Belden, as he's the only thing hereabouts big enough to bother with. Aside from the fact that Pride Bloom is a grudge-holdin' skunk and you'd best sport an extra eye in the back of your head, George'll just naturally stomp you if he finds you in his way."

McGivern smiled at her perception, but said lazily, "Maybe I came out of my way to see an old friend."

"Hell, I saw your face when you saw me. You was surprised." Ma swung her hefty bulk up from the chair. "I got to check on the gamblin' room. Don't go away; I'll be back. I'll send you company, meantime."

"Don't bother," McGivern said quickly, but Ma was already moving back to the gambling room at her heavy, rolling walk. A minute later a girl came through the beaded curtains and over to McGivern's table.

"May I sit down?" Her voice was low, musical.

He didn't want to talk to this or any girl, pleasant as she might be, but it was Ma's gesture for old time's sake, he knew. He only nodded, yet an impulse made him stand quickly as the girl drew the chair out and wait till she was seated.

She regarded him intently, curiously, and he returned

31

the look. She was tall, willow slim, with clear gray eyes widely set in a slimly molded face. Her hair was arranged in a high coif that caught the tawdry lampglow as a blaze of white gold. She was young and strikingly attractive, this alone setting her apart from the usual percentage girl. But it wasn't that which prompted his curiosity. An indefinable air of well-bred dignity touched her voice, her carriage and movements. Even the knee-length gown that bared her arms and shoulders was simple, unspangled, ungarish, though of a rich material.

"Are you a friend of Mrs. Gates, Mr. McGivern?" she asked. He noted now the crisp New England accent of her words—affected-sounding to the Western ear, but somehow admirable with the low, pleasing modulation of her voice.

"Yes'm. Will you have a drink?"

"No, thank you. They call me Georgette."

He glanced up, startled. "That's—" He bit the sentence off, wondering what had prompted it. Few things should surprise him any more.

She nodded calmly, but a faint brittleness edged her words. "Yes, it is a bawd's name. Not my real one, of course, but still not inappropriate. There are many ways of prostituting one's self."

McGivern felt his face burn. He couldn't reconcile the well-bred, quiet restraint of this girl's manner with her unconcerned candor, nor was he certain of the meaning of her enigmatic words. "I didn't mean—"

"It hardly matters. However, I happen to be a singer. The Silver Thrush of the Belle Fourche. Mrs. Gates has tempered the otherwise tawdry title by playing up what she calls my natural 'class' ... the idea being that the customers get a forbidden thrill out of watching and hearing a lady-apparent with high-toned airs singing inelegant ballads. If these airs puzzle you, consider them part of the act. I deliberately project 'class'—or its illusion. Often there's little difference, don't you think?"

He stirred uncomfortably. "I wouldn't know."

32

She eyed him with measuring candor. "You don't look as though you'd know, either. Especially after I saw you rough up that man. But why did Mrs. Gates ask me to sit with you? Why not one of the other girls? Rough-looking customers are quite uneasy with me—while they appreciate me when they're part of a mob."

The brittleness had mounted in her voice, and he felt an inward stir of protest. "I liked your voice before."

"Has it changed?" She sounded startled.

"It has. It's cold, harsh."

Her clear eyes took a fresh measure of him. "You notice things, don't you?"

"That's my business. Or was. Army scout."

She smiled suddenly, erasing the bitter harshness that had settled around her mouth. "I've seen Army scouts before. But none that—"

"I beg your pardon."

The man spoke stiffly, quietly; McGivern was surprised and mildly annoyed that talking to this girl had relaxed his usual alertness to where he hadn't seen the man approach.

"Good evening, Clyde," the girl said. "Mr. McGivern, this is Mr. Prentiss."

Prentiss extended a soft hand, murmured something, and looked back at the girl. He was about thirty, balding, not over five and a half feet in height. He wore a cheap, neat suit of dark material and his celluloid collar dug high and stiff against his chin. There was something prim and cloistered about him, like any bookish clerk who had worked a lifetime for bigger men and endured a thousand small indignities without complaint.

"Would you care to go for a ride after I finish work tomorrow afternoon, Julia?" Prentiss asked. He glanced nervously over his shoulder, plainly ill at ease in this smoke-filled din of drink and gambling.

"Yes, of course, Clyde," she said, faint irritation in her words. At the man's prissiness, McGivern guessed; he almost smiled at the incongruity of such a man courting a casino girl, and idly wondered about that.

33

McGivern looked at the girl and was about to speak when Ma Gates bustled back. "All right, honey, back to your stand."

The girl stood, saying quietly, "Perhaps you'll come to hear me sing soon, Mr. McGivern. I can't promise you'll like the fare—"

"He'll like it, honey," Ma Gates said sharply, waving a plump hand in dismissal.

McGivern had stood when the girl rose to leave; as she turned back into the gambling hall, he sat down, facing Ma, who leaned her heavy, black-clad arms on the table. "You like Georgette?"

He nodded.

"Figured you would. I remembered how you like 'em—quiet and smart. She's different from the other girls. Reads books, poetry, toney magazines."

"Who's Clyde Prentiss?"

Ma's thin lips twitched. "Bookkeeper over at Belden's Freight Company. Maybe her and him's got something in common, at that. Georgette's real name is Julia Lanphere, and she's from Boston. One of them Beacon Hill swells. Something happened to her back East. Dunno what, and I never asked." Ma showed her thin old harridan's grin. "You could take her away from that mouse, was you minded."

"I'm not."

Ma Gates' snort was eloquent. "Look, this is an old Ma you're talking to—remember?"

"I ran out of wild oats a long time ago, Ma."

"The hell. What are you now—thirty-four, five?" She paused, her wise eyes thoughtful. "You *have* changed, Mac. It shows around your eyes and mouth. It's sort of mean."

"I'll see you tomorrow, Ma," McGivern said quietly. He stood, clamped on his hat, and walked out.

On the boardwalk he paused, breathing the fragrant darkness, mentally checking what he'd learned. George Belden was his man, no doubt of that. He was aware now of a marrow-deep tiredness, and he started across

34

to the hotel. Tomorrow he'd begin the tough job of marshaling evidence, and sleeping on his plans had always been a help. He wondered if Pride's choosing him out had been arranged, and he decided not; still, he'd better move carefully. . . .

5

THE MORNING SUN had already touched the clap-
boarded fronts of Saguaro's main street from a mellow
softness to a brassy glare as Reggie Harlan turned onto
the street and headed down toward the freighting yard
at its south end. As he drew abreast of the little
millinery store, Reggie glanced at Melissa Belden's rig
pulled up in front. He had seen her leaving Chain
Anchor earlier and now he idly wondered at her frequent trips to town. The ranch cook brought out all the
supplies they needed, and Lissa already had enough
clothes to outfit a regiment of dowagers. Likely it was
boredom that drove her to town, if only to make a few
trivial purchases.

Still looking toward the shop, Reggie saw Melissa
come out, swinging a hatbox in her hand. Beside her
walked Sheriff Paul Hornbeck, carrying two more boxes.
Lissa was handsome as always in a gray riding habit, a
pert straw hat on the shining auburn coils of her hair,
but her face, usually cold and withdrawn as a pale
cameo, was faintly flushed as she smiled up at Hornbeck.
Both of them saw Reggie then, and Melissa's smile
vanished. Harlan lifted his hat, an ironic grin on his
wide lips. Hornbeck quickly dropped the purchases in

36

the buckboard, touched his hat to Lissa and walked away.

Reggie rode on, whistling under his breath. Belden's spendthrift wife and Belden's ex-drunk of a sheriff. He almost laughed aloud, wondering if the Old Man knew about this. It looked innocent enough, nothing you could pin down; but Lissa had never blushed, never smiled, for any man, her husband included, in the three years Reggie had worked for Belden.

Harlan's thoughts veered as he passed the hotel veranda and saw a tall, spare man slacked in one of the chairs, watching the currents of life along the main street. So McGivern hadn't ridden on; he was staying over, and the possibilities this suggested were disturbing. Reggie gave the man a neutral nod as he passed, and McGivern nodded back impassively.

Belden's Freighting Company was at street's end. A narrow frame building fronted the street, with the company's name painted across its weathered upper front. A high board fence with an arched entrance began here and ran on for many yards, enclosing the building and off to the right the big wagon yard with its labyrinth of barns and sheds and corrals. Reggie rode through the archway and tied his horse at the rail just off the drive. He mounted the steps leading to the front office.

Halting in the doorway, a fresh amusement deepened in his face as he saw Clyde Prentiss at his high desk and stool. Prentiss was in his shirtsleeves, his narrow shoulders hunched over his ledgers.

"Hello, Clyde," Reggie said loudly. "How's the girl friend?"

Prentiss looked up, quick dislike pinching his face. Since the prim bookkeeper had started to court a honkytonk girl, Reggie's occasional baitings had become a daily ritual. "Quite well, thank you."

Reggie winked slyly. "Always wondered how she was. Damned if I thought you'd find out, though."

Prentiss' thin fist knotted around his pen and he flushed with anger, but his eyes fell from Reggie's

37

hard, merry gaze. Harlan laughed, clapped him on the shoulder, said lazily, "Attaboy, Clyde, up and at 'em," and walked to the inner office. Beyond this was a short hallway with another door at the end, and from here he walked unannounced into Belden's office.

The inner office was a shabby cubbyhole with a high, grubby window facing the street and another opening on the back lot. The only furniture besides the battered iron filing cabinet in one corner was a roll-top desk with a swivel chair, and a straight-backed visitor's chair. The swivel chair creaked dangerously as its occupant ponderously turned to face the door.

George Belden was a gross tub of a man who must have scaled over three hundred pounds of immense trunk set on short, stocky legs. The best tailor could not have altered his baggy black suit to fit his grotesque form. His keglike thighs almost split his trousers. His belt vanished in his belly under a shocking expanse of yellow-and-green-checked waistcoat. His features were incongruously small and delicate in his egg-bald head with its gray fringing of hair. He might once have been handsome in a cold, incisive way before his lower face became swallowed in its bulging wattles.

"Good morning, Reggie," he wheezed, "and close the window before you sit down. The draft stimulates my arthritis."

He wouldn't breathe if he didn't have me to blow his nose, Reggie thought, stepping to the window and slamming down the sash. He toed the visitor's chair around and sank into it, cuffing his hat back on his head. He took a straw from his pocket and chewed it, thoughtfully eyeing Belden.

"Saw your wife this morning."

Belden cocked a brow over one fish-cold eye. "At the ranch, of course."

"There, and in town. Your boozehead sheriff was carrying her packages."

"Ha ha ha," Belden said. He didn't laugh; he said it. Belden never laughed. "If fair Lissa and pious Paul find mutual pleasure in a tête-à-tête, why not? Swine

38

who are contended to rut are less likely to gore the stykeeper. And I keep a full sty, don't you agree, Reginald?"

Reggie stared at the fat man through half-veiled eyes, silently hating him. George Belden, he had long since discovered, had no emotional direction at all except his ruthless ambition, toward which all legitimate or crooked activities were aimed. Even Reggie, with his own comfortably slack ethics, caviled at this contemptuous, ice-like indifference to humanity.

Reggie Harlan, scion of one of New York's oldest families, had been kicked out of a half-dozen excellent schools for as many raw escapades, until his father had disowned him completely. Afterward he'd drifted slowly West, going from drinking and wenching to stealing, gun brawls, and worse. He had no regrets, because he had no more ambition at thirty than he'd had at twenty. He did have an intense and energetic love of life, and luxuriated in his small and large vices; whereas Belden was dominated by single-minded greed that ruled out everything else.

"Consider," Belden murmured now. "Lissa's assets of beauty and background will someday be useful to a man who is going places, perhaps to the governor's chair. I can't afford to have her run off because of discontent."

"She might just," Reggie said softly, "run off with Hornbeck."

"Ha ha ha," Belden said, his wattles shaking. "Lissa's first love is the clothes, money, and luxury which *I* provide. Hornbeck, that worm? The only thing holding him from the bottle is a slender thread of respectability—which *I* gave him. Let them have their rosy little affair." He switched subjects without changing the reedy tonelessness of his voice. "Nachito is to make contact with the ranch today. Why aren't you out there?"

"I came to find out if the last shipment of guns came in this morning. Our deal with the 'Paches is for two hundred rifles, like before."

Belden scowled. "The wagons haven't arrived yet,

and they were due yesterday. It's a long overland haul; they could have gotten tied up at a river crossing, stalled in mud, anything. We have one hundred and fifty rifles and fifteen thousand rounds ready for Nachito. Can't you promise him the rest?"

Harlan smiled thinly. "Look, I've done all our business with that Apache; you ain't met him. He's a businessman and politician in a breechclout. He has to dicker through us, but that don't mean he trusts us farther'n a grasshopper can spit."

"Wise redskin," Belden wheezed sarcastically. "You'll tell him to come again in a week, exactly."

Reggie nodded and started to rise, then hesitated. "That McGivern's still around. Saw him as I rode in."

Belden shifted his elephantine bulk, and the chair shrieked. "You really think he's dangerous?"

"You saw Pride last night after McGivern finished with him," Reggie said flatly. "Pride's dumb, but he's a tough customer. McGivern wasn't even marked."

Belden nodded broodingly. "Then, Pride did tell us McGivern was a scout at Fort Laughlin—when he caught that whisky-running pal of Pride's. But that was six years ago. Still, it wouldn't hurt to check on McGivern's movements. Send two of the men in to see me when you get back to the ranch. They'll tail him."

Reggie smiled sardonically. He'd noted McGivern's watchfulness; the man wouldn't be fooled. But this was the best that could be done. "Don't reckon you want me to send Pride?"

"Of course not," Belden snapped. "Keep that hothead out at the ranch from now on. After the way he jumped McGivern, contrary to your orders. . . ."

"I can give him his walking papers."

"No." Belden pursed his thin lips. "Once free of our outfit, the fool would likely brace McGivern. There must be no trouble till we're sure of McGivern—who he is, his purpose here. If he *is* working for the Army, as you surmised, his death would fasten suspicion on us for certain. If it has to come to that, we'll remove him carefully . . ." He paused, steepling his pudgy fingers.

"Maybe you'd better tell Nachito to come back in three days. Those rifles are the only proof of our activity, and the sooner we get them off our hands the better . . . with McGivern around. The rest of the arms should be here then. Meanwhile, have a guard posted over the guns we have. Post it day and night."

"All right."

Belden nodded dismissal and Reggie rose and tramped out thoughtfully. He went through the inner office so preoccupied he forgot to bait Clyde in passing. Pausing at the outer office door, he leaned against the jamb and built one of the Mexican cigarettes he favored, letting his gaze move absently over the wagon yard.

Abruptly his hands stilled around the makings; his eyes snapped to focus on the tall form of McGivern. The man was conversing with one of the teamsters over by the corral. As Reggie watched, they shook hands, then McGivern turned and walked back to the archway to leave.

Reggie took a step backward, cutting him from McGivern's view. When he'd looked out cautiously and seen that McGivern was gone, he leisurely finished shaping his twirly and went down the steps. He crossed the wagon yard to the teamster, who had a wagon up on blocks with the wheels off and was greasing the hubs. He said, "Morning, Lafe."

Lafe Elberg returned the greeting and straightened from his job with a grin, wiping his hands on a rag. He was a tough banty of a man whose face was sun-boiled a darker red than his flame-colored whiskers.

"That this McGivern fellow you were talking to?" Harlan asked idly. "The one who massacred Pride?"

Lafe's was the grin of a born brawler. "That's him. I used to work for him."

"Oh?" Reggie casually bent his head, cupped his hands to light his cigarette. "Doesn't look much like a freighting man."

"Hell, yes; got a big outfit in Silver City."

Face expressionless, Reggie waved the match out. "And he wanted to talk over old times?"

41

"Oh, he ast some questions ... you know, shop talk."

"About the goods we freight, markets, routes, stuff like that, eh?"

Reggie felt a nudge of surprise when Lafe answered, "Nope. Wanted to know about the men working here, said he might be expanding business and be needin' more teamsters. Our bunch is nothing but the best, and I told him so."

Harlan smiled. "Hope we won't be losing you, Lafe."

"Not a chance; Mr. Belden pays the most and treats you the best."

Always provided you keep on his side, Reggie thought dryly. He switched the subject, exchanged a few moments of small talk with Lafe, then said good-bye and walked back to his horse. He mounted and turned the animal, riding as far as the archway.

Here Harlan halted, glancing up and down the street, his attention sharp. Exactly what McGivern had been digging for mystified him, but he felt uneasily sure that the man's questioning of Lafe had been no idle whim.

In a moment he saw McGivern ride from the livery barn a block down and turn his horse west from town. When McGivern had swung out of sight, Reggie nudged his mount forward, his face grim. McGivern was taking the wagon road that connected Chain Anchor with town. Any stable boy could have told him the way to Belden's ranch ... but what, if McGivern knew, had triggered his certainty?

6

HE'D BEEN LUCKY, McGivern reflected as he jogged his sorrel past the last house. His first reaction at the sight of Belden's sprawling wagon yard had been a fatalistic despair. The guns could be cached anywhere in that maze of sheds. Then he had spotted Lafe, a former man of his, and a few questions had convinced him there were no illegal caches in the yard. The men who worked Belden's Freighting Company were rough, bluff, and honest, like Lafe himself. McGivern hadn't risked further querying, but he knew that gunrunners would not store hundreds of rifles under the noses of honest men. The Winchester '73's were in big demand, distributed for sale as fast as they were freighted into an area, and large numbers in storage would certainly smell amiss; the gunrunner was a breed despised and hated everywhere.

It was only logical that once the guns had reached Saguaro they had passed into the care of those who would see them safely into the eager hands of Apache renegades. Ma Gates had said that Belden's big ranch ten miles east of town was his real headquarters, stocked with toughs and gunnies, and it was only good sense to carry on liaison with the Apaches from an isolated ranch rather than from town. The guns could be taken to the ranch a few at a time, concealed in the usual ranch supplies.

McGivern knew that it could prove more difficult to locate a rifle cache there than at the freight yard; a stranger might be shot on sight, and no one the wiser. For now, he just wanted to size up the layout of Chain Anchor. Then he would lay his plans. He gave brief thought to Reggie Harlan, whom he'd noticed watching him from the office as he spoke to Lafe; Harlan had ducked back, but not fast enough. He would question Lafe, of course, and Lafe could only tell him that McGivern was a Silver City freighter looking for men. That would baffle Harlan and his boss still more, McGivern thought with satisfaction.

As he rode, McGivern's preoccupation did not dull his alert senses. Small things—the twirling trail of a rattler which had crossed the road an hour ago, the wagon ruts and Harlan's horsetracks that had been made since, the distant speck of a vulture hovering on static wings over something below, the thud of his mount's hoofs in the heavy dust of the road, betraying the time since the last rain—these were catalogued in the back of his mind and analyzed meaningfully. The terrain was not flat. The road took its way over humpy dunes, skirted lava outcrops. Because his vision was limited here, McGivern's other senses sharpened.

A single sound at his back, a sound not coupled with ordinary desert noises, made him pull up sharply. He slid from his saddle with a fluid twist of his body, Indian-fashion. He knelt and laid his ear to the road. He knew then that a rider was deliberately pacing him at perhaps a hundred yards' distance. He was being followed.

He led his sorrel off the road, circling a broad, flat-topped outcrop split by a great crevice. He guided his horse into the crevice, then took a running jump and landed lightly atop it. He lowered himself on his belly and took off his hat. From here he had an unin-

terrupted view of the road, though few white men could
have detected his hiding place or where he'd left the
road.

He was able to pick out the man's approach long
before he rode into sight over a rise. It was Reggie
Harlan. *Followed me, all right,* McGivern thought with
a silent token of respect: Harlan had had his number
from the start, and after speaking to Lafe, he had an
inkling of what McGivern had in mind.

When the big man had passed out of view beyond a
dune, McGivern slid off the rock. He mounted and
reined the sorrel around; he could not follow the road to
Chain Anchor now. Harlan, forewarned, would see
that he didn't get within a half mile of the place by
road. That meant he'd have to circle wide and come
up from the north or south. It would take time, with
his ignorance of this rugged terrain, McGivern knew
resignedly. But he had to assess the ranch layout by
daylight before he could lay a definite plan. . . .

He began a broad swing to the north. After a half
hour of steady traveling, the land ironed out and flattened away to the north and east. He carefully gauged
the illusive, heat-dancing distances. The ranch was ten
miles east of town, and he'd come a good two miles from
town before leaving the road. He would head due east
for eight miles, then turn south to hit the ranch.

The land held its flat, hard-baked appearance as he
ate up the remaining miles, with the sun hot against
his right side, then swung south by instinct. Ahead
now a sandstone-and-shale hogback ridge gleamed
crimson. He slowed, frowning. The ridge was a good
hundred feet high, with steep walls insurmountable by
a horseman, and it cut directly across his path for
miles, as far as he could see. Then he made out where a
canyon deeply scored the rimrock, as though a giant
wedge had been driven from top to base. Coming nearer, he cut sign on wheel ruts leading into the canyon
mouth. That meant that the V-cleft made a handy
route which pierced to the hogback's opposite side. The

tracks had been made by a heavily weighted vehicle; he considered that thoughtfully.

He put his horse directly into the canyon—and halted almost at once. He dismounted, eyes fixed on horsetracks tramped into the soft, sandy floor. They were fresh, yet not cleanly etched. He stooped and touched them, feeling a cold sensation along his spine. These tracks had been made only a few minutes ago—by a horse neither barefoot nor iron-shod. The hoofs had been bound up in thin, tough hides; and he knew that only Chiricahua Apaches muffled their ponies' hoofs with deerhide stockings.

He mounted and made his way cautiously up the canyon. A heavy rubble of shale chunks, dislodged from above, littered the floor. McGivern couldn't keep his sorrel's hoofs from clipping an occasional rock with small tinny ehcoes that made him wince. If the Apache rider were only minutes ahead, he'd surely pick up the sound.

McGivern's eyes were ceaselessly ferreting out the trail, and just short of a sharp bend in the canyon ahead he saw a change in the Apache pony's steady lope. The rider had briefly halted and then the tracks continued, deep-dug and hurried. *Stopped when he heard my horse, then he kicked it up,* McGivern thought. He spurred his own animal, but came to an abrupt halt before he reached the narrow-angled turn. The pony's imprints continued, but the sudden lessening of weight was perceptible.

He left his horse, but it kept going, McGivern thought in brief puzzlement. Where had the man gone? Then he understood. Crowded against the inner turn was a lava buttress about head high to a standing man. The Apache had quirted his pony hard, at the same time springing from its back onto the buttress. There was the faint scraping of loose stone atop the buttress, where he'd landed on his feet. Then he'd proceeded to scale the almost vertical wall like a cat, taking advantage of every hold. Now he was out of sight somewhere high on the talus just beyond the turn, balled in a crouch on one of the protruding shale ledges that laced the upper gorge.

McGivern considered these things in the flash of a second—and also that the Apache thought he had to deal with a sense-dulled white-eyes. Nor would a white man look for an enemy high on these walls—unless he knew that conditioning to dizzy heights was part of the Apache puberty-ritual test. This one's agility proved his youth.

McGivern soundlessly released a held breath. The sharp-eared brave would be suspicious of his sudden halt . . . he kicked his animal into motion and swerved around the turn, his eyes instantly whipping up to scan the rugged cliffside. Yet it came swiftly, instantly, before he had even a glimpse of his enemy.

An arrow breathed past his ear. He flung himself from the saddle, a second arrow grazing his jacket even as he leaped off. He rolled to break his fall on the soft earth, and was for a moment sheltered by the sorrel's body. He scrambled up, made a short crouching run that carried him back to the lava buttress. He dived behind its cover as a third shaft drove into the rock a foot above his back. The quartz tip, splintering, pock-marked his jacket.

He drew his pistol and edged his face around the buttress till he could see the whole wall. Then he saw the blued tip of a rifle barrel nudged over the rim of a shale ledge tilting a good twenty feet above the gorge floor. It had been a matter of pride with the buck to strike first at a lone white man with primitive bow and arrows; these had failed.

McGivern deliberately exposed his shoulder and arm, extending his pistol at arm's length as he fired. Chips flew from the ledge. Suddenly the Apache sprang to his feet, teased into view by his enemy's exposure; he threw his rifle to his shoulder and fired as quick as thought, then immediately dropped prone again.

McGivern felt the slug fan his temple; he yelled and fell backward, out of sight. He rolled on his belly, his gun drawn up by his head and ready. Face pressed to

47

the hot sand, he waited. He heard the Apache's eager descent of the talus, his moccasins clattering down a few shale fragments. With a thud the Indian landed lithely on the sand. He paced slowly forward, warily circling the buttress into McGivern's field of vision. McGivern watched through slitted lids. The Apache was holding the rifle steady, to finish the white man at a twitch of movement.

McGivern's movement was no more than the upflick of his fist that held the cocked .45; he fired point blank from the ground. The Apache's rifle thundered in his hands, but it was pure reflex. The bullet ricocheted down-canyon. McGivern's heavy slug spun him like a rag doll and hammered him in a twisting fall.

McGivern got to his feet and tramped to the fallen man, the .45 still pointed. He placed his foot on the naked shoulder and shoved, turning the youth on his back. The rifle rolled from his limp hands. McGivern stooped and picked it up. The Winchester repeater was still new, but it had seen use. The stock was scratched, the barrel rubbed with vegetable matter to dull the glint.

For a long moment McGivern looked down at the Apache. He was unconscious, his breathing hoarse; blood welled a fiery pattern across the coppery torso from a hole high on the left side. He wasn't over twenty-one, clean-limbed as a young stallion. His was not the usual flat, broad Apache face; it was aquiline and boyish, spanned by a broad band of vermilion paint, with stripes of blue above and below. He wore only a breechclout, a warband to confine his straight black hair, and hip-length moccasins folded down at the knees.

A real old-time broncho Apache, McGivern thought grimly. His hand tightened on the still-leveled pistol. *Why not?* The Winchester was like a cold, hard indictment against his palm. This buck might have been at Creagh Canyon that day . . . *he might have done it.*

The thought beat against McGivern's brain like an angry pulse. His finger made a beginning pressure on the trigger, and as slowly relaxed. This was only a boy, wounded and helpless; the finer sensibilities of a civilized upbringing held his hand. It was the folly and stupid greed of white men that had set off the massacre; the Apaches were fighting for existence itself. Finally there was the cold practical knowledge that this buck had been heading for Chain Anchor, probably a lone agent to arrange for the next liaison of guns. McGivern knew well that force, or its threat, would get nothing out of an Apache; still, an Apache might be wiled out of valuable information by one who knew his language and his people.

With this settled in his mind, McGivern's actions became swift and decisive. He dug a none-too-clean spare shirt from his saddlebag and tore it into strips. He knelt by the unconscious boy and raised him to a sitting position against his knee, finding that the bullet had ranged between his short ribs and gone clear through. Both wounds were bleeding cleanly. McGivern fashioned a makeshift wraparound bandage.

Afterward he walked downcanyon till he found the Indian pony grazing in a grassy pocket. It caught the white man's smell, flattened its ears and sidled away. McGivern spoke a few guttural Apache words, and the pony—evidently a favorite of its brave—became motionless, and he picked up the trailing reins. Leading it back, he hoisted the body of its master onto it and with his lariat tied the boy's feet together beneath the pony's barrel. Mounting the sorrel, he led the pony to the canyon mouth. There he dismounted and went back on foot to erase the signs of the struggle, systematically brushing out tracks back to the canyon mouth.

Mounted again, he struck eastward, hugging the base of the ridge, where air currents would shift the sands and erase their trail. He restlessly scanned the crumbling, broken surface of the cliff till he located a thirty-foot-high ledge, almost inaccessible. He swung stiffly down, ground-haltered the horses and picked out his route from the ground. Then he began to climb, moccasined toeholds bringing him swiftly to the ledge.

Past its rim he saw a shallow cave eroded into the cliffs. This was ideal; it would provide both shade and concealment.

Packing up the brave's limp weight was the hardest part; the third ascent, with saddlebags slung from his shoulder, was easy, but he was exhausted when he rolled onto the ledge. He lay on his back sucking deep breaths, drenched with sweat. Then he crawled on hands and knees into the cave, and knelt by the brave where he had stretched him on his side. He unbound the blood-stiffened bandages and washed the wounds with water from his canteen. They had almost ceased bleeding, and the Apache's rugged constitution would finish the cure. The buck would not travel for a while, though; and he was still unconscious, evidently in shock.

McGivern made a compress and a fresh bandage. Then, as he lifted his canteen to drink, the Apache suddenly spoke. "The first arrow was badly feathered, or you would be dead, white-eyed son of a coyote."

He lowered the canteen, seeing the black eyes glinting with mockery in the gloom. How had the buck known that his captor understood Apache? Then he realized that the boy had spoken only to convey a cold comtempt by his tone. Yet he was surprised; it was the way of an Apache prisoner to remain sullenly taciturn.

McGivern answered then, speaking casually: "Did your blind grandmother feather it, boy?"

Only a faint flicker of eyelids betrayed the buck's surprise. Then: "How is it that a white-eyes speaks the tongue of the *Shis-in-day* like one born to it?"

"I have lived at San Carlos. Also I guided the pony soldiers against the *Be-don-ko-he* and the *Ned-ni.*"

"I am *Be-don-ko-he*—what you *pinda-likoye* call 'Cherry-cows.'"

McGivern nodded soberly. "They are brave fighters, greatly led."

The youth grunted. "You know our chiefs?"

"At San Carlos I drank *tulapai* with Cochise."

50

The youth's lips twisted faintly. "Cochise is a sick old man. His belly is sour with the white man's whisky."

"I led troops against Tana."

"What are you called?"

"McGivern."

"Ma-giv-urn. It is sour in my mouth. Your mouth is full of lies, I think." He stared bitterly at McGivern. "I am the grandson of Tana. Yours is not a name celebrated in our clan."

"Then try the name of Day-zen on your tongue, *ish-kay-nay;* it will taste truer."

The youth's eyes widened now; he raised his head, winced, and sank back against the saddle-blanket pallet. The Chiricahua warriors had long ago dubbed McGivern *dazen,* the Apache word for mule, because of his stubborn tenacity which had tracked down more than one war party. It was a name feared and respected, yet rarely spoken of with hatred, by the Apaches.

"How is the grandson of Tana called?"

"Gian-nah-tah."

They talked freely then, the Indian's bitter contempt evaporated before the white man all Apaches knew was not as other *pinda-likoye* . . . an honored enemy in war, a fair-dealing friend in peace. After the last outbreak of hostilities, McGivern's recent reception at San Carlos has been cold, but this youth, whose garrulity with an enemy proved his free-wheeling ways, seemed unaware of the boycott. He spoke of old battles recounted by the elders, in which McGivern had figured prominently; he mentioned warriors McGivern had met in peace and war.

McGivern did notice that Gian-nah-tah carefully veered from speaking of himself or his exploits, yet Apaches were notorious boasters. Nor did he make mention of Maco or his famous feud with the scout; and so McGivern was sure that Gian-nah-tah was one of the band dually led by Maco and Nachito. The Chiricahua was wary of betraying military secrets to a known enemy. McGivern wanted information, but he knew better than to press for it directly.

51

He was mulling over this as Gian-nah-tah asked suddenly: "Why did you spare my life? Has the heart of Day-zen turned to water?" He spat sideways. "Perhaps you have become a woman."

"I sprang, like Gian-nah-tah, from a woman's parts. Maybe it is that part, in me, that finds no warrior's honor in slaying the helpless."

Instead of the expected sneer, he saw a puzzled frown knit the Apache's forehead. "I understand—yet do not understand. When I see my brothers maiming and torturing small animals; when I see them drive white-hot king bolts into screaming white men as Maco—" Gian-nah-tah broke off at the slip of the tongue. "When I see these things," he went on slowly, "I feel a shame to which I cannot give a name, of my sire and his, and all my brothers. I do not mutilate, I do not torture. Once the others laughed, and their eyes said 'coward.' They do not laugh now," he finished grimly, as though he had said too much.

"Then we are alike," McGivern said quietly, and was silent, knowing men lost such a feeling by speaking too much of it. Gian-nah-tah said nothing, but his eyes held on McGivern's face with probing curiosity.

"I go now." McGivern pulled his cramped knees to a crouch. "I leave this." He indicated the canteen and a folded oilcloth containing a little jerked beef.

"And when you return?" Gian-nah-tah asked softly.

"When you are well, I take you to a white man's fort."

"I will be gone from here before another sun," Gian-nah-tah said matter-of-factly.

"You will not ride for a quarter of a moon. The wound will open and kill you."

A glint touched Gian-nah-tah's eyes, though he did not smile. "If we were at San Carlos, I would wager my best pony."

"Perhaps we will drink *tulapai* there."

"No." The calm matter-of-factness again. "If I return to San Carlos, it will be in death."

McGivern slung the saddlebags from his shoulder,

crawled from the cave and stood erect on the outer ledge. He was surprised to see the far westering of the sun crowning the desert rim with rose-gold. The day's happenings had seemed crowded into a small time. He would not be seeing Belden's ranch by daylight now, he reflected coldly, and time might be running out. Tomorrow, then. Meanwhile he felt drained to exhaustion, and ravenously hungry. There was food and a bed in Saguaro.

You're getting old, McGivern, he thought sourly, *or soft in more ways than one.*

7

IT WAS FULL DARK when McGivern reached Saguaro. After turning the sorrel in at the livery, he headed for the hotel to clean up. Two men were sitting on the front steps, their cigarettes glowing cherry-red. Their low talk broke off as he stepped onto the porch. Their heads turned to follow him, light from a lobby window crossing their faces. One was dark, narrow-shouldered, and sallow-faced; the other was chunky and straw-haired, with eyes like dirty ice. Both wore filthy denims and both returned McGivern's regard with tough, cynical stares.

McGivern tramped on past into the lobby, knowing they'd been waiting for him. *I'll be watched from here on,* he thought, and bleakly accepted that and let his mind run ahead of it. He went up to his room and washed, then slapped most of the dust from his clothes. Afterward, since it was past the hotel supper hour, he left for the Cattlemen's Cafe downstreet. He didn't have to glance back to know that the two men were following him.

The Cattlemen's was a spacious eatery with linen-covered tables, and looked clean enough. A few late patrons were still eating. McGivern took a corner table where he could watch the room. A harried-looking waitress took his order—a double helping of beef stew, apple pie, and a pot of coffee—then went to wait on the two toughs who'd taken a table near the door. The straw-haired one raised his wicked gaze. "Forget it, sister," he said flatly. The girl backed off, eyes wide, and hurried to the kitchen.

McGivern sat back to wait for his food, letting his gaze slowly travel the room. His eyes halted on a bald, enormously fat man in a loud waistcoat who appeared to be finishing off a whole roast chicken by himself. The fat man glanced over at the two toughs, then at McGivern—with open curiosity. His eyes were slate-colored, the coldest McGivern had ever seen.

When the girl brought his food, McGivern attacked it hungrily, ignoring the toughs and the fat man. He finished his pie leisurely, poured a third cup of coffee and lighted a cigar. The door opened and Reggie Harlan came in. He went directly to the fat man's table and leaned toward him, talking in a low voice. The fat man cut him off with a word, nodding toward McGivern. Harlan turned in his chair, faint humor in his eyes as they met McGivern's. The fat one would be George Belden, McGivern now realized.

Harlan rose and came over to McGivern's table. "Pleasant ride, sport?" There was a pale malice in his eyes. "Like the country, do you?"

McGivern tapped cigar ash into a saucer. "It's not bad," he said idly. "I'd have to see more."

Reggie grinned derisively. "I'll bet."

"Those two clowns belong to you?"

Reggie's grin didn't alter. "If they do?"

"Pull them off," McGivern said softly. "I'm telling you."

"Free country, a man rides where he likes. Them as well as you."

"I wonder," McGivern murmured, "if they'd push over as easy as Pride."

"Pride jumped you, friend," Reggie said amiably. "You could have got the sheriff to serve a warrant and had Pride's heels cooling in the lock-up. Kruger and Mills ain't bothered you. Now you bother *them*—" He paused meaningfully. "Well, it's a nice, tight lock-up, friend."

"A nice tight frame-up."

"You said it, not me." Reggie chuckled. "See you in church, sport." He went back to Belden's table.

McGivern sat scowling at his empty plate, his cigar going cold between his fingers while his mind raced furiously over his dilemma. Reggie had plainly inferred that wherever he rode, the two gunnies would not be far away. If he chose them out, they'd have the sheriff pick him up. Even if he left the hotel by the back way and got his horse, the desk clerk and the livery hostler were both in Belden's pay. His tired mind picked at the problem confusedly. Maybe a drink would help; he stood, dropped a half-dollar on the table and walked out. Kruger and Mills were less than a dozen paces behind as he went through the batwings of the Belle Fourche. A girl was singing in a clear soprano, and the men at the tables and bar were silent, their attention on her.

Pushing through the crowd, McGivern saw Georgette, nee Julia Lanphere, sitting on the far end of the bar, legs crossed and hand on her hip as she sang. McGivern ordered a drink, with Belden's toughs bellying up a yard away. The customers were respectfully silent and rapt as Georgette gave sweet, staid renditions of "Annie Laurie" and "Sweet Afton." Without changing the inflection or mood of her style, she launched into a bawdy trail-herders' ballad. She did not belt it out as you expected a casino singer to, and the men broke their silence with a roar of laughter.

A hand touched his arm. "Something, ain't she, Mac?"

"Evening, Ma. The clientele thinks so," McGivern said dryly.

Ma Gates' vast bosom stirred with her chuckle. "Honest to God, you ought to run for chairman of a civic busybody league. Your blood's gone deader'n flat beer."

"Age creeping up."

"My stars, don't I know it." Ma sighed. "But you . . . old?"

"Matter of fact," he smiled, "I was wondering if your singer would like more conversation with a beat-up old scout."

"Sounds more like McGivern," Ma grunted. "Sit yourself. I'll have her come to the table. All right?"

"Fine," he said absently. His mind was ticking now; Georgette might be able to help him unknowingly.

He ordered another drink and carried it to a table. Ma Gates moved over to speak to the girl; she nodded, giving McGivern a smile of recognition. She finished her song to wild applause and yells of "More, Georgie, more," and shook her head in cool refusal. A grinning cowboy swung her to the floor.

McGivern was on his feet holding a chair for her, and she slipped into it with a murmured, "Thank you." He took his seat opposite her, offered to buy a drink, which she declined, and cudgeled his brain for an amenity. He said uncomfortably that he'd liked her first songs.

"Thank you again."

"Even if you didn't like it much . . . up there."

Her candid eyes searched his face. "I've had cowhands pour out their troubles to me when they've drunk themselves past shyness. Then tell me I don't belong here . . . offer to take me away from all this. You are the first to notice how *I* felt, what I thought."

"That's true most anywhere." He shrugged. "Civilization hasn't got to the stage where men care what women feel—or they once did and have since stopped caring. Some of the tribes . . . the Cheyenne . . . admit women to council, value their advice."

Pleased surprise touched her face. "You think about these things. Now I am curious. Do you like to read?"

"Winter's the time when I read, when things slow down. No poetry or tea-time stuff, I'm afraid."

"But you have read seriously."

"When you spend a lot of time on the desert, alone, you think a lot. You want to learn more." He shifted with discomfort. This talk was as personal as he'd ever gotten with any woman . . . and he wasn't here for that. "Maybe you'd like to talk it over tomorrow morning. We could go riding. Though I haven't a buggy," he added, remembering Clyde Prentiss.

There was pleasure in her face, and a humorous understanding. "Why, I have riding clothes—and haven't had a chance to wear them."

"Tomorrow morning, then . . ." He let his voice trail, turning his head. Clyde Prentiss had just come in and was moving toward their table. He nodded to McGivern, a hint of displeasure on his sharp pale features.

"The usual ride tomorrow, Julia?" Prentiss asked curtly.

Her response was cool. "If I'm back in time. Mr. McGivern has asked me to ride with him; we're starting early."

"I see," Prentiss said primly, a flush mounting from his high collar. "Try not to be late, Julia." He turned without waiting for a reply, and stalked out.

She looked at McGivern, who said nothing. She colored slightly. "You're thinking that Clyde takes me for granted."

"Something like that."

She fingered a bracelet on her wrist, looking at it musingly. "Clyde and I come of the same background, though of different classes. Out here class doesn't matter." She looked up half-angrily, half-defensively. "If you can find three men in this town who've read five good books, have taste and at least occasional manners. . . ."

"I wasn't judging," McGivern said quietly. "Just thinking. My privilege. Yours too."

The stiffness relaxed from her face; she laughed, a little sharply. "At least you don't pretend you're not thinking."

He only nodded and stood up. "Tomorrow morning. I'll bring your horse here. About seven?"

"About nine," she said dryly. "I'm a late worker. At that, it will be early. Good night, Mr. McGivern."

Back in his hotel room, McGivern went to the window without lighting his lamp. Across the street, leaning against a gallery post of the Belle Fourche, was one of Belden's toughs, the light hitting his bare, tousled straw thatch. He was smoking, his head tilted back to watch McGivern's window. They would watch the hotel in alternate shifts through the night, he guessed. Tomorrow both would be bleary and short-tempered from little sleep. Georgette—Julia—would help him do the rest.

8

I BELIEVE THOSE MEN are following us," Julia said
calmly. She and Tom were a mile from Saguaro as she
looked back across the flats, shading her eyes with her
hand. She was wearing a green riding habit with a
divided skirt. A matching porkpie hat was perched on
her high-coiled pale hair, and she carried an Eastern
riding crop.

"Pair of saloon loafers with nothing better to do,"
McGivern said idly.

"It does make you nervous, though. What an odd
pastime. I never will understand Western man . . . In
properly sloughing decorum," she added, "suppose you
call me Julia."

"Tom, then, or Mac." To pull her attention from
Kruger and Mills, he motioned with his hand. "Look
there." Julia gave a little scream. A huge rattler was
coiled in the shade of a shelving outcrop well to their
right. "Let him alone," McGivern said, smiling, "and
he'll let you alone."

"I—it startled me."

"This desert is a bigger book than you'll ever read,
Julia. I've lived in it and I know it."

"I'd like to learn." Her eyes were bright as an eager

child's, and somehow it was pleasing to see that her strangely mingled sophistication of Beacon Hill and the Belle Fourche was only skin deep.

So he talked as they rode slowly through the gathering heat of midmorning, occasionally stopping to point out a giant *sahuaro* cactus, an unusual shrub or a darting lizard. Julia quickly and easily followed his shifting attention. It came to him with an unbidden suddenness that he was enjoying this, and he knew a twinge of guilt that he could be distracted for fleeting minutes from his mind-locked goal. Yet he knew that the timeless desert could work its own spell, erasing disillusion and hurtful memories as its healing herbs known by the Indians could alleviate physical sickness. They were two cynical people who needed that balm, but it was dangerous balm for a man and a woman alone. And McGivern thought: *Why not? The rest of it belongs to the past, the dead past. Maybe you're beginning to want to forget.*

His conscience flailed the thought, angrily denying it. He was all right now, he told himself; he straightened in his saddle, scanning the flat landscape. There was a jumbled rise of shale formations about two miles distant, he judged; imperceptibly he neck-reined his horse in that direction. Kruger and Mills were hanging back about a mile, easily keeping within eyeshot of these flats. The trick now was to lull their attention. . . .

It was close to noon when McGivern and Julia had ranged leisurely to the edge of the shale rise. The horses picked their way over the crumbling slate to a narrow height of land. Here McGivern halted, dismounted, and helped Julia down. He broke out sandwiches from his saddlebags, two cups, and a bottle of *rioja alta* wine.

"A little warm," he said in apology as they sat tailor-fashion on the warm rock and he poured the wine.

"But this is wonderful. I know wines, and this is a good one. How did you ever find it in Saguaro?"

"Got the hotel cook to put up the lunch. Learned he

61

used to be a *chef de maître* in New Orleans. Came out here as a lunger. This is from his private stock. I thought it would please you."

"You're thoughtful, Tom. Thank you." She sipped the wine, her eyes fixing him disturbingly.

He looked away, across the shimmering flats. Kruger and Mills had dismounted from their horses and were squatting on the ground with smokes. They were bored and they were angry. They hadn't slept much, and they'd been riding a hot desert at a slow gait. Now they were hunkered down, with empty bellies, cursing Harlan and Belden and wondering why the hell they were trailing McGivern on a picnic outing with a honkytonk girl. They were undisciplined hell-raisers, and this trailing took patience. McGivern guessed he could throw them off without difficulty; they'd look around half-heartedly, swear a little, then ride back to town and wait for him.

When he and Julia had finished eating, McGivern packed the saddlebags unhurriedly and told her "Let's lose those two."

She nodded, her eyes bright, and he thought uneasily that a heady combination of sun and wine was giving her the wrong idea, and she was not averse to it. They mounted and rode lengthwise across the height without haste and in plain view, McGivern in the lead. "Now," he said quietly, and abruptly put his horse down a steep incline. Shale rattled away ahead of him, and Julia gamely held his pace. He kicked his mount into a canter up a small canyon full of angled turns. The whole formation was crosshatched with miniature gorges, and McGivern led recklessly through the labyrinth, working toward the south and east.

Within a half hour they broke again onto open flats, and he called over his shoulder, "Let your horse out." They settled into a mile-eating gallop which McGivern shortly halted, knowing the horses could not weather such a pace in this heat.

Julia reined up beside him, laughing shakily. "That was fun."

62

"You haven't laughed before."

Her face sobered; she said gently, "I hadn't much to laugh about—before."

He hastily changed the subject. "Thought we'd head south now, then swing back to town." Without waiting for her reply, he nudged the sorrel into motion. He meant to leave her at the town outskirts, then strike for Chain Anchor alone.

He could make out the great ridge formation that lay north of Belden's ranch, and he idly wondered how the wounded Apache was. He'd thought little of the Indian youth since yesterday. As a cog in Belden's intrigues, he was negligible; the Apaches could sent another man, but at least the gun liaison was delayed. Aside from the seed of personal liking that had begun between them, he had no reason to concern himself further with Gian-nah-tah. He was still an enemy, and McGivern had done no more than their common humanity dictated.

There was a more pressing concern to occupy his attention: locating the cache of Winchesters. That settled, he would return to the cave—and what? McGivern wondered cynically. Take the Apache to Belden's sheriff and Belden's jail in Belden's town? Or let him return to his war party to kill more whites? McGivern could not delay his self-imposed task of seeing the gun smuggling completely smashed, to take the Apache hundreds of miles to a fort. He shook his head wearily; moral decisions were infinitely more complicated than the black-and-white judgments made by his stiff-necked Covenanter parents.

The ridge rose nearer with their steady pace, and now McGivern saw several buzzards wheeling against the brassy sky. For three minutes as they rode he watched the carrion birds swoop and hover and hesitate to settle; their prey was not yet dead. Without telling Julia, McGivern reined casually in that direction.

Shortly they topped a dune and looked into a small, brush-filled swale. Gian-nah-tah's paint stood there, placidly switching flies off its flanks. Yesterday

63

McGivern had left the pony tethered in some shrubbery at the base of the ridge.

"What is it?" Julia asked sharply.

McGivern didn't answer. He slid from his saddle and ran down the slope. Gian-nah-tah was sprawled on his face in the brush at the bottom of this swale to which his desertcraft had guided him before his strength failed. His clawed fingers sunk in scrabbled clay showed where he'd started to dig for water. Exertion had reopened his wounds; fresh bloodstains welted the flannel bandage. McGivern ran back to his horse and fetched his canteen. He turned Gian-nah-tah's limp body on its back, supporting the boy's head against his arm as he tilted the canteen to his lips. The Apache stirred; his eyes opened and his throat muscles worked convulsively. McGivern let him have a few swallows, then corked his canteen and set it aside.

As his head was turned, Gian-nah-tah exploded beneath him. McGivern was flung joltingly on his side and like a striking snake the Chiricahua was on him, snatching McGivern's knife from its hip sheath. The blade made a silvery arc in the sun as his arm went back. For a moment it hung in the air like Julia's startled scream, and in that moment McGivern grabbed the wiry wrist and twisted.

Gian-nah-tah groaned, weakly trying to smother McGivern's leverage with his leaning weight, and the Apache smell that was grease and sweat and woodsmoke was rank and full in McGivern's face. An upsweep of his arm would have smashed his elbow cruelly into Gian-nah-tah's wounded side. Instead McGivern scissored his legs around the Apache's hips and rolled him aside. With another hard twist he forced Gian-nah-tah to release the knife. He snatched it up and sprang to his feet. Gian-nah-tah lay on his back panting, eyes filled with pain.

"It was a good try, *pinda-likoye*," he whispered. "I will not go back to San Carlos—alive."

McGivern sheathed his knife. "A fool try, *ish-kay-nay*. You might have reached San Carlos alive—with

64

me—had you waited in the cave. You would not have made it back to Maco's band alone. You almost died here."

"In the night a fever ate my brain; I drank all the water you left, and still my thirst raged. You did not return; shall a warrior die in a hole like a wounded animal?"

Gian-nah-tah struggled slowly to his feet, disdaining McGivern's extended hand. He backed off at an unsteady pace, almost falling. Then with a burst of reserve energy that again caught McGivern off-guard, Gian-nah-tah wheeled, swift as thought, sprang to the paint and snatched the Winchester from its buckskin sheath. He wheeled back in the same movement, leveling the rifle, but McGivern had already palmed up and cocked his pistol. Yesterday McGivern had cached the Apache's weapons under a flat rock near the pony; evidently Gian-nah-tah had easily found them.

The Apache grinned wolfishly. "What do you call this, Day-zen?"

"The white-eyes call it a Mexican stand-off."

"No. If you were a *nak-kai-ye*, we would both shoot." He meant the hereditary hatred between the Mexicans and the Apaches. "There is liking between us."

McGivern nodded watchfully. "Yet you tried to kill me, as I would in your place ... The liking counts for nothing here."

"A little, maybe. Also we are neither of us fools. I shall withdraw now, and neither will shoot, for both will surely die. Another day we may fight and one shall die. Or, if Yusn wills, in a better time I will take the hand I refused."

McGivern shook his head. "To come this far, you almost died. Another mile will finish you."

Gian-nah-tah's right hand braced the ready rifle against his hip as he inched forward to McGivern's canteen on the ground between them. With a swift movement he lifted it, slung the strap to his shoulder and straightened. "Your water gave back my life; it will keep me alive till I reach my people."

He backed to his horse and swung astride, bowing with a wince of pain across his horse's mane. "It is a great thing to fox Day-zen twice. *Adios*." The Apache sidled his horse away a good thirty paces, bent low over the withers, and quirted the paint into a run toward the north. He had brains to match his courage, and he was an Apache; he would win through. McGivern didn't want to think about that. He'd unwarily let free an enemy who could kill more whites.

He tramped up the slope to where Julia waited wide-eyed, her reins twisted between her hands. As he stepped into his saddle, she burst out, "What happened between you and him?"

McGivern shrugged. "You saw the story. A stand-off."

She shook her head slowly, her eyes puzzled. "You knew each other before. Why—he was almost friendly!"

"Knew him at San Carlos. I lived there once."

"I believe that . . . the way you knew the language . . . but I think there's more. I think those two men were following us for a reason. I think that wounded Apache was here for a reason. I think, Mr. McGivern, that you even brought me with you for a reason."

Her words were firm with conviction, edged with a faint scorn. McGivern's face felt hot at her accuracy. "Anything else?"

"Yes. I think you're too friendly with a hostile. I've seen peaceful Apaches. Didn't he wear the paint designs of a hostile?"

McGivern nodded wearily; she would have to know it all now, knowing as much as she did and putting a wrong interpretation on it. Yet how far could he trust a woman he'd met two days ago?

He talked as they headed their horses back toward Saguaro, telling in a toneless, factual way everything that had happened since he'd received a telegram from Colonel Cahill over three months ago. She rode without looking at him, but watching her face now and again he saw the tenseness relax and shades of concerned emotion replace it.

66

When he'd finished they jogged on in a full minute's silence, before Julia spoke in a hushed voice. "This girl ... you knew her for a long time, Tom?"

"Since we were kids," he said quietly. "Our families had neighboring farms in Ohio. When I reached eighteen, my feet got too itchy; I had to ride out and see the world. Ann understood—and she said she'd wait. I hit the deep West, and what with one thing and another I forgot that I'd ever promised to come back. Thirteen years. Then, a year ago, my freight business was prospering and I got an urge to go back to Ohio. Mostly, that was a mistake. Mam and Pap were dead, my old friends were strangers."

He paused humbly. "But Ann had waited. At least, she hadn't forgotten, as I had."

"I don't quite understand," Julia said in soft admission. "It isn't human nature to just ... wait."

McGivern looked at her quickly, his glance a little hard. "That's your judgment, an easy one. You're a beautiful woman. She wasn't pretty, even as a girl. She was thirty-one when I went back."

"A lot of women marry who aren't attractive," Julia said defensively. But she added thoughtfully, "I suppose a plain girl would find it easier ... to wait."

"Waiting is never easy," he said flatly. "I know this: I went back. And she was there. And it was the same between us again. She had a beauty that ..." He stopped, searching for words. "It wasn't so easy to see because it was inside."

"The only kind that counts," Julia murmured. There was reluctance that was almost pain in her words that made him look at her strangely.

There was another silence before she spoke again, the brittleness sharply accenting her voice. "I was a vain, fuzzy-minded little girl once, my friend; all that, though I was nineteen. Beacon Hill upper crust, and a minister's daughter at that. Our life was luxurious, yet conservative, and always you lived by the book. Not the Scriptures, the social register. There were rules and rules. I tired of them all."

She hesitated, her tongue touching her lips. "There was a musician, a traveling European pianist, who played concerts in drawing rooms. I met him at a party. He was continental to the core, with dark sad eyes and long pale hands. He coughed a great deal—what you call 'a lunger,' I suppose—and he spouted long stanzas of unintelligible verses in French: he called himself an aesthetic rebel. Being what I told you, I used to meet him secretly in a rose-petal-and-pink-tea haze. And when he left Boston, I went with him."

She smiled palely. "We were married in the first town we came to, if that's important. I soon found Raoul drank when the coughing fits became too severe. And when he drank, he . . . never mind. One night in Albany after a concert, he shot himself through the head." She turned her head away, looking across the desert. "They said the West was a new land for a new start. I found one here . . . of sorts."

"Your family," McGivern said quietly.

"I wrote letters. They all came back with a concise note. To the effect that the Reverend Mr. Jonathan Lanphere no longer had a daughter. She ran off with an immoral 'show person,' and so ceased to exist." She shook her head in puzzled bitterness. "Well, the life isn't so bad by some standards. I have my honor, whatever that means, and I eat three meals a day. I don't ask for pity; for five years I've weltered in self-pity till I'm sick of it. And of myself."

McGivern was silent now as the buildings of Saguaro came into view. *Not bad by some standards*. Yet by contrast with a Beacon Hill upbringing, he could see casino life would tear a sensitive, well-bred woman apart. As it would Julia unless, somehow, she freed herself.

He reined in behind a swell of low dunes, and she looked at him questioningly. "I'm riding to Belden's ranch," he said. "What happens there is my business. I'll have to trust you, Julia."

"I'll keep your secret." She smiled tiredly. "You keep

mine—no, more; forget it. I'm sorry. I had to tell someone, that was all."

"You can bottle a thing up just so long," he agreed softly. "But I won't forget, Julia."

"Strange. I know that you rode with me today under a pretense, and yet I find myself telling you everything." She watched him a concerned moment. "You'll be careful, Tom . . ." She reined her horse quickly away, heading for town.

McGivern watched her until she was out of sight beyond the dunes, then swung east again at a brisk clip. In an hour he achieved the hogback and the southward-running canyon which bisected it. He rode warily into the winding gorge, ready for anything; Chain Anchor might have outriders patrolling the drift lines, and if they'd been expecting an Apache contact, they'd know by now that something had gone wrong. Wariness heightened when he found fresh sign where a lone shod horse had traversed the canyon only hours ago, then turned back. Perhaps Harlan himself, though it wasn't likely he'd unriddled what had happened.

The canyon ended high on the far side of the ridge and spilled down in a broken shale slide to its base. The character of the land altered sharply, as though the ridge made a clean demarcation between the desert to its north and the grassy plains here that undulated away to south and east. The ridge was Chain Anchor's northern range boundary, McGivern guessed as he halted at the canyon exit; a several-branched creek sparkled between the richly grassed hills, the source of their fertility.

He had to spur the sorrel to braving the treacherous slide, and at its bottom he immediately struck due south through the grass, following the faint ruts of the wagon trail. For an hour he rode steadily, spooking up occasional bunches of decrepit or half-wild steers ranging along the creek bottoms. All bore the brand of an anchor with two chain links. Obviously Belden hadn't driven to market for several years, and his neglected ranch was, as Ma Gates had said, only a cover-up.

Ahead, the land rose to a low wooded ridge where McGivern dismounted and tethered his horse. He cat-footed through the trees to the summit of the slope. He could see into the gradual dip of a wide bowl where Chain Anchor headquarters lay.

The low ridge formed a timber-cloaked horseshoe, enclosing the ranch on three sides, but open to the west. His vantage was from the north arm of the horseshoe. The bowl flattened off at the bottom in a vista of rolling park dotted with big isolated cotton-woods. The thick, rich lawn that surrounded the build-ings might once have been well-tended, but now the grass was knee-deep and rank, and the near buildings, a bunkhouse, a cookshack, and a maze of barns, sheds, the pole corrals, showed a careless lack of repair.

The main house was built of massive timbers, flanked by wings of fieldstone. It, along with a carriage shed and stables, was set off at the entrance to the horse-shoe. Unlike the working part of the ranch, with its look of weatherbeaten neglect, the owner's part was well-kept, with trimmed hedges, a gravel drive, and a well-clipped lawn.

McGivern took stock of it all, charting it indelibly in his mind as he hunkered down in the timber above to wait out the day. He saw little activity. Some crewmen were loafing on a bench in front of the bunkhouse, apparently with nothing to do. A red-haired woman in a print dress came out of the big house and sat in the porch swing. McGivern had seen her in town yesterday morning, talking to the sheriff; curiously, he wondered what her place here was. From this distance she looked slender and youthful, surely not the wife of the gross, aging Belden. His daughter or housekeeper, probably.

Toward sunset a buggy accompanied by two horsemen drove in from the west along the town road and turned in at the gravel drive. McGivern identified Belden in the buggy, flanked by Harlan and Sheriff Paul Hornbeck. The girl rose and met them on the steps, and all went inside.

The vultures are gathering, was McGivern's wry

thought, and he guessed that the missing Apache contact, and his own possible role in the Apache's failure to show up, would be the center of the discussion. His nerves were beginning to hairtrigger, and he called on his old stolid patience to wait till darkness. Tonight, if a gun cache was on this ranch, he would find it. And when he was through with the rifles, none would be usable by the Apaches or anyone else.

9

JULIA RETURNED HER HORSE to the livery stable and walked slowly back to the Belle Fourche. She felt slack and bone-weary, and knew that tomorrow she would pay with a hundred aches and twinges for these unaccustomed hours in the saddle. But now the weariness was a pleasant one, permeating body and mind with a deep restfulness. Men turned to stare as she went by, and she thought, *I must be a sight*. Her green habit was covered with dust; her skin felt sweaty and gritty, pleasantly so. A lifetime as a society and saloon prima donna had cut her off from such direct sensations.

It wasn't till she turned in at the side door of the Belle Fourche and started up the stairway to her room that she learned why the men had stared. Ma Gates met her at the head of the stairwell, hands at hips, regarding her with amazement.

"God's sake, Georgie. Expected you to be wore out, and here you're pert as fresh daisies. Just a little sunburned. You look great. What'n hell happened?"

"Why—nothing," Julia said in confusion. "Your friend is quite a gentleman."

Ma grunted. "You can't tell me nothin' about Tom

McGivern. The mouse was here an hour ago, askin' after you."

"Clyde?" She'd forgotten about Clyde. "What did he want?"

"Asked if you was back from your ride with that McGivern person." Ma grunted furiously. "Damned hoity-toity runt. Sent him packin' with red ears."

Julia felt a swift irritation that Clyde had been probing at her personal life in his sly way. Then she remembered she'd promised him the usual buggy ride when he finished work. "I have an engagement, Mrs. Gates. Could you have Charley bring hot water up?"

"Best rest, girl," Ma snapped. "You got to go to work at six. Can't have my girls' personal lives pushing on their work."

"I'm sorry, Mrs. Gates. I promised."

Ma grumbled as Julia went on to her room, but Julia heard her bawl for Charley the swamper to ready up a hot bath for Georgette. Behind a screen, she struggled with the buttons of her limp riding habit, while Charley, a hunchbacked old derelict, brought up buckets from the kitchen and filled a washtub improvised for the girls' baths. Afterward she locked her door, slipped into the tub and let the water slide like a hot soothing cloak over her. She closed her eyes, enjoying the sense of languid ease. Not the least of it was due to unburdening herself to McGivern; she hadn't realized how badly she'd needed to tell someone all. It had seemed oddly natural to unburden herself to this man she hardly knew.

She had never considered telling Clyde Prentiss of her past; Clyde had already guessed much of it, and she was too used to his iron judgments in moral matters. She could always retaliate by deliberately saying things to shock him, though at times she thought there was a sly, ferocious hypocrisy behind Clyde's prim front.

Distastefully she put Clyde out of mind, and smiled secretly, enjoying the tingling warmth that was not wholly from the hot water. She'd thought she would never have any more illusions about men, yet she had known the old romantic stirrings of girlhood today. The desert, the wine, the incident with the Apache, had all contributed—but she couldn't deny that all these had centered about the man at her side, releasing a torrent of long pent-up feeling in her. *You're a fool,* she thought suddenly, bitingly; *you were nothing but a pretty accessory to him, and now you know why he is here and what he is fighting. A man alone against all Belden's crooked power. You will probably not see him again . . . not alive.*

A fear almost like a physical sickness struck her. She stepped from the tub, toweled briskly, automatically selected a dress from her closet. She thought with distaste of the hour ahead with Clyde Prentiss. Usually she nostalgically enjoyed his knowledgeable range of talk, from business to Emerson's philosophy and the novels of Hawthorne, all related in his crisp Massachusetts nasality; but today she viewed the prospect of the next hour with him as almost unbearable. Should she plead a headache? But McGivern had put his trust in her; she must behave naturally and graciously, particularly to Clyde, whose ferreting curiosity and jealousy already filled him with unspoken suspicion of McGivern. Then, she thought, Clyde worked for George Belden; how deeply was he immersed in the man's enterprises?

She was ready at the side door when Clyde reined his buggy in front at exactly three o'clock, stepped down and came briskly up the alley. He halted on the steps, eyes widening with almost reluctant admiration. "I must say, Julia, that you've never looked lovelier."

"Thank you, Clyde," she murmured in quiet concealment of her lack of pleasure. Yet he seemed to sense this and was silent as he handed her to the seat, took up the reins, and crisply put the livery bays into motion. Clyde took a western road from town, which followed a sluggish, cottonwood-bordered creek. He halted in the dappled shade, jabbed the buggy whip back in its socket with a sharp motion and turned a disapproving face to her.

"I hadn't mentioned it before, Julia; it was none of

74

my business. But do you think it best that you see this McGivern so regularly? The man is rough, semiliterate, at best. Not," he added hastily, "that this is an index to his true character. But he *is* a stranger of whom we know nothing—"

"As you say, Clyde, it's none of your business," she said tartly. "However, Mrs. Gates knows him—most approvingly."

"That old harridan—" Clyde began, but a stormy hint in Julia's glance cut him off. He looked sullenly down the creek, nervously fingering the reins. Julia was satisfied to let him stew. A good share of their relationship was built on tacit or spoken conflict which amused her. But now she was not amused, only bored and angry. . . .

Back in Boston, Clyde would have been of the serving class that clerked in the stores patronized by her wealthy relatives; in this blunt land where even the cattle baron was often on first-name terms with his sorriest puncher, she knew that much of Clyde's attraction to her was a sense of class which would have been off-limits to him back East. His occasional hints of marriage, which she deftly fended off, were founded, she guessed, on a vicarious thrill the staid bookkeeper received from consorting with a debutante-turned-casino-singer, and the sense of righteousness he would receive from lifting her to respectability—on his terms. It would satisfyingly wipe out the ingrained inferiority he couldn't help feeling, and out of sheer gratitude she would become a demure and decorous wife.

So much for Clyde, she thought a trifle grimly; her own feelings she had already summed up. That left McGivern, the cause of their immediate bickering. McGivern, who'd left her and headed into danger, perhaps death; and she could do nothing for him. The clammy fear came back like an icy blow in the stomach. If only there were a safe way for him to collect the evidence he needed to smash the gunrunners. . . .

Maybe there is. The thought was like another blow, bright and relieving. Clyde Prentiss might be humanly

75

small, but she had no reason to doubt his honesty; wasn't he forever prating of business ethics and some employers' lack of them? There was something mealy-mouthed in the way he hinted at George Belden's underhandedness, which he would never dare mention to Belden's face. But no man who'd never achieved the depths of depravity could condone gunrunning; Clyde's ignorance was almost certain, yet he was in a position to undermine the vicious operation.

She turned suddenly to him. "Clyde, have you received any large shipments of Winchester rifles lately? Were they noted in the company books?"

He swung his head, facing her warily. "What brought on that question?"

Julia hesitated only a moment before telling him, slowly and carefully, that George Belden was almost certainly running guns to an Apache band. For proof, she drew on all McGivern had told her about his experiences since arriving in Saguaro, omitting his true reason for coming here, explaining that he was acting at the Army's behest, and had traced large shipments of Winchesters to Saguaro.

"I see," Clyde murmured when she had finished. All animosity had vanished, and his voice was sharp with interest. "Strange. We've received a number of sizable crates of the sort used to pack rifles at intervals during the last months. I've watched the yard men unload them. Once a crate broke open and spilled out its load—yes, new Winchesters." He stroked his chin thoughtfully, repeating, "Strange. The crates were always transferred to a yard warehouse, yet I've often been in that warehouse and found no rifles in storage. I assumed they must have been taken away after I was off work, almost with an air of secrecy. They were not distributed to local merchants—and the Army doesn't contract for Winchesters. There was never mention of them on invoices, no record entered in my book. Of course all this seemed odd, but it isn't discreet to question an employer too closely. And I know nothing of gunrunners or their methods; it never occurred—" He broke off flatly, his eyes narrowed and cautious. "Of course, you had a reason for asking."

"Yes, Clyde," she said steadily. "I want you to write the commandant at Fort Laughlin—Colonel Cahill, Tom McGivern's friend. I want you to tell him what you told me. It should be enough to warrant a full investigation of George Belden's freighting activities and his company's books . . . perhaps enough to bring him to trial . . . with your testimony of what you know. Some of the teamsters must be honest men who can corroborate that the guns *were* delivered. Neither Tom nor the Army can do anything on mere suspicion— but your testimony as Belden's bookkeeper—"

"Would save risk to Mr. McGivern's precious neck, eh, Julia?"

"Don't be small, Clyde!" she said vehemently. "Don't think small, for heaven's sake—where the lives of hundreds of innocent people are at stake. You haven't been out here long; you haven't lived close to an Indian uprising. I have. It's horrible!"

"Yes," Prentiss said softly, musingly, as though her vehemence hadn't touched him. "All right, Julia. I'll see what I can do. I'll check the books over again, tonight, to make certain. I have an office passkey for night work."

"See me afterward. Tell me what you found out."

He nodded, clucked to the horses and swung their buggy around, headed back for town. Julia afforded herself only a slight relief. McGivern was still in danger, until she could tell him of Clyde's agreement to help. *Let him come back,* she prayed. *Let him come soon.*

CROUCHED IN THE BRUSH on the ridge, McGivern slowly chewed a strip of jerky, let the tough, fibrous mouthful slide down his throat. He smiled wryly at this old ritual. Town life softened a man, yet he'd often lived for weeks on jerky and a little water. Down below, lights shone in the main house. Belden and his group would be finishing supper, and the crew had finished straggling back from the bunkhouse.

It was full dark and time to move. He left concealment and worked down the slope, coming up behind the wall of the nearest shed. He hugged the wall, edging to its far corner. A thorough search of rambling sheds might consume hours, but he had the whole night.

He started to ease around the corner, then flattened to the wall as the door of the huge hay barn creaked open a scant twenty yards away. A man stepped out, paused to shape a cigarette and light it. Then he paced on, headed for the bunkhouse, a rifle swinging from his hand. *That's it,* McGivern thought with a stir of excitement. *The barn. That was a guard.* He was lucky, but he could have been as unlucky, if he'd entered the barn and run full into the guard. This must be a change of shifts, and the relief would be along shortly. He'd have to work fast.

McGivern melted through the shadows to the double doors which the guard had neglected to close. Just inside, he struck a match and hand-cupped its flare away from the doorway. The wash of light before the flare died to a steady flame showed him a bare clay floor, a loft above with a wooden ladder. He pinched out the match and in utter darkness took two steps that brought him to the ladder. He groped for a rung and started to climb. When he felt the board floor of the loft, he swung his weight up and forward and crouched at its edge, listening.

Satisfied, he struck another match. In its feeble flicker he saw a pile of hay against a far wall. He stood, bending his tall frame under the low rafters, and moved to the hay. He swept his foot through it, encountering the hollow side of a box. He stooped and pulled away the hay, exposing four long rectangular cases. There were no stamps or identifying marks, he saw before the match singed his fingers and went out. Carefully he struck another, pulled his knife from its sheath, drove the blade under the slatted cover of the topmost box, and pried upward. There was a thin shriek of nails, and he stopped, holding his breath, listening to the silence. Then, getting purchase with his fingertips, he lifted the cover.

They were there . . . spanking new Winchester '73's tiered in compact rows. This was what he had come to find. There was no time to wreck each one systematically by dislodging the firing pin, as he'd planned; he had to think of getting out before the guard was renewed. He extinguished the match, moved back to the loft edge, and there froze to immobility.

A man's booted steps were moving casually across the trampled ranchyard toward the barn. He couldn't get out in time; he'd wait for the guard to take up his position and then get the drop on him. He slipped his .45 from its holster, with the bleak knowledge that the guard could identify him to Belden, and from then on

McGivern would be free game in an open field for Belden's gunnies. If he escaped the ranch. . . .

Unsteady lantern glow filled the doorway as the guard approached, and then he stepped inside, a tall, wavering shadow in the saffron glow. He paused in the doorway to glance around, the high-held lantern illumining his battered face. It was Pride Bloom, hat cuffed back on his greasy hair. A dirty bandage laid a grimy streak across his broken nose. McGivern watched tensely from the loft shadow as Pride walked to the ladder, shifting his rifle to the hand that held the lantern, holding both awkwardly as he reached up to grab the ladder rung with his free hand.

McGivern leaned out to view, pistol leveled. "Hold it there. Keep that hand up and stand off."

Pride jerked, looked up, and then took two steps back, his arms stiffly erect. "Do it all slow. Pull your sidearm and drop it," McGivern ordered. Pride did so, unspeaking as his malignant gaze picked out and identified McGivern. "The rifle. Reach out and get it with your free hand, drop it. Now lower that lantern to the floor and straighten up with your hands high."

Pride obeyed, still wordlessly. McGivern, still facing Pride, started to swing down to the top rung to descend. In that instant, with McGivern's body twisted awkwardly, Pride's foot lashed out, hit the lantern and sailed it against a supporting post. The light shattered and died. McGivern held his fire and then, hearing Pride scramble for his guns, leaped off into the darkness, hitting the clay floor lightly, pivoting to face Pride's gunflash. The shot made an echoing boom, the slug hammering into the wall at McGivern's back. At the end of his pivot, pulling his gun with him in a tight arc, McGivern saw Pride outlined against the lesser darkness of the doorway. Then he fired.

Pride jerked back with the slug's impact, but somehow kept his feet. He shot again, blindly, and fired a third time as his legs gave and he went down on his face, gunflame blistering the floor ahead of his falling body. McGivern ran for the door, slipping to one knee

80

on the wet clay and hearing a shout from the bunk-house before he regained his feet and whipped out the door. Careening on his heel, he charged across the open yard for the slope. Lantern light spilled out the bunk-house door as a flood of men poured through.

Shots buffeted the night. The close whir of a lead hornet told McGivern he was seen, and he dived side-ways, into the deep and pooling shadows of a shed.On his hands and knees he skirted the wall, hugging its shadow, and came against a pole fence which ended at the shed corner. He heard confused shouts, as he slipped between the fence poles. He glanced back and saw additional lanterns and lamps bobbing across the yard now as the men fanned out. Reggie Harlan's voice was raised in a question, then roared orders.

McGivern backed off from the fence, came against something yielding and warm that snorted with fear and sprang away. *It's the horse corral,* he thought. Now the nearing lamplight picked out the shadowy forms of the horses, milling nervously, and he moved swiftly and noiselessly among them, crouching low as he worked across the corral. In the uncertain light, crouching groundward amid the milling horses, he misjudged his direction. Suddenly he came up against the fence, and instead of attaining the slope side and the safe dark-ness beyond, he saw more sheds beyond the fence.

Cursing under his breath, he started to step through the poles, and then two men jogged his way, circling the corral on this side with a lantern picking out their path. He drew his leg back, shot a glance around and saw the black hulk of a water trough. He dived, hit the dirt behind it and lay motionless as the two men ran past, a bare yard away, their lantern making a brief tawny aura around the narrow pocket of shadow that hid him, and then receding. He came to his feet and slipped out between the poles, making for a shed a few feet away.

He ducked through the low doorway and sank into a corner, his heart pounding. The darkness was heavy with the smell of coiled leather, and he knew that this was the harness shed. He couldn't stay here; soon Harlan would be organizing a search of each building.

Cautiously he edged to the doorway, gun palmed and ready. The bobbing flare of lanterns told him that the search was temporarily concentrating toward the shed where they'd last seen him, and now was the time to move. He looked out—and stepped quickly back at sight of a vague figure approaching the shed from the main house, walking fast. He flattened against the wall by the door; he could only wait for the man to enter, buffalo him fast, and then make a run for it.

The figure paused in the doorway. McGivern's hand shot out and caught a handful of collar, his fist tensed to strike. There was a muffled little scream. He released the woman at once, shoved her aside, swung and broke for the door.

She caught his arm and he started to shake her off, but instantly froze when he heard her sharp, imperative whisper: "Be still! Be quiet! They saw me; they're coming."

"Who's in there?" Harlan bellowed.

The woman brushed past McGivern, stepping out into the nearing lantern glow. "It's me," she said calmly.

McGivern heard Harlan halt, heard the hesitation as he digested this, the disgusted anger in his reply. "You picked a hell of a time to go riding."

"That would be entirely my business and none of yours. What is all this?"

"A prowler . . . around somewhere. Better get back to the house till we find him."

"I'll ask for your advice when I want it, and that will be never," she said tartly.

"Have it your way," Reggie said surlily, and McGivern heard him move off, bellowing more orders.

The woman stepped back to the doorway. "Make your run now," she whispered urgently. McGivern moved past her and circled the shed, fading like a shadow into the brush that backed it. A scraggly overgrowth of trees and thickets covered his retreat to the slope and its dense timber. He was safe now; the sounds and lanterns of the searchers were thinning away as he climbed the dark slope and found his unerring way down its opposite side to his tethered horse. Here he waited till he was certain the search for him was being confined to headquarters proper. Then he mounted, started to rein north.

An instinctive thought caused him to feel for the knife in his hip sheath, and the cold realization that it was not there made him rein in. In his haste to uncover the guns, he'd left the knife in the loft. It would surely be found, but only possibly would it be identified as his. He bleakly considered this and then shrugged. His knife would make little difference to Belden and Harlan in fixing the prowler's identity; they would suspect nobody but him. He thought briefly of Pride Bloom, knowing his bullet had been a fatal hit, and felt only a slight regret. Pride had been a human wolf, like his friend Jack Hurdy.

Starting to squeeze the sorrel into motion, he checked himself at the soft whicker of a horse nearby. He listened intently and picked out only the usual nocturnal sounds. Yet a horse was close by and he placed it in an island of timber below the tip of the ridge's north arm. Perhaps a stray animal . . . yet he was prompted to dismount and leg it toward the grove.

He wormed easily, noiselessly, between cottonwood boles free of underbrush. At the heart of the grove lay a small clearing, and in the hazy light of the moon now topping the eastern horizon he saw a standing horse, its reins trailing, in the center of the clearing. A man sat on a rock, nervously puffing a cigarette, face shadowed by his hatbrim. Even as McGivern sank to his haunches, eyes narrowed in puzzlement, he heard a horse plowing through the grove opposite to where he crouched.

The man heard it too; he stood swiftly, grinding his cigarette under his heel, and the moonlight caught on his gaunt face. Sheriff Paul Hornbeck. He must have come straight here from Belden's house, McGivern reasoned, but who was he waiting for? The approaching rider broke from the trees and swung down at the clearing's edge. It was the woman who had helped him; she wore a dark riding habit and her shining auburn hair was bared to the moonlight. She came forward to meet Hornbeck, running the last few steps into his arms.

There was a moment's silence, then her voice, released on a ragged breath: "I can't stand it any more, Paul . . . his indifference, his smug inferences—"

"He—he knows about us?" Hornbeck said thinly.

"Harlan saw us together, and Harlan is his eyes and ears. He knows that much, suspects the rest. And he doesn't even care. But he torments me with his oily hints. He sickens me. Everything about him is disgusting. Paul, if you care at all, you won't leave me under his roof another night!"

Hornbeck swallowed audibly. He took her arms, moved her gently away. "What do you want me to do, Melissa?"

"Not fight him, Paul. Just come away with me. All we need are two horses and some food and water."

"But what would we do, where would we go?"

"Anywhere, away from him!" Her words were a bitter, vehement outpour. "Paul, for once in your life, stand up and fight for something you want! Don't hide behind that mock star you wear, don't crawl behind a bottle—"

She broke off at something she saw in his face, then added softly: "Paul, Paul, I'm sorry. But you don't know; you haven't been married to George Belden for fifteen years."

"Lissa, you're the only thing I ever cared for," Hornbeck said in a dogged, tormented way. "You must know that's why I really quit drinking." It was a rare moment of honesty for the man, McGivern guessed.

"I gave you that much," she said tonelessly. "But no more?" He was silent and she made a small, weary gesture. "Well, I don't blame you. Anyway—he'd find us, no matter how far we went."

"It wouldn't be right, Lissa." Hornbeck's voice was low, shamed.

"You need to believe that, don't you?" she said gently. "Neither of us can help what we are . . . and talking only makes it worse. You'd better go."

He gave her a brief, almost hungry, look and walked with slumped shoulders to his horse; stepped into the saddle. "When will I see you again?"

"Does it matter? Good night, Paul."

She stood in mid-clearing, head bowed, unmoving as Hornbeck wheeled his horse into the dense hedge of trees. When the sounds of his going had died away, McGivern rose and stepped into the clearing.

"I forgot to thank you, Mrs. Belden."

She turned, a startled hand lifting to her mouth. Surprise altered to a bitter, defiant stare as he crossed the clearing to her. "You have a strange way of thanks— Mr. McGivern, isn't it?—eavesdropping and having the gall to let me know it."

"I'm here by chance. Since it happened, I'll ask why you helped me."

She gave a slight, indifferent shrug. "I only know you're George's enemy. Anything that hurts my husband is worth helping."

"Yes'm. How much do you know about his activities?"

A braided riding quirt dangled from her wrist. Irritably she slapped it against her skirt. "That they're mostly crooked, and only gossip tells me that much. George is careful to see that I learn nothing that could be used against him. He keeps his private papers and all legal documents locked in his company safe. Don't waste time pumping me; I'd help you if I could—but I can't."

"Maybe," he murmured. "What can you tell me about Hornbeck?"

"Paul?" Her tone was guarded and defensive. "What do you want to know about Paul?"

"How deep he is with your husband," McGivern said bluntly.

"Oh." She laughed shortly, almost deprecatingly.

85

"Paul is a tool, only. He hears the same gossip I do, and pretends he hears nothing. George, you see, gave him respectability—and Paul feels guilty because of me. He can't believe, still, that George is as black as I paint him. Paul is quite honest. Just—weak."

"And you, Mrs. Belden?"

"What of me, Mr. McGivern?"

"You live on with a man you despise."

A wry, painful smile touched her lips. "Oh, yes—*my* weakness. It's simple enough. I've stayed with George because one doesn't easily outgrow a silken and perfumed girlhood . . . and I lack for nothing, in that way. But you can give up anything—if you become desperate enough."

McGivern regarded her with mounting curiosity. In spite of the faint lines around her eyes and mouth, she was still a beautiful woman; the soft accents of the old South tempered her tones with a hint of antebellum graciousness. "I'm puzzled, ma'am. That's why you married him?"

"You're overcurious, sir," she said stiffly.

"About people, always."

Surprisingly, she gave a small, relaxed laugh. "That's honest, anyway. You're a strange man, Mr. McGivern, in that you invite confidence . . . Would you like to hear the silly story of a silly girl? My family's holdings were ransacked and burned by Sherman's army. George was just one of many carpetbagger politicians who came in to prey on the leavings. Even if my Southern pride hadn't been humbled by poverty—well—fifteen years ago, George was quite handsome in a mature, fortyish way. And I was only eighteen, starry-eyed and ripe for the plucking. Too late, I realized he was completely cold and grasping, that he married me for my social value alone. So I languish in luxury on an isolated ranch, waiting to be used again when circumstance is ripe. George can't afford to lose me; no other woman would have him now, for love *or* money."

"Least of all one as beautiful, ma'am."

"Why—thank you." She flushed faintly. "I'm still a

86

starry-eyed fool, you see; I like to hear nonsense from a man."

"The simple truth." He touched his hat. "Thanks. You've been a help."

"I have? How?"

"Hornbeck. He's not so tangled with Belden he can't free himself. And he's the law. I may need his help."

She shook her head with a small, sad smile. "Paul is hopeless. I wish it were otherwise. I haven't only been seeing him because I wanted him to take me away. I'm foolish enough to think that together we could have salvaged what's left of our lives. But Paul—"

McGivern interrupted. "There aren't many drunks who can quit, even for a woman. He did. That's something. There might be more to him than you know, than he knows. Time he found out."

"But how can he help you?"

"There you'll have to trust me," he said shortly. "Good night." He left her and cut back through the grove to his horse. She was a good woman, he decided, though vain and pampered, but he reserved trust on short acquaintance. On her relations with Hornbeck he made no judgment; it was no business of his. Though if Hornbeck felt guilty about merely meeting the woman, it was unlikely their affair had gone beyond a few almost decorous meetings.

Mounting up, McGivern kneed his horse into a trot, swinging in a roughly northeastern direction across the sweltering desert. He'd make night camp out there, and tomorrow set about establishing a permanent camp on some local promontory from which he could spot any effort to move the rifles from Chain Anchor. It should come soon, now that they knew he had definite knowledge of the gun cache.

He was sure that Belden would not carry on the actual trade, with a war party nearby. Each Apache warrior was his own man; even the tribal chief served only as a sort of senior counselor. On the warpath, an Apache made a grudging concession to the command of his war chiefs, but it was a thin check, and no sane

87

white man would permit a whole band of blood-lusting Apaches on his ranch. Belden would do direct business with one or a few of the steadier heads of the party, and transport the rifles to an agreed rendezvous. Rifles in quantity would be conveyed only by wagon, and McGivern remembered the old wheel tracks he'd seen in the ridge canyon to the north. That was the place to watch; a weighted, slow-moving wagon would be easy to spot.

He raised his head, smelling the desert air; it held a rare, uneasy stir of air currents that he knew well: a storm, a bad one, was brewing. He'd have to choose this night's camp with an eye to good shelter.

He had already considered and rejected the idea of riding to Fort Laughlin and returning with a detachment of cavalry. Colonel Cahill would be swift to oblige on only McGivern's word, but the trip there and back would consume precious days, and during that time the guns could be moved, delivered, and the evidence gone. No, he'd wait and watch; when the guns moved out, he'd get another man and follow the gun wagon to rendezvous . . . and where could he find a more accredited witness than a lawman? That meant Sheriff Paul Hornbeck. McGivern thought grimly that Hornbeck would accompany him if he had to hogtie the sheriff. No matter how Hornbeck had blinded himself to Belden's machinations, he could not deny the plain evidence. With Mrs. Belden's persuasive help, Hornbeck's testimony would be secured at the proper time.

Their dual testimony would destroy Belden and future gun-running here, but what of the present shipment of rifles? McGivern knew that he must somehow prevent these guns from actually passing into Apache hands, and that would be the hardest trick of all to turn.

11

REGGIE HARLAN WAS in a temper when he finally ordered the men to break off the search and get back to the bunkhouse. As he stood in the ranchyard, hands on hips as he watched them disperse, his back and belly felt clammy with more than this day's furnace-like heat that had long since sweated him to irritability. *It had to be McGivern,* he thought sourly. *The damned Indian. We had him boxed, surrounded, and he slipped out. The Old Man'll be fit to be tied.*

He and Belden had been sure McGivern was responsible for the failure of Nachito or Maco or one of their men to show up at the ranch the day before yesterday, the date they'd set with Nachito a month ago, when the war chief had delivered the Army payroll chest to the ranch. That was in full payment for the first two hundred rifles Reggie had delivered to the Apaches four months earlier. Nachito was a man of his word. Besides, he'd been steadily gathering more reservation breakaways into his band, which he planned to build to army size with mixed youthful hotbloods from all six Apache tribes. He would need many more rifles—and the Army would send out more payroll trains.

McGivern was the fly in the ointment. Reggie's suspicions of the man had crystallized two days ago when he'd lost McGivern on the road to Chain Anchor after talking to Lafe Elberg; the failure of the Apache agent to show up on that same day—for Nachito was always dependable—could be logically traced to his running head on into McGivern. This morning Reggie had ridden to the ridge canyon and traced it from one end to the other for telltale spoor; here and there the ground had been recently disturbed and all definite sign carefully obliterated, not enough left to follow up. Then today, those fools Kruger and Mills had let McGivern give them the slip.

McGivern was clever and thorough, and now he'd entered the ranch unseen, got into the barn between the guard change, found the cache, and killed Pride Bloom. Pride was a negligible loss. But McGivern's interest in what was going on was certain now, and the question was—what would he do next?

Reggie's hand shifted on his hip, touched the bone-handled knife he'd found by the torn-open gun crate in the loft. McGivern's. He drew it from his belt, turned it in his hands with the wry thought that he'd rather have the man. It was small comfort to know that McGivern could make a mistake like any other man.

Wearily Harlan pivoted on his heel and tramped up to the house, across the wide veranda, through the propped-open door into the parlor. Belden's flaccid bulk was stretched like a jelled mass on the leather divan. His shirt collar was open, his tie loose, and he was fanning himself with a folded newspaper. Opalescent drops of sweat shone on his oily moon face.

"Well, Reggie; and what luck?"

"None," Reggie growled as he pulled a straight-backed chair around, straddled it, and leaned his arms on the backrest. He glanced at the open book that lay face down on Belden's mounded stomach—*The Prince*, Machiavelli's classic study of dictatorship. Reggie had once begun it himself, only to toss it aside when he found there was nothing in it applicable to his wants. It was Belden's meat, though; man-of-power sort of thing.

Money and prestige were fine, Reggie thought, for what they could get you—liquor, women, good times— but as an end in themselves, why bother?

"You fool," Belden wheezed softly. "Did he get into the barn?"

"He did, and into a gun crate. Killed Pride Bloom when Pride found him . . . and left his calling card." Reggie handed him the knife. "Must have dropped it. . . ."

"Why, this is fine," Belden said dryly, dropping the knife on the floor after a glance at it. Faint lights coalesced in his icy eyes. "It was McGivern, of course— and what will he do now?"

Reggie shrugged. There was a wintry silence which Reggie uneasily broke. "What about the rest of the gun shipment? You said the wagons from N'Orleans finally got here today."

Belden nodded coldly. "You'll send Kruger and Mills to bring them from the warehouse to the ranch tomorrow. Since I'm surrounded by incompetents, they're as good as any."

"The whole shipment'll be ready then," Reggie mused, "and still no word from Nachito."

"He's probably cautious—since his other man failed to return. The question is—" Belden's snappish tone broke off at a light sound of feet ascending the veranda. Lissa came in, riding crop in hand, her face a lovely mask.

"What do you mean," Belden wheezed, "riding out, with a prowler around?"

"Don't shout at the stars, George; they can't hear you."

"Ah," Belden murmured, "but you're somewhat more attainable than the cold and distant stars—eh, my dear?"

She flushed, bit back an angry retort, walked swiftly from the room down a corridor branching into one of the wings. A door banged behind her.

"Hornbeck," Belden murmured. "He left only a few minutes before the excitement—and Lissa went to her room for her riding togs."

"What do you care?" Reggie asked dryly.

"Ha ha ha," Belden said. "I don't; that's the beauty of it."

"You better let up on her. Innuendoes can rub hard, and you want to keep her happy."

"Let them rub the stupid wench," Belden said flatly. "Nobody knows Melissa better than I. The pleasures of a luxurious existence will more than balance the scales."

Reggie thought with quiet hate, *one of these days, Jumbo, you'll make a wrong judgment about someone in that cold, fishy way, and it'll kick back on you.* He swung his glance idly from Belden and it froze on the doorway to the big dining room, darkened now. He made out the hulking shadow of a man standing there in utter silence.

"What is it?" Belden demanded.

The shadow advanced noiselessly into the parlor and became a squat bull of a man, not tall, with short legs and abnormally long arms. His copper-hued face was flat-featured and bigoted, distorted by a great scar which twisted transversely from his left lower eyelid across his broad nose, cutting deeply into his upper lip and pulling it into a cruel grimace. His shoulder-length black hair was partly confined by a greasy warband, and he wore cotton pants stuffed into knee-length moccasins. A filthy calico shirt strained across his barrel chest; over it he wore a faded blue Army officer's tunic with one epaulette and all the buttons missing. An old cap-and-ball dragoon pistol was shoved in the trousers' waist.

Reggie had seen this Apache only once before, when he'd delivered the first shipment of guns to the rendezvous, but even a white man who thought all Indians looked alike could never forget this one. He had a chill sensation of wondering how long the fellow had been standing in the dining room—watching and listening.

"This is Maco," he told Belden.

The fat man wheezed himself up on his elbows, staring with interest at the co-leader of the Apache raiders. "Welcome, sir; we've been waiting on you. Reggie—your chair for the gentleman."

Maco grunted his contempt and squatted down a few feet from the divan. He stared with impassive fascination at Belden's obese hugeness before saying gutturally: "Where guns?"

Harlan hesitated before replying. Heretofore he had done business directly with Nachito or his lieutenant, Tah-zay. These two were the soul of honor, the half-Apache wrangler who worked for Chain Anchor had told Harlan when he'd first quizzed the man. The same wrangler had put Harlan in touch with some relatives at San Carlos, and through them arranged a meeting with Nachito. Nachito would always deliver full payment for the guns, would risk his life to keep his given word. How far could Maco be trusted?

"Nachito couldn't make it, eh?" Harlan said uneasily.

Maco's lip curled in undisguised contempt. "Nachito say not worry, you get money. Where guns?"

"Ready to go," Reggie said. "Only we might have to hold 'em up a while. . . ." Quietly, briefly, he explained the situation to the war chief. At mention of McGivern's name, he saw Maco start, mutter, *"Day-zen!"* and a glint of stark hatred fill the narrow eyes. It meant nothing to Reggie, and he went on, finishing: "You understand how it is."

"Enju. When get guns?"

"Ask him why Nachito or his man didn't show up two days ago," Belden put in.

"Him come back camp, bad hurt. Say only that white man shoot him; he not want talk. So Maco come through white man *hacienda* at back, listen. Think maybe white man goddamn liar, make doublecross Apache."

"And now you know differently, eh, Maco?" Belden smiled urbanely.

"When get guns?"

Belden scowled. "We can't move till we're sure it's safe. Listen, Maco; bring your people to rendezvous, and wait. We'll show up in a week at the outside."

Maco rose in a fluid movement, setting a hand to his

93

knife hilt. "Fat *pinda-likoye*, voice like burro but smooth tongue like snake. Make trap, Maco come back, cut through fat to your heart. *Sabe?*"

"Ha ha ha," Belden said. "Perfectly. It's agreed, then."

Without another word, Maco glided to the doorway, vanished through it and was swallowed by the night.

Belden mopped his forehead with a silk handkerchief. "That's settled. Double the guards over those guns. That McGivern's Injun enough to come back, catch us off-guard and wreck them."

"Assume he's working for the Army," Reggie said. "Now he's got the guns spotted, won't he leave to fetch the soldiers, give us a chance to move the guns out?"

"I think not. Fort Laughlin is the closest Army outpost, several days' ride. He'd know we could move the guns in his absence, and then where would his evidence be? No—McGivern will stay to watch us."

"He might send someone for the Army, then."

"From *my* town? Come now . . ."

"He's friendly with Ma Gates," Reggie insisted. "That old bat's not afraid of us by a damn sight—and she's got people working for her."

"Very well. Station some men to watch her place and its employees. Get the rest of the crew out scouring the local range. Hunt McGivern down. *Get him.*"

"Easier said than done," Reggie said wryly.

"See to it, or it'll be your hide," Belden said flatly. As an afterthought, he added, "Get that fool Pride under the ground and out of the way."

Reggie nodded and left the house. On the veranda he paused to roll a cigarette, his mind a cold welter of hatred for the fat man. *Well, you're still footloose; you can always drift. But not,* he told himself, *till you've cut a bug hunk out of either George's profits or his fat carcass.*

He bent his head to light the cigarette, then raised it sharply, listening . . . A horseman was swinging across the ranchyard from the town road. As he cantered into the soft spill of lamplight from the front windows, Reggie, with a start of surprise, recognized Clyde

Prentiss. He stepped awkwardly down at the tie rail. Reggie saw that his hands were shaking, his shirt wilted with perspiration. His eyes jumped nervously. "I've got to see Mr. Belden."

Reggie waved a hand at the open door and followed Clyde inside. Curiously amused, Harlan took a position leaning against the doorjamb. He watched Clyde hesitate before approaching the divan where the fat man reclined.

"Yes, Clyde?" Belden said unconcernedly, not even glancing at the bookkeeper's paste-colored face.

Clyde's words poured out in a nervous rush. As he listened, Reggie's bored smile thinned, vanished. He straightened, his muscles tensing. Belden merely grunted, continuing to fan himself with the newspaper. When Clyde had finished, he glanced up at the bookkeeper, his murmur benevolent. "How much money do you want, Clyde?"

Clyde moistened his lips, his voice thin and high-pitched. "How much is my silence worth to you, sir?"

"Come, come, Clyde," Belden said jovially. "A good blackmailer calls his own shots. By the way," he added casually, "you hid the books in a safe place, of course, after examining them; presumably in the care of one or more people who knew you were coming here tonight."

"Why-why—" Prentiss' stammer, his vacant-eyed nervousness, gave him away.

"You didn't," Belden purred. "Of course anyone you confided in would want a cut of whatever you get out of me. But I'm very much afraid, my boy, that—" The divan creaked as he broke off speech and swung his bulk to a sitting position, facing Clyde with malevolent, mountainous calm.

"Wait a minute!" Clyde's voice rose shrilly, edged with panic; and Reggie guessed that Prentiss's greed had overruled his rabbity, cautious ways, given him the false confidence to come here tonight—and that he was only now getting an inkling of his danger. "Julia Lanphere told me about the gun-running—she knows—"

"Your saloon chippy? Does she know that you came

here to blackmail me? I thought not. What could she do if something . . . happened to you? What proof can she offer? The word of a saloon singer against George Belden?" Belden's wattles stirred with his gentle shake of the head. "You poor, pathetic fool," he said softly. "You've stepped far out of your depth, trying your game with professionals."

Prentiss flung about with a thin groan and ducked for the doorway. With an easy movement, Reggie pulled his Colt and slammed the barrel against Clyde's temple. Clyde plunged to the floor and lay motionless on his face. Reggie's wicked glance lifted to Belden. "Now?"

"A moment," the fat man said. He stooped, picked the bone-handled knife off the floor where he'd dropped it and examined it thoughtfully. "McGivern has also been friendly with this singer—what's her name? —Lanphere. If we killed McGivern and he's working for the Army—we'd be in trouble. But if McGivern and Clyde fought over the girl, and McGivern were hunted down as a murderer, he'd be safely out of our way and no danger to us."

Reggie scowled. "McGivern kill Clyde? How do you figure that?"

"Ha ha ha. Why," Belden wheezed softly, "when Clyde is found with McGivern's knife stuck in him, what else can folks think?"

THAT NIGHT McGIVERN made camp in the lee of a shelving outcrop on Chain Anchor's north range. He rolled into his blankets and went to sleep with the first thin rumblings of thunder in his ears. He was awakened at midnight when the storm broke in a torrential downpour. Near-solid sheets of wind-borne rain lashed the ground. He pulled his blankets deeper against the inner wall of the outcrop. Making certain his bed was high enough to drain away ground water and spare him a soaking, he rolled back in the blankets, hat over his eyes to shut out the blinding flare of lightning, and went stoically back to sleep, despite the roar of storm.

He awoke in the gray and dismal pre-dawn and looked out at a dripping, mist-bound world. There was a chill in the air. His horse had been tethered just outside, in the lee of the rock, to escape the full fury of the storm, and now it rolled shivering to its feet. McGivern briskly rubbed down its matted, glistening hide. His clothes were clammy with the heavy moisture in the air, and the only way to keep warm was to move.

He saddled the sorrel, mounted and rode briskly away toward Saguaro. It should take him an hour to reach town, and he would still have time to get what he needed before the townspeople were awake and stirring. He needed food, a good-sized bundle of it, to cache up on Chain Anchor's north boundary ridge; there might be days of waiting before the gun wagons moved out.

When the sprawl of town took bleak, vague shape out of the fog, he slackened his pace because of an inner caution. He had the cold conviction that after last night he would be hunted from one end of the range to the other by Belden's hardcases. Not that this greatly concerned him; he had foraged in the heart of Apache country and eluded the grim, canny warriors of Delgadito, Sal Juan, and Geronimo. Like the Apaches, he had found the plains and desert his natural element, as some men found theirs on the high seas. He'd never felt quite at ease in towns. After taking up residence in Silver City he'd often made long, lonely camping trips.

As he neared the buildings, they made a drab and cheerless prospect: it was a town full of enemies. His only friends there were Ma Gates and Julia Lanphere. Two friends, both women; they couldn't help. They might be closely watched from now on, and his own position would be dangerous enough without embroiling them.

He reined in at the southern outskirts beyond a hedgerow of cottonwoods, picking out the general store at the middle of the main block. He'd swing back of the buildings and come up on the rear of the general store. It would be a simple matter to force the back-door lock, enter the storeroom, take his wants and leave payment. He rode in close behind the first building; reaching its far corner, he started to knee the animal on past the alleyway that separated it from the adjoining saloon.

Suddenly a cracked and quavering voice halted him with its unsteady warning: "Hold it there, mister."

McGivern turned slowly in his saddle, holding the reins high in his hands, careful to make no move that might be misinterpreted. An old man whose shrunken frame was muffled in an oversized slicker hobbled from

98

the alley, a shotgun leveled shakily in his veined hands.

"Easy, Pop," McGivern counseled quietly. "That thing could cut a man in two."

The old man halted a few careful feet beyond McGivern's stirruped foot. "You damned murderin' skunk, I'd like nothing better," he husked in the same unsteady timbre. "Pile off, slow and on this side." The shotgun muzzle moved in a menacing semicircle.

McGivern swung stiffly down, threw his reins and faced the old man. "What is this?"

"You can pester the sheriff with your questions," snarled the old man. His head was bare above his glistening slicker, thin gray hair matted wetly to his angular skull. "He don't listen, the jedge will. Move!"

He stepped carefully aside, motioning with the shotgun at the alleyway. McGivern started down it, and the old man fell in behind. When they reached the street, the oldster said tersely, "Stop here." He faced the north end of town, raising his voice in a shrill yell: "Paul! Paul, I got him! Come a-hyperin'!"

A stocky figure emerged from an alley at the far end of the street and legged it toward them, a slicker flapping about its legs. *Hornbeck,* McGivern thought. *He and the old man were waiting for me to show up. Whatever this is, it's serious. Watch yourself.*

The sheriff hauled up breathlessly in front of them. His face was flushed with a kind of vindictive righteousness; his glistening slicker arms lifted and pointed a Greener at McGivern's stomach. "I knew you'd show up if I waited long enough. You had to come back—to get grub, or to see that saloon slut. Don't say anything, McGivern; don't even breathe hard. Just walk. The jail's on your right."

McGivern tramped toward the sheriff's office, the cold fury in him dampened by the threat of the two shotguns. Either man would be glad of a chance to use them. He entered the office, a bare room whose brick walls were almost solidly papered with reward dodgers. He stood with Hornbeck's weapon targeting him

99

while the old man skirted the rolltop desk and lifted a ring of keys from a wall peg. He unlocked the corridor door to the cell block and stood aside while Hornbeck nudged McGivern through. They halted before an end cell, and McGivern stepped inside. The door rang shut with an echo of finality, and the old man turned the key.

McGivern gripped the bars tight in an effort to hold his voice steady. "You want to tell me about this, Sheriff?"

"Is it anything you don't know?" Hornbeck asked sardonically.

"So far you haven't said a damned thing. If that tin star makes you holier-than-thou, it also gives me a right or so, like hearing why I'm charged."

"I don't need the law read to me by your likes," Hornbeck said glacially. "All right, keep your little pose. About four hours ago Clyde Prentiss was found over by the creek—knifed to death."

McGivern's stomach recoiled as from an icy sledge-hammer blow; he said slowly, "You in the habit of nailing a stranger for murder because he's convenient?"

With a smug, bitter smile, Hornbeck unbuttoned his slicker, reached in an inside pocket and brought out a handkerchief-wrapped object. He opened it in his palm, and McGivern saw the knife he'd left in Chain Anchor's barn loft last night—the knife with an oddly designed bone haft he'd carved himself, the razor-edged blade honed from an old file and now covered with rusty stains.

"Yours, isn't it?"

"That's for you to find out," McGivern said, his face impassive as stone.

"I already questioned the girl. She identified the knife as yours."

"Julia Lanphere, you mean?"

"That's the slut."

"Hornbeck," McGivern said softly, "use that word again—"

"And you'll tear down the bars to reach me?"

100

Hornbeck's lip curled. "You arrogant, uncivilized desert rats are all alike ... crowing your mockery of society and its laws even after you're caged. The girl was seen often with you or Prentiss. It's obvious ... a jealous quarrel. The two of you go off from town a ways to settle it. Prentiss is unarmed, no match for a brute like you. One thrust to the heart is all that's needed."

"And the knife left for you to find."

"Panic, sure. Why not? Your kind is all bluff and bluster. You can kick a man silly in a dirty saloon brawl, but murder is something else. You struck in anger—then lost your head and ran." Hornbeck's thick fist closed around the handkerchief and knife. "You're sewed up, McGivern. Your confession will save us both time and trouble—because I mean to sweat one out of you."

McGivern disciplined his wild-running thoughts, steadied his voice. "Sheriff," he said mildly, "Miss Lanphere told you about the knife. Did she also explain our relationship?"

Hornbeck frowned. "Gave me a lengthy cock-and-bull story about your working for the Army, trying to locate guns that Mr. Belden, of all people, is smuggling to the Apaches. That Clyde Prentiss was trying to help, and must have been found out—and murdered by Mr. Belden."

"It didn't strike that logical mind of yours that the story was a shade involved to be made up on short notice."

"It was made up," Hornbeck said grimly, "but not by her. *You*. You told her that to make yourself a hero in her eyes, turn her attention from Prentiss to yourself."

"Look—" McGivern masked his desperation with quiet-toned patience—"you can check my story with Colonel Cahill—Fort Laughlin."

"Sonny," the old jailor jeered, "don't you fret none; he will."

"But it'll take days by letter, and Saguaro has no telegraph. By that time.... Listen to me, Sheriff."

"I've listened to enough damned slander about the town's foremost citizen," Hornbeck shouted.

"One question, inside my rights. Who found Prentiss' body . . . in the middle of the night?"

"One of the Chain Anchor hands—Kruger by name," Hornbeck snapped. "It was just after the storm ended. He came to rouse me out, took me to the spot. We brought the body to Doc Beeman's—he's the coroner—and had the knife removed. Then I went to question the Lanphere girl, and afterward stationed myself and my deputy at opposite ends of town to wait for you. I counted on your desert rat's gall, not your guts, to bring you back."

"The coroner found no other marks on the body?"

Hornbeck scowled, shrugged curtly. "A bruise on the temple—doubtless made when Prentiss fell with your knife in him."

"And Kruger, one of Belden's hands, happened to be drifting down by the creek in the middle of the night and discovered the body."

"McGivern," Hornbeck said in an edged voice, "one more! One more inference about Mr. Belden and I'll open this cell—"

"And work me over with a bottle?" McGivern jeered softly, thinking, *if I could rawhide him close enough to grab that Greener. . . .* He went on cuttingly, "I hear that's how you work best, bottle in your hand."

Abruptly Hornbeck calmed. He pointed a finger, shaking it gently. "All right, McGivern. I can wait. To watch you swing. Laugh yourself blue in the face while you think about it." To the old jailer he said curtly, "Come on, Eph," and the two tramped down the corridor.

The cell door closed and McGivern sank onto the edge of the narrow cot, a slow, cold despair settling to his marrow. He felt a swift flare of anger at Julia Lanphere, but it died as quickly. It had been his own fault for trusting a woman. Yet that wasn't right; she had tried to enlist help sensibly . . . through Clyde Prentiss, who alone was in a position to collate material that might smash Belden, with no personal risk.

But Prentiss had been careless or unlucky; McGivern's knife in his body, plus the fact that Julia had been seen with both men, would add up to a jealous quarrel. Even a fair-minded lawman would be obliged to think as Hornbeck had; the inquest would lead to a murder trial.

From time to time McGivern had sent Colonel Cahill reports on the progress of his long quest, but even if the colonel produced those letters, the scales would balance toward the scaffold. If Belden had had McGivern murdered, the colonel could have turned McGivern's reports over to the U. S. Marshal; there would be dangerous investigations by government agents. Successfully framing McGivern for murder would discredit those reports; only Cahill and McGivern would know the truth—truth that would die with McGivern, and leave the colonel helpless.

From the street, McGivern heard a familiar sound that brought him to the high, barred window facing an alley. Squeezing his face to the bars, he brought his angle of vision to the patch of street showing between the jail and the adjacent building. A wagon was creaking past, from the direction of Belden's freight yards toward the south road, and on the seat he caught a glimpse of Kruger and Mills. The small load in the wagon bed was tarp-covered. That would be the last of the guns for the present quota, on their way to join the others.

Voices in the outer office brought him back to the cell door, straining his ears. He recognized Reggie Harlan's amiable, deep-chested drawl. "So he's caught. I was going to send the crew out to help run him down, but this saves us trouble. Good work, Sheriff. It's news that'll please Mr. Belden. Got to keep this town clean of such murdering riffraff."

"It's my job," was Hornbeck's reply, but his voice held a note of obvious pleasure.

Because Mr. Belden will be pleased, McGivern thought with weary irony—and he guessed that inside an hour, when Belden was informed that McGivern was safely in jail, the completed shipment of guns would be on its way to the Apaches.

Restlessly he paced the cell, hardly hearing the door close behind Harlan and then Hornbeck saying magnanimously, "You've been up half the night, Eph; go home and get some sleep ... Oh, you might take McGivern's horse to the stable; and put his keep on the county bill."

"Yessir, Paul; thankee."

An hour and more passed, and then McGivern lost track of time. Along the savage run of his thoughts, his mind trailed up a dozen false spoors and backtracked relentlessly to a solitary checkmate of all Belden's moves: he had to escape and follow his original plan—to track down and destroy the guns. But he had an additional reason for needing an accompanying witness: only by seeing the evidence of Belden's gunrunning would Hornbeck be persuaded that Belden had framed McGivern for Prentiss' murder.

He halted in the middle of his cell, turning slowly to scan it for the twentieth time. The jail had been built to last; the floors were of solid oak, the walls of tightly mortared fieldstone. He fisted the barred door in both hands, braced his body and shook it. The lock rattled faintly; that was all. The door was anchored to an oak frame by three deep-sunk bolts in each hinge. Even with a prying or bolting tool, he'd be discovered long before he could remove the door, and there would still be the cellblock door and Hornbeck or his jailer to get past. McGivern flung himself on his back across the cot, a hand rubbing his aching eyes. Hopeless. It was hopeless. . . .

Another familiar voice brought him back to his feet, his heart pounding. It was Ma Gates' raucous tones flailing Hornbeck out in the office.

"I don't care what you think," Hornbeck shouted exasperatedly. "I have plenty of evidence to hold him. Anyway I don't know how you heard."

"That mouthy mothbag of an Eph Johnson was shootin' his trap off over in the Belle Fourche not five minutes ago," Ma snapped back. "Now lemme lay down a law, knothead. One statin', to wit, that we get five minutes with a prisoner. Georgie and me aim to have 'em."

"Very well," Hornbeck said coldly, then after a moment's hesitation: "I can't very well search women, so I'll have to go with you. Leave your handbags on the desk."

Ma Gates gave a contemptuous snort. McGivern stepped back, sinking onto the cot as Ma and Julia Lanphere came in, followed by Hornbeck with a drawn Colt in one hand and a key ring in the other. Curtly motioning the women to stand away, he unlocked the cell door and stepped back to the far wall, keeping his gun out.

Julia was first inside, tall and statuesque in a dark blue dress that contrasted with the pallor of her face. Her usual poise was shaken by a frightened concern. "Tom," she said softly. "I'm sorry. I didn't mean this to happen. I tried to tell Hornbeck—"

"Forget it," he broke in quietly. "It's done."

She made a small, unhappy gesture, biting her lower lip. Ma Gates brushed past her, the cot squawking as she lowered her hefty bulk alongside McGivern. "So what can we do for you, Mac? Better name it now; your head's in a noose."

"Afraid the warbag's all sewed up, Ma—for now." He was astonished then to see the big woman sniffle, fumble inside the voluminous bosom of her black dress and bring out a handkerchief. She raised it to her nose and blew loudly. He knew at once that she was putting on an act; she'd come to help him, but how? For friendship's sake and to spite the law—and no doubt with some persuasion from Julia—Ma Gates, once she'd made her decision, would go all the way. He fell in with her pretense, saying gently, "Now, Ma."

Her hand came down and covered his at his side. "Aaaahh," she said, fashioning a husky note for Hornbeck's benefit, "You know me. Heart of stone."

"Sure."

"Just that you're a favorite of mine, always was, always will be. Even if you done it, poor boy." McGivern winced inwardly, thinking, *don't overplay it, Ma.*

She turned her hand then and let something hard and cold slip from the folded handkerchief against his hand. At the same time, Julia had moved a step sideways, her full skirt momentarily cutting between them and Hornbeck's intense and watchful gaze. The sheriff cleared his throat irritably, and Julia stepped away, a second after McGivern had jammed the object under his thigh, recognizing its shape and feel without looking down.

Ma stood with a brusque movement, one glinting eye fashioning a broad wink, on the side away from Hornbeck. "Need anything, you get word to Ma. Make a hell of a character witness, but anything else. . . ." Her majestic head turned toward Julia. "Got anything on your mind, girl, spill it."

"I'll just say again—I'm sorry, Tom." Her face and voice held a desperate plea for understanding that was not part of the act, and McGivern said gently, putting into it all the sincerity he dared, "It was enough, your coming here, Julia. You and Ma."

The women left the cell. Sitting tautly, McGivern listened to their waning footsteps, wanting to give them time to get clear. Hornbeck moved to the cell door and locked it. He turned away, sheathing his gun, and started back to the office.

McGivern heard the street door close behind Julia and Ma Gates. He moved swiftly and silently to the front of his cell and shoved his arm between the bars, rapping a sharp order: "Stop there, Sheriff. Get your hands up before you turn."

13

HORNBECK HALTED IN his tracks, just ahead of the
cellblock door, his broad back stiffening. Slowly his
hands went up as he came around, blood mounting to
his face; he stared at the derringer in McGivern's
extended hand. "Come on," McGivern said harshly.
"The keys. . . ."

Hornbeck tramped back to the cell, his face a study
in frustrated wrath. McGivern drew his arm in, motioning at the lock. "Lower your left hand with the keys.
That's all you'll need."

Hornbeck fumbled with the lock; as the key turned,
McGivern pushed the door wide, and almost in the
same motion scooped Hornbeck's Colt from its holster.
With an ungentle hand he turned Hornbeck and shoved
him against the wall, facing it. Swiftly he broke the
loading gate of the Colt, shucked out the shells, jammed
the empty gun in Hornbeck's holster. "Fast, now. You
got handcuffs?"

"Left—hip pocket," Hornbeck said in a low, choked
way.

McGivern lifted out the manacles and clamped one
over his own right wrist, the other over Hornbeck's
left. With a rough yank he turned Hornbeck to face

him, slamming the derringer in his fisted left hand into Hornbeck's stomach. The sheriff grunted, doubling in a way that brought his face within three inches of McGivern's.

"Listen. I'll say it just once." McGivern's quiet voice held dead certainty. "We're walking out together, you and I. You'll keep your free hand resting on your gun, not forgetting it's empty. My hand'll be in my pocket, around this derringer. We'll go to the stables and pick up our horses. If anyone asks, you're taking me over to the creek where Prentiss' body was found; we're going to check for sign. That'll be the truth. And hear me. . . ." McGivern moved the derringer till the short muzzle jammed deep in Hornbeck's throat. The sheriff's Adam's apple moved convulsively. "One wrong word, one wrong move, and you're dead. Understand that. What's at stake is more important than your life or mine."

He swung away from Hornbeck, shoving the hand with the gun into the pocket of his buckskin jacket, then tugging the sheriff with him down the corridor, into the office. He paused long enough to get his gun and shell belt from Hornbeck's desk and buckle the belt under his jacket. They stepped out. The sky was still overcast, with a dreary nip to the air; a few people moved along the street, giving the two men only curious glances.

"The stable," McGivern murmured. "And keep your hand on your gun. You're being careful with me."

The boardwalk echoed solidly beneath their feet as they tramped a full block to the livery. In spite of the chill, McGivern felt warm sweat gather along his back and belly; his eyes quested the street restlessly for sign of any of Belden's gunnies. Probably they had all been summoned in to help move the rifles.

The two men turned in at the livery archway, and the ancient holster showed no curiosity at all as Hornbeck curtly ordered him to saddle their horses. McGivern stood tensely in the runway, watching the street, voicelessly cursing the hostler's infuriating slowness as he readied the horses. With a jerk on the handcuffs, McGivern signed Hornbeck to mount first; as the sheriff settled heavily into leather, McGivern made a twisting leap that carried him astride the sorrel. Their mounts were crowded close because of the awkward length of chain fettering their wrists. McGivern kneed his horse into motion, and Hornbeck hesitated only a moment before following suit.

They rode slowly apace down south Main street, then turned right at the end of the block, hitting the cottonwood-bordered creek road where it wended southwest along the stream bed. The desert rolled flat as a griddlecake away from the low banks. The fog was dissipated now, but iron-gray still mantled the sky and laid its grim pallor across the land.

Hornbeck's voice, freighted with contempt, broke the silence. "I don't know what you hope to gain by this."

"You'll see. Just don't miss the place."

"Those women are accessories. They smuggled a gun to a killer. I'll see they're called to reckoning." Hornbeck's tone held a smug note of satisfaction.

He feels very righteous now, McGivern thought. *He's tied it all into one neat moral bundle.* A saloon proprietress and ex-madam, with the help of a honky-tonk slut, had manipulated the escape of a murderer. A cold resentment drove McGivern to say bitingly, "Your sense of respectability extend to other men's wives, Hornbeck?"

For a moment his outraged awareness that McGivern knew about Melissa Belden was stark in Hornbeck's face; then it sheathed with a protective aloofness. He said distantly, "What do you know of medieval times, McGivern—of knighthood?"

"Not a hell of a lot."

"Men of old extended their protection and affection to a lady in return for her favor. It was a mark of high breeding and courtliness. Nothing that you'd understand."

"Oh," McGivern said soberly, "it's crystal clear."

Hornbeck gave him a stony glance, then hunched his black-suited shoulders and grimly shut his mouth.

McGivern wondered wryly whether the man was only a sounding board for the opinions and manners he'd heard. In the narrowly drawn lines of Hornbeck's thoughts, there were only "good" women or "bad" women—never people who were women. Not even Mrs. Belden's condemnation of her husband could shake Hornbeck's black-and-white ruling that George Belden had raised him, a drunkard, from a social abyss of evil. Hornbeck had despised his fault, but had been too weak to change by himself: a good woman had helped; somehow he'd rationalized away the fact that the "good" woman wanted to run off with him, obviously a sin in Hornbeck's rule book. Still, he had changed outwardly, even to copying some solid citizen's neat, careful speech. And gave a prating of dead chivalric custom as an excuse for the only honest feeling he had, his love for Melissa Belden. Or was that too a self-imposed illusion, part of the man's total pose? Maybe the man was hopeless, McGivern thought despairingly, a useless pig in the poke for this desperate gamble . . . but it was too late to turn back.

"That's the place," Hornbeck had reined in, and McGivern checked the sorrel, following the sheriff's pointing finger to a small, willow-fringed swale at the water's edge. Awkwardly the two of them dismounted, left the horses with trailing reins and clambered down the bank. McGivern quickly read the story in the soft, trampled mud left by last night's rain.

He began to talk quietly, pointing out obvious signs to Hornbeck, who followed his explanation with surly reluctance. "There were two horses here, Sheriff. A man dismounted from one, dragged something heavy and limp off the other—a body—carried it a few yards— see the double weight on the footprints—and dropped it . . . here. That where you found Prentiss?"

Hornbeck muttered an assent, his face intent now in spite of himself. "Man walked back to his horse and mounted," he continued. "Walloped the other horse into a run—let's say back toward Belden's ranch. Then he put his mount up the bank to the road, and—let's say again—went to town to fetch you. Here's where the two of you came down the bank to pick up Prentiss' body."

He turned to meet a hostile glare; Hornbeck said: "You could have left Prentiss here yourself—after you killed him."

McGivern nodded wearily. "You've seen I wear moccasins; this fellow had boots. Don't say I could have changed to boots; let it ride. Just remember what you see, that's all. No time to waste . . . The key to those cuffs." Hornbeck fumbled out the key and extended it. "Your pleasure," McGivern added, balancing his Colt in his left hand.

After Hornbeck had stowed the cuffs and key in his pocket, McGivern said, "Go ahead of me to your horse."

"Where to now—if you don't mind saying?"

"You had supper there last night."

"Chain Anchor? How far do you intend carrying this farce, McGivern?"

McGivern smiled faintly. "It's likely to be a long ride, Sheriff; a long, long ride. It's your duty though, and you get paid for it. I get nothing but satisfaction."

Hornbeck released a soft groan, facing McGivern with clenched fists.

"You heard me, Sheriff."

Hornbeck's stolid shape slogged up the muddy bank, and he mounted and fisted his reins with a furious resignation, waiting for McGivern to mount and motion him into the lead. They struck due east, swinging to give the town a wide berth on the south, and soon hit the Chain Anchor road. The murkiness was thinning at last and banked clouds rolled in, these in turn giving way to colorless sunlight hazily shafting their soft bellies. McGivern placed the position of the hidden sun, gauging the time as midmorning; there would be plenty of time to catch the slow-moving gun wagon.

When they achieved the mouth of the horseshoe ridge that enclosed the ranch headquarters, McGivern cautiously slowed and ordered Hornbeck to ride a horse's length ahead. The whole layout appeared deserted,

111

but a few of the crew might have remained. He rode slowly behind Hornbeck, his drawn gun lying ready against his thigh.

As they neared the gravel drive fronting the main house, the front door swung open. The first creak of hinges pulled McGivern to a halt, his gun lifting. He heard a raucous voice wheeze, "Lissa—come back! I'll shoot." Then Melissa Belden came running out, her face as white as her shirtwaist. She started across the yard, then wheeled with a little cry as George Belden's rotund form waddled out, a rifle in his hands. He halted with a startled grunt at sight of the two men, began to swing the rifle awkwardly up across his stomach.

McGivern fired from the hip. Shards of wood flew from the doorframe a foot from Belden's head. "Drop it," McGivern ordered.

Belden froze in mid-movement, glaring like some grotesque gargoyle, half-raised rifle pointed groundward. Slowly he unclenched his hands and the rifle clattered to the veranda. Melissa Belden let out an inheld breath, then turned and walked to Hornbeck's stirrup. "Paul, what is it? *What's happening?*"

Hornbeck had been watching Belden; now his dumbfounded stare lowered to her, speechlessly. McGivern kneed his horse to the tie rail and stepped down. He walked up to Belden, slapped his clothes for concealed weapons, then said sharply, "Come over here, Mrs. Belden. Tell me what happened."

Melissa came back to the veranda, followed by Hornbeck. The sheriff's face was a bewildered study at what he was seeing and hearing. Melissa told them, a stiff, automatic quality to her words, that she usually slept late, that this morning a noise had awakened her. She had thrown on a wrap and come outside, to see her husband, Harlan, and the crew over by the barn. The crew were loading oblong-shaped boxes onto a freight wagon. She'd been puzzled, but then Harlan had turned and seen her, and his look had been frightening. She had hurried inside.

Shortly Belden had come in and told her to forget what she had seen. She had known something was wrong, and then she'd remembered how McGivern had come to the ranch the night before and knew that his coming had something to do with this secrecy. Belden had read her thought in her face; he'd twisted her arm and forced out of her how she had helped McGivern escape. She swore she knew nothing else, and it left him undecided. Soon the wagon had rolled, accompanied by the entire crew, and all the while since her husband had plied her with questions she could not answer.

"McGivern," she pleaded, "please—will you tell me what this is all about?"

"What I tried to tell Hornbeck here," McGivern said tersely, grimly. "Your husband is running guns to hostile Apaches."

Hornbeck raised one hand in a gestured plea. "George, you're not denying it!"

Belden's toadlike gaze held a fathomless contempt.

"He knows better than to say anything," McGivern said softly, "before he sees his lawyer. Nothing I have so far would stand in a court of law, and he knows it. Now I'll say why I brought you with me, Sheriff. You and I are following that wagon. You're going to see the proof with your own eyes."

Hornbeck's expression was vacant and stunned. "It can't be true."

"It *is* true, Paul!" Melissa said passionately. "It's got to be." She caught him by the arms, almost shaking him. "You didn't believe me before—about George. This isn't just hearsay, this will *prove* it!"

Hornbeck said dully. "Is there something between you and McGivern?"

"Paul, for the love of heaven—"

"Hornbeck," McGivern cut in coldly and positively, "there's no time to argue with you." He tilted up his gun a half inch. "You're coming if I have to buffalo you and tie you across your saddle."

Slowly and doggedly Hornbeck shook his head. "No.

113

I can't. This could ruin everything. It will. No, not that."

"Ah, that's it," Melissa breathed. "George gave you a comfortable little niche of status. You can't stand on your feet without it. You'd rather live out your life under a shoddy pretense."

Hornbeck shrugged dully. "This badge was supposed to mean something. What does it mean now, Lissa?"

"Whatever meaning you give it!" she said vehemently. "No more, no less. If George pinned it on you to serve his own ends and you let him have his way, you'll prove yourself to be exactly what he thought you were . . . a weakling who can be twisted for anyone's purpose, but never your own. Oh, Paul, there's a limit to how far anybody can help you, even me. You've got to help yourself!"

McGivern spoke with a flat edge of impatience. "Say how it's to be, Hornbeck. Now."

"Yes, Paul, decide." Melissa's face was filled with angry color. "You can go with McGivern the hard way . . . or make your choice now, for yourself. Else you've seen me for the last time."

"Not that, Lissa," he said weakly.

"That. I'm leaving George. I can leave you as easily." Her voice faltered slightly, then strengthened. "I can, Paul."

Belden started to chuckle, his vast gut trembling. He made no sound, yet the chuckle mounted to a noiseless, mirthless laugh. Melissa turned on him, her voice low and hate-filled. "Stop it, George, stop it."

Hornbeck looked up; his eyes focused, narrowed down. "Don't do that, George." McGivern wisely held his tongue, watching the slow, crazed anger fill Hornbeck's face. "Pious Paul," Belden wheezed between chortles. "Pious Paul and lovely, luxury-struck Melissa. I give you much joy of each other."

Something ugly and warped behind the fat man's Olympian benevolence was naked, and the sight of it seemed to snap whatever cowed fantasy Hornbeck held about the man. He lunged between McGivern and

114

Lissa, his long fingers fastening around Belden's throat. His lunge sent them both stumbling back through the open door, Belden's weight crashing to the parlor floor with an impact that shook the house.

Hornbeck was on him, thick hands choking the laugh to a gurgle. Belden's eyes popped fishlike in his skull, a last breath clawing noisily from his throat before the deepening force of Hornbeck's fingers pinched off his wind. His small, womanish hands pulled futilely at Hornbeck's wrists. The tide of red that filled his jowls shaded to a swollen purple.

McGivern watched, his gun hanging loosely fisted at his side, a faint, grim smile on his lips. "Oh, stop it!" Lissa cried. "Stop it!"

McGivern took two steps and closed his hand on Hornbeck's shoulder. "That's enough."

Hornbeck seemed not to hear. When McGivern tried to pull him off, his stocky body was rigid with unleashed fury. McGivern whipped his Colt up and down in a short, chopping arc that ended against Hornbeck's temple. He caught the sheriff's limp weight and supported him to a leather divan.

Hornbeck sat up with a grimace of pain as Melissa came over, kneeling at his side with eyes full of compassion. He looked at her stupidly, then at McGivern. "You hit me."

"After you'd proved your point."

"By God," Hornbeck muttered, ducking his head and gingerly rubbing it. He looked up again. "By God."

"Feels that way, doesn't it?" McGivern smiled faintly. "Can you ride?"

A kind of surprised intelligence mingled with a half-baffled exultance filled Hornbeck's long face. His eyes met McGivern's with a level regard. "Any time."

14

THEY GOT BELDEN into his room and handcuffed him to the iron bedstead. The fat man was wheezing like a fish out of water, still unable to speak when Hornbeck and McGivern left him asprawl the bed and went out to their horses.

Melissa stepped onto the veranda, her eyes troubled as she watched them mount. "Paul," she said then, "I—I want to go with you. There's nothing for me here."

"I'll be back, Lissa."

"If you don't come back?" It left her like a lost cry.

"I'll be back." He frowned, holding in his fiddlefooting horse. "It'll be dangerous enough without a woman. You'll be all right here . . . George can't hurt you now. It has to be this way." He looked at McGivern for confirmation. The scout nodded. Melissa said nothing. She watched in silence as they rode from the ranchyard.

McGivern wordlessly led the way, cutting north from the ranch along the fresh-rutted wheel tracks. Harlan and the others had a broad start, but even so they'd make slow time with the heavily loaded wagon. Once the pursuers were close it would be simple to trail them at a distance to the rendezvous. What happened afterward would be the difficult and dangerous part . . .

Hornbeck rode jauntily, shoulders squared against his horse's rocking gait, and McGivern knew that the man had found himself with a vengeance. Heady wine for a man in his mid-thirties who had spent half a lifetime leaning on outward props—whisky and then false prestige and a woman's sympathy—rather than find strength in the hard, independent core of himself. McGivern wondered if Hornbeck was only caught up in a reaction of extreme bravado after a cowed lifetime. He considered that carefully and decided that the man's self-finding was real; he'd only needed the sudden triggering of Belden's mockery to release it. The reaction might still leave him over-confident for a while, overbalanced to rashness; the business facing them called for cool thinking and steady hands. *Cross that bridge when it comes up,* McGivern thought then. He bent his full attention to the trail.

There was a thrum of hoofbeats from behind, which McGivern was the first to hear. He reined in and quartered his animal around facing their backtrail. Hornbeck ranged over beside him, squinting against the sun. Then the sheriff blurted, "It's Lissa."

"Not surprising," McGivern said shortly, "is it?"

She pulled to a halt, flushed and a little breathless. She had changed to rough trousers and a man's hickory shirt, her rich auburn hair topped by a floppy hat. A breath of wind toiled with and loosened a few wisps of hair across her face, and she pushed them back with a hand, the gesture oddly defiant, as was the strong determination in her face.

She touched a bulging knapsack slung from her saddlehorn. "You'll need food and water. I've brought both."

"We'd have made out, but thank you nonetheless," McGivern said with elaborate dryness. "I see you also brought yourself dressed for a trip. It's no go, Mrs. Belden."

Her chin lifted. "Yes? And why not?" Her eyes softened a little, looking at Hornbeck. "I'm going with you, Paul. If you don't come back, neither do I. It's that simple. There's nothing else I can do."

A harried anger stirred in Hornbeck's face. "Listen, Melissa . . ." His voice trailed off helplessly. "McGivern, can't you say something?"

"Nothing I haven't said . . . and nothing I didn't mean."

"You're overlooking a practical point, Mr. McGivern," she observed flatly. "The more witnesses to this, the better. Particularly when—when one or more may not return alive."

"A woman can't testify against her husband, and I'm after Belden's scalp—his alone."

The defiance drained from her face, to be replaced by a softened, begging plea. "You're a hard, self-sufficient man, but you must understand . . . a little. Didn't you ever care for someone enough that—that everything else came second in your life?"

McGivern's hand fisted on his lifted reins. Her words had broken through his defense; and he knew by the wondering triumph in her expression that she had seen it. "Once," he said in a tight undertone.

Melissa seized on it with a woman's intuitive accuracy. "A girl. Did something happen to her?"

"Yes."

"You were there?"

He shook his head in negation, then avoided her eyes.

"Didn't you wish that you could have shared . . . what happened?"

"Mrs. Belden—"

"You understand that much, then," she said softly. "It's worse for a woman. A man who loses his woman still has his work—his ambitions—his life interests. Or revenge, if nothing else." He winced faintly. She said then: "A woman who loses, loses everything. I can't lose him and go on alone, not when there's this last chance for us both. That's why I'm coming."

"Melissa," Hornbeck said humbly.

"I won't be in your way. I may even be of some help."

"That's not likely," McGivern said roughly, to cover his feelings; a curt jerk of his head motioned her to fall

118

in behind, ignoring the half-angry, half-sheepish reproach in Hornbeck's face.

At high noon they halted deep on Chain Anchor's north range, just short of the barrier ridge, to rest and eat. Melissa had packed a practical grubsack of staples ideal for a dry and fireless camp. Since it would probably be bite-and-run later, McGivern warned them to eat their fill and get some rest afterward.

By midafternoon they had penetrated to the end of the canyon bisecting the ridge and were on the sterile and waterless wastes to the north. From the flats with which McGivern had become familiarized by previous excursions, the land rose to a semi-plateau which rolled limitlessly to the north and east, desolate and broken irregularly by massive lava formations. Only a few twisted, scraggly juniper and piñon were lodged in the shattered, tortured rocks that reared like menacing sentries on every side of the wagon trail straggling between them over hard-baked clay levels. The trail was the only sign of white man's invasion of this wild country, which still belonged to the buzzard, the snake, and roaming bands of renegade Apaches. The broiling sun slanting ruthlessly against their backs began its slow sapping of the strength of Hornbeck and the woman; McGivern had to caution them to conserve their water.

Because McGivern had deliberately held a slow pace to spare the horses and keep a careful distance between them and the wagon and its armed guards, it was late afternoon before the wagon hove briefly into view, then jolted again out of sight behind a rocky shoulder. Hornbeck and Melissa, drooping with heat exhaustion, failed to notice anything, and McGivern said nothing. Harlan had no suspicion he was being followed; to his knowledge McGivern was safely jailed. It accounted for his confident failure to put out flankers or a rear guard.

The land became higher and more rugged. This was not mountain country, but McGivern suspected they were mounting the lower spine of a northern range where it petered out. That would account for the heightening, choppy aspect of the terrain. He guessed the rendezvous would be deep in the heart of this area. It was ideal: accessible even to a heavy wagon, but remote and rugged enough to throw off an unskilled tracker. Already the clay floor of the plateau had thinned away to broken, treacherous shale, and McGivern had to dismount frequently to check sign. Sometimes it was the work of minutes to discover even a fragment of shale freshly clipped by a shod hoof, or a rare horse dropping. Several times he lost sign altogether and had to work the backtrail patiently in a concentric circle to find where the wagon had made a sudden turn.

At last they rode over a humped jag of creosote and saw the distant wagon entering a rounded, saddle-shaped break in a gigantic serrated hogback. McGivern motioned the others swiftly back behind the creosote. That hogback must be the atrophied spine of this high terrain, and on its other side the land would fall away again. *Close to rendezvous now,* he hazarded. That was why he wanted to hold to shelter for a few minutes. The Apaches could have sentinels on that ridge, watching for the wagon, and its arrival would bring them down. *It better,* he thought.

He squeezed the sorrel into motion, some of his excitement communicated to the animal; it pricked its ear and fiddlefooted foolishly as he put it across the creosote hump. Hornbeck and Melissa fell in with his lead without words, and he knew that they too, alerted by his sudden halt, had seen the wagon.

In fifteen minutes they reached the saddle. McGivern took swift note of a narrow niche cleaving the ridge wall, barely wide enough for one horseman to enter at a time. It afforded concealment beneath the beetling upper ramparts of the ridge. He ordered Melissa and the sheriff to head their horses into it and await his return.

"What'll you do?" Hornbeck asked quickly.

"Go over that saddle on foot. See the other side."

"Alone?"

"Mister," McGivern said patiently, "you're in hostile
120

country. Your enemy's the sharpest, toughest desert fighter alive. I told you before, your life or mine don't matter. We just have to stay alive long enough to spike the enemy's guns. That means scouting the layout by someone who can meet an Apache on his home ground, and that means me. You'd be in the way. Lie low and keep quiet."

Without waiting for a reply, he slid to the ground with his pair of Army fieldglasses in hand, turning his horse into the niche with a slap on the rump. At an easy, low-bent lope he entered the saddle dip without looking back. The trail sloped up for a good hundred yards, and then downward at a treacherous angle. McGivern now found himself looking across a limitless plain that hazed into the far horizon, and the sight brought him to a surprised standstill. Instead of the gentle tapering-off of the heights he'd expected, the far side of the ridge dropped sharply. The incline was fairly gentle up here, but soon it sheered off in a steep drop hundreds of feet to a slow-crawling river at its base, heavily silted to a murky yellow.

Moving on a few yards, he lowered himself to his belly and lay in watchful immobility. The majestic pitch of the wall below was broken only by an occasional flat ledge of tilted shale. One such ledge protruded from the gentler upper incline, and toward this the wagon was careering and jolting. The hoorawing of the driver, the squeal of brake shoes, drifted up. It was a tricky negotiation, but the driver expertly achieved the ledge and hauled up the team.

The horsemen crowded around the wagon and dismounted. McGivern's gaze moved on, taking in a second, larger ledge somewhat below and well to the left of the first. On the ledge a jumble of monolithic rocks formed a rough circle, as though a giant hand had playfully swiped at the cliff above and hurled down a massive handful to the ledge, afterward carelessly arranging them around a sandy amphitheater. Within this natural cordon was the Apache camp. The pony remuda stood rump to rump along a picket rope strung

121

between two boulders. Supper fires burned by a few brush wickiups, and dusky forms were moving from the camp. This wasn't the main band, that was certain; he counted only a dozen braves.

And no guard on the ridge above. Damnfool young bucks had carelessly deserted their posts to see the wagon, and no doubt would get a fierce castigation from the leader for it. Just now the whole camp was converging on the higher ledge where the wagon had stopped. The white guards were fingering their rifles nervously.

Suddenly one buck wheeled in his tracks, bawled an order. The others halted and straggled sullenly back to camp. The buck who'd given the order went on alone toward the whites. That would be the war chief. McGivern lifted the binoculars and steadied blurrily on the climbing man. He swore softly and fined down the adjustment. The flat cruel features of the Apache swam into focus.

Maco.

Recognition of his old enemy sent a still, quiet hate crawling along McGivern's spine, but his hand held steady, following the war chief's ascent to the ledge. The tall figure of Harlan moved off from the others, and he and Maco met at the juncture of ledge and slope. Words passed. Heated words, for Maco made an angry, slicing gesture with his hand. There was no love lost between these white and Indian renegades; only their dual purpose preserved a thin harmony. Maco had been careful not to let his warriors get near the whites. McGivern thought fleetingly of the Indian youth Giannah-tah whose life he had spared, wondered if he was down there in the Apache camp.

Maco ended the caucus by pivoting on his heel and stalking back to his camp. Reggie hesitated a moment, then swung back to his men and barked orders. The crew off-saddled, threw down blanket rolls and gear. Two men unhitched the team, another threw back the tarp on the wagon and lifted out a peeled log roughly the thickness of a corral pole. This he thrust between

122

the spokes of the back wheels, then lashed it securely to the wagon frame. A rough lock, to brake the wagon solidly on the precarious ledge.

McGivern watched them set up camp. Whatever had passed between Harlan and Maco, it was evident that the rifles would not be unloaded tonight. That could be a stroke of luck. McGivern moved the binoculars down, studying the jagged face of the escarpment to the churning river below. Yes, there was the way . . . with Hornbeck's help and the aid of darkness.

He inched back a yard on his belly, rose to his feet and dogtrotted back across the saddle to where Hornbeck and Lissa waited. They had driven the horses to the far end of the cranny. Both squatted on their heels within its mouth. They stirred aside to make room as he sank to his haunches facing them.

"Well?" Hornbeck said impatiently.

"The 'Paches are there, an even dozen. Maco's band, all right. I saw him. But not the main bunch."

"What does that mean?"

"One of two things. Maco's broken with Nachito, which I doubt, or Nachito is holding the rest of the band nearby . . . because Harlan refused to bring his half-dozen men near half a hundred wartailing 'Paches—which was good sense." He paused grimly. "Tall odds for us, all the same. Seven whites, twice that many Apaches."

Hornbeck glanced at Melissa, nervously rubbed his hands together. "What do you have in mind?"

McGivern said flatly, "Those guns have to be destroyed. There's only one way. If we're lucky, we'll only have to take on Harlan's bunch, and we can get the drop on them."

Quietly he outlined it for them. Melissa bit her lips. "It will be risky . . . for you both. There's no other way?"

"No."

"And I just hold the horses ready—and wait?"

"That's it." He drew the derringer Ma Gates had slipped him from his pocket. "If we don't make it . . . ," he hesitated, ". . . you'll need this."

123

She took it wordlessly. Hornbeck was pale, but he nodded his determination as he gently pressed her hand. They ate and drank a little from the knapsack, crouching in a tight circle to wait for nightfall. They spoke little except to go over the plan. The cramped inactivity, coupled with bleak anticipation, dragged minutes to eternities. Sunset crowned the heights, rosy strata that faded to gray twilight, then darkness. First moonrise shed a silvery complexion across the rocky landscape; it seemed the dead face of another world, making the tense vigil somehow unreal.

It brought McGivern face to face with the grim riddle of the death he might taste soon. He could cope with the knowledge, as he often had. He could only guess at Hornbeck's thoughts. The sheriff was tense-postured, no hint of hysteria about him. He and Melissa sat close, a wordless communion in that closeness that touched the scout with an unsettling sadness. Strangely, it was not a dead girl for whom his memory fumbled, but a living one. A man might love a memory, but he did not think of death when death was so close.

He remembered Julia as she had looked that day when a casual outing had suddenly become more for them both—the sunlight on her bright hair and the flush of sun and wine in her face and the awakening to a sense of life she had never known . . . He faced his thoughts with a puzzled self-amazement, a fresh excitement. He had not realized how nearly a hurtful memory had scarred over, yet he could not deny it. *If I come out of this,* he thought, *there'll be time, time to know her.* He'd forgotten how life went quickly on in this new, yet ageless, country of unceasing change.

When he judged that both the Apaches and the Chain Anchor crew were turned into their blankets, McGivern rose and touched Hornbeck's arm. With a half sob Melissa reached up and drew Hornbeck's face to hers; then she was on her feet, groping to the rear of the shadow-blackened niche to lead out the horses.

McGivern went ahead of Hornbeck through the deep vale of shadows that pooled in the saddle dip. They reached the vantage point where he had lain earlier. He sank to a crouch, waiting for Hornbeck to move up beside him. Below the blanketed forms of Harlan's men ringed a large fire. A long guard hunkered down against a wagon wheel, a blanket thrown over his shoulders against the high-country chill. Off to the lower right the Apache camp lay in utter darkness, the cookfires extinguished. The Apaches would have a hidden sentry in camp, but the high location of Harlan's camp would cut off his view, luckily.

McGivern pointed to indicate a shallow arroyo which cut wormlike down the rotted talus of the slope, the alluvial fan at its lower end spilling onto the shale ledge of Harlan's bivouac. Hornbeck nodded his understanding. He was close at McGivern's heels as the scout slipped into the arroyo, flattened himself on its sandy bottom, dug in his elbows and inched his body forward in short lurches. *Lucky it's a white camp we're stalking,* he thought wryly, hearing Hornbeck behind him, breathing heavily, his body scraping along as he clumsily followed McGivern's example.

They stopped just beyond the fitful rim of high-tossed firelight. The back of the wagon was a dozen yards distant; to its left the fire blazed, with its circle of sleeping men. The guard was half dozing against the wheel, his head jerking a little in an unconscious effort to hold to wakefulness, his rifle tipped slackly in his hands.

Signaling to Hornbeck not to move, McGivern came to his feet now, sixgun in hand. He skirted the sleeping men like a flitting shadow, and was halfway around the camp before the guard's head snapped erect at some half-sensed movement. McGivern covered him, raising a finger to his lips. Hornbeck rose, stepped up beside the open-mouthed guard and lifted the rifle from his nerveless fingers. A curt whisper from the lawman ordered the guard down on his face. McGivern moved soundlessly among the sleeping men, collecting their rifles and handguns that lay in sight, tossing these to the soft sand away from the fire.

As he stepped across to the last sleeper, this one suddenly threw his blanket aside and came to a sitting position with a gun in his fist. His mouth opened, hauling in breath to release a shout. With a swift merciless violence, McGivern clubbed the man across the jaw with his Colt, laid him out cold. The crack of metal on flesh and bone brought two others erect in their blankets. They stared, blearily taking this in, then slowly lifted their hands. The remaining three, Harlan included, snored on in their blankets. McGivern was relieved; of them all, only Harlan was likely to resist.

With McGivern covering the crew, Hornbeck pulled out his pocket knife and cut the lashings on the wagon's rough lock. Gingerly he dragged out the log from between the spokes and laid it on the ground. Then he put his shoulder to a rear wheel, gripped the spokes, dug in his heels, and shoved. At McGivern's murmured order, the guard and the aroused sleepers moved over to the wagon with a cowed wariness. With a man straining at each wheel, the wagon budged a few inches, rocked, settled.

"Put your backs into it!" Hornbeck hissed with a savage warning that threw a genuine effort into the other three. The wagon began its soundless roll through the soft sand that covered the ledge rock, slowly at first, then with a ponderous gain of momentum. Harlan grunted in his blankets and settled back with a snoring sigh as McGivern watched unblinkingly. The wagon had reached the outer rim of the ledge, where its pitch took an abrupt plunge. As the front wheels touched the incline, the men leaped away. The heavy wagon careened out over the lip-rock, and then nothing in the world could have stopped it.

There was a moment's silence as the wagon vanished into the darkness below, then a slack, jolting roar as it hit the steep shale beneath and rushed on and downward. McGivern and Hornbeck backed swiftly away toward the upper slope as Harlan and the others rolled out of their blankets. The three who'd helped stared

126

stupidly at the threat of leveled guns in the hands of the pair backing away. With a baffled, bull-chested roar, Harlan was clawing out of his blankets, reaching for a gun that wasn't there. Then the thunderous crash of splitting wood resounded from far below as the loaded wagon hit the lower slope and the river, its destruction muffling its own splash. Harlan stood a stunned moment with the firelight playing on his golden curls; then he lunged for one of the rifles on the ground.

McGivern snapped a shot at him and missed, then wheeled and loped up the arroyo, with the lawman scrambling ahead. Now the guns opened up behind, but the crew was still half blinded by firelight after their rude awakening. Bullets sang off rocks with deep angry whines. For a few seconds Hornbeck and McGivern were highlighted by flickering firelight before they were lost in the deeper shadows upslope.

McGivern heard Hornbeck ahead of him, climbing and panting, then a low groan as Hornbeck's leg buckled under him and he fell. McGivern dragged him to his feet.

"Ricochet—got me in the leg," the sheriff gasped. "Go on."

"Give me your gun and *move!* I'll cover you." McGivern turned as he spoke, firing at the man in the lead as the whole gang poured up the arroyo. The man yelled and shrank against a cutbank. McGivern shot again, and the others scattered behind the rocks. "Go on," McGivern yelled savagely as Hornbeck hesitated.

Hornbeck swore at him, thrust his gun at the scout's hand and resumed his stumbling ascent. McGivern crouched, making himself small between the banks. The bulky figure of Harlan plunged up the arroyo, waving his gun, trying to pull his men into a charge. McGivern fired twice, too hastily. Harlan faltered and cursed blisteringly as he fell back to shelter. Now the bedlam in the Apache camp reached McGivern as a flurry of shouts. He guessed the hostiles' first reaction was that they'd been attacked by Harlan's crew.

McGivern emptied his gun at the rocks below, then palmed up Hornbeck's and fired again. The Chain Anchor men fired wildly at his gun flashes, but McGivern had already moved to a higher position. Now he could make out a few dusky figures bounding up the moonlit slope off to his right, Maco's gutturals raised in harsh command. The crafty war chief had summed up the situation and was rallying his braves to help the *pinda-likoye* with *pesh-e-gar,* the guns. McGivern turned his attention on the lean, elusive shadows of two Apaches who were bounding like mountain goats ahead of their fellows, up toward the rose-fire winks of McGivern's gun. He turned and raced up the gully, knowing he could not pin down the Apaches as he had Harlan's men.

As he achieved the top of the gully, he saw Hornbeck's limping shape just disappearing into the shadow-filled saddle pass. He'd have to stall pursuit till Hornbeck and Melissa could get a start on horseback. He heard Harlan's crew leave cover and pound up the arroyo.

McGivern pivoted to face the fast-coming Apaches, laying his pistol across his forearm, braced against the uncertain light and a moving target, and steadied down. The .45 bucked against his palm, and the first Apache doubled in midstride and went down.

The second foeman hauled up, nocking an arrow to his gut-strung bow and whipping it level. McGivern fired and knew he'd missed as the Apache, untouched, released his shaft.

It made a close and hateful *whir,* struck an outcrop two feet from the scout's head. For a split second McGivern saw that the arrow had been deflected at an angle—before it ripped sidelong through his hair and scalp. The blinding pain staggered him. His moccasined foot slipped on a smooth shale fragment and turned at the ankle. He tried to twist as he fell sideways, tried to throw out his arms to catch his weight. Something smashed him in the face and he hit the ground, rolling on his back. The stars blazed near, pinwheeled whitely in his blurring eyes, and that was all.

A LARGER BLAZE that glared and throbbed redly
behind his eyelids brought him slowly awake. He knew
that he was lying on his back on warm sand with hot
sunlight on his face. He remembered with a kind of
obscure panic that Apaches would cut off a captive's
eyelids and stake him out under the sun. He blinked
frantically and found his lashes crusted with blood. He
strained them open. The sun, midmorning high, washed
with a full painful glare against his sight as he raised
his head.

He was in the rock-bounded amphitheater of the
Apache bivouac, his wrists tied across his belly. Copper-
skinned warriors hunkered in the shade of the monolithic
rocks, talking or working on their gear. There was a
subdued and ominous quiet about their low gutturals. It
hung like a poised knife in the sun-drenched air. Of this
he was keenly aware. A youth in his teens, squatting
nearby with a rifle across his knees, glanced at McGivern
and rose to his feet, then looked at a wickiup a few
paces away and grunted a single word: "Maco."

The stiffened hide hinged from a crossbeam over the
entrance swung outward, pushed by the war chief's
great shoulders as he squeezed through. He stood and

was motionless, eyeing McGivern with a contained hatred. He glanced at the young buck. "Go to the camp of *pinda-likoye* with *pesh-e-gar*. Bring the big white-eyes with yellow hair." The youth loped obediently from camp, heading for Harlan's bivouac.

"How do you feel, *Nantan* Day-zen?" Maco's tone bore a cold, cynical edge of humor. He was savoring this moment.

"Well, I thank you." McGivern's reply was even, calm, from a throat parched and swollen. He sat up and covered his painful wince stolidly. He inched his body back against the cool shade of a monolith, only now noting that his feet were tied. He set his teeth against the tortured throbbing of his head. "It is a surprise," he said then. "I had thought your braves would be working on me."

"The *nantan* must have the pleasure of knowing it," Maco said. "Since *Chigo-na-ay's* first beams rose from the desert, my braves have searched by the river. The current is too deep and swift. The *pesh-e-gar* are lost to us. For that, Day-zen, you will scream for death through many days and nights."

"But many white-eyes will live. Can you live with that thought, Maco?"

Maco's smile showed stained and broken teeth. "You will help me bear it, Day-zen. It is a time I have long awaited; that I am not quick to end."

A rattle of shale up the slope announced Harlan's arrival. He trudged across the camp, stopped a few feet away. "You know, sport, this almost makes losing the guns worthwhile."

"Losing the gun-running, too?" McGivern murmured.

Reggie laughed silently. "Why? You're all here." McGivern's back stiffened, his gaze automatically circled the camp. "Hornbeck and the woman are in one of the *jacales*," Reggie said. "It wasn't hard running 'em to ground after Maco's boys took you, McGivern."

"You fool," McGivern grated flatly. "Have you forgotten she's Belden's wife? With anyone but Maco,

130

she'd be made a slave, not harmed. But Maco! And you turned her over to them . . ."

Irritation shaded Harlan's stare. He shifted his feet uncomfortably. "No choice," he growled. "Maco demanded all three of you. He outnumbers me. Any story'll do for Belden. He'll not be caring, her knowing what she does. Belden had a use for her, but this ends it. Same for Paul. It's too damned bad."

"What about you?"

"How's that?"

"A man who'll run guns to hostiles is low enough," McGivern said steadily, "but I didn't stamp you as one who'd throw a white woman to Maco."

Harlan flushed darkly. "God damn you, McGivern . . . there was nothing else I could do!" His momentary twinge of angry conscience vanished. A cold, vicious brutality that almost matched Maco's supplanted his easy blandness. "You bought into this, McGivern . . . kept poking and prying. And Prentiss had to try blackmail. When her and Hornbeck bought in with you, they earned your rations. Now you can all choke."

With a savage movement, he swung to the war chief. "Let's dicker. I want to be moving out." The two of them talked for a half hour, squatting in front of McGivern, contemptuous of his presence. They made furious ultimatums, swore at each other with the heated arrogance of two overbearing personalities who wouldn't give an ell. McGivern gathered that Harlan wanted to barter directly with Nachito, whom he trusted, but the younger chief was holding the rest of the band out of sight. Harlan's quarrel with Maco yesterday had resulted in the failure to unload the guns, and their subsequent loss. The fact of their double defection worsened their tempers.

Yet they arrived at a compromise. Harlan promised another shipment of two hundred rifles, to be delivered in three months, and got Maco to promise cash on delivery this time, but was unable to wheedle the war chief out of even a quarter payment for the guns McGivern had lost them. McGivern listened with a dull detachment, wondering whether men like these would always stand between the two races and the panacea of brotherhood for which he himself had worked . . . hopelessly, it seemed.

When they had ironed out the last detail, Harlan rose without a handshake, without a parting word, and tramped from the camp. Maco was scowling with the thought of his commitment as he vanished inside his wickiup. McGivern leaned his aching head against the cool rock and closed his eyes, trying to cudgel his dulled brain. This was a vise of circumstance as hopelessly tight as he'd ever known.

He listened to the sounds of horses moving upslope as Harlan's men broke camp and headed back. He set the ringing hoof falls to a mechanical refrain with the sick beat of blood in his temples. Strangely, the dwindling sound seemed to become louder.

He opened his eyes. The warriors jabbered excitedly as they converged on the east end of the camp. McGivern eased to his feet by straightening his legs and sliding his back up the slippery rock face. He saw the cause of the commotion.

Along the eastward-running wall of the gigantic hogback spine was a crude trail formed by a slipped fault in its bedrock. From where the wall curved out of sight, a line of riders slowly wended single file along the narrow trail coming into the camp. Chiricahua braves . . . ten . . . twenty . . . thirty and more, painted and armed for war. The main body of the band, held at a nearby bivouac till Harlan's men were gone. Like those in camp, the newcomers were young men, many not out of their teens. Yet they were seasoned to the warpath. A few favored badly tended wounds. Some carried Army saddle gear, canteens, cartridge pouches and belts, saddlebags. Others wore Army campaign hats and pieces of uniform. A strutting buck in the lead sported a lance-ripped frock coat and an ancient beaver hat. All carried the Winchester '73's.

As they came off the slope into camp, there was an exchange of joshing camaraderie. Near the end of the long file stepped two horses with the twin poles of a travois litter lashed between them. A youthful brave sat the rocking litter, a slow smile breaking his dark face as the braves began jostling around him, all talking and joking at once. McGivern knew a stunned surprise, almost like a padded blow: the Apache on the litter was the boy he'd saved three days ago, who had neatly turned the tables on him to ride off half dead on a drooping pinto.

Two husky warriors caught Gian-nah-tah's arms, swung him to the ground. He grunted and said something that made them laugh. Maco had emerged from his shelter, his black scowl not breaking as he went over to the youth. They spoke briefly, the youth nodding gravely, stoically facing Maco's angry news.

With a sharp word, he chopped Maco off in mid-speech, and only then looked over at McGivern. Motioning the others about their business, Gian-nah-tah trudged over to where the scout leaned. He walked carefully but erect. He looked exactly as he had three days ago, showing little outward effect from his wound. A fresh calico rag was bound over his midriff, where a poultice made a flat bulge.

"This is not a *nak-kai-ye* stand-off, eh, Day-zen?"

"So," McGivern said coldly, "you are Nachito."

"I did not deceive you." The youth was unsmiling, but his eyes glinted his amusement. "I won the name of Gian-nah-tah at ten summers, when I warned my tribe of a nearby patrol of *rurales* before the scouts saw them. I became a warrior at fourteen, a war chief at eighteen, when alone I slew four white-eyes who came to tear up our land for *pesh-litzogue*, the yellow iron. And with Geronimo, I earned the name of Nachito from the Meh-hi-kanos in Sonora. Did I deceive, Day-zen?"

McGivern shook his head. "Had I known you were Nachito, you would not have escaped so easily."

"This I knew." And now Nachito smiled openly; it did not dull the wicked edge to his next words. "Maco says you came last night with a man and a woman to the

133

camp of the *pinda-likoye* with guns, and those guns lie out of our reach in the river below."

"He speaks straight."

Maco, with a few curious braves straggling behind, had come up and now stood impassively with folded arms. His murky eyes boiled with hate. "Does Nachito question this?" he demanded.

Nachito did not even glance at him, but continued to regard McGivern with curious serenity. "It is known everywhere that Day-zen is a just man. Why did you destroy our guns? Do you not think we have the right to defend ourselves?"

McGivern tilted his head wearily back against the rock. No one knew better the endless record of white treachery that had triggered every Apache atrocity. "Of course you have the right. As it is my right to meet you in the war field, a man against a man. But those who brought the guns were men of my race. Would Nachito crush the snake who warms itself in his blankets?"

"It is a good reason. But in the past you have not fought us this way."

"No." McGivern paused, marshaling himself to speak without emotion. "There was a girl in the land of my youth. She came from where the sun rises, to be my woman. A stagecoach was attacked in the great canyon east of Fort Laughlin. The woman was killed by an Apache lance."

"I remember," Nachito said simply. "The lance was mine."

"You—" McGivern lunged away from the rock. His bound legs twisted beneath him and he fell helplessly on his back at Nachito's feet. A buck leaped forward, his lance lowering its keen tip to McGivern's throat.

"As I do not war on women, my heart was sore," Nachito said quietly. "But as you are my enemy, I tell you to hear me, or die."

"Now or later," McGivern panted. "And I gave you your life. . . ."

"You will listen," Nachito said inexorably. "The soldiers and men of the stagecoach fought furiously before we killed them all. We overturned the coach and set fire to it, and only then heard the white woman cry out. We did not see her lying inside. Maco dragged her out and laughed as he put his torch to her hair. Such, for Maco, is but a beginning. Before he could stop me, I ran my lance through her heart. Since that moment, Maco has hated me." He motioned at the buck, and the lance point was withdrawn from McGivern's throat.

McGivern sat up and felt sweat crawl down his face, felt the shaking of his body with released tension, and did not care that the Apaches saw it. Nor did Maco's scarred face make him hide his grimace of satisfaction. "A man who earns the hatred of Maco sleeps lightly," McGivern said huskily; it was his token of thanks to Nachito.

"A war chief of the *Be-don-ko-he* whose heart turns to water at a white-eyed woman's screams, who admits this to a white-eyes," Maco sneered. "Gladly I took the war trail with Nachito—the grandson of Tana, the lieutenant of Geronimo. If they knew this, both would spit on you."

Nachito turned slowly to face the older man, a hand falling to the hilt of his knife. "They knew," Nachito said softly, "and they did not spit. Perhaps Maco would like to spit."

"I do not spit on crippled boys."

"Then keep it in your mouth with your foolish words. You talk like old Naka-do-klunni, the medicine man. Nobody listens to him but the squaws and the children."

The listening braves grinned; one chuckled aloud and was silenced by Maco's cold glare. McGivern guessed that the co-leadership of this band was an unsatisfactory arrangement for both war chiefs. A note of icy casualness to their insults suggested that they'd quarreled before. Nachito had needed Maco's seniority at first, in winning his reputation with these northern Apaches, but McGivern sensed that there had been a slow shift in the balance of leadership.

The young bucks liked Nachito, with his youth, his

humor, and his brash courage. Even his non-Apache quirks, his refusal to torture and his amiable discourse with an enemy, were eccentricities which added to the colorful personality of a born leader. It was Nachito who'd taken the initiative in the gun liaison with Belden. And McGivern guessed that to Nachito's mind Maco had become so much dead wood that the junior chief would be glad of an excuse to sweep out. If Maco had a similar notion, he was stymied by Nachito's popularity. *Maybe,* McGivern thought with the glimmer of a hunch, *just maybe, if I scratch Nachito's back, he'll scratch mine.*

Nachito said thoughtfully, "It is spoken by our brothers at San Carlos that you asked questions. They told you nothing, yet you learned all!"

"I am called Day-zen."

"Well-named. And now you are here." Nachito regarded him with mock perplexity. "What shall I do with you, Day-zen?"

"He is mine," growled Maco, "as are the other white-eyes. . . ."

"That we shall see," Nachito said serenely. "Have the man and woman brought here."

Three braves loped to a wickiup at the north end of camp. Shortly they returned with Melissa Belden and Paul Hornbeck in tow. One buck forced Melissa to her knees in front of Nachito, his fist fastened in the red-gold mass of her hair. Her clothes were torn and her smudged face bore a dazed, uncomprehending look. Hornbeck's mouth was bleeding; a filthy rag was tied around his thick calf. He kicked furiously at the two Apaches who held his arms. One of them clouted him across the head, and he subsided. The buck who held Melissa jerked her head back at a painful angle, drew his knife and passed it suggestively around the bright tangle of her hair. Nachito spoke sharply, and the buck quit clowning.

"What are these to you, Day-zen?" Nachito asked.

"Friends. The man wears the white-eyes' star of law, the woman is Belden's."

136

"These things I know. Harlan told Maco that Belden is tired of his woman. She has spirit, to go to war with men. *Enju,* I have need of a servant with spirit." The watching braves grinned and nodded at each other.

"Here you step too far," Maco rumbled. "The woman is mine. Day-zen, too, and the *pinda-likoye* with the star."

McGivern came to his feet now, teetering precariously on his heels and catching his balance. He faced Maco squarely. His heart was triphammering with the knowledge that he, Hornbeck, and Lissa had one thin chance for life. It depended on how far Maco could be goaded, on how far McGivern could push a tacit alliance with Nachito. As he felt the Apaches' attention focus upon him, he made his words strong and steady.

"Nachito is hurt. He cannot make a contest. I will fight you, Maco, in the Apache fashion."

Surprise flickered in Nachito's eyes; he said nothing, only watched McGivern intently. A murmur ran through the listening braves. Maco spoke, sneering: "For your freedom, white man?"

"For slavery," McGivern said quietly. "Who would not rather be Nachito's slave than Maco's victim? Then—" he lowered his voice, directing its hard challenge at Maco alone— "we have fought often, you and I, but never as a man facing a man."

"A prisoner does not name terms," Maco growled.

"Our quarrel is not as the quarrel between our people. You know this well."

Excited talk broke out. Who did not know of the almost legendary enmity between Maco and the white-eyed scout? It would be a great thing to witness the final reckoning—a thing of which a man could boast to his grandchildren. McGivern covertly studied the two chiefs, seeing the thoughtful calculation behind Nachito's eyes. If they dueled, and Maco were killed, it would rid Nachito of a powerful enemy-in-rank. The youth's half-friendly feeling for McGivern and sense of obligation for McGivern's sparing his life were of lesser consideration, but not to be discounted either. And it was

137

Nachito's sentiment which could sway the opinion of the braves by a single word.

Maco only saw himself being cheated of torture victims, and this seemed a symptom of his waning power. He tried to salvage face with a half-snarled, "Are these the warriors of the *Be-don-ko-he,* to snivel at the torment of enemies? When you return to your lodges, the women will spit on you and turn from your blankets. Women do not bed with women."

The words were ill-chosen. The excited flurry of talk sweeping the braves became tinged with ugly resentment. Nachito squelched it all by raising his hand. "It is done. Maco shall fight Day-zen, or we will strip him of his weapons and drive him afoot from camp."

The crowd had only needed a single firm ultimatum to crystallize their wavering intent. Nachito, canny politician, had voiced it at the psychological moment. They were solidly behind him now, cheering their approval.

Maco proudly folded his arms, his cruel face stoical. He might win the duel, but he had lost more, and the word would spread through Apacheland ... Maco would slide into oblivion. Seeing him fearlessly, almost contemptuously, accepting this knowledge, McGivern knew a reluctant admiration for his old enemy.

Nachito drew McGivern aside, pulled his knife and severed the scout's bonds. McGivern stood flexing his cramped muscles, rubbing circulation back to his arms and legs. Nachito eyed him quizzically. "Once more you have done me a service," the young chief said in a low voice. "First you spared my life—"

"And maybe just spared my own," McGivern said dryly, grimly. "As your slave. . . ."

"You can watch for a chance to escape, though you will not escape. Still, I thank you, *pinda-nantan.*"

"That you can prove. I would talk with my friends." Nachito's eyes narrowed, and McGivern knew it was his wits against the war chief's now. He shrugged casually. "Maco may kill me. There is a feeling between me and this man and woman. My last words would be a comfort."

"It is so. If Maco wins, he wins them." Nachito hesitated, touched McGivern's shoulder. "A friend is a good thing. I have many followers, few friends. I did not tell my people how I was shot; they would not understand why you did not kill me. You and I know. Go to your friends, Day-zen."

The braves were all talking at once, hashing over the old quarrel between the duelists, and making bets. McGivern moved over to where Hornbeck and Melissa sat in numb misery in the shadow of an isolated monolith. A single guard squatted by with a rifle.

"I don't understand all this," Hornbeck burst out, motioning at the Apaches. "What's going on, McGivern?"

He hunkered down by them. "Our lives are up for stakes," he said quietly. "I'm going to fight Maco. If I win, the three of us become Nachito's property." He didn't add what would happen if he lost. He glanced now at the Apache guard, a boy of fifteen or so, whose soft face had already seasoned to capable manhood. He was gambling that the lad understood little or no English as, rather than lower his voice and rouse suspicion, he spoke to Melissa in a normal tone. "They find the derringer I gave you?"

Her dazed eyes lifted, her forehead puckering mechanically as though fixing on his words was an effort. "I . . . hid it in my boot. They didn't find it."

"When the fight starts, slip it to Paul. They'll all be watching me and Maco."

"What's on your mind, McGivern?" Hornbeck asked, intent now.

"It's our only way out. I'm going to grab Nachito for a hostage."

16

IF I CAN KILL MACO," McGivern said steadily, "if I can bring him down by Nachito, and get my hands on Nachito before they know what's happened . . . we'll have a chance. Not much, I warrant. But we can't wait."

Hornbeck said hesitantly, "Wouldn't it be better to wait—and lull their suspicions?"

"This may be the only time I'll have my hands free and a knife in them. Nachito's still weak from his wound; he won't fight much. He promised us our lives. But he couldn't keep his braves from your throat or mine for more than a day or so. It's their custom to take only women or children captive. A war party won't be saddled with watching grown male prisoners. And the Apaches know me, consider me dangerous."

Hornbeck was silent for a time, and McGivern gave him unspoken tribute for his poise. The man had unshakably found himself. "All right," he said. "What can I do?"

"Lissa'll give you the pocket pistol. When I grab Nachito, you shoot the guard."

"That boy?"

"Then wing him," McGivern said quietly, insistently, "but get his rifle. If I threaten to kill Nachito, the guard can use the same threat on you two—unless you move first."

Hornbeck wet his lips. "Yes.. All right. But if Maco kills you—"

"There's two bullets in the derringer."

"I know. A bullet for me, and. . . ." He swallowed. McGivern's hand went out, gripped his shoulder in a quick hard squeeze. The scout rose and walked through the Apaches, who respectfully made way for him. He halted at the edge of the cleared spot.

Maco was waiting. He'd stripped himself to the waist. He was average height for an Apache—a full head shorter than McGivern—but his broad shoulders and chest swelled with ox-like thews. Sheer strength had long given him the prestige that other war chiefs had won by personality, though he matched any in craft, cunning, and fighting prowess. His obsidian eyes lanced hatred at McGivern and he faintly flexed his long arms, rippling the knotted muscles under his copper hide. McGivern knew he'd have to rely on speed and his knife and try not to close with the Apache, thinking coldly now: *he'd break a man in half if he got his hands on him.*

McGivern shrugged out of his shirt and jacket, tossed them aside. The sun beat against his lean back as he moved toward the middle of the cleared area. The Apaches murmured and pointed at the long knife scar seared into his flesh. Nachito walked out, with the tip of his lance drew a circle roughly fifteen feet in diameter. He lifted two knives from his breech-clout and murmured some ceremonial words above them, of which McGivern caught only the last five: "That life may ebb cleanly." He stooped painfully and laid the knives in the center of the circle. Then he walked back to where the warriors were ranked in a ragged cordon around the clearing.

Nachito squatted down a little ahead of the others, and McGivern took note of his position. All of an Apache's training was directed toward vigilance to protect him from surprise; the unexpected caught him completely off guard, undone by his own carelessness. McGivern was depending on the laxity of excitement and the unexpectedness of his move to enable him to seize Nachito, hold him helpless before the braves could rally.

Sunlight pooled wickedly along the waiting blades. The adversaries wove warily toward the weapons from opposite sides, an easy grace to the mincing shift of their moccasined feet. McGivern moved first, lunging, stooping and picking up a knife, in the same movement flicking out a foot to kick Maco's knife away. It slid only about a foot. Maco, moving with surprising agility, dipped a long arm and snatched up the knife at the same time leaping aside to escape the vicious orbit of steel swung at his shoulder by McGivern. Pivoting gracefully on a heel, Maco countered with a straight-arm lunge that carried his pointed knife over McGivern's shoulder as the scout ducked. He tried to whip under Maco's guard, to slash at his abdomen, and again Maco leaped back.

Now Maco moved in on him, his knife making wide glittering arcs at the end of his long arm, holding McGivern off and at the same time forcing the scout back step by step to the circle of bystanders. McGivern must either leap aside or meet the attack. With a lightning kick to Maco's thigh, he sent the Indian reeling back a pace and then lunged to meet him. He ducked beneath Maco's full-armed swing, again sought to bring his blade up under Maco's guard.

The Apache's free hand clamped powerfully over McGivern's knife wrist. As Maco's knife swung back, McGivern flung his left arm around the Apache's waist, lifted, threw his hip behind Maco's right buttock, and swung him off his feet. Maco crashed on his back, but still held McGivern's wrist. He fought to pull McGivern on top of him; the scout stiffened his legs, braced wide, and Maco gave up. He swung his knife at McGivern's leg. McGivern jerked the leg away, and it threw him off balance. He kicked blindly at Maco's hand, and the knife flew from it, the point burying itself in the earth eight feet away.

But the maneuver let Maco give a powerful tug on McGivern's wrist that brought the scout down onto him with a grunting impact. Maco's long arms whipped around him like crushing snakes. His left hand still holding McGivern's wrist pulled the scout's own knife against the small of his back, point outward. McGivern was on top, but helpless . . . and now Maco had the hold he had feared. The tremendous power of his arms tightened, straining, until McGivern felt his breath choke in his throat. His ribs constricted against his lungs; bright lights exploded in his eyes.

Savagely he bent his head, fastened his teeth in Maco's shoulder, bit through the flesh and hung on. The war chief squirmed, making no sound, but McGivern felt the pain loosen Maco's arm grips. Throwing all his strength into the effort, McGivern pulled his knife hand free, whipped it beneath Maco's body. The Apache grabbed at the wrist again, awkwardly, but now the knife was at *his* back, flattened against the flesh. He tried to tug it away; McGivern hung on. He could have turned the blade into Maco's back, but an icy warning beat through his red fury: *get him by Nachito first*.

He heaved sideways and they rolled, Maco on top for an instant, but McGivern throwing his weight up and rolling again, using the impetus to roll them both over a third time, locked together, till they lay on their sides not two feet from where Nachito squatted.

For a moment it was almost as though they were resting, gathering strength, strained chest to chest. Not once had McGivern relaxed his jaws on Maco's shoulder. Now McGivern relentlessly turned the knife, the razored steel breaking flesh. McGivern's biting hold practically immobilized Maco's upper body, yet he strained awkwardly to tug McGivern's hand from his back, his own right arm keeping its crushing hug on the scout's body. McGivern now thrust with all his power, felt steel grate against a rib and slip past, and

143

then the blade sank to the hilt. Blood gushed warmly over his hand.

Maco's bull-like frame stiffened, heaved with a mighty spasm that jolted loose McGivern's hold and flung him on his back by Nachito's knees. He still held to the knife, and he pulled savagely, and it stuck. He wrenched and twisted, Maco's body turning with the pull, and the blade slipped free. The war chief's legs twitched once; then his great carcass was motionless.

Sucking in a deep breath, McGivern sat up slowly, as though fully spent with the effort. Then, before the awed braves could even begin to react from the tensely stiff spell that bound them, his hand shot out, closed on Nachito's throat, and yanked powerfully. McGivern's legs thrust up, bringing him to his feet and dragging Nachito up with him. He swung the young war chief around, back to him, wrapped his left arm around Nachito's neck and locked him helplessly. His right hand held the point of his wet knife against Nachito's throat just under the ear.

The braves were utterly stunned, paralyzed for the moment, as McGivern had known they would be. He had to move only a few steps to put his back against a towering rock slab at one side of the circle. As he swung his back against it, he rapped into the silence: "A move—the smallest move—and he dies."

Then the cracking bark of the derringer. Hornbeck had waited almost too long.

The shot brought the Apaches to their senses; Nachito was the first to recover. He strained his body away from McGivern's, his hand tugging at McGivern's death-like grip. The scout ground his elbow cruelly into the youth's wound, and Nachito, too weak to resist, relaxed shudderingly.

A wicked murmur of sound, like a rising storm, swept through the warriors; through the stir of dusky bodies, McGivern saw the boy guard on the ground, clutching a bloody shoulder. Hornbeck had already snatched up the rifle and leaped in front of Melissa.

McGivern sent his words flat and cold across the

144

rising voices: "A move, I said, and Nachito dies. Hear me, men of the *Be-don-ko-he*. One of you will get our horses . . . the rest stand as you are. We will ride from here, taking Nachito with us. When we reach the white man's town, Nachito will be freed."

A wrenched laugh gurgled from Nachito's throat. "Day-zen is a fox, but the *Be-don-ko-he* are not rabbits to leap to his bidding. Brothers, you have guns. Shoot him through my body."

"Maco is dead," McGivern cried out challengingly. "If Nachito dies, who will lead you?"

"Tah-zay," Nachito gasped. A lanky warrior who towered inches above his fellows took a hesitant step forward. "Careful," McGivern murmured.

"Tah-zay," Nachito said. "To you—my friend—I have told my plans and hopes for the people. Kill Day-zen and lead the way."

Tah-zay's wiry arm moved in protest. "The plans were yours, *sheekasay*. I cannot lead. The feeling of the men is for you." The braves murmured their agreement.

Nachito gave a strangled cry, and McGivern felt the keen disgrace of this tremor through the war chief's body. "Nachito has been tricked like a child that rides the *tsoch* on its mother's back. I am not fit. *Shoot!*"

"Hornbeck." McGivern raised his voice. "The tall Indian. Put your gun on him." The lawman butted the rifle to his shoulder and sighted along Tah-zay's back. "Yes, shoot," McGivern gibed. "We will die, so will Nachito; and his plans will die with Tah-zay. Is there another among you who can lead as Nachito hopes?"

A warrior at the edge of the throng suddenly moved, shadow-silent, slipping behind a near rock. "Stop that man," McGivern said sharply, knowing the Apache meant to get above him.

"Pi-on-sen-ay," Tah-zay shouted. "Come back! The craft of Day-zen is as ours." The warrior must have hesitated, for Tah-zay cursed him. "Spawn of a coyote, I do not fear to die—*but Nachito must live.*"

Pi-on-sen-ay came into sight off a rock, dropping like

145

a cat back to the ledge. He said sullenly, "You take the word of a white-eyes?"

"Of this white-eyes alone. Is there an Apache who does not know the heart of Day-zen? Once at San Carlos, my mother, Tes-al-bes-tin-ay, was near to death; it was Day-zen who brought the white-eyed medicine man who cured her." His gaze leveled on McGivern. "You will let Nachito go?"

"I gave the promise. Are Tah-zay's ears bad?"

"Pi-on-sen-ay, bring three horses." At Tah-zay's quiet command, a groan rose deep from Nachito's chest. "Be still," McGivern whispered. "You will be a child in truth if you cannot take defeat like a man."

Pi-on-sen-ay went to the picket line and led back the horses. He left them between McGivern and the crowd, reins trailing. McGivern called to Hornbeck to bring Melissa and circle widely around the Apaches, keeping his rifle ready, and mount up, after catching up the reins of McGivern's horse.

Only when this was done did McGivern push away from the rock. His knife did not leave Nachito's throat. He moved to his own rangy sorrel. As he quickly brought his knife hand down to lift Nachito's foot to stirrup, the war chief tried feebly to wrench away. In a flash, with Nachito stirruped, McGivern lifted him bodily into the saddle, at the same time swinging up behind, his knife at Nachito's ear again. It was accomplished smoothly in the space of a few seconds, before anyone knew what was happening.

He kneed the sorrel lightly. It followed Hornbeck's mount, the sheriff guiding both horses.

All the way for the length of the slope above the camp, McGivern's back crawled, expecting any moment the smash of an arrow or a bullet as some impulsive brave broke. But only Maco could have rallied them to sacrifice Nachito, and Maco was dead. The camp lay silent and unmoving behind. . . .

McGivern realized how deep-seated was the voluntary loyalty of these braves toward their leader. Only a dozen years ago, Nachito would have been another

146

Mangus Colorado or Victorio or Cochise—a personality like a living flame, which could draw followers from beyond his own tribe. Even now, with old hatreds still rankling, such a one as this could be the rallying point for hundreds of young Apaches . . . and another interlude of bloody and hopeless warfare.

It cannot, it must not happen, McGivern thought, and the thought stayed with him. He knew what he would have to do, soon, after Nachito was released.

Once they had reached the upper ridge with its saddle framed pass, McGivern quickened pace. He knew that the Apaches would follow, that they would have an unseen escort for many hot, dry miles. He only hoped they could reach Saguaro before nightfall.

"You had better be sure, very sure," Belden said softly.

"Hell," Harlan answered irritably, "I left all three in Maco's hands. Man, he's an Apache."

"So is McGivern, very nearly."

Reggie grunted, slacked back in his chair with his legs crossed, thumbs hooked in his belt. It had been the work of fifteen minutes for Hosmer, the ranch blacksmith, to liberate Belden when Harlan and the crew had returned to find him handcuffed to his bed. Afterward the crew threw a drunken spree, Harlen warning them to confine it to the ranch. He and Belden had ridden to town and the seclusion of Belden's freight office to discuss what had happened and weigh their future moves.

"At least," Belden had told him, "you were wise to turn Paul and Lissa over to Maco. It saves us a nasty job. With what they know, neither would be useful now; on the contrary, they're dangerous."

Looking at the fat man now, sprawled like an immobile toad in his chair, the lamp on the desk between them throwing Belden's features into weird relief, making them agelessly craggy and evil, Harlan knew a full resurgence of his hatred. He couldn't deny that he himself had taken the easy way of handing the sheriff and Melissa to the Apaches, but McGivern's condemnation had stung. Belden hadn't even a twinge of regret. He hated the fat man the more for being able to escape living with his acts.

"So nothing's changed?" Reggie asked softly.

"Nothing. Learn to accept what happens, my boy. The loss of Paul and Melissa is merely an irritant which can be hurdled. Meanwhile, you did well, bluffing Maco into promising cash on delivery. A letter to my brother in New Orleans will resume the gun traffic."

Reggie hesitated. "Maybe we'd better soft-pedal it awhile. If McGivern sent what he learned on to the Army. . . ."

"It will prove nothing, in itself. One man's words—discredited by the fact that he is a murderer who broke jail and forced the sheriff to leave with him. Neither are heard of again. What does that prove? Nothing. McGivern's friends will need more than that to launch a Federal inquiry. Now kindly get out of here. I have work to do."

He bent his head over some papers; it was as though Reggie had ceased to exist. Harlan rose, opened the door, and carefully slammed it behind him as he went out. He grinned with a truant boy's satisfaction as he groped his way through the darkened outer office. Outside, he went to his horse, mounted, and swung toward the archway.

Abruptly he pulled the reins and brought the animal to a halt. He pulled back into the shadows of the high fence, his heart pounding with a scared savagery that left him faint. The archway was wide, allowing anyone just inside to gain a full view of the street for a block in either direction. A first fleeting glimpse of the south end had shown him three riders coming in. An orange outwash of light from a store window had picked out the three plainly.

McGivern. Hornbeck. Melissa. Hanging with weariness across their drooping horses . . . *but alive and well*. All of them.

After the initial presence of mind that led his retreat

to shadows, Reggie's brain drew a numbed blank. Then it functioned chaotically, first with the impulse to shoot McGivern and the sheriff as they drew abreast of the archway. He saw the madness of that notion as it occured.

What to do; stay and bluff it out? He rejected that at once; he'd never feared any man, but he suddenly feared McGivern with a clammy and paralyzing fear. There was something unresistible about a man who could free himself and two others from a camp of armed Apaches. What had gone wrong, he did not know. He did know with an iron certainty that McGivern had effected it.

He let out a long, sighing breath of relief as McGivern and Hornbeck did not turn in at the archway, but continued downstreet. *But they've seen the light in the Old Man's window, sure as hell. They'll come here for George. All he can tell them is you left a while ago. If they look for you, it'll be at the ranch.*

The thought steadied him. George was through, with three witnesses to the illicit gun traffic. But he, Reggie Harlan, could get out of this with a sizable stake if he played his hand coolly.... There was at least ten thousand dollars in Belden's office safe, and it was a week's ride to the Mexican border. Plenty of country for a man to lose himself in.

He cursed softly, then, remembering that he didn't know the combination of the safe. He could go in and put a gun on George and force him to open it, but McGivern and the sheriff might come in at any moment. He would wait until they had taken Belden and left ... then open the safe. How?

Black powder. There were three kegs in one of the yard sheds, and he'd seen safes blown open by experts in his younger, wilder days. He'd tether his horse at the rear of the yard where there was a gate in the back fence. Crack the safe ... dump the paper money in a sack ... get out through the rear office window ... circle the sheds and reach his horse by the time the first spectators were drawn by the explosion.

149

He put his horse across the yard toward the isolated shed where explosives were kept. From its door he could see by the street lights anyone who came or left through the front archway.

Once in the shed, he lighted a lantern, closed the door, and kept his eye close to a knothole facing the yard as he set about opening a powder keg with a crowbar. He smiled thinly, thinking of the family fortune he'd rejected years ago. Really, it was the tag of pompous responsibility he'd have had to assume with it that he'd rejected ... Ten thousand to spend as he pleased in the land of *mañana* was better than a million in a social straightjacket.

17

ALL THREE OF THEM had breathed easier when the lights of Saguaro grew into view across the flats. It was late darkness, long after twilight. Hornbeck and Melissa were swinging numbly, half dead with exhaustion, to their horses' mechanical gait. McGivern could feel his own trained vitality sapped to its limit by the ordeal of the past two days.

The closeness of town summoned a spark of outrage to Hornbeck's words as he returned to the bitter controversy that had divided them an hour ago. McGivern had set Nachito afoot and the young chief had headed back north across the tawny flats to meet his warriors, invisible on the backtrail.

"I'll give it to you once more," McGivern said wearily. "I had to keep my promise to free Nachito. There was something bigger at stake than my word of honor. . . ."

"A thin argument—that he'd be martyred in a white man's jail," Hornbeck flared back.

"He would, though. . . . Years ago, Mangus Colorado, big chief of the Mimbrenos, went alone to the diggings of some white prospectors and told them in a nice way to move on, out of Apache country. They tied him up and whipped him almost to death. He lived to start the first of the Apache wars, and men from every Apache tribe followed him. Later, when Mangus Colorado surrendered to white soldiers, they shot him down in cold blood. And that set off the worst uprisings of all . . . took twenty years to put down. To a broncho Apache, jail is as disgraceful as a whipping, worse than death." McGivern paused pointedly. "If you didn't see—back there—that Nachito is the same kind of leader, you're blind."

"But this is 1881. The Apaches are on reservation, except for a few renegade bands like Geronimo's."

"And Nachito's. And the hundreds of young men who'd break away to follow him. Why trade for that many rifles unless he had more braves lined up . . . reservation bucks ready to break at a word from him? Jailing him would have the same effect as jailing Mangus Colorado, just possibly worse. There's something else, too. Day-zen—me—is one of the few whites who's always treated honestly with the Apaches. If I'd failed to release him, it would have been a master stroke of betrayal by the white-eyes. In some ways they're like children . . . if complete confidence in a man's honor is childlike. They depended on me to keep my word—or else none of us would be alive."

"But Nachito will go on," Hornbeck said doggedly, "to raid and kill again. Good God, McGivern, after what you told me about your fiancee, how can you give those devils an inch of advantage? Even granted what you said, that Nachito is the man to draw hundreds behind him?"

"That'll take time," McGivern said grimly. "He'll lose face for a while, when it gets around how I tricked him and took him as a live hostage from forty of his fighting men. Not for long, but long enough for me to get information to Colonel Cahill that will stir the top brass to sending hundreds of troops into the field to round up the renegades. I'll offer my services as scout free. I know some now about how Nachito's mind works . . . and that's half the battle won. I'll chase him and harry him, give him time to do nothing but run till he's cornered. It'll be a lesson no Apache will forget."

Hornbeck lapsed into gloomy silence, and there was only the thin *clop* of horses' hoof falls through the darkness, nearing town. McGivern thought back with a sad dispirit to Nachito's last words before they'd parted: "You were right to call me *ish-kay-nay,* a boy, when first we met, Day-zen. See how you have foxed the boy."

"Then now I call you man," McGivern had replied gruffly. "You had not tasted defeat, and it made you careless. A man gains by every mistake. Soon you will see the greater mistake of your father, and his, in fighting the *pinda-likoye.* When the Apaches were many and the white-eyes few, your greatest chiefs could not drive them out. Now the white-eyes are many, and Nachito is playing a fool's game. When he knows this, he will go to the reservation and lead his people in the ways of peace and change."

"The ways of our fathers were good," Nachito had said angrily. "What right have the *pinda-likoye* to force their ways on us?"

"The right of might," McGivern had replied wearily, "and of broken treaties and crooked agency men and other treachery. These things will pass with time. You cannot change them by more killing."

"Then I can die fighting their wrongness," Nachito had said bitterly. "It is too bad, Day-zen. It was near my heart that we were almost *nejeunee,* friends."

"Yes." These were their last words, and Nachito was gone, back to his brave and hopeless fight against history.

Now as they rode through the first rectangles of light thrown from windows onto the soft dust of the street, Melissa released an audible sigh. Even McGivern felt a faint sense of homecoming.

Yet he pushed the thought of Julia Lanphere back in his mind. Belden had to be taken. Automatically he glanced across the board fence that skirted the freight yard, seeing the light in the high front window of the office.

Hornbeck followed his glance and said, "Not without me you don't. I'm taking Melissa to the hotel first. Belden is my job."

Mine, McGivern corrected grimly, but not aloud. They rode on to the livery stable and left their horses, evading the startled hostler's questions. By now the whole town knew that the sheriff had ridden away early yesterday with a shackled prisoner in tow. A small crowd gathered behind the three of them as they crossed to the hotel. Hornbeck, limping a little, was supporting Melissa with an arm around her waist as they went inside. McGivern halted in the doorway, turning to face the townsmen. "Go on about your business, you people."

They took in his gaunt height and trail-stained clothes, the harried warning in his face. They slowly dispersed, muttering sullenly. He waited on the porch till Hornbeck came back, and without a word the two men went to the sheriff's office. Hornbeck buckled on a spare shell belt and gun, and found an extra .45 which he loaded and handed to McGivern, who shoved it in his belt. Then they angled downstreet toward the freight office, McGivern slowing his pace to accommodate Hornbeck's limp. "Better see a doc."

"Afterward," was Hornbeck's stubborn reply.

They went through the archway, crossed the yard, and went up the steps. "I know the office," Hornbeck murmured, stepping ahead of McGivern. He softly opened the door and eased into the outer office, guiding McGivern with a hand on his wrist. They moved across the murky dimness till McGivern heard the lawman grip a doorknob and turn it. The door opened into a short corridor; at its end, a crack of light showed beneath a door. Hornbeck's gun whispered from leather, and McGivern palmed his own and moved after him.

Hornbeck opened the door suddenly and kicked it

154

wide; it crashed with a pistol-shot impact against the wall. Belden sat behind his desk. His face was like a grotesque totem carving, showing nothing at all. The flame of the desk lamp guttered faintly in the draft, exaggerating the shadows to weird, wavering patterns. The air of this musty little cubbyhole was stifling and motionless; it was like a den where some malign being conjured dark spells against mankind.

They stepped into the room and moved tacitly apart. Hornbeck rapped crisply, "On your feet, George. I'm holding you for the United States Marshal."

"Why, that fool. That blundering, swaggering fool," Belden said almost pleasantly, and McGivern knew he meant Harlan.

A desk drawer was open at the fat man's elbow. With incredible swiftness his small hand blurred down and dipped a small-caliber gun from the drawer, fired. The hasty shot whipped between the standing men. McGivern's hand lashed out and batted Hornbeck's gun down as the sheriff fired, the roar of his gun merging with McGivern's own.

Belden plunged backward like a dying buffalo, his swivel chair skidding away from its occupant's tilting weight. The room trembled with the impact of his fall. McGivern skirted the desk, looked, and rammed the gun back in his belt. Hornbeck came around beside him, finally dragged his hot-eyed glance to meet McGivern's.

"Why did you knock my gun down?"

"I thought you might have forgot he was Melissa's husband."

Hornbeck slowly holstered his gun, staring bitterly down at the bloated hulk whose gaudy waistcoat clashed with a deep ugly stain, whose bulbous eyes were frozen in the iced-dead stare they had worn in life. "No," he said hollowly. "No, I didn't forget."

"Better see the doc now," McGivern suggested. He turned quietly and left the office. It was Hornbeck's job now, his to finish. His somehow to whip the long-compromised townsmen into a posse and clean up the leaderless riffraff at Chain Anchor. McGivern's job was done, and the single-minded intensity that had burned in him these many months drained away. About Belden he felt no regret. He had warred on and killed Apaches who deserved better. . . .

He stood a full minute on the porch, breathing a hot wind off the desert, with its myriad of clean smells. Then he turned out of the yard and headed for the hotel. He was aware of the rancid sweat and filth that caked his body. The aftertaste of grime that summed up this whole job was strong in his mind, and maybe cleansing his body would help. Yet he came abreast of the Belle Fourche, and a sudden impatience to see Julia, hear her voice, turned him through the swing doors.

He heard her before he saw her—sitting on the bar with a hand on her hip and teamsters and cowhands ringing her with rapt attention as she sang. He went to the bar, leaned against a deserted end and watched her till her head turned toward him. Her face went white; her eyes widened, dark with the residue of some unguessable strain. Her voice broke in mid-note. He smiled, and nodded assurance. She picked up the thread of her song again. When it was ended, the men overrode her protests, demanded more. She shrugged a little, smiled her resignation at McGivern, and began singing again.

He listened, toying with a drink he didn't want, thinking sleepily of what he wanted to say to her and wondering how to begin. His head began to tilt unconsciously.

The roar of a muffled explosion shuddered across Julia's voice, and she broke off. The whole building trembled. A babble of talk started as men broke for the door. McGivern was first through the batwings, veering in his run to meet Hornbeck limping from the doctor's office by the hotel.

"What is it?"

"Don't know," Hornbeck grunted over his shoulder.

"Sounded like it was from the freight yard ... but I just left there, and nobody. . . ."

His voice trailed off as McGivern raced ahead in long, loping strides. Smoke was pouring from a broken window of the freight office building. *From Belden's room,* McGivern thought, and was lunging for the porch when he braced swiftly to a stop. A man, something bulky dangling from his hand, was dashing across a moonlit patch of ground at the rear of the building, to vanish in a shadowy tangle of sheds.

McGivern ran after him, tugging the gun from his belt. He saw the running man dart between two sheds and break for an open space beyond, clearly highlighted by moonglow. A horse stood tethered against the back fence that hedged the yard, and the man headed for it. McGivern pounded after him and the man heard him and wheeled around so quickly he stumbled. He caught his balance and McGivern saw the light strike off his gun as he swung it up. His hat rolled off with his sharp turn and the moonlight silvered his golden hair.

McGivern stopped. A dozen yards separated them. He called: "Harlan!"

The man's great shoulders hunched high and stiff with surprise; he cursed in recognition. An orange tongue of flame spewed hip-high to his big body. McGivern felt the bullet furrow hotly along his lifting forearm. But his arm continued to lift, holding steady till Harlan's hulking upper body blacked the sights of his sixgun. He squeezed the trigger as Harlan's gun bellowed again.

Harlan was jolted back two steps and then he braced his legs apart, still clutching the sack in his left hand as his right arm chopped up and down, firing again and again as though he were throwing each shot in his fury. McGivern felt a numbing blow in his shoulder, but he kept his feet and aimed again carefully and shot. Harlan's whole body shuddered with the hit. His gun fell to his side. He took a single long, almost careful-seeming, step forward and then his footing

157

skidded away and he plunged face first in the dust. It moiled up around him in a silvery haze and settled thinly.

McGivern walked to him, reached out with a toe and stirred the sack away from Harlan's outflung hand. It fell open and spilled out packages of greenbacks. He knelt and picked one up, hefting it gently in his palm before he dropped it by the dead man. He said aloud, yet softly, "You bought it all, you and Belden. Every damned cent's worth."

"I'm glad you told me about Clyde," Julia Lanphere said quietly.

He looked at her across the table. He had been thinking that the dark dress she wore was like a mourning gown, and her words startled him. "Glad?"

"Perhaps that was a poor thing to say . . . but I've felt so guilty, terribly guilty . . . that I sent him to his death when I asked his help. I thought he'd been caught in an attempt to gather evidence for us. When you told me what Harlan said about his attempt to blackmail the gunrunners—no doubt using that same evidence—well, it was a relief."

McGivern lightly, restlessly rubbed his bandaged shoulder where Harlan's bullet had made a trifling flesh wound. "I thought maybe you and Prentiss. . . ."

She looked at him quickly. "No." A sadness shaped her mouth. "I am sorry for Clyde, truly sorry. Perhaps he took too much for too long off bigger men, until it warped his better feelings. Or . . . he wanted to marry me. Perhaps he thought the blackmail money would persuade me. But even if I hadn't known, I would have told him no."

They were sitting in the deserted Belle Fourche. It was still early in the morning, but McGivern had already said his farewells to Paul Hornbeck and Melissa Belden. Hornbeck meant to finish out his term of office here, he had said—do his best to clean up the corruption that Belden had sowed. Meanwhile he'd personally clarify the testimony at the inquest for Clyde Prentiss, and McGivern was free to go.

158

"You'll get small thanks from the town," McGivern had advised him. "They've lived on their knees to Belden too long."

"So did I," Hornbeck had said quietly. "I won't do it for thanks; it just has to be done. After that, we'll go to Georgia and see about some land holdings Lissa's family owned. It may be a start. We're going to try."

And Melissa's face had been drawn and worn, yet with a composed happiness overlaying it. "We're not deceived that it will be easy, Tom. But we can do it." She'd added, almost defiantly, "Do you think we have that right?"

"You have every right," McGivern had said.

Afterward he had gone to the Belle Fourche, where Ma Gates had said a warm good-bye, then discreetly left McGivern and Julia alone.

Out of the deep reserve of his lifetime, McGivern had to struggle for words. No matter how he framed what he wanted to say, he thought that it would sound too bald for the occasion. So much had happened. There was Clyde Prentiss, among other things. Without knowing whether he was acting wisely, he'd told her about Clyde. And felt a strong relief at her reaction. Yet he had no certainty of her real feelings, and he told himself heavily, *maybe you're just a damned fool. You still need more time.*

He pushed his chair back and stood, saying, "I've got to be going. It's a long way to the fort."

Julia rose too and followed him out to the tie rail. The sorrel, inexhaustibly rugged and rested now, pricked up its ears eagerly. McGivern stepped up into the saddle and looked down at Julia. She reached out and laid a hand on the sorrel's shaggy mane. "How long will you be gone?"

She expects me to come back. He felt a little foolish, and suddenly good. "We may be in the field a long time, rounding up Nachito. Weeks, months maybe."

She said gently: "We're not just two lonely people grabbing at straws, Tom. I know that—and so do you. When you come back it will be easier. We'll have the

159

time then, and the words." She paused, her eyes bright again, and proud. "Go along, Tom, and God bless you."

The sorrel sensed its rider's mood and pranced fool ishly the whole length of the street. McGivern's shoulder caught an aching twinge with each strike of the hoofs, but he gave the animal its head.

THE HARD MEN

One

Rocking on its creaking thoroughbraces, the stage rolled to a stop by the stage depot. The four passengers filed off. First to step down was the seedy-looking drummer with bad nerves, clutching his sample case like a talisman. He was followed by a big, rawboned man in a dusty suit of old-fashioned cut, who then formally handed down a plump blonde woman with knowing eyes. She leaned close to the big man before letting go of his hand, giving him a heavy scent of the perfume that had stifled him for the last twenty miles.

"Well, a gentleman," she murmured huskily and smiled. "You ever come by Maudie's place, and that's one block down, you ask for . . ."

Her voice faded as she met the man's eyes directly for the first time, eyes that reflected no feeling as personal as indignation or even scorn. She took a step backward and whispered, "Excuse me," then brushed past him and walked to the rear boot to receive her luggage from the driver.

Not sparing her another glance, the big man gave a hand to the fourth and last passenger who now stepped from the coach. This was a girl in her late teens, small but not slight of build; the sturdy fullness of her mocked the drab and soiled dress she wore. It was made of a cheap material that matched the frayed traveling cape she carried over one arm and the little dilapidated straw hat that topped the heavy wealth of her whitegold hair. Her face was a pretty one, oval and strong-boned; her young smooth skin had a fine translucence, a milky freshness with a tint of budding roses, but her one really beautiful feature was her eyes. As remarkable as the big man's eyes, they were totally different—warm and wide open, clear as gray crystal, and so honest that meeting them made a man think uncomfortably of forgotten sins.

She said now, with a smile that was curious and faintly chiding, "Papa, what did that woman say?"

"Nothing for your ears," the big man said gruffly. "You have the list I made, Thera? Of the things we will need, eh?"

The girl gave a little sigh, opening the shabby reticule she carried. "Here it is, Papa. But I thought we could get some rooms at the hotel now."

"We will rest when we are home, not before," Krag Soderstrom said brusquely. "There is a general merchandise store across the street. Have the list filled, girl, while I do the other things."

As Thera started across the street, the driver who was unstrapping luggage lashed to the coach top called down, "Mister, you want to help me with this trunk?"

Soderstrom started to turn, and then his gaze was snapped back to the street by a sudden rattle of sound. An instant later six horsemen thundered around the corner of the hotel adjacent to the stage depot, veering in a hard-riding body down the center of the street.

There was no hesitation, or even pause for thought between Soderstrom's awareness of the coming riders and his movement. He took three long steps to reach his daughter. She was halfway across the street when he caught her by the shoulders and dragged her back with a rough power that swung her feet clear of the ground. The riders surged past with a savage momentum, voicing high wild whoops.

Krag Soderstrom drew a deep angry breath, tasting the haze of bitter dust that hung in the air. He said harshly, "You are all right?"

"Yes, all right," Thera said calmly, but she winced as she passed a palm over her upper arm where his fingers had cruelly bruised her.

"That hurt, eh? Not so much as getting rode down, I think."

She smiled at his unyielding gruffness. "No, Papa. Now I will do the shopping."

Soderstrom grimly waited till she had crossed the street and entered the store. He turned to the driver, nodding at the half-dozen riders as they piled off their horses in front of the Alhambra Saloon a block down. "Who are those fools?"

The driver spat over his shoulder, saying, "Wagontree men," as if it explained everything. "Good men. Would of been right sorry if they had rode down your little gal. Here, take aholt on your trunk."

Grunting, he heaved one end of the big brassbound leather trunk over the side rail, and Soderstrom clamped his long arm around it and shifted it easily to his shoulder. Walking slowly but straight as a pine under a burden that had taxed the strength of the two men who had loaded it, Soderstrom tramped into the depot. There he asked for and received permission from the agent to leave behind the ticket counter the trunk which contained all of his and Thera's belongings except the clothes on their backs.

Afterward he stood on the depot's rickety steps and passed his iron glance across the ramshackle cluster of frame and adobe buildings that made up Mimbreno. It was no different from a dozen other sunbaked, sprawling hamlets he had come through in the last few days, and only the fact that it marked the journey's end made it deserving of his particular attention. A hot wind passed up the dusty ribbon of street and riffled the tired leaves of the few cottonwoods drooping in the forenoon heat. A pair of loafers drowsing in barrel chairs on the hotel veranda gave him a lazily curious scrutiny.

Krag Soderstrom's size alone would mark him even in this land where big, hard, and weathered men were no exception. His heavy-boned body towering inches above most men carried little excess flesh, and at thirty-seven, despite his near-ungainly size and build, all his movements had the effortless grace imparted by superb musculature. He had a long Scandinavian face, squarish and bony, with a rumpled mane of flaxen hair and a ragged pale mustache whose drooping points hid his upper lip. His jaw shelved out like a granite ledge, and his sharp high cheekbones and craggy nose might have been chipped from the flank of a mountain. His eyes, under a straight ridge of whiteblond brows, were an ice-blue so penetrating that few people could bear their direct glance. But that frozen quality went deeper than surface; it tunneled from the cold irises into the inner man in a way that shook and repelled perceptive strangers.

Having taken his bleak, totally unimpressed look at the town, Soderstrom came off the veranda and swung briskly upstreet toward the newspaper building he had noted as the stage rolled in. His walk was hampered by the tightness across chest and shoulders of his old wedding suit which he had hardly worn in eighteen years. Now it was wrinkled and dust-creased by long days and nights on cross-country trains and coaches, and his boiled white shirt was smudged and stale, the high stiff collar wilted by sweat. Soderstrom had never sweated so much in his life. It was the dead simmer of oppressive heat, and not the jolting discomfort of a long journey broken only by fitful snatches of sleep, that laid a dull exhaustion on his northlander's constitution and temperament. That, and the vagrant currents of loud talk and explosive laughter from the Alhambra across the way, did nothing to improve his always dour temper.

The newspaper was a narrow single-story 'dobe building wedged between two larger ones; the lower half of its big front window was painted white to banner the black block wording, BUCKMASTER COUNTY WEEKLY PRESS. JOB PRINTING. H. KINGERY, ED. AND PROP. Entering, Soderstrom paused inside the doorway. The long gloomy room was a scene of monumental order and disorder. The side walls were piled with a clutter of boxes and cartons and yellowing stacks of newspapers. To his left was an iron safe and a clothes commode, to his right a swivel chair and a desk heaped with neatly stacked papers and proofs. The room was divided midway by a wooden railing, and from the print shop at the rear came a curious, steady sound of metal striking metal.

A man, short and hunched and white-haired, swinging a stiffed-up leg, was sweeping the floor with slow, jerky movements. His back was to the door, and now as he turned Soderstrom saw that his nut-brown face was networked with wrinkles and scars. His eyes had the blankness of pale blue marbles, and something not quite definable in his look made a man's flesh crawl.

"You want something?" His scarred lips contorted in forming speech.

"You are the owner?"

The man gave an inarticulate mutter and tilted his white head toward the rear, then went on sweeping. Soderstrom went across the office and through the railing gate. As he circled a tall cabinet he removed his old slouch hat. Behind the cabinet a young woman was seated on a high stool. She was wearing a drab and worn workdress and an ink-stained apron, and her right hand moved with deftness and speed as she selected type from two cases set on a sloping frame and slapped it into a stick in her left hand.

Without looking up, she said evenly, "Well, what do you want?"

"I want to place an ad."

"It had better be a short one. We go to press this afternoon and the forms are almost filled." She set down the composing stick and picked up another, looking at him for the first time. He was used to people's half-startled scrutinies at first meetings, but she gave him only a cool appraisal.

She was about twenty-eight, a willowy woman with hair that was a flaming red even in its tight bun under the dim overhead lamp. Her face was angular and clean-lined, with a liberal dusting of freckles across the nose and cheeks; she was far from pretty, but definitely not plain.

She looked tired and slightly harried, and now she said irritably, "Well?" He looked at her blankly, and the faintest smile touched her wide mouth. "I can set type as fast as you dictate. Go ahead."

"Wanted," Soderstrom said, and paused to watch her ink-stained fingers blur into motion. A moment later she looked up, and he went on, "Experienced riders. Forty a month and keep—"

"Thirty."

"What, missus?"

"Thirty a month is the going rate in these parts."

"All right," Soderstrom said coldly. "Apply K. R. Soderstrom, Ladder Ranch."

Her fingers ceased movement and she looked up with open curiosity, half-pointing the stick at him. "You're Soderstrom?"

He nodded stiffly; this young woman's manner was too forward to be seemly. And what sort of work was this for a woman?

"Then I take it old Angus Horne has sold Ladder to you."

"That is right. We met at a Grange convention in Minneapolis. There we talked, and the deal was made."

She nodded. "I knew that old Angus had gone to live with his son on a farm up north. Then you're not from Wisconsin, Mr. Soderstrom?"

"There are a few Swedes in Minnesota, too," Soderstrom said gruffly.

That drew a merry, gamin laugh from her as she gave him her hand. "Do excuse my manners, sir. I'm Hannah Kingery, and I own this newspaper."

A half-conscious scowl of stolid disapproval touched his long face, even as he noted the surprising strength of her grip. Her slenderness belied a sturdy robustness, but the fact deepened his disapproval; a fine strong woman like this should be busy with keeping house and bearing children.

Hannah Kingery said quietly, "You wear your opinion of independent women even more frankly than most men, I should say."

Soderstrom grunted, "That is your husband's concern, missus, not mine."

"My husband is dead," she said evenly, and turning back to the typecases, completed the composition of his ad with a brisk deftness. "That will be two dollars."

Soderstrom took out his shabby purse and counted out the coins. As he raised his eyes on handing over the money, he surprised a mounting curiosity in her face, and then she said, "I don't mean to be rude, but could you tell me a couple of things without scowling?"

Soderstrom scowled. "What are they?"

"I was just wondering—I presume you have had experience at ranching?" Her tone presumed that he had none.

"I worked on a cattle outfit in Dakota Territory when I was a kid. Four, five months."

"Oh, I see. Four, five months." She hitched her feet to a higher rung on the stool and awkwardly crossed her arms on her knees. "Second, how much did you pay Angus Horne for his Ladder, sight unseen?"

Soderstrom eyed her darkly. "Five thousand dollars for a few thousand acres good riverbottom grass, a ranch headquarters developed already, and about nine hundred head branded stock. The price was plenty low, all right, but Mr. Horne's son is a good friend of mine. His word I take that this is a good outfit." He paused deliberately. "What you think, missus, is you are talking to one big dumb squarehead, eh?"

Not squareheaded, narrowminded," Mrs. Kingery said sweetly. "No, you hardly impress me as stupid. Which increases the puzzle, unless old Angus neglected to bring up a point. Or did he mention Wagontree?"

"Wagontree and the Buckmasters," Soderstrom said stolidly. "I will take care of anything they want to start."

"Oh, indeed. Well, well." She nodded gravely and tapped the composing stick against her chin, leaving a smudge there. "Angus was pushing seventy, of course, and fed up with trouble. That's why he pulled his stakes from here. Perhaps he thought that he could pass his problems on to a younger man in clear conscience. Though if you'll forgive my saying so—"

"I know," Soderstrom grunted. "I'm green as grass, I ain't dry behind the ears, and Loftus Buckmaster is half mustang and half bull buffalo."

"Then old Angus did give you fair warning." A faint smile tugged at her lips, and she was about to say more when the hunched white-haired man came around the cabinet, still clutching the broom.

"Anythin' else you want tended to, Miss Hannah?"

"That will be all today, Waco." Her voice was gentle; she jingled Soderstrom's coins in her palm and impulsively handed them to the white-haired man. "Here. A small bonus, and please—buy yourself one good meal before you start drinking."

"Thankee, Miss Hannah." The man gave Soderstrom a vacant, incurious glance, then went to the wall, leaned his broom there, took a ragged coat from a hook and shuffled out.

"A case in point," Hannah Kingery murmured. "That poor wreck is Waco Millard. He used to be the best bronc-buster in the valley. Now he ekes out a bare living swamping out saloons and stables and the like."

"So?"

"He worked for Loftus Buckmaster, breaking rough string mustangs. One day when Waco was sick, Loftus made him top a killer mustang—it was that or lose his job. The horse threw him, but Waco got a foot hung in a stirrup and the brute bolted through a gate that some fool had left partly open. It was five minutes before a rider was able to overtake the horse." She grimaced faintly, as if at some firsthand memory. "Waco was broken up pretty badly, but Dr. Enever pulled him through, no thanks to Loftus Buckmaster. He had no use for a stove-up hand, and he discharged Waco on the spot with what he had earned to the day, not a penny more."

Soderstrom gave a bleak grunt. "That's plain sense anyhow."

Her eyes clearly mirrored her shock. "Do you mean that as it sounds? That years of loyal service to a brand should count for no more than—"

"Look, missus," Soderstrom cut in harshly. "A man looks out for his own. Good or bad, another man's luck is his own lookout. He has got coming what he earns, not a cent more or less." He arced a callused thumb against his chest. "Me, Krag Soderstrom, I come out here to raise cows, to look out for my own, to tend to my business. That's the way it should be. If this Buckmaster knows that, good. If he don't, maybe he will find out fast."

"Your position is clear enough," Mrs. Kingery said coldly. "I can see that I was wasting my breath. Loftus Buckmaster owns half this valley and is well on his way to taking the rest. In the process he has destroyed a number of people, not by murder. By worse—killing dreams and hopes. Well, perhaps it takes one to oppose one. I wish you not luck but good hunting. You are the same kind of man."

Soderstrom's ice-blue gaze held on her face. "Maybe you will spell that out. What kind of man?"

"Why should you wonder," she retorted with thrusting irony, "if you know yourself as well as you obviously do?

Then you know your enemy. But, very well—Loftus Buckmaster is a man who fought Apaches, rustlers, drought, to carve out a piece of God's earth for himself—the trouble being that he got a taste for carving and could not learn to stop. The times he knew, rough and brutal times to be sure, turned him as hard as stone, as if that were any excuse."

"You think it is not, eh?"

"Not," she countered flatly, "unless a man lets it be. Loftus Buckmaster drove the one person who loved him, his wife, to her grave. He pushed his only daughter into making a bad marriage in her simple desperation to get away from him. He made—is still making—his two sons into his own spittin' image. All that is really mild stuff next to his treatment of non-relatives ... all of the little people he's bullied and terrorized. That, of course, is no concern of yours, except as it bears on the fact that you just wasted two dollars."

"Wasted?"

"For the ad. I doubt there is even one rider in Buckmaster County who will dare answer it. Well, even if your days are numbered, I hope you prove mean enough to hurt him even a little—that will make it worth it."

Wondering at the bitter vehemence with which she spoke Soderstrom said, frowning, "This is Buckmaster you're talking about?"

She gave a low, brittle laugh. "I would rather not admit why, but the fact provokes its own admission. Loftus Buckmaster is my father." Briskly she swung back to the typecases, saying matter-of-factly, "If you'll excuse me, I have a form to complete. Your advertisement will appear in today's paper. Good day."

Soderstrom clamped on his hat and tramped toward the front office. He was halfway across the room when he caught a faint, muffled cry from somewhere outside.

That was Thera. Even as the thought crossed his mind he was quickening pace, and three running steps carried him out to the street.

Two

While the elderly storekeeper filled her order, rummaging stiffly among the stacks of goods on shelves and counters, Thera Soderstrom peered out the window at the currents of life on the main street. A great curiosity was in her, mingling with her high excitement. Her zest for life had never been remotely satisfied by her seventeen sheltered years on a little Minnesota farm. Now, within two short weeks thrust into totally new surroundings and situations, her lively young mind was still dazzled by all she had seen, and she could not take in enough of it.

This was Saturday, and now as the morning wore on, the street and sidewalks bustled with the increasing traffic. She was surprised at the number of cowboys thronging the town, wondering why they were not at work; but she remembered how in sawmill towns in the northern woods the lumberjacks would flock in for a payday spree. The sight of so many young Western men quite took Thera's breath away; somehow they seemed invested with a glamour she had never associated with loggers. Almost every one of them was decked out fit to kill, in spanking clean shirts and silk scarves and tight boots so pinch-toed it seemed they must cause the wearers untold miseries. They strutted and swaggered whenever a town belle, high-nosed and parasoled, went by; Thera smiled . . . *They look different, that is all; they are not, really.*

There was one difference: the guns. Although most of the workaday cowhands were unarmed, or wore their pistols stuck in the waist bands of their overalls, a few carried their six-guns in holsters slung from cartridge-studded belts, and she could not help thinking that the more hard-bitten individuals were really of a different breed.

Thera's glance was drawn to the doorway of the stage depot as her father stepped out and headed upstreet with his long, swinging stride. She watched his tall, big-shouldered form till he turned into the newspaper office, and then she sighed, a small sadness tucking the corners of her full lips. How lonely he always looked, even in a crowd; she saw what others did not because she remembered and she knew. Krag Soderstrom had always been a gruff and brief-spoken man, that was simply his way, but she could remember, when *Mor* was alive, how Papa's chill eyes had sometimes lightened and danced with flecks of humor. Yes, she could remember, but not very well, for that had been a long time ago.

When the storekeeper had assembled the articles on her list and she had paid him, she asked whether she might leave them there until her father had bought a wagon on which to load their goods. He agreed readily.

Thera was not beautiful, but her smile was; it was like the goodness of sun and wind on a rippling field of ripe wheat, so rich and full that a man's fading eyes stung with the memories, real or fancied, that it provoked.

She thanked him and went out the door, her eyes bent downward as she restored her change purse to her reticule. A man's arm jostled hers in passing, knocking the reticule from her hands.

"Beg par'n, miss," the young man murmured as he paused, bending to pick it up. He doffed his hard derby with a sweep as he handed her the reticule with a crooked little grin. Thera smiled back, her frank gaze admittedly liking him; he was almost as tall as Papa, but very thin, and his shabby slopshop trousers and coat, the latter opened to a frayed dark turtleneck sweater, were a disreputable match for his age-tarnished derby. But she was a little alarmed that such a nice face could have its fine clean lines so stressed by thinness and pallor.

"Thank you," she murmured, and the young man seemed to start when he met her eyes, then lower his own in shame. She saw him stumble as he walked away, and realized with a swift shock that he was drunk. *Oh—poor young man!* He had been drunk long and often, that was plain from his sickly look.

Flustered, she started the other way, almost bumping into a man in soiled range clothes. He was long and angular and wolf-faced, with a great beak of a nose and wicked saffron eyes. He removed his black hat, showing a bald and shining dome.

"Look here at the little lady, Richie," he said in a deep, whimsical drawl. "Where are you-all bound to in a fine hurry, little lady?"

The man's face was ruddy with liquor, and the odor from his breath was sweetish. "Please," she said firmly. "You will let me pass."

"Aw no, now. Not till I have innerduced myself and friend. Jack Early of Nacogdoches, Texas, ma'am. Richie Sears here of, uh, where you from, Richie?"

His companion, standing to his left and a little behind him, was a desiccated wisp of a man whose wiry body indicated that he was younger than he looked. His face was a wry and shriveled mask, and the slack folds of his chin and his bright, half-lidded eyes gave him the appearance of a tired lizard. There was a trimness about his elaborately fringed trousers and embroidered jacket.

"I'm from most everywhere, Jack, but I know better'n you," Sears said quietly.

Early eyed him a fuddled moment. "Better'n what?"

"A Texan, drunk or sober, ought to know. Man don't fool with a decent woman, Jack."

The small man's meager speech was soft, but like the somber disillusionment in his bright eyes, somehow chilling. Thera did not like either of these men who wore their guns so handily, but she instinctively knew that of the two the smaller one was the more dangerous. A core of quiet viciousness underlaid his soft speech; he was simply a man who had nothing to prove and knew it.

Jack Early laughed and lifted a big-knuckled hand to touch her, saying, "Tell us your name, pretty." Another hand struck Early's aside before it reached her shoulder. Glancing around in surprise, Thera saw the lanky youth in the derby.

174

"Leave the young lady alone, you damned ruffian, or I will—" He grunted and staggered backward as Early backhanded him on the chest with a contemptuous rap.

"What you gonna do, dude," he murmured, "is back your big mouth. Or you be eatin' that funny hat."

Thera shuttled a frightened glance from one to the other, saying softly, "Please," but all three men ignored her. Richie Sears looked indifferent and faintly bored as he put his back to the building and tucked his thumbs in his belt.

A second cuff by Jack Early knocked the derby spinning into the street. The youth braced his feet apart, drawing himself erect. Thera's heart sank; he was quite drunk, and almost frail-looking beside Early. "That," said the youth, "was quite enough," and stepped in with his fists awkwardly cocked to swing wildly at Early's jutting jaw. His fist bounced lightly off the man's shoulder. Early's lips peeled away from his teeth; he smashed a long looping overhand into the youth's mouth. The young man gasped and dropped his hands. Early drove a leisurely fist into his middle, and he doubled and sank down retching.

Early took a fistful of his shirt and kept him upright and carried him backward into the alley between the store and the feed company. Pinning him to the wall, Early proceeded to work him over with carefully pulled punches.

Thera wheeled on the small man to cry that he stop it; his chill fish-lidded eyes changed her mind. She turned and hurried diagonally across the dusty street toward the newspaper building, holding her skirt high. "Papa." She let the word out in a shrill cry.

Almost at once Soderstrom exited from the building, coming to meet her in lunging strides. "Papa, help me—they are killing him!" Getting a shaky control on her voice then, she made an explanation.

Solderstrom gave only a stolid grunt. "That is not my lookout."

"Papa, don't you understand? He is getting killed because he tried to help me!"

Soderstrom's eyes swept the group of curious onlookers. His face wore a scowl which might have been mild embarrassment. He growled, "All right, all right," and almost before the words were out of his mouth Thera had seized his arm and was pulling him after her.

As they reached the alley, the youth was still upright, holding onto a dwindling consciousness, for Early was in no hurry, dragging it out almost scientifically.

"Here," grunted Soderstrom, "you," taking a long step into the alley as he spoke. Early turned his head, and Soderstrom's big fist met his shelving jaw like a cleaver hitting beef. Early spun about and fell on his face.

Instantly Richie Sears pushed away from the building. Thera's low warning word brought Soderstrom around to face the small man, his fist still lifted.

"You touch that gun, mister, and you will have a busted arm before you get it out." His voice matched his eyes, which were cold and ugly, and suddenly Thera, who had never feared her father, was afraid of him.

Richie Sears said, "Maybe you should back off now," in a whisper-dry voice.

He looked ready to fight, but now someone called from across the street, "You men slow down." Thera saw a man coming from a building with barred windows and SHERIFF black-lettered above the entrance. He was a tall old man with a gaunt, dour face beneath a smooth cap of dead-white hair. A star of office was pinned to the lapel of his neat well-worn suit. He came across the street with a stiff rheumatic stride.

Richie Sears said in his arid, toneless way, "Maybe we'll forget it." He stepped carefully around Soderstrom and gave a hand to Early who was pawing on his hands and knees. Supporting his groggy partner, Sears moved down the walk past the sheriff who did not even look at the two men. His mournful and faded eyes studied Soderstrom.

"You bought yourself a sack of hell, son, stirring up trouble in my town.".

Thera had taken vague notice of a young red-haired woman who had come up at the same moment the sheriff had. Before Soderstrom could answer, the red-haired lady said sharply, "You never forget who you're working for, do you, Otis?"

176

The sheriff eyed her mournfully. "You got a shrewish tongue in your head."

"Be that as it may, this man is a new county resident, land owner and taxpayer—he's bought Angus Horne's place—and anyway, Otis, I doubt he'll bully as easily as the average whiskeyed-up vagrant."

Ignoring her gibe, the sheriff said wearily, "You got any paper to show it?"

Soderstrom chewed his mustache and glowered, but Thera knew that he would not go against the law. He opened his coat and from an inner pocket withdrew a paper, unfolding it. The sheriff laboriously took out a pair of spectacles, set them on his nose, and pored over the paper with a testy care. Thera knew that it was perfectly valid, the property description being based on an exact government survey, and so turned her attention to the lank youth who was bracing himself against the wall, holding a soiled handkerchief to his bloody nose and mouth. His eyes were glazed with a residue of shock and liquor, and she said anxiously, "Please, you are all right?"

"Not—" His first word dissolved into a fit of terrible coughing, and when it had ebbed, he smiled feebly. "Not at all, Miss, but good of you. Very good."

The sheriff sighed and handed back the deed, then folded his spectacles and put them away. "You bought yourself a sack of hell."

The red-haired lady said with a hint of derision, "He's entitled to protection under the law if he needs it, Otis."

"I don't," Soderstrom overrode her words curtly. "I don't need trouble either, but any starting up will be finished by me. Just so that is understood."

The red-haired lady chuckled. "Don't worry, you can depend on Otis not to lift a finger on your behalf."

The old lawman gave her a look of weary disdain and then, moving with a stiff tired care, crossed back to his office. The lanky youth essayed an unsteady step away from the wall and nearly fell. Soderstrom caught him roughly by the arm. "Bring him over to the office," the red-haired lady suggested.

"He can clean up there." She gave Thera a friendly smile. "Are you with Mr. Soderstrom?"

"My daughter," Soderstrom said with what sounded like gruff reluctance. "Thera, this is Mrs. Kingery who owns the paper."

Thera breathed an "Oh" of fascination before remembering her father's very fixed ideas about a woman's place.

They crossed to the *Weekly Press* building, and Thera gazed about in wide-eyed wonder as Mrs. Kingery led them through the office and print shop to her quarters at the rear. These were a couple of simply furnished rooms with facilities for cooking and sleeping, and in small ways reflected a woman's touch as the brisk practicality of her office did not, Thera noticed.

The young man, who gave his name as David McIver of New York City, stripped off his coat and splashed water on his face. He seemed alert and clear-eyed then as he dried himself on a strip of worn towel, but Thera was still troubled by his thin, pale look. The frayed holes at the elbows of his sweater told of poverty; his sickly condition told of worse.

"Much better, ma'am. Thank you."

"Fine," said Mrs. Kingery. "Could you tell me what happened?"

Soderstrom frowned. "You mean to write this in a story?"

"Why not?" She gave him a level-eyed look. "Tell me, Mr. Soderstrom, is there anything of which you *do* approve?"

Thera said quickly, partly to forestall her father's temper, but also with an eager interest, "Oh, do you write?"

"I do everything," Mrs. Kingery said humorously. "Running a weekly paper is ordinarily a two-man job, but I'm only one woman. I have a nice modern treadle-press which is some help. Would you like to watch me set up a few lines of type?" She took Thera's arm as she led the way out to the typestand. "A very pretty name, Thera, but I'm afraid you'll have to tell me exactly how to spell it. Mine is Hannah, by the way. . . ."

Thera watched Hannah's typesetting skill with unconcealed awe, thinking, *She is wonderful! And how she stood up to Papa—I have never seen even a man do that for long*. Yet she was uncomfortably aware of her father's dark look. At least he gave civil responses as Hannah Kingery extracted the story from the three of them.

"There," she said, "all completed. If you'll come around later, you can see yourselves in print."

Soderstrom said, "We will be leaving town in a couple hours."

"Of course; you'll want to see your new place." She eyed him a speculative moment. "By the way, if the deed you showed Otis is the original, you'd better get it filed in the county records."

"You think somebody will try to steal it, missus?"

"If you're lucky, that's all that will happen," she said dryly as she slipped off the high stool. "I wouldn't guarantee the safety of your papers even in the county courthouse. Now you've met our sheriff, you may be inclined to agree."

"A foolish old man," Soderstrom grunted.

"That foolish old man is Otis Crashaw—a name that meant a good deal in the Kansas and Nebraska trail towns of twenty years ago. He was as fine a peace officer as the West has known."

"And now?"

"Now he's become an ineffectual relic coasting on his reputation in the comparative obscurity of a backwoods county, kowtowing to the powers that be. Mr. Soderstrom—perhaps you'll understand now. This town, this whole county, fits in my father's pocket with room to spare. Loftus Buckmaster built this country and built it to his taste. The Homestead Act, Pre-Emption Act, Timber Culture Act—he developed Wagontree by having his riders file land under all of them, then waiting out whatever time the law specified before they could sell and buy them out for a few dollars. And God help any man who crossed him."

Narrow-eyed, Soderstrom said, "But there were other home-steaders. And men like Angus Horne who bought up land and built good outfits for their own. He let them grow and stay, eh?"

"In those early days, yes. He wasn't nearly so big, and he was careful never to overextend himself. And some of them, like Mr. Horne, were friends of his. A few are still around.

But, as Angus may have told you, he and Pa had a falling-out and then Angus was cold turkey like the rest—the newcomers who've tried to homestead the remaining open range. He has held it so long, he can't conceive of letting it go. He's become, well, a fanatic." She smiled tiredly, tucking a straying wisp of red hair into place. "That is where I was foolish enough to think I had him where the hair is short. Pa had 'legally' deposed a number of government homesteaders by scaring them off before their prove-up time was ended. Twisting the big bad federal tail, so to speak. It was a good hook, so I wrote scathing articles on the terrorizing of government homesteaders and laxity of federal protection and ran off handbill-sized copies on my job press and sent them to every member of the U.S. Congress and every large newspaper in the country. Well, a minor rumble began in official circles, but I hadn't counted on Pa's influential friends in Washington—senators and lawyers who've prepared briefs on his behalf and now have the whole thing bogged down in red tape."

"Suppose a man owns his land and he stands on it with both feet planted solid. What can your pa do then?"

She shrugged lightly. "What did he do to Angus Horne? Anything short of outright murder, and usually it doesn't take much. How long anyone lasts depends on the quality of his nerves. I still have a mild suspicion that you are human, Mr. Soderstrom, and that no matter how tough you are you have nerves that can be worked on—that is how my father fights. Or rather hires men like Richie Sears to fight. If the law is bought off, what can you do? You sell out to my father at his price, if only to salvage something."

Thera's lively curiosity was greatly aroused, wondering why this remarkable woman should hate her father so; was it only his ruthlessness? But Ma, who had been a stickler for correct manners, had always warned her not to voice such thoughts.

Young David McIver gently cleared his throat. "I'll be on my way now. I want to thank—"

Thera had an inspiration; she said quickly, "Do you want work?"

180

McIver gave a bitter chuckle. "Want it? Miss, I've got to have work and soon."

"Papa, you need men—"

Soderstrom jerked out a dry laugh. "Him? You want me to hire this white-livered college boy?"

"He helped me and has been hurt for it. We should help him if we can." She gave a firm little nod. "That is only right."

"Girl, I'm too green myself to afford the hiring of greenhorn hands. I need men who know the work, able-bodied men." He tilted his head contemptuously. "Look at him. He drinks, too. No."

Hannah Kingery put in dryly, "Mr. Soderstrom, how many men can you name offhand who don't drink?"

Soderstrom turned his iron look on her, and Thera thought, *She knows already how he thinks and how to needle him; she enjoys it, too.* The interplay between them bemused Thera, and she said nothing now; it was McIver himself who spoke up defensively:

"About the drinking, I'll be honest. I'm consumptive. I came out from New York because my physician recommended a high, dry climate. I had barely enough funds to get this far, only to find myself unable to get a job of any sort. Your opinion, sir, is widely shared. Lately the spells have become so severe that I drink to kill the pain. If no liquor were available," he added quickly, "I could not very well drink. I would be willing to do any work assigned me for meals and board alone. And I can learn the work—everyone has to learn."

Soderstrom's regard was totally bleak; at last he said, "All right, college boy. You want to come on them terms you come. But by God, you will work, and anytime you slack off, out you go."

Thera touched her father's arm, smiling a little. Mrs. Kingery, as she accompanied them to the door, said pointedly, "Somehow I find it hard to believe that you have a grown daughter."

Soderstrom halted with a hand on the latch. "Why do you say this?"

"Certainly you had a wife."

"*Ja.*"

"That," Mrs. Kingery murmured, "is what I never would have suspected. You don't like women."

"Some women, maybe. There's something else you don't suspect."

"Oh, and what's that?"

"You have got ink on your chin. *Adjo,* missus."

Three

Before leaving town, Soderstrom had a last chore about which he took his time: the selection and purchase of a sturdy, well-seasoned spring wagon and a team of good horses. The proprietor of the livery barn had a number of rigs for rent or sale in back of his building, and Soderstrom ignored his spiel and made his round of the vehicles, studying each in turn.

A diffident voice spoke up behind him. "Mister?" Soderstrom turned, his bleak gaze settling on the hunched, scar-faced man he had seen in the newspaper office. He was holding a shovel and long-handled brush, and had evidently been swamping out the livery's stable.

"You seen me before. Waco Millard."

"*Ja,* I know. What do you want?"

Waco Millard took a hesitant step forward; his eyes were strangely bright. "I heard what you told Miss Hannah, that you aim to ranch under Buckmaster's nose. Didn't take much notice till I seen you put down that tough Jack Early. You ain't like these scared clodhoppers Buckmaster is pushed off. You'll make a fight, by God." His scarred face twitched. "Mister, hire me on. I don't want nothing but to side a man who'll take on Buckmaster."

182

Soderstrom was already shaking his head brusquely. "I have no use for you."

"You wouldn't never be sorry," Waco Millard said feverishly. "I was a top hand once and I know plenty. You need a man like that. You listen, mister."

"I don't need busted-up cripples," Soderstrom snapped. "They're no good to nobody." He pushed past the man, moving on to inspect another likely rig. Halting by it, he shot Millard a scowling look as the hunched swamper moved slowly back to the barn. There was something wrong in that man's head, he could swear; not all the damage was to his body.

Soderstrom found what he was looking for: a secondhand rig scarred with use but sound in every piece and joint. He called to the proprietor, who was chatting with Thera and McIver, and after many minutes of fierce dickering wore the price down to half the first offer.

Afterward they drove down to the general store where he picked up the heavy trunk he had left at the depot, loading it in the wagon bed. Then inside the store he checked over the articles Thera had purchased from his list. He had based his choice of gear and provisions on an outdoorsman's longtime experience—dried staple foods, cooking utensils, and blankets. Now he also carefully chose from the store's guncase a new Colt .45 and two secondhand Winchesters in good condition; he asked for ammunition, too.

With the supplies loaded, Thera beside him on the seat and McIver sitting awkwardly doubled in the wagon bed, Soderstrom took the reins and clucked up the team. Leaving town, he drove northeast onto the alkali flats as the scorching eye of the sun climbed against a dazzling blue. There was not a cloud in the sky, and already Soderstrom felt the suffocating pressure of the day's full heat. He began to sweat; he soon abandoned his coat and collar.

Following the directions given him by the livery owner, he took his bearings north-northeast by the loaf-shaped height of a black butte which tapered off toward a canyon-riddled valley. In many places the old road was almost obscured by wind-gusted dust, for Angus Horne had left his ranch a good eight months ago. He had discharged the last of his crew and left the Ladder shut down and deserted.

Squinting across the ridges dancing in the heat and the rim of distant gauzed peaks beyond, Soderstrom felt the dual discomforts of a northerner in a hot climate and a stranger in a new land coming to a home he hadn't seen.

Ah, what did you expect, Soderstrom? What did you think you were coming to—a little paradise, eh? No, that is not what you want; heaven is only for saints. But why did you come?

It might be only that all the old roots had gone bad; it might be no more than that. After Hedda had died, the meaning had gone out of his life. Then one bad year after another with his wheat farm; if it was not flattening hail, it was devouring locusts or a plunging market. It seemed that a man could not win, that he was besieged on all sides by enemies he could not touch. The relentless pressures on a man over many years came to fill his life, his whole outlook, with a bitter and brutal quality.

A need to shed bad memories or to make a new start or to satisfy a nameless, restless ache—what did it matter? A man who jarred himself in one deliberate move out of an ancient rut was not a man looking for the tame, the curried. This land of raw challenge could offer only abrasive new life or sudden death, and he welcomed the choice; he had been sparring with ghosts too long, and that was no good for a man.

They left the flats and moved across the broken valley through the heightening heat of forenoon, crossing rough talus slopes and crooked ridges. Past the valley, they mounted the slant of a shallow mesa bearded by a scrub growth of close-paced juniper and tangled mesquite. Here the old road made a plain and winding track through the timber. Soon it dipped into what he knew was the Salt Creek Valley and paralleled the creek itself, a meandering southward flow that had died to a shallow trickle in the blasting heat of late summer.

The surrounding valley was well-grassed, and time and time again they spooked up bunches of fat cattle branded and ear-marked Wagontree. This was his land, Soderstrom knew, and the sight of the alien cattle was fuel to his flint-edged mood.

He also saw a lone horseman on a not-distant hillock to the south, apparently following their progress across the valley. As Soderstrom watched, the man abruptly turned and vanished down the far slope. Something about the horsebacker and his action was disquieting; neither Thera nor McIver had taken notice of the rider and Soderstrom said nothing.

Presently the trail curved around a heavy shoulder of rock, and beyond this, snugged back within a deep fold formed by two granite hills and cut deeper by the roiling flow of the Salt Creek, was the Ladder layout. A few ratty cottonwoods shaded the rambling, one-storied adobe house. There was a 'dobe combination bunkhouse-cookshack, a frame barn and stable and outsheds, and a maze of pole corrals.

Soderstrom had seen enough ranch headquarters in Dakota to tell that the place had long ago become badly run-down, but then Angus Horne had not deceived him on that point. As he drove across the grassless barn lot toward the house, he noted the broken fences and the fouled corrals, and the stray pieces of old gear that had never been stored out of the weather.

Soderstrom halted the team in the cottonwood shade, came off the seat, and handed Thera down. McIver slipped to the ground on rubbery legs and was promptly doubled up by a coughing fit. Soderstrom shook his head with a dour disgust; he would be lucky to get the price of grub and a bunk out of this sick, ravaged college boy. But he had tried to help Thera, and this made a debt; also he would work wageless, a fact that almost balanced Soderstrom's need for experienced riders.

Sale of the farm had not brought a large sum, and as relatively small as Angus Horne's asking price had been, the buying of Ladder had left him desperately short on cash. Even the purchase of this wagon and team and a few supplies had eaten uncomfortably into his little reserve.

Moving up onto the sagging porch, he tried the latch. The door was wedged tightly; he kicked it twice before it creaked inward on rawhide hinges worn nearly through. He saw a rat scurry for cover in the gloom. Hazy sunlight streamed through cracks in the heavy wooden shutters, and old bullet scars pocking the adobe walls told of the days when the Apache marauders had held forth in the mountains to the west. The ancient hand-carved furniture, rough and serviceable token of Angus Horne's long tenure as a widower, was covered by thick dust which gave a mustiness to the air.

Each room, as they inspected it, was a study in disorder. The kitchen, which Horne had evidently made his all-purpose quarters, was the worst, bringing a choked little gasp from Thera. A Swedish girl absorbed a fetish for tidiness almost with her earliest understanding, and this lesson Thera had learned well from her immigrant mother. As she took in the floor and table littered with scraps of gear, magazines, and even dirty dishes and crusts of food, she bit her trembling underlip in consternation. But when she stepped into the room and her foot hit an empty bottle, an angry set came to her chin. "We will have to fix things up. We will start now."

Soderstrom grunted, stolidly kicking the wreckage of a broken chair from his path as he went to the shutters and threw them open. He turned to McIver. "There is a lean-to back of the place where grub is stored. Drive the wagon around there, then unhitch and water the team. Put them in the barn for now till we have got the fences fixed."

There was much to do, a fact grimly welcomed by Soderstrom as he discarded his wrinkled, sweaty suit trousers and boiled shirt in the room he had chosen for himself in the west wing. The afternoon sunlight streaming through the window gilded the bare mud-plastered walls; both bedrooms were innocent of furniture or fooferaw, except for a single narrow cot and moldy straw tick in the room that Thera had taken. He would have to throw his own blankets on the packed clay floor or bed down in the bunkhouse with McIver till he had constructed suitable beds and commodes. The slipshod condition that pervaded the whole place was what happened when a man's pride went out the window. A pride of a harsh and bitter sort that Krag Soderstrom had never lost.

He had questioned Angus Horne extensively, pored over cattleman's journals till his eyes ached; he still needed to familiarize himself with his own range and stock, but even that could wait. Until he had acquired an experienced hand or two for the actual work, there would be plenty of work just fixing up the place. He changed to thick-soled workshoes and well-worn duck pants and a fresh-bought workshirt whose prickly newness irritated his neck, retaining only his old slouch hat. He would break in his uncomfortable new half-boots when the time came.

Thera quickly whipped together a late midday meal of beans, biscuits, and coffee, and both Soderstroms ate with robust appetite. McIver could barely put down a few mouthfuls, though he drank a great deal of coffee. Soderstrom knew that the college boy was dying for a drink of whiskey—he had gone through a long bout with the bottle himself after Hedda died—but he felt no mercy for McIver. Either he would sweat out his craving or he would crack; there would be no halfway living on Krag Soderstrom's place.

The two men spent the afternoon carrying armloads of the useless trash that littered the house, bunkhouse, barn, and yard to a bonfire that Soderstrom set on a bare spot off back of the barn. Meantime Thera was everywhere at once, briskly directing the whole operation; she carried dozens of things outside to air out in the sunlight; she found a bar of strong yellow soap from which she pared shavings into a pail of water and set to scrubbing down the kitchen, the bedrooms and part of the bunkhouse "so we will all sleep good tonight." Only then would she permit the food and utensils, blankets and belongings, to be brought inside.

She, with her high spirits and quiet laughter, made a game of the work; Soderstrom, driving himself with a dogged grimness, several times caught her talking and laughing with McIver and was not pleased. They were too young to take things seriously enough, and while McIver seemed a decent sort, he did not fancy Thera taking to a sick college boy; somehow it did not seem right.

Muttering and chewing the tips of his mustaches, Soderstrom gathered up the two empty water buckets in the kitchen and tramped out past the barn and the trash fire, swinging up the creek where it meandered past the outbuildings. Angus Horne had said that the well was off back of the place. He found it above the brushy creek-bank, and it boasted plenty of clear water.

As he dipped the first bucket full, Soderstrom made out a sound of horses coming from downcreek. Setting down the bucket, he headed back along the bank, keeping the barn between himself and the house. He heard a man's voice, loud and strident, and had a moment of regret that he had not strapped on his new Colt. But he had left a rifle leaning by the barn wall against emergency, and now as he picked it up, feeling the good familiarity of stock and barrel, he felt better. He had been a hunter all his life, and this was his kind of weapon.

He flattened himself along the wall by the corner, exposing his head enough to pick out the five men sitting their horses in the front yard. Among them he identified the two with whom he had clashed in town—Thera had caught their names as Early and Sears—which meant that these were Wagontree men. All five were armed to the teeth, and Soderstrom did not wait to see more.

Wheeling about, he moved along the barn wall till he achieved the brush that rimmed one of the flanking hills. He made his way with noiseless care along the base of the hill, keeping always behind the wall of shrubbery, and emerged from it well downcreek; he came to the cover of the rocky shoulder where the road turned into the place. Stepping around the shoulder now, as he brought up his rifle, he was not sixty feet behind the horsemen.

Both McIver and Thera, who had been in the house, were now in the yard facing the men. One, a huge and thick-bodied fellow who had reined out ahead of the others, said, "All right, so your pa is the boss. Where is he?"

Thera spoke quietly and shook her head, and the huge man turned his prancing black on a rough rein and spoke to the others, "Spread out and find him then."

Soderstrom levered the Winchester and said in a tight and ugly way, "No. You stay all together. Keep your hands in sight." He saw Sears and Early exchange glances as they recognized him. The other two hands, a slim mustachioed fellow and a heavy-set blond youth, appeared to be of a common stripe—gun-hung, dangerous men.

The leader paced his black around the others to get a clear look at Soderstrom. A muscled mountain of a man in the dust-soiled dignity of a black suit, he was massive in every part of his body. Kidskin gloves sheathed the hamlike fists knotted around his lifted reins. His black-bearded face was heavily fleshed, filled with bluff arrogance; his low black nests of eyebrows made a perpetual scowl. He was in his mid-thirties, which meant that he was not Loftus Buckmaster, whom Angus Horne had described as a white-haired giant. One of the sons, Soderstrom guessed.

"Your name is Buckmaster?"

"Garth Buckmaster."

"I will give you maybe ten seconds to say what you want," Soderstrom said in a quiet tone of iron. "Then you will ride. I know you, and I tell you don't waste my time. I have bought the deed on this place, and I am here to stay."

The huge man rumbled his laughter. "That don't matter, fella. Horne had paper on this outfit and he couldn't hold it. Neither will you."

Soderstrom was not impressed. Garth Buckmaster's habit of authority sat him like a heavy fist, but whatever directed the fist was not here. "You figured you would show us that now," Soderstrom said softly. "Riding straight in with four armed men at your back. You have had it easy, pushing around people who are scared, eh? You did not figure on a man who is ready for you. Maybe here is something else you did not figure on."

Deliberately he swung the rifle level, and Buckmaster smiled, "You won't use—" The crash of the rifle shattered the warm stillness; the black reared with a squeal of pain, rump-seared. The big man pitched from his saddle, and the impact of his fall shook the ground. He rolled heavily to his hands and knees, then scrubbed a gloved hand over his face. Soderstrom saw the sudden furtive fear in his eyes and felt a long-delayed pleasure; a wolfish grin bared his teeth.

"So. You are trespassers, and a man can shoot his trespassers."

"You don't want to kill a man for—"

"I want to," Soderstrom murmured. "You don't know me yet, mister. Now you find out. Get off your horses. I hit the horse where I shot at him; think of this before you try anything."

The four men still mounted made a cautious dismount and then, at Soderstrom's curt order, let their shell belts and pistols drop. He was about to tell them to remove their boots, when it occurred to him that this tight vain cowman's footgear was not made for walking.

"I will turn your horses loose tomorrow," he said, and pointed his rifle sideways at the ground. "The guns you can come get sometime, if you dare. Now. There is the road."

The small man called Sears spat quietly at the ground; his eyes were like coals in his lined and wattled face, and there was no fear in him. He walked straight ahead, not even looking at Soderstrom as he tramped a bare yard away from him. The others shuffled forward. Buckmaster got to his feet and beat his hat uncertainly against his pants, then followed his men. The four filed around Soderstrom at a tense, careful distance.

"Papa," Thera called hesitantly. "Maybe this is not—"

Soderstrom rapped out harshly, "Be still," and watched the five men as they struck south across the rolling grass. He had settled nothing, he knew grimly. But for Thera's presence, he would have shot them up some at least. He was not sure, but he thought it might even be easy to kill such men.

Four

Soderstrom kept working steadily until well after dark. He and McIver were repairing a broken section of corral by lanternlight when Thera called them to supper. By now the college boy was exhausted; he literally collapsed into his chair. Probably, Soderstrom thought grimly, he had not put in such a day in his soft citified life. Actually this had been only a half-day; tomorrow and the tomorrows to follow would be far more grueling. A healthy man could have done the same work in half the time—still, McIver came free. And he would lose his softness or die trying. *No, not that,* Soderstrom amended contemptuously. *Not the college boy; he will quit first.* But he was no longer so sure, grudgingly having to concede that McIver threw himself into whatever he did without a grimace of complaint.

Thera bustled back and forth between stove and table, laying out a savory meal of bacon, hot smoking cornbread, and good coffee as her father liked it, black and strong. "David," she rebuked, "you do not eat like you mean it. My cooking is so bad?"

"No," the youth said with a lame haste. "All very good, I'm sure, but I may be a while getting back my appetite."

Soderstrom gave him a small cold grin. "The drinking, eh?"

"Partly." McIver flushed slightly, but resentment tinged his voice. "Sickness can also contribute, or so I've been told."

Thera said with her firm and sunny faith, "Soon you will eat good," and moved briskly back to the stove. She opened the oven, lifted out a canned-apple pie and carried it to the table; she sat down to eat and chatted lightly with McIver, refusing to look at her father. She had not spoken directly to him since he had harshly silenced her this afternoon.

Soderstrom was troubled. No matter how gruff his moods, he had hardly ever raised an angry word to Thera.

Her fair skin was still pinkened by stoveheat as she began to clear the table. Watching her brisk young grace, the reflection in her face of a liveliness that never seemed to touch the grave gray eyes, Krag Soderstrom felt a deep and sudden pang. How like Hedda she was . . . and not a day younger than Hedda on that day some eighteen years ago when a fresh-faced immigrant girl hardly two weeks out of a ship's steerage, less than two months from her native Sweden, had come as hired girl to the midwest farm where he was working and saving wages for a place of his own. Within the week she was his bride, and in the ten years they had had together he had not regretted once that fast, impulsive courtship. His bride—so quick, so young, so suddenly cold in her grave. Again the pang, cutting as a knife, swiftly smothered with iron gruffness. The sad ache hardly lessened with each passing year, and he wished that it would; for it made intolerable the many good memories he would have liked to relive. Yet oddly now, one memory did bring a lightness that relaxed his mouth under the drooping mustache. For Thera was censuring his harshness in exactly her mother's old manner: he was nothing, he did not exist, till she should choose to notice him again.

"Go to bed," he told McIver. "It will be dark yet when we are up tomorrow." Rising, Soderstrom passed through the house and stepped out onto the sagging front veranda. An autumn chill touched the early evening. He took out his tobacco pouch and stubby blackened pipe, absently filling it as he swung his gaze around the dark layout. He could not see much, but his mind's eye was busily reconstructing the run-down outbuildings and broken fences; this would again be a good place. Impatience threaded his thoughts; tiredness laid only a slight drag on his muscles. Tomorrow they would ache a little, and then he would be back in the zesty swing of living and working; to Krag Soderstrom there was little difference any more.

A horse, probably one of the restless Wagontree ponies, nickered faintly in the barn. He struck a match and cupped the flare to his pipebowl; his lips were set around the stem or he would have grinned. Those men had expected an easy mark; they would be back. Perhaps with others. Soderstrom took the pipe from his mouth to let the grin form; he did not mind the odds being tough and big. But his lips sobered; there was Thera to consider. And the college boy too since he could not fight. Maybe he could shoot a little, though Soderstrom dourly doubted it. That was a qualification he should have specified in his ad. But remembering Hannah Kingery's words about the riders hereabouts being skittish of her father, he thought, *No matter, they will know.* As he would soon enough know whether the ad produced results.

A curious turn veered his thought wholly to Hannah Kingery. She was a strange sugar-with-spice sort of young woman, flippant and tart-tongued and gentle by turns, and with a well of hidden reserve that he sharply sensed without knowing why. She was clever and several-sided, which tended to discourage any judgment he might make; if asked he would say he did not like her, but privately he was sure only that he disapproved of her. His idle musings carried him from the thought that, clever or not, she was probably useless in a kitchen, to a mild wonderment that such a woman could be the sister of a thick-headed brute like the Buckmaster he had met this afternoon. But maybe someone who knew Thera and himself would be as greatly surprised.

Soderstrom shook himself, irritated at this thinking. He knocked out his pipe against a veranda post, then turned to enter the house. As he opened the door, a bullet hammered into the jamb inches from his left shoulder.

Not sparing even an instant to glance backward, he lunged through the doorway as the shot echoes rattled between the granite hills. Soderstrom slammed the door, shot the boltlock, and wheeled for the wall to snuff the lamp; he detoured slightly to snatch up his rifle.

Even as the room ebbed into darkness a fusillade of rifle shots opened in concert from the embracing hills. Bending low, Soderstrom moved from window to window, securing the shutters of each while a steady hail of slugs pattered the outside walls. He heard quick steps as his daughter and

McIver entered the parlor, their voices excited; he barked, "Thera!"

After a moment she said calmly, "Here, Papa," from over by the first shuttered window. There he caught a gleam of steel where moonlight streamed through the shooting port that perforated a shutter and that was usually covered by a hinged block of wood. Soderstrom uttered a quiet oath. He knocked over a chair getting to her and roughly took the second rifle from her. "Down! Stay down on the floor, I tell you. McIver, this gun, take it and shoot. Shoot at the flashes. A bad shot or good, in the dark and at this range, it makes no difference."

When he felt McIver's hand close on the gun, he returned to the last window he had secured and took his position at the port. He opened up with a steady drumming fire at the stabs of gunflame high on the slopes. As he had told McIver, there was little hope of hitting anything when your only targets were elusive powder-flashes.

So this was Wagontree's retribution. He did not know whether they meant to kill or only frighten, but that first bullet had been dangerously near. The thick shutters absorbed the hail of lead so efficiently that no more bullets found their way inside; but the advantage still lay with the enemy. The random sprinkling of gunflashes showed them scattered widely in a straggling line about two-thirds of the way upslope; also, the shifting pattern of shots showed the riflemen to be always changing position, offering no constant target. Meantime they had only to direct a steady fire on the stationary fire from the two shooting ports.

Now, as Soderstrom had feared, they were getting the range, difficult in downhill shooting. As he pulled back from the port to refill his magazine, a whistling slug found the aperture and caromed off the inside walls.

At the other port McIver was keeping up an even, competent fire. Obviously he was no stranger to a rifle, and he did not shrink from danger: even in this chaotic moment these facts left a strong impression on Krag Soderstrom.

"Sir, I will need more cartridges."

"You need nothing," Soderstrom growled, "but to get down on the floor and stay there. Do it now."

"But—"

"Do as I say and get your fool head down or lose it. They are finding the range and bullets don't bounce off these holes. Get down!" As he spoke Soderstrom crossed the room intending to hurry through the house to the rear. He'd had the cold thought that probably this frontal assault was a diversion; there were three more sides to the house, all undefended. He would secure all shutters and bar the back door.

Then McIver's excited voice brought him to a stop. "Sir, look. Something's happened out there. Someone on top of the hill seems to be shooting. Can't be sure, but I think it's at them—"

"Eh?" Soderstrom returned to his port, squinting at the black loaf of the hill. The boy was right. An isolated gun was speaking from the topmost height, and the ragged pocks of gunfire below were disappearing. A confused outbreak of voices drifted off the dark slope, and now it was plain: the Wagontree men were pulling out. There was, shortly, a muted clatter of hooves as the whole body of riders headed away upvalley.

At last Thera broke the trailing silence. "There is a friend out there. Papa, we—"

"Be still. Maybe this is a trick."

Soderstrom moved back to the port and placed his eye to the opening, watching the moonlit yard. After a long while he saw a man's lanky form detach itself from the black shape of the hill and start across the yard. Soderstrom levered his Winchester, the noise carrying with a metallic sharpness.

The man out in the night halted beyond a fence. "Halloo, the house."

"Who are you?"

"Man looking for a bait and a bunk."

"You got a rifle," Soderstrom called.

"Sure I got a rifle. I used it on them yahoos shooting at you."

"What I mean, you put down the rifle before you come on. I

can see you good, mister. Keep the hands away from your body."

Soderstrom watched until assured that his directions were being followed; he stepped back to the table and struck a match. Again the soft lamprays spread through the room. He saw with some anger that McIver had stayed at his window, and worse, that Thera had quietly taken her post at the unoccupied port. She had the Colt .45, holding it ready, though she disliked guns and could not have hit a bull broadside even with a rifle.

Wordlessly Soderstrom took her by the shoulders and propelled her firmly to a chair, then stepped to the doorway. He eased back the bolt and nudged open the door with a foot, then cut sideways behind it. Steps sounded on the veranda. As the man stepped inside, blinking against the light, Soderstrom closed the door and in doing so moved behind him.

The man whirled. "Mister, don't ever come behind a man that way."

Soderstrom roughly nudged his belly with the Winchester, edging him backward. "You do not give the orders. Move ahead of me. Move!"

They entered the kitchen, where Soderstrom turned up the lamp. The newcomer's blinking, temper-worn glance touched each of them in turn. He was about thirty and narrow as a lath, with a pugnacious, long-jawed face. His hair was red and unruly and untrimmed under his horse-thief hat, and the lamplight gilded a week's growth of fiery whiskers. His faded denims were soft with age and use, worn almost chalky at the knees and elbows. There was a feel of something untamed and free-ranging about him that, in a less prickly moment, might be oddly engaging.

"Sit down," Soderstrom said coldly. The man straddled the bench and folded his scarred hands on the table, tight-lipped.

"Why do you come here, mister?"

"Can I move my hand?"

"So you keep it in sight."

The man reached for a folded newspaper protruding from

196

his jacket pocket, and unfolded it on the table. "If that's your ad in the corner, I'm answering it."

Soderstrom's bleak gaze did not change. "Now tell what happened out there."

The rider's bony shoulders faintly stirred. "That ain't much of a say. I was coming on the road and seen a passel of men riding up from the south. I pulled off the road and waited—"

"Why?"

"Because I knew why they was here. Hell, anybody in the county who knows there's a new owner on Ladder could tell that. I saw 'em leave their horses and take to the high ground, and lay up there. When it was clear what they was about, I tied my horse and came up the other side of the hill. I got above them and shot down. I nicked one for sure, and hit or scared another from his bellowing. Then they cleared out."

"Why do you come looking for a job this time of night?"

"Because I live way back in the hills and got into town late today and didn't see a paper till then. I decided right off and saw no sense waiting." The man placed his palms on the table and half-rose, slightly bristling. "I don't fancy hard-nose questions off a man I pulled out of a jackpot. I had better receiving than this from folks don't owe me a thing."

"Sit down," Soderstrom said quietly. "There is another question. Can you work cows?"

"Yes, by God, man and boy."

"Thera, bring food. Your name, mister?"

"Rafe Catron."

"If you have your own blankets, there is a place in the bunkhouse."

The rider sank back on the bench and stared dourly at the table. Soderstrom briefly introduced himself and his daughter and McIver as Thera set a loaded plate and a cup of steaming coffee in front of the stranger. He attacked the food with a fury that indicated most of his days were lean ones. Soderstrom sensed that only a rawhide pride provoked the man's refusal when Thera offered seconds; he let his coffee cup be freshened. Then he picked up his hat and rose. "Obliged. I left my horse back of the hill. I'll see to him and throw my stuff in your bunkhouse."

Soderstrom told him to come to the house afterward. Catron nodded and went out; and Soderstrom inspected the newspaper he had brought. It featured an editorial blistering Hannah Kingery's father; she might have been writing about a stranger.

Rafe Catron returned, accepted a third cup of coffee, and got a cigarette going. Soderstrom said then: "I am told, mister, I would have it hard getting riders. About the time I am thinking all I can get is maybe college boys, you come. All right. You say you know cow work. And you don't look stove-up anyway I can guess."

"I ain't."

"Then why you this out at the heels, eh?"

Catron looked ready to bristle again, but then as if in concession that the contradictions about him deserved explanation, he grunted, "Never liked working for another man. Never stick long. Plenty times I've said I'd sooner starve by my lonesome than take another man's guff, and plenty times I came close to it." He paused, then added grudgingly, "That is part of it. Maybe you should know the rest."

"If there is more, you tell it."

"You always this hard-nosed?"

"That is right," Soderstrom said flatly.

"I got a place back in the hills," Catron snapped. "It ain't much. I make do by hunting, trapping, wolfing for bounty. I raise a few goats and a little truck. Once in a while I come down to the valley and work cows a spell.

"Last year I was doing some spring branding for Henderson, a one-loop rancher over east of here. Was out in the brush by myself and about to draw a straight iron on a new calf when some Wagontree riders showed up. Both Buckmaster boys, Garth and Chad, was with 'em. There is a dim view of mavericking hereabouts, and we had words. Then the Wagontree crowd hazed over the cow which was nearby and clipped the winter hair off her brand. It was Wagontree, sure enough. They called it rustling. I called it a mistake. Said I was working for Tom Henderson, and was about to put on his brand. Hell, I ran a few head some years back and I got a brand registered in the county book. Everyone knows that.

Garth Buckmaster said it was time they showed a lot of long-looping poor trash the what-for of things.

"I said it wouldn't take an hour to check with Tom Henderson. He would bear me out. Chad said that sounded all right. He is the sly one of the two and a heap more careful. Garth is all beef and cussedness, but is the oldest and has got the say-so for his pa. So he give the word and they strung me up and rode away. I was kicking away black in the face when this tree branch busted and dumped me down. It was an hour before I could get about. Then I made it home and laid up for a week."

Catron tipped up his pugnacious chin and exposed his throat. The long rope-scar made a raddled shine under the light. "When I was up and about I done nothing for a month but practice with my guns, rifle and handguns. I had had luck trapping, and every cent has gone for shells. I been ready for anything, but I ain't made a fight. No lonesome man can make a fight. I come across your ad, so thought I would have a look at you."

"Well," Soderstrom said grimly, "you seen me."

"I see you, and mostly I wouldn't put up with your hard-nosed sort in a year of Sundays." Catron's ruddily weathered face darkened. "But you'll fight."

"You think so?"

"They'll bring the fight to you and you won't back off. That's clear as day." Catron lounged to his feet, a deep satisfaction in his tough face. "I'd work a job for beans and biscuits for a chance like this."

"You think there'll be more hoorawing like tonight, eh?"

"Not much." Catron chuckled "They will think that was one of you shooting from above 'em tonight. They'll think you outsmarted 'em and put someone up there. That will make 'em take a long second look, and next time they will come for keeps. They have been pushing folks off by playin' pat-a-cake so long they may be slow about toughing up. But you wait."

"Tomorrow," Soderstrom said, "we will start working cattle."

Catron gave a bare nod that included them all and tramped out the back door. McIver said good night, and doubled up in a coughing fit as he went out. Thera went to the doorway and called after him, "David, keep warm tonight. Make a good fire in the stove." She closed the door and leaned her back to it momentarily, her face softened by lamplight and hidden thoughts.

Soderstrom made a gruff sound in his chest as he stood, fumbling with his dead pipe. "I did not mean to shout at you."

She laughed, "Heavens, I had forgot," but her brief-touching glance irritated him. Maybe it was not pity in her face just then. But something uncomfortably close to it.

Five

Rafe Catron moved his few belongings from his deep-hill place to Ladder. After he had helped Soderstrom with the selection and buying of some good horseflesh, the bitter business of hazing the scrawny, half-wild steers out of the eastern foot-hill country began. It was a region studded with steep-pitched ridges, mazed by abrupt coulees, and choked with tangled thickets. Catron said that after Angus Horne had abandoned Ladder, the Wagontree riders had pushed much of the Ladder beef back into this barren, broken country, fit only for scanty browsing. Meantime their own cattle had been quietly drifted onto the long rolling slopes and grass flats. At Catron's advice, Soderstrom did not now waste time chousing off these trespassing beefs except when they chanced on good-sized bunches; these would be driven back toward Wagontree at a tallow-shedding pace.

On the first day Thera aroused her father's genuine wrath when she appeared wearing an outfit she had bought the day before unbeknown to him: a man's shirt and trousers, as well as a panama hat and cowman's half-boots, all somewhat oversize.

"I will not have you showing yourself about in man's clothes," Soderstrom roared.

"Papa, with only two men, you will need me. Till David is better I will help."

That settled the matter, Soderstrom finding some release for his seething temper by blaming young McIver. He saw to it that McIver rode the meanest trails, ate more than his share of dust, and handled the most grueling chores. McIver took the full brunt of his savage cussings which, when Thera was not nearby, were pungent and frequent.

Day after day the steady grind continued. Where the rugged terrain was not boxed by sheer sandstone walls or treacherous slides, it was masked by a rioting overgrowth. Daily they broke trail through canyons choked by catclaw and yucca to herd out handfuls of rib-lean steers that had penetrated the cruel cover to slake their thirst at some isolated sink containing a few inches of slime-covered water. They were in pathetic condition, but once moved to the good lower grasses they would add poundage quickly, Catron said.

Soderstrom dourly hoped so, for he was fighting time. He was nearly flat broke, and he could not look for credit in a town where the guiding hand was Loftus Buckmaster's. His only hope of lasting out this year was to fatten enough beefs for an early trail drive to a railhead market while the stock prices held high.

For all of them the first two weeks were a nadir of nightmarish exhaustion. It was stagger out of your blankets in the murky pre-dawn and enter a world composed of dust and sweat and broiling heat, the creak of leather, the sting and tear of brushy barbs, the crackle of branding fires, the bawling of cattle, and the stench of burning hair and flesh. Always the dull ache of a deadly mechanical routine where one frustrating day melted into the next. You came not to notice the rankness of your clothes ingrained with dirt and old sweat. At day's end you sought your blankets and a gray dreamless stupor. And rolled out before dawn to begin the savage circle all over again.

Thera's fair skin burned badly, and she suffered with the heat. She was a sturdy girl, but still this was a man's work

201

whose demands she could not meet. She did her best, with a fortitude and good cheer that was incredible. Even Soderstrom, driving himself harder than any of them if only because even if they had their limits he would admit none, shed every ounce of excess tallow and was dehydrated to clean sinew and muscle. The same with Rafe Catron, who admitted he'd tackled no such job as this in his life. The indifferent currents of his existence hadn't before been so doggedly channeled toward the goals of a Krag Soderstrom.

But it was McIver who suffered the most. His soft hands blistered till even rein-guiding a horse was an agony. His sallow face, where a dirty beard did not obscure it, burned beet-red and peeled and burned again. His slender frame was pared to bony angles, and he tottered about like a gaunt, hollow-eyed ghost. Long after the want of drink ceased to burn like a fever in his cheeks, his coughing fits worsened; he ate little and his stomach retained less. Twice he passed out on particularly tough chores and had to be packed back to headquarters. At these times only Thera's intercession prevented her father from carrying out his promise and discharging him outright.

"You are goddamn lucky, college boy," Soderstrom would rumble darkly, and was always there to goad him whenever McIver began to slip with sickness and exhaustion. "I found a bottle of whiskey old man Horne left on the place, college boy. You want me to tell you where it is, eh? Maybe that would give you some belly."

Even the taciturn Rafe Catron was moved to some spare words in McIver's defense: "You ought to leave Mac alone, Mr. Soderstrom. The boy has got guts to stick on, sick as he is." Soderstrom's reply was not fit for Thera's ears, but he began to let up on McIver all the same. The boy's sheer tenacity provoked his respect, and he could only surlily guess at why he would not knuckle under. Certainly McIver must hate him; maybe it was that acid spur of fury that drove him on. Or maybe it was mostly Thera, with the words or smiles that were a sunny extension of her whole spirit: "You did better today, David; tomorrow you will do better yet. You will see."

And McIver's rock-bottom misery did lessen a little. His appetite got better; his color improved somewhat and his coughing fits were less severe, partly perhaps because Soderstrom abandoned his savage pressures on the boy entirely as he came to the realization that the more he hazed McIver, the more Thera stubbornly took his part. She was coming to like him too much, and you could never tell about a slick-tongued college boy. Although had Soderstrom been asked to explain from his knowledge of McIver's character exactly why he took a bitter exception to him, he couldn't have done so.

As the work went on, Soderstrom kept an iron alert against trouble. He saw that nobody's duty took them out of hailing distance of the others. More than once they spotted distant riders watching from open heights of land, which meant that Wagontree was keeping a watchful eye on their progress. And would not let this threat to their habitual authority go unchallenged. But when and how would they strike?

The day came when Catron gave it as his opinion that the bulk of Soderstrom's scrub stock had been combed out of the breaks. At supper that night Soderstrom announced his intention of starting a gather of as many now-fattened cattle as they could handle for a drive. Thera then made the practical observation that their food supply was low and decided in the same breath that McIver would accompany her to Mimbreno. Soderstrom did not object, partly because her tone settled the matter, partly because it would be improper for a young girl to go alone to town, though he put his assent typically: "He might as well go along with you, girl, for all he gets done around here."

Next day, while a drowsing coolness still clung to the morning, McIver stiffly took his place on the seat of the spring wagon beside Thera. Soderstrom frowningly checked the harness and regretfully found that the college boy had hitched up properly.

Thera gave her father a happy smile as he looked up from a headstall. She made a picture of unbelievable freshness and radiance in her crisp fresh calico, bell-skirted and fitted gently to her upper body. She was a bit thinner now, and her last sunburn, a mild one, had peeled to a golden tan. Her starched bonnet lay in her lap; the sun made a pale blaze of the heavy braid wrapped like a gleaming coronet around her head. A catch of memory stung Soderstrom's throat; he scowled at McIver. "You keep your nose clean, mister, you hear?"

That could mean almost anything, and McIver's lobster-burned face colored a faint shade deeper. He tilted his battered derby to a mildly defiant angle and clucked up the team. Soderstrom stood watching them wheel down the road. Then he briskly went to the corral where Catron had their ponies saddled.

The two men spent the day selecting and driving jags of the fattest steers to a large box canyon, confining them inside with a pair of maguey ropes stretched across the mouth. Catron thought they could start driving north to Taskerville in three days. At sunset they returned dog-tired to headquarters and threw together a supper of bacon and warmed-up beans and cold biscuits. McIver and Thera had not returned, and Soderstrom gruffly confessed to some concern.

"Hell," Catron said, holding a sputtering lucifer to his after-supper cigarette. "You know for a couple of kids going to town is like a pardon from stony lonesome. No cause to worry."

Soderstrom grunted as he packed his pipe; he went to the fireplace and puffed the tobacco alight from a flaming twig, eyeing Catron's back through the smoke. Rafe was a hard worker who had brought a needed know-how to the job; yet Soderstrom mistrusted the current of hidden tension he felt in the man. Catron had been aboveboard in stating his reason for hiring on: to strike at Wagontree and the Buckmasters when the chance came. But still Soderstrom was not quite sure of him, and he did not know why.

He stepped out on the porch; his pipesmoke made a frosty ribbon on the nipping, still air. He let his glance circle with satisfaction the headquarters area in the lowering dusk. The litter of trash had been cleaned up; a broken fence boasted freshly peeled rails; the warped and sagging door on the tack shed was replaced, these and other improvements having been made in what odd moments could be found after a day's work.

A restless irritation touched him so that he was about to saddle up and learn what had delayed McIver and Thera. Then he heard the wagon approaching on the road. Frowning, he knocked out his pipe and grimly considered the blistering what-for he would give them. He did not, in the growing darkness, make out the two people until the wagon rolled into the outspill of window light. Then he saw that the man beside Thera on the seat was not McIver; it was the hunched old cripple called Waco Millard who had wasted his time asking to hire on . .

Thera was already scrambling to the ground as Waco halted the team; she ran into her father's arms, and she was trembling wildly. "Here, girl," he growled. "Stop shaking and say what this is about."

"Papa, oh papa, he is hurt so bad! Get the doctor please!" She caught his arm and drew him to the wagon bed. Here McIver lay on his back between the stacked supplies, and Soderstrom roared for Catron to bring out the lamp.

McIver's face, in the sickly light, was almost unrecognizable. His clothes were torn to shreds; his whole body was savagely lacerated. His breath was a bubbling rasp through his broken nose.

Soderstrom let the picture etch with a raw bleakness into his mind and said quietly, "We get him inside, Catron. Give Thera the lamp. Now mind you lift careful so we don't mash a lot of bones."

Six

When they had gotten McIver into Soderstrom's own room and applied carbolic to the worst of his hurts, Soderstrom asked the brittle question. It was Waco Millard, hovering by the doorway like a bird of bad omen, who croaked up at once, "It was a Dutch ride. He got dragged on a rope."

Soderstrom darted him an agate-hard stare, then looked at his daughter. "Tell it all, girl. Leave out nothing."

As Thera told the story she did not take her eyes off the boy's mangled face.

After they had done the shopping in town and had loaded the wagon, she had gone to the newspaper office to chat with Hannah Kingery while McIver went to a saloon for a drink. There he had encountered four of the men from Wagontree, two of them Jack Early and Richie Sears. Early had wanted to take up the quarrel from weeks before when he had beat McIver with his fists, and so he had pushed David to a fight.

"Then dragged him behind a horse," Rafe Catron said bitterly. "What was that damned sheriff doing?"

No, Thera said impatiently, that was not how it was. McIver had met the drunken, blustering Early out on the street and shot him down. Then—

"Mac done for Early?" Catron could not believe it. "But he don't even pack a gun."

Waco Millard cackled softly. "I give him mine." And tugged a rusty old pistol from his belt and held it up. "I was swamping in the place when Early called him out. Early said he had better have a gun in five minutes because he would come smoking then whether he did or not. He was powerful drunk, Early was. McIver was pretty pale but was bound to defend his honor, he says, so I fetched him this old gun hid in

206

my poke. Told him to aim like he was pointing a finger and take his time. Hell, Early had a slip gun; he come at this boy fanning bullets like he was spraying ladies' coloney, and by God, this Mac took aim and shot once and busted him wide open."

Catron whistled quietly, and Soderstrom motioned for his daughter to go on.

Then, she said, the sheriff had been ready to jail McIver. Surprisingly, it had been Early's friend Richie Sears who had laconically enjoined Sheriff Crashaw to let McIver go his way, as the case was one of clear-cut self-defense. Sears and the other two Wagontree hands had taken Early to the undertaking parlor, and then promptly left town.

Thera had been afraid as they drove home toward Ladder, remembering the look on Sears' face. They had been alert for trouble during the ride, not relaxing until they were well past the turnoff to Wagontree headquarters and within a couple of miles of home. Then, as they rode around an abutting shoulder, Sears and the pair of toughs were waiting.

Thera shuddered; she would never forget the small man's words or the tone of them. *Jack Early had a big mouth and he was a fool. Still he was the only partner I ever had, boy. I ain't about to do for you; old Buckmaster don't want killing. Maybe you will wish you was dead. . . .*

Soderstrom shook her insistently by the shoulders. "The man who dragged him, this was Sears, eh? Thera?"

"Yes, yes, but please get a doctor now, papa. We were so close to home I brought him on here, but now he must have a doctor."

"I'll go," Rafe said, and tramped out.

Soderstrom stood by the window as Catron's horse drummed away on the road. *They will pay for this night's work,* he thought with a massive certainty, and finally settled his frosty stare on Waco Millard. "What does he do here?"

"Why, if he had not given David the gun, that Early would have shot David down. And then he asked if maybe now you would hire him. So I told him to come along, and papa, please do not tell him no."

"Give a man a chance, mister," husked Waco Millard. "I

will do anything you set me to." His scarred face twitched. "I will work for 'most nothing."

"All right, you have got a chance coming. I need another man for the trail drive. But you will put in a whole man's work. You pull your freight or out you go."

Rafe returned with Dr. Enever, a sandy-haired young man with conspicuous jaundice and a temper. He made his examination and said that McIver appeared internally sound except for a dislocated arm which he had set. The damage to his slashed and welted face, bad as it looked, was superficial; he put a bandage on the nose. What the boy needed now was rest and care. Once McIver came to long enough to whisper through puffy lips, "Working for you can be rather a harrowing adventure, Mr. Soderstrom."

Soderstrom was impatient to deal with Richie Sears; he meant to go to Wagontree headquarters and keep a watch on the place as long as necessary to catch Sears alone. He would need Rafe Catron's knowledge of the country to help form his strategy. But Catron said, "Let's don't go off half-cocked, Mr. Soderstrom. Wagontree is a hell of a big outfit; they got line camps the size of your Ladder layout. We better make sure where Sears is. I can pick up his trail from where he dragged Mac last night."

There was no talk as the two men headed up the road in the tepid afterlight of false dawn. They came to the rocky abutment where the three Wagontree men had ambushed the spring wagon, and Catron had no difficulty tracing the ground where Sears' horse had dragged McIver. Afterward the three crewmen had cut south toward Wagontree land. Much of the near-straight trail crossed an almost barren flat stippled by ironwood and mesquite; Rafe was able to track easily from horseback.

Presently he halted and dismounted to check the ground. Here Sears' mount, with its bent-calked right hind shoe, had plainly split off from the others. "The other two went clear on to Wagontree headquarters," Rafe explained. "Sears headed for the lower Salt Creek, meaning he has a berth at the line camp there. Nearest Wagontree camp to your place."

"Then we go there," Soderstrom said grimly. "I want only Sears."

Rafe stepped into his saddle and settled an uneasy glance on the older man. "You mind saying what you got in mind when we find him?"

"Wait and see, mister." Soderstrom reined on toward the straggling line of the Salt Creek. They followed it for a mile or so and came into the long narrow valley where the Wagontree lineshack lay. Tying their horses in a thin skirmish line of timber, they waited for the gray light to give vague form to the shack and its outsheds.

The place lay dark but not deserted; animals were stirring in the corrals. The shack was widely exposed on all sides where brush had been cleared away, and out beyond this the brush flourished in a dense and tangled perimeter. Soderstrom inspected the layout and in several spare phrases told Catron exactly what they would do.

When true daylight paled the east and outlines gained sharp profile, he gave the order. Rafe made off toward the left through the brush, Soderstrom to the right, crouching low. When he was less than fifty yards from the shack, Soderstrom chose a vantage point and sank down on his haunches. He dug out three boxes of shells from his jumper pocket and broke them open. Afterward, rifle across his knees and biting his pipestem, he waited. The air was cool and still. Soderstrom breathed of it deeply; the rifle had an easy, accustomed feel against his palm.

The shack door opened and a man stepped into the yard. He was shirtless, and he looked about and yawned and scratched his gray underwear above his ribs. Afterward he sauntered off toward the corral and leaned on a pole. Soderstrom carefully put his pipe away and sighted up, levered in a shell, and fired.

Splinters flew less than a yard from the man's hand. Even in the still-ghostly light Soderstrom saw his jaw drop, and then he wheeled and lunged for the shack. Deliberately Soderstrom shot again; the man fell grabbing his leg, and a hoarse, panicked cry escaped him.

The door burst open and Richie Sears and another man

came out, guns in hand. Now Rafe's rifle spoke from the brush off east of the shack, kicking up dust in front of them. Sears, moving like a lean ghost, sprang back inside. The other hesitated and moved toward the fallen man. Soderstrom fired again and the rider swore loudly and wheeled into the shack, banging the door. The man on the ground continued to groan his fear and pain.

Soderstrom put two shots into the shack door and then rose and loped off, low bent, to a fresh position. Rafe was laying down a steady hammering fire at the east wall now. Crouching in a fresh spot, Soderstrom saw a rifle barrel nudge across the front window sill and bead on his former position. He fired and heard a savage curse as it was withdrawn.

They peppered the windows and the weathered walls with a steady fire, and after a brief rally the two occupants quit shooting. Soderstrom guessed they were both hugging the floor to avoid the slugs that found cracks and windows—his, for Catron was carefully laying his shots high. Now Rafe put a casual fire on the smokestack till it broke and clanged and clattered off the roof. Soderstrom shoved in fresh shells and turned his attention on the door, smashing the upper, then lower, hinges. The bottom one broke and the door fell crazily askew of its own weight. He felt a deep pleasure in this destruction.

"All right—all right!"

There was a note of sheer panic to that yell from inside—it did not come from Sears—and Soderstrom shouted for Rafe to hold fire. He called to the two men to throw out their guns and come out with hands high. After three rifles and a pair of handguns had been tossed out a window, they emerged. Sears held his hands shoulder-high. The other man was clutching a bloody arm and a blood-soaked bandanna was tied around his scalp.

Soderstrom and Rafe both stepped out to view, moving in from either side. Abruptly Richie Sears spun sidelong, running almost double-bent for the brush. Soderstrom yelled for Rafe to hold fire, and Sears crashed into the brush and wallowed through it. "Get your horse and bring him back," Soderstrom called, adding, "I don't rope so good."

Rafe grinned his understanding and wheeled, dashing back toward his ground-hitched animal. Soderstrom approached the two wounded men; he motioned at the one on the ground and said to the other curtly, "Tend him."

The thin rider with the bloody scalp knelt to examine the other's leg. His probing fingers drew a hoarse yell of pain; the man's face was pasty. "Busted," the thin rider said. "All to hell, it feels like." He looked at Soderstrom. "No call for that, mister. We're just working hands, him and me. He needs his leg. If he don't lose it altogether, he maybe won't use it again."

Soderstrom's eyes were flinty. "You should of picked your company better, him and you."

The thin rider cursed him, then dug out a pocket bandanna and started to tourniquet the wound. "Hold on now, Joe. She is got to be tied off."

Rafe was breaking brush in a careless gallop, and now he came into the clearing and streaked past them, swinging his coiled rope. Again the brush swallowed him, and his crackling passage through it followed west across the valley. Unless Sears had managed to reach the hills that bounded the valley, he would be run down in short order.

Then Rafe was circling back, and in a minute he rode into the clearing with Sears dragging at the end of his dallied rope. Sears lay belly-down panting after Rafe halted; he rested on his elbows and spat dirt. He had taken a few bruises, but Rafe had hauled him not very fast over soft ground. It was Soderstrom whom Sears eyed with an unflinching hatred; he spat again.

Without a word Soderstrom went to the brush corral and drove out the horses, hoorawing them off. Afterward he gathered up the guns the men had thrown out, then tramped into the shack and dropped them on the floor. Picking up the heavy lamp from the table he broke it against the wall; he struck a match and tossed it in the streaming coal oil. He wheeled outside then and walked over to Sears, saying, "Get up," in a quietly savage tone.

Sears staggered to his feet and Soderstrom removed Sears' belt and roughly secured his hands at his back. The shack

211

was spewing oily billows of smoke backed by a wicked crackle of flames as Soderstrom, with a word to Rafe, skirted it. Rafe followed him on horseback, tugging Sears along. By the holding corral a lone big cottonwood flourished and sometimes dropped a scanty shade for the corraled animals. Here Soderstrom stopped. "Give me the rope."

Rafe, not understanding, said, "What?"

"The rope," Soderstrom snapped. "Then step down. I will want your help."

Rafe's weathered face altered with comprehension. "You ain't meanin' this."

For answer Soderstrom jerked the noose that circled Sears' chest and arms up around his neck, then secured it with a fixed knot. "I am going all the way, mister. If you don't like it, clear out."

"But God, Mr. Soderstrom! That is plain-out murder. You'll get strung up yourself for it."

The insensate rage held in a tight ball in Soderstrom's belly snapped its thin checkrein and he walked straight toward Rafe. Catron quickly threw down the rope half he still held coiled. He reined off as Soderstrom bent to pick up the rope but did not go far, watching in mounting disbelief as Soderstrom tossed the coils over a spreading limb, then seized the end and drew the rope up tight.

Sears' head was pulled tightly at an angle to his body. All the intensity had washed out of his bright lizard's eyes; they held a total hopelessness that went beyond fear. Sears expected to die now, and he was not afraid. Somehow this cooled Soderstrom's rage back to a simmer, and the sense of Catron's last words reached him. *But by God, I will serve him and his big boss a lesson they will not forget.*

He leaned his weight on the rope and stretched Sears' wattled neck. The man gagged and began to choke. His face darkened; his eyes started to glaze over, and only then was Soderstrom about to ease off. But Rafe Catron shouted with a wild timbre, "Jesus! That's enough, Mr. Soderstrom. Let it up!"

Soderstrom turned his head and saw that Catron's face was dead white, and that he had his six-gun out and loosely pointed. Deliberately Soderstrom turned his back to Catron and gave the rope more pressure. Sears was in the first throes of real strangulation, face purpling and tongue distended, before Soderstrom finally released the rope. Sears' legs folded and he slipped to the ground, retching and gasping.

Soderstrom looked again at Rafe Catron who sat his saddle with the gun limp in his hand, his face etched with sour defeat. "You still working for me, Catron?"

"Sure," Rafe said sullenly. "I guess so."

"Then hear this," Soderstrom said gently. "You ever pull a gun on my back again, you better use it." Turning on his heel, he walked back to the burning shack. The two Wagontree hands were silently watching the shack and all their belongings go up in smoke.

"You men know why this happened?"

"We know," the thin rider said bitterly. "Sears told us. Goddamn his kind, and damn the old man for taking them on."

Soderstrom said, "You might find other ranges more to your taste," and went back to the tree. Sears was sitting with his knees drawn up, wheezing fitfully; his sick eyes turning on Soderstrom held the same fearless hate.

Soderstrom untied his hands. "Get up. Take off your boots first." Sears wordlessly jerked them off and stood up in his sock feet. He flexed his thin hands; he seemed to have an idea what was coming. Soderstrom nodded brusquely to Catron who was looking on dourly. "All right, now we are done here. Get my horse. We go now to Wagontree."

For a moment Catron was speechless. "But what the hell for?"

"I want this old man, Buckmaster, to see his prize gunman who has walked maybe three-four hours with a rope on his neck and no boots."

Richie Sears said in a paper-dry drone, "Don't do that, mister. Not to me."

Soderstrom ignored him. "Most of the Wagontree people will be out on roundup, eh? The few that are left we can handle." He saw Rafe's hesitation and said flatly, "Mister, I asked you if you was still working for me. Now I do not ask, I tell you. Take my orders or get out for good."

"All right." Catron's voice was low and harried. "But you push a man, by God. You push a man."

"There, mister, you are damned right."

Seven

Having forestalled trouble from the two hands by driving off the horses, Soderstrom pushed unhurriedly toward the southwest and Wagontree headquarters. Sears walked ahead of them, the rope on his neck fastened to Soderstrom's pommel. He carried himself as straight as a ramrod in his humiliation, but this was only the start of what he would endure.

They rode downcreek unspeaking, until Rafe ventured carefully, "That was going too far. Busting that Joe's leg and then burning all their stuff."

Soderstrom turned slowly to stare at him. "You joined me to see them get hit. Now I am hitting them, don't read me no scripture."

"I want to see the Buckmasters hurt, sure," Rafe said sullenly. "But these was just poor hands, like I been myself."

"You think Sears is another grubby hand, too, eh?"

"No. Hell, I fancy doing for him myself but not enough to swing for it. I thought of that."

"So did I. But till I did, what I done was my business." Soderstrom's voice was grim. "You pulled a gun on my back."

Rafe traced a callused thumb along the rope scar on his throat. "I had a taste of a rope. That is a godawful way to punish a man. I couldn't think of nothing else."

"Next time you better think only of what I said."

The brisk pace afoot was beginning to tell on Sears. Like

214

any rider he walked as rarely as possible; his feet were tender and misshapen from years in tight vain cowman's boots. They hit a stretch covered with coarse gravel and sparse bunchgrasses; Sears began to stumble. Whenever he slowed down, Soderstrom gave a vicious flick to the rope, urging him on. Then Soderstrom halted his horse, bringing Sears to a painful stop. A rider had topped a ridge fifty yards away and was coming on at a rapid lope. Rafe shaded his eyes, and after a moment said, "That's Chad Buckmaster."

Soderstrom lifted his Winchester from its scabbard and laid it across his pommel, waiting. The rider pulled up his well-gaited black some yards off; he sat his saddle with an easy grace. He was about thirty and gave the impression of being big all over though his flanks and waist were spare as whipcord. Black curling hair lay like a close cap against his head, from which his ears were faintly batwinged. His face was heavily handsome; he wore a faint provocative smile. His calico shirt, rawhide chaps, and flat-crowned hat were those of any working hand; the thick dust coating them indicated he was on roundup.

The younger brother, Soderstrom thought. Chad Buckmaster was dark like his brother Garth, with much of Garth's considerable size; his smiling and unruffled stare reflected the pleasant irony of his sister Hannah. But he bore little real resemblance to either one; there was a feel about him of potential for either good or bad; you couldn't be sure.

Chad Buckmaster said lazily, "Hello Rafe," and passed a half-shuttered look over Soderstrom. "Ah, the neighbor. Not planning to pay a call like this, were you, neighbor?" Without waiting for an answer, he tilted a nod toward the spume of lifting smoke at their backs. "I was coming to see about that. Our linecamp, I believe." He cocked his head almost politely. "Your work?"

"We will talk on that maybe, when Rafe has taken your pistol."

Young Buckmaster clucked his tongue with a wry grin and shrugged, turning his hands upward. Rafe rode close and disarmed him, ramming Chad's gun in his own belt.

"I'm Chad Buckmaster."

"It is your pa I want to see."

"All right," Chad said agreeably. "I'll take you to him. But not so you can gun him in his own house."

Soderstrom gestured toward Richie Sears. "Is he dead? The other two at the lineshack, they are alive also. But next time it will be different. That is what your pa must know. Maybe if I tell him myself, he will believe it."

Chad frowned slightly, checking his fretting black. "I don't understand this. Something happen?"

"I will talk to your pa only."

"Sure thing," Chad murmured. He fell into loose pace with their mounts as they moved on.

Soderstrom gave him an oblique cold study, saying, "Your big brother is the wolf maybe and you are the rabbit, eh?"

Chad turned his head, smiling handsomely. "The diplomat, let's say. Pa sends Garth when he wants to show his teeth."

"Your brother keeps busy then."

Chad laughed. "Well, he is generally moving some. Look, I want to show you something. Mind turning enough to top that rise yonder?"

"Lead on, but no tricks, mister." Soderstrom guessed from the drift of sound beyond the rise what Buckmaster wanted him to see, but he was still curious.

They swung slightly east and swerved onto the long height that terminated the high rolling land toward this end of the valley. Soderstrom had his first look at a big roundup camp. It lay in a mile-long dip laced with scrub juniper. At one end was the remuda corral filled with fresh mounts, tended by three wranglers. A hundred yards on, the vast sprawl of the camp proper began, a hodgepodge of warbags, spare saddles, blankets, and assorted gear. At one side stood the freight-, chuck-, and calf-wagons with their tailgates down. Two swampers were unloading a wagon, and the cook and his roustabout were butchering a calf. Over the far flat hung an alkaline haze of dust, making half-visible a panoramic beehive of activity—flickering branding fires, the black bodies and white faces of countless cattle, the shadowy forms of riders moving back and forth.

Chad Buckmaster said idly, flicking his horse's mane with

216

his quirt, "That's what you have picked a fight with, my friend. Something to think about, eh?"

Soderstrom could see that the burning of one lineshack made a very minor fleabite on this empire. He gave a stony nod that was also a gesture to motion them back off the slope. Again they set off southwest by the sun.

Richie Sears no longer walked with pride; his head hung to his chest, and occasionally he staggered. Chad said with a thoughtful glance at Soderstrom, "A long way to herd a man like this. We won't be in sight of headquarters in some three hours or more if—"

"Good."

There was no more talk. Sears plugged doggedly on, never looking backward. The sun broiled overhead. Soderstrom called a horse rest finally, and the men dismounted to stretch their legs. Sears collapsed on the ground, his chin on his chest. Chad Buckmaster uncapped his canteen and drank, then said mildly, "Mind if I give him—"

"Not a drop." Soderstrom noticed that the bottoms of Sears' socks were shredded to nothing and the dirt-ground soles of his feet were scratched and bleeding. When he gave the order to go on, Sears climbed at once to his feet and began plodding. Oddly, as if getting a second wind, he walked for a time with an erect and even stride. But Soderstrom could see the aching tautness of his neck muscles and knew each step was an effort; occasional dabs of dark wetness stippled his footprints. And then it came to Soderstrom with a dawning unease that Richie Sears was determined not to break, to somehow turn his humiliation into a victory of sorts.

By the time they came in sight of the Wagontree buildings, the gunman's stamina had broken. He was staggering worse than before. But he lurched on until, blindly missing a stride, he pitched on his face. Groaning, he got his hands braced and crawled to his knees.

Rafe Catron swore, and stepped from his saddle. "That's enough, by God. Shoot me or fire me, but I am giving him a hand."

Soderstrom chewed his mustaches. "All right, load him on in front of you."

Sears raised his head. He said in a parched croak to Soderstrom, "Go to hell, you snorky bastard," and stumbled with a violence to his feet. He went on with his body straight, holding his legs carefully stiff as his bloody swollen feet accepted the alternating agony of his full weight.

They had not reached the outbuildings when he fell again and lay quivering against the ground. Again Rafe got down and this time, against Sears' feeble struggling, lifted him to the saddle. Rafe went ahead on foot leading the horse as they threaded into the working part of the ranch.

Soderstrom could not begin to take in the vast maze of barns and stables and corrals. The area comprising the living quarters was set off on a slight incline. As they approached its huge combination stable and carriage shed, a Mexican stableboy came running out.

"The horses will wait, Luis," Chad said as he swung to the ground. "This *pistolero* has sore feet. Take him to the bunkhouse, then get your grandmother to care for him."

"I'll go along," Rafe Catron said, giving Soderstrom a questioning look. He got a curt nod and started to lead the horse away when Chad said, "I'll take my gun now." Again Soderstrom nodded, and Rafe passed over the pistol.

Richie Sears raised his slumped head. His fancy vaquero's outfit was dirty and torn, and his face was drawn with pain. Only his reptilian eyes were unchanging. "Snorky, I'll remember this a long time."

"I think you will," Soderstrom said, and looked at Chad. "This is far enough. I have come so far, now your pa can come here."

Chad shook his head. "Afraid that's not possible. My father has lost the use of his legs."

After a moment Soderstrom nodded, and the two of them rode on to the main house. Catron had once mentioned how Loftus Buckmaster had started with a 'dobe *jacal* and added a room a year ever since. The construction somehow made a pleasant blend with the sage-dotted hillside it followed upward in a rambling sprawl, the lesser rooms terraced along it above the main house and joined by short flights of open steps. The main part was adobe and two-storied with a broad stone porch supporting gallery columns and an iron-railinged balcony.

They were admitted by a young woman in her late twenties whom Chad introduced as his sister-in-law. Garth's wife was rather slight and delicate with a slim pretty face framed by light brown hair pulled back in a Psyche knot. There was a shy meekness about Naomi Buckmaster, and her words were almost inaudible. She trailed a faint scent of heliotrope; her dress of watered silk rustled as she led the way up a short stairway and down a hallway.

An oak-paneled door opened on a broad well-lighted parlor. Garth Buckmaster, massive and bearded, leaned against a fieldstone fireplace scowling into a whiskey glass dwarfed by his thick paw. His glance found Soderstrom bulking in the doorway; recognition came and a savage curse left him.

Soderstrom said, "Do your feet still hurt?"

Garth made a guttural sound, dropping his arm from the mantel. His great weight tensed, coming forward on the balls of his feet. Then a cavernous voice rumbled from a deep armchair, "Hold still, son, damn it. That walk done you good."

The man who had spoken was a bear-huge man, but he was in the twilight of his life. The years had grizzled his shaggy hair and beard, though the fiery black of his eyes was undimmed. His short truculent neck thrust forward a craggy heavy-jawed head. His great-boned frame was shrunken even in the quilted robe he wore, and the big horny hands resting on his knees had a wasted look. His voice was like distant thunder; it fitted his patriarchal arrogance which, a man had to admit, he wore well.

Chad went to the old man's side, and bending over, spoke quietly and earnestly as if to placate him. Occasionally he nodded at Soderstrom. "All right, all right," old Loftus rumbled at last. Chad sat down then, and Naomi Buckmaster also slipped into a chair and made a pretty pose, looking little and fragile in a room with four hulking men.

Old Loftus pierced Soderstrom with a stare. "Heard plenty about you, Swenska. Can see why, now I clapped eyes on you. So you're the man Angus sold out to."

"Maybe," Soderstrom murmured, "you never thought someone would not sell to you."

"Nope," old Loftus said affably. "Never did. That's plenty small talk; let's have why you're here."

Soderstrom told him and old Loftus chuckled tiredly. "Now listen, I never ordered Early to crowd your boy and I never ordered Sears to give him a Dutch ride. None of my doing."

"Having men shoot up my place my first night there, that was not your doing, too, eh?"

"Hell, yes. But I judged you would crawl out with a mild prodding. You're a real tiger, son. Something else I never counted on." He picked up a hickory cane beside him and butted it to the floor, leaning his wasted hands on it. "Let's quit all this hemming and hawing. You rough up a tough nut like Richie Sears and haze him barefoot into enemy territory to make a point. All right, I'm impressed. Now let's get to horse-trading. I'll buy you out, land, buildings and cattle for fifteen thousand dollars. Fair?"

"Only if I wanted to sell, mister. I don't."

"Just what do you want, son?"

"I will settle for being left alone. Now you know what happens when I'm not."

Old Loftus seemed to deliberate; he thumped his cane gently on the floor. "How much more land will you be wanting?"

"I got all I need."

"More cattle?"

"Maybe a few over the years, if my range can support them. We have modest ways, us Swedes."

Loftus Buckmaster smiled. "Well, that sounds reasonable. How you feel about me rubbing up agin other folks now and then?"

Soderstrom shrugged. "That is their own lookout."

Old Loftus leaned back, still smiling. "That sure does sound reasonable. Don't puff your crop about this, son. Anything you can do to me ain't enough to rouse the hackles on a feist. I am just weighing what your dab of a Ladder is worth to me, and it ain't worth the trouble of a fight."

Garth Buckmaster was pacing heavily back and forth; he halted and scowled. "Pa—"

"Shut your mouth," old Loftus said mildly. "You have got my size and Chad has got my brains, but together you don't add up to the man I was. I give you some say-so now and again because you got to learn; won't be nobody to brace your backs when I'm gone. You listen, boy. I always knew when to pull in my horns and when to crowd. That is why I have lasted as well as growed."

Garth dropped his gaze, a flush mounting to his fleshy face. His big hand threatened to crack the glass it held.

Old Loftus seemed suddenly tired; he shut his eyes and let his head drop back. "You got what you come for, Swenska. See him out, Chadwick."

Coming out with Chad Buckmaster into the midday brightness, he found Rafe Catron waiting on the steps. As the three of them mounted and started back among the sprawl of outbuildings, Chad said genially, "Quite a concession from the old man."

"Was it?"

"You're too suspicious," Chad grinned, and pulled up. "Well, I'll leave you here and head back for roundup. If you're going directly to your headquarters, you'll find the road is best." He touched his hat and loped off toward the north.

Soderstrom and Catron left the headquarters on its left flank and put their horses to the wagon road. Rafe said, "The old greaser woman was making a poultice for Sears' feet when I left him. A wonder for easing a man, them old remedies."

Soderstrom, peering down the sun-touched switchbacks of the road, hardly heard him. And shortly Rafe said, "Who is that coming?"

"His daughter."

"Who?"

"Buckmaster's girl. She runs the newspaper."

"Hell, I know that. But man, you have the eyes." Rafe tipped down his hat and squinted at the coming rider, and shook his head. "Yes sir, you have the eyes."

When they met, Hannah Kingery pulled up her sleepy-looking livery nag. Even on horseback, she looked quite statuesque, wearing a gabardine riding habit and a flat-crowned hat. She gave the reserved hello of acquaintance, and then Soderstrom said bluntly to Rafe, "Ride on. I will catch up."

Catron looked curious, but not very; he touched his hat and rode wordlessly on. Hannah Kingery eyed Soderstrom with a thoughtful smile, not disconcerted. "Were we about to ask each other the same question?"

"Maybe. I thought you did not like your pa."

"I don't have to like him to love a place where I grew up. Often I ride out from town, and if my way takes me near, I always drop in. Besides, Naomi—my brother's wife—has been my closest friend since we were children."

"She is not much like you, missus."

"Don't call me 'missus'," she said a shade crossly. "I can't be over eight or nine years younger than you." The wind had whipped fresh color to her face; she tapped a horsehair quirt against her palm. "Everything you say seems to have the bark on it, Mr. Soderstrom."

"That was not meant badly."

Surprisingly she smiled a little. "I know. And you are right, but when we were children there were no other girls of our age about. Besides, she needs a woman to talk with now and then—or she'd go crazy." She watched him coolly. "I wouldn't have taken you for liking him either, or has the gaff gotten so rough you're selling out?"

"Not this year, missus. He has promised to trouble me no more."

"I told you not to—he what?"

Soderstrom told what had happened to McIver and his own retaliation, and Hannah only shook her head. "But surely you don't believe him."

Soderstrom smiled very faintly. "There is a man I can look at eye to eye. Even crippled up—with arthritis?—there is a man. If I have him right, his pride is too big for what he says. Also if one man could laugh in his face and make it stick, others will know they can. That is why he must drive me off and why today settled nothing. But if I wanted to put a man off his guard, I would tell him otherwise. If I didn't think he would believe, still I would tell him so."

"Of course," she said without inflection. "I said you were alike, didn't I? As a journalist, or snooper, may I inquire as to how Pa has gone about making your life pleasant these last weeks?"

Soderstrom frowned and lifted his shoulders. "He has done nothing. Except to have my place shot up the first night, and then Catron came and drove his men off—"

"I meant to ask you about Catron. He's a suspected cow thief, you know."

"He says he stole nothing. He has worked well and hard, and now I will need him to get my cows to Taskerville."

"You're driving there soon? Be careful. Cattle in a herd are rather a handy target; possibly my father was waiting for something of the sort." She seemed to hesitate. "By the way, your daughter visited me in town yesterday. And you're scowling again."

"*Ja*, so?"

"I was about to ask where she will stay while you're on the drive. Surely not at the ranch."

"She won't. She will come along and drive the wagon with the grub and blankets."

"I suggest that she come to Mimbreno and stay with me while—"

"It ain't I want her doing man's work," Soderstrom said roughly. "I need my three men to herd the cows, and someone must drive the wagon."

She gave him a careful, silent regard. He felt strangely uncomfortable; he had seen no women in weeks outside of Thera and now Naomi Buckmaster, and neither of them had made him aware of his grimy, unshaven, and work-wasted appearance.

"Oh, I see. You're afraid of my influence on her. Isn't that really the thing?"

Soderstrom's first impulse was to growl a denial, but he was uneasily aware of the deep impression this woman had made on his daughter. He liked directness and honesty, and he would not repay Hannah Kingery with less than she had shown.

"What you do," he told her flatly, "is not fit work for a woman."

"My husband was a printer and I assisted him until he died and left me that modicum of experience and nothing else. How would you suggest I make a living, Mr. Soderstrom?"

"Usually a young widowed woman marries again and makes a new home. My mother, my wife, they were good women who worked hard to make their homes good ones."

"Yes," she said coldly. "And died quite young, I shouldn't wonder."

Soderstrom's face closed like a mask; he started to ride on, and swiftly she reached out a hand. "Oh, please—I'm sorry. I did not mean that as it sounded. But a new day is coming for women; young as she is, a girl of Thera's spirit is bound to be caught up in it. Sir, you can't stop it from happening."

Soderstrom snapped, "Happening don't make any damnfool thing good," and put his horse past her on the road.

Eight

In a few days Soderstrom, Catron and Waco Millard had finished up the beef gather. On the evening that they drove the last of the cattle into the holding canyon, a rough count was made. A dozen or so sick and near-starved ones were culled out. They had already separated and branded the late calves and hazed them loose into some coulee cutbacks. These would be turned onto Ladder's open range later, now that the beef cut was complete.

For these last few nights, the three men had made camp close by the holding canyon, splitting up a night watch into three two-hour shifts. So far no sign of trouble; but as he squatted by the fire tonight, brooding at the crumbling cherry coals, Soderstrom's thoughts budged dourly to Hannah's warning that a herd on the move would make a prime target. Rafe came from checking the horses; he hunkered by the fire, lifting the boiling coffeepot in a callused hand impervious to heat, and filled a cup. Against the night chill he wore a bulky coat of goathide with the hair side turned out. He took a deep swig of the scalding brew, burned his tongue, and swore.

Soderstrom took out his pipe, but did not light it. He rubbed it between his palms, staring into the bowl. "Millard is keeping good watch by the canyon?"

"Don't worry. He knows what's at stake." Rafe scowled into the cup, nursing his burned tongue. "We both do."

I wonder if you do, Soderstrom thought grimly. He had a prize crew in this pair, two men moved only by a feral hatred for Wagontree and Buckmaster. Not that this counted against them; he wanted men with the stomach for a fight. Then there was McIver who, he grudgingly had to admit, had turned out far better than he had expected, though he would be in no shape for the drive.

Catron said, "With the calves and culls all separated, about four hundred head for market. We come across enough carcasses and leavings that I'd allow for a heavy kill, but we got more than three men can rightly handle anyway. You want to leave at first light, I reckon?"

"What do you think?"

"My old pappy always said, 'Leave the boss say it, son, and keep your nose clean.'" Catron grinned, then lifted his head. "Sounds like the wagon."

Soderstrom came to his feet, listening as he peered across a star-silvered meadow. Thera, who had stayed at the ranch tending the wounded McIver, was to have arrived earlier today with a wagonload of supplies. Now as she wheeled into the firelight and halted the team, he was surprised to see McIver beside her on the seat. She dropped lightly to the ground, distress in her face. "I did not want him to come," she said, watching McIver carefully step down.

The boy's left arm was in a sling and he moved as if his

body were one vast ache. His stitched and half-healed face was very pale as he limped to the fire. "I am ready to return to work, sir," he said, and Soderstrom only grunted. Rafe gave both of them a mildly incredulous glance, then quietly spat, tossed out his coffee dregs, rose and walked away to his soogans.

When McIver had spread his blankets by the fire and dropped into a fitful sleep, Thera murmured, "I would not say it before and shame David, but Papa, you must send him back to the ranch. He is still sick. He can get about a little, but he must have rest now. When we get back—"

"I tell him nothing," Soderstrom said roughly. "He hired on to work; if he cannot work, let him say so."

"But he will not." Thera's voice held a puzzled, injured note. "You know he won't, a young man so proud. Only if you say to go back, then he will. Won't you tell him?"

"Let him say it," Soderstrom said flatly. He rapped his pipebowl against his boot from habit, then stood up. "No more of this."

She stood too, the pink firelight glinting on her sudden tears. "I thought maybe when you were so mad because they hurt him . . . but no, you never cared about David being hurt. I know that now. It was just that they spit in the eye of Soderstrom."

"Thera!"

But she had already swung away and, without looking at him again, walked to the wagon and got her blankets. Soderstrom bit deeply into his pipestem. There was both a curse and a cry in his thoughts, and he could give voice to neither.

Thera, beating a ladle on a skillet, roused them out in the gray dawn. She had a coffeepot bubbling on banked coals and leftover son-of-a-gun stew (as Rafe considerately described it for her ears) warming in the Dutch oven. Within the half-hour they were on the move, driving the small herd out of the box canyon; they swung up through a wide draw and followed it out of the rough country to the flats beyond. Rafe and Waco took the points while Soderstrom and McIver ate dust in the drag. Thera followed fifty yards behind with the wagon.

At Rafe's suggestion, they were avoiding the regular cattle route at the outset. They would make a wide loop north and later swing back toward the trail. Wagontree had probably kept a watch of sorts on their operations and would know they were ready to drive. But Wagontree would have the old trail spotted, and the longer they could be thrown off, the wider Soderstrom's margin of safety. There was no need to scout the terrain ahead; Rafe knew the country well, and had every draw and pothole mentally charted. He allowed that it would make for some mean travel, but there was good grass here and there, and he knew the waterholes.

But as the day wore on, Soderstrom began to uneasily feel that the good prospects had been exaggerated. By his admission, it had been a long time since Rafe had covered this country, and this summer had been unusually hot and dry. Scattered patches of graze gave way to stretches where bone-dry dust rose in impalpable clouds around the plodding beefs, choking animals and riders. The horses had to work without relief, since there was no spare string. The men dismounted from time to time to clean the clogged dust from their mounts' nostrils. The furnace-like heat danced in shimmering waves on every side, and the sun reflected off the alkaline *playas* with a dazzling whiteness that hurt the eye. The men sweated and coughed through a fog of heat and dust, and hoorawed the cattle from parched throats.

Rafe gave the orders, bawling them in husky volleys. He dropped back and told McIver to take over at point. The boy was in bad straits, hunched deeply in his saddle, and he roused himself sluggishly, barely raising his head, at Rafe's voice, then reined over to the position vacated by Rafe.

Soderstrom knew that it was no place for a green rider, and he ranged over by Rafe to say as much. Rafe's grimace cracked the dusty mask of his face. "Jesus, Mr. Soderstrom, you think this eating dust is for a sick man?"

"You want to eat his dust, mister, you do it, but anything goes wrong on his point, it's on your head."

"He'll do all right. Anyhow we're crowding these mossies

too hard. Let's ease down. This is a spooky bunch, and there's a way to push before nightfall."

"You said Lost Sink is the first good water?"

Rafe nodded, wiping a hand over his mouth as he squinted off at the horizon dancing in the heat. "I hope. Seen three-four dried-up seeps already. Water in the Sink will be down, more than like. Never knew her to go dry, though."

The apprehension was more than justified when, toward sunset, they drove the herd up over a sandhill and saw below nothing but a shallow bowl of mud rimmed by white mud that was dried and sun-cracked. Lost Sink had gone dry. Soderstrom put his horse around the flank of the herd, squinting his way through the haze of wind-tattered dust. It made dim forms of the lowing, thirst-crazed cattle, milling back and forth.

When he reached Rafe, the redhead was sitting his horse and softly, monotonously taxing his spare but evil vocabulary. "Bad mistake, and it was mine. Them beefs was thirsting enough this morning they should of been driven to water first, but I thought Lost Sink'd be water high anyways."

Soderstrom's jaw was ridgelike under its dust-powdered beard, but this of all times allowed no luxury of temper. He squinted against the bannering dust from eyes red-rimmed with sunglare and said softly, "The thing is, what now, eh?"

"There's a choice. We keep pushing the way I mapped her and hit Pima Tanks by tomorrow noon. Take the chance the Tanks ain't down, too. If it is, these critters won't last it out. Else we swing around back the way we come and hit the regular route. Hate to think of that, now we come this far, and we're driving enough tallow off these scrubs as it is."

Soderstrom thought it over. "All right, tonight we bed down here. You get a couple hours' sleep and ride on ahead to check Pima Tanks. You will be back before dawn, then we can lay the plans."

Rafe glumly assented, and they herded the cattle on to a good-sized flat below a looming granite ridge. They made camp under the rim and drove the horses back into a narrow fissure in the cliff wall. Here was grass, and a small spring bubbling out of the rocks. They washed their faces and drank

228

their fill, except for McIver who tumbled into his soogans like a drugged man and fell asleep at once. When they had wolfed the simple meal Thera prepared, Rafe also sought his blankets for some sleep preparatory to his long ride.

Thera carried the dishes and utensils back into the canyon and washed them at the spring. Waco Millard was saddling up for nighthawk duty as she returned, her arms loaded, and he said in a shrill half-whisper, "Mind how you set them things down, Missy. Recollect one night on the Red, back in '68. I was with a trail crew pushing a thousand head to Abilene. Quiet night like this one. Fool roustabout was stashing away pots and pans and dropped a whole armload. Cattle was bedded down a half mile off, but the sound set 'em off like Chinee firecrackers. Two men got killed trying to turn 'em."

"Thank you, Mr. Millard." She laid the utensils down carefully, one by one, on the outspread pack tarp. Waco nodded, his scarred face grotesquely twitching, and then mounted and rode out to the skittish, lowing herd.

Soderstrom lay stretched out, head propped on his saddle, puffing at his pipe. Millard's words made him thoughtful; everything depended on this herd, and the number of things that could go wrong made unpleasant thinking. He had kept an eye out all day for any sign that they were being followed. He had seen none, but if Wagontree had been watching them off and on and had caught his herd heading out today, they might have followed up at any distance simply waiting their chance. Hannah had warned him that her father could be holding off only in anticipation of a moment when the herd would be vulnerable. But Soderstrom was satisfied with this bedground; he had open country on three sides and a cliff at his back. There was a full moon. What could the Buckmasters try?

He dozed that way, awkwardly propped against his saddle. When he woke, his neck was sore and stiff; rubbing out the kinks, he became aware of voices. He realized that Thera and McIver were talking on the other side of the wagon, and now Thera was saying in her grave, quiet way, "I wish that you try not to hate my father, David."

229

"I don't—" McIver broke off as if embarrassed, and she, as though he had not spoken at all, went on, "Life has been hard to him. Once he was different, but always he was strong. And when the bad things happened, again and again, because he could not act as a weak man would and let it break him, he could only turn hard. Now that we have come out here, in time maybe the change will turn things different again. I hope for this."

McIver said nothing for a while, as if reluctant to voice a contradiction, and finally he said rather lamely, "I was wondering . . . do you read, Thera? None of my business, except that if you've had no opportunity to learn, I'd be happy to teach you."

"What that says is that my English is so very bad, eh?" He protested, missing the grave teasing in her tone. "No, that's only the truth, David; I was born in America, but Papa and Mama were both from the old country and talked only Swedish at home. So did all the people around where we lived. I did not learn English till I go to school; then it has come hard for I have not needed it till now. I don't think I ever learn English good, David. I read it very bad. I read the Swedish newspapers," she added half-defensively.

"You don't speak English so badly, Thera," he said earnestly. "Why, you know two languages and both quite well; that's an accomplishment. And you can learn to read English as well, if you'll let me teach you."

"Yes," she said very slowly. "I would like this. Then I will ask Hannah to show me how she sets the type. I would like—"

"Who? Oh, Mrs. Kingery." He did not sound pleased. "You want to become a lady journalist."

She laughed. "No. But I have never worked outside my home. This I would like to do, for a little while."

Soderstrom had heard enough; he came to his feet and tramped around behind the wagon. They were sitting tailor-fashion on the ground, and it was all innocent enough, but he felt a slow temper that made blades of his words. "Get out and relieve Millard, college boy."

McIver got gingerly to his feet and limped back into the

canyon to fetch his horse. Thera stood too, saying, "You should not—"

"Be still. You will not hire out to work; I say so and you are my daughter. You hear me good, Thera?"

"Yes." Her face was suddenly very white, but her words held only a proper obedience. "Yes, I hear you."

"And don't ever apologize for me to anyone like I just heard you do," he said harshly. "Never again."

"No, Papa." Her eyes held an icy control, and they seemed to look through him. "I will never speak for you again."

Soderstrom wheeled and stalked back to the fire. The blaze seemed to burn into his eyes; his head started to ache. *Helvete!* Why had he spoken to her in such a way? Maybe Hannah Kingery had been right and he feared losing the one remaining thing for which he cared. Only he had no words to say so, and must fall back on the habit of command. And, in forcing her obedience, was driving her farther and farther from him; but even if the right words had come, he could not have brought himself to say them. Soderstrom sank back on his blankets and, finding no answer, fell into a troubled sleep.

It might have been an hour later that he was sluggishly roused by a hard, insistent hand shaking him by the shoulder. The fire was dead, and dimly now he made out Rafe Catron bending over him. "What—"

"Keep it low, Mr. Soderstrom. Get on your feet, but be still about it."

Soderstrom did, and then whispered, "What is it?"

"Nothing for sure. Was rousting myself to saddle up and heard something make a stir on the rim."

Soderstrom squinted up at the black cliff silhouetted against the stars, a good eighty feet above their camp. He strained his eyes and listened. "An animal."

"On the safe side, would sooner guess it ain't. A fine place for someone to start rolling rock, eh? Better collect the gear and move out quiet as we can. I'll get the horses, you roust out Waco and your girl."

Rafe moved off like a shadow toward the dark mouth of the canyon. Soderstrom yanked on his boots and went to shake

Waco up. The scar-faced man grunted assent to the swift explanation and began reaching for his gear in the dark, rolling it into his soogans. Thera's sleeping place was inside the wagonbed, and Soderstrom had started toward the wagon when he stiffened to the sound of dislodged pebbles rolling down from above.

Suddenly the confined roar of an explosion shook the earth. Soderstrom ran for the wagon with a hoarse yell; he stumbled and fell as a thin shower of stone and earth rained over him. Off right of the camp he heard a massive slab of rimrock shift and tilt and plunge downward. The ground trembled to the impact of collapsing rock. Out in the night, a stir of movement rippled through the herd as the first surge of panic took hold of it. There was a shout and a few shots as McIver made his token effort to contain the panicked animals.

Soderstrom was already on his feet lunging toward the wagon, then was forced to take a sprawling dive to one side, barely in time to avoid being run down by the frightened horses bolting from the canyon, Rafe's savage voice urging them on. At the same time came a roar of grinding rock. Even as he leaped up, Soderstrom was aware that the rotted shale rimrock along this entire section of cliff, weakened by the tremors, was about to go.

Rafe came running from the canyon, yelling, "She's sloughing off on our heads—run for it!" Soderstrom plunged over to the wagon, bawling Thera's name, his words drowned by a thunderous cascade of falling boulders as the rimrock went. A mass of rock and rubble crashed into the wagonbed, and before his mind could even seize on the chaos of what had happened, he was blinded by a rise of bitter choking dust. He felt a tug on his arm. He was obscurely aware, as the roar of the avalanche dwindled off, of a rumble of hooves as the herd juggernauted into a full stampede, but it did not pierce his consciousness.

Rafe was pulling on his arm, dragging him away, and then before the rattle of landsliding rock had died away, the stunning shock of full knowledge brought Soderstrom tearing from Rafe's hold, blindly wheeling back toward the wagon.

The camp was gone, wagon and fire and gear, buried under

tons of massive rubble, the silent dust settling over it. A berserker's roar burst from Soderstrom's chest, a sound of madness and pain that was flung against the cliffs and back.

"Papa—"

He came blindly around, only half-believing his eyes even when he saw her coming quickly, lightly running, from the darkness. He smothered her in his big arms, shaking like a man in fever as he wrested sense from her breathless, broken words. "See, if I hadn't been mad at you . . . so mad I went off walking by myself . . . oh Papa, it is all right!"

Nine

As they squatted around their cook fire in the cool dawn, a kind of sick and exhausted apathy gripped all of them. No one was hungry. They drank black scalding coffee and said little. Beyond the general mood, each of them was preoccupied with his own individual problem; for Soderstrom, it was the recognition of utter defeat.

He couldn't justly attach blame to McIver, since even a number of experienced hands could have done little to halt the wild stampede. By the time he and Rafe and Waco had caught up, the herd had run itself pell-mell into a stretch of razor-edged *malpais* and broken canyons. A number had rushed over sheer drops to death; others, crippled and hamstrung, had to be dispatched one at a time. A few sound head remained, barely enough to bother rounding up. The destruction of the herd, not the herders, had been the Buckmasters' sole intent, otherwise the dynamite charge would have been set directly above the camp.

Hunched by the fire, Soderstrom sipped his coffee and numbly let his scattered thoughts converge. He raised his head, feeling the intent regard of them all and, behind this, a silent question.

"First," he said slowly, "I will go to town and ask the sheriff to do something. He will do nothing. Then I'll have all the excuse I need to hit them in any way I want."

"Well," Rafe said around his cigarette, and paused, squinting against the smoke. "I dunno. We got no proof who dynamited that cliff. Maybe part of what they wanted was to make us redheaded enough to try to settle the score. Be all the excuse they'd need to see us dead."

"You are afraid, then?" Soderstrom's voice was freighted with disdain. "Of them? Of their bought law, eh?"

"Law's still law. As my old pappy would say, don't fancy it and don't buck agin it, either. Anyway we're four men against their whole crew."

"There are ways," Soderstrom said softly. "They like to fight in the dark, eh? Good. Numbers mean nothing in the dark, and it's hard to prove anything. All right, they have shown me the way to fight. And now I have nothing to lose; they have much. That is the way, too." His gaze shot across them. "Well?"

Waco's white hair plumed on the mild wind; his eyes glittered. "That sure shines to me, mister."

Rafe Catron frowned and drew on his cigarette once more, then pinched it out and dropped it. He nodded once; that was all. McIver alone looked uncertain as he raised a drawn and haggard face. "I don't know. I would need time to think about that."

"You have till I get back from town," Soderstrom said, and set down his cup and stood. "Thera will come with me. You men get together what is left of them cows and head them home and turn them loose."

As the two Soderstroms pointed their mounts southeast, Thera made a few attempts at talk, but after a few curt replies, they rode in silence. Obliquely Soderstrom knew that he was letting a feeling of raw defeat crowd him to a reckless action. For last night had seen the ground cut cleanly from under him; he hadn't the funds to make even a start toward restocking his ranch. No matter what sort of fight he carried

234

to the enemy, he could not avoid the overriding, bitter truth: he was finished here. A sense of gray and total futility seized him, but in a minute, remorseless as a sea tide, his unspent rage swept back and held in him like a tight hot ball.

By the early afternoon they reached Mimbreno. The main street, bathing in the heat, was livened by the bustle of Saturday traffic. Rigs and saddle horses crowded the tie rails. Bonneted women flocked the sidewalks in gossiping coveys, and a mob of kids were playing kick-the-can in the middle of the street. They skirted the confusion, and Soderstrom pulled up by the hotel, a two-storied and unpainted building weathered and warped past any redemption of paint or whitewash. His gaze angled across the way to the tie rail of the Alhambra Bar. Among the animals tied there was Garth Buckmaster's big black. He and maybe some other Wagontree men were off to an early start this payday, and Soderstrom thought, *Yes, they would be celebrating,* and felt the anger lift like flame, high and scouring.

He swung to the ground and helped Thera dismount. "Go and get us two rooms," he told her. "Then wait for me."

Her eyes searching his face held a half-plea, and he could read the thought which by now she knew better than to voice; it would do no good. Her eyes were sad and troubled, and she went slowly up the steps into the hotel.

Soderstrom went to the livery and left their horses, and came back downstreet carrying his saddlebags and rifle. Then, seeing the giant form of Garth Buckmaster leaving the Alhambra, he quickened pace. Garth swung around the tie rail to his black, caught up his reins and was swinging heavily astride when Soderstrom came swiftly up behind him. Without a word he reached a long arm and hooked his fingers in Garth's belt and gave a savage yank, stepping back.

Garth plunged backward into the dust. He scrambled onto his hands and knees with a roar. Then grew awkwardly motionless as Soderstrom's rifle was rammed against his ribs.

"You have wiped me out, mister. Maybe I should wipe you out."

Garth's eyes rolled and lifted; sweat and dust stained his shirt and the side of his bearded face. He tried to rumble a laugh, but one look at the hard and angled face of the man above him shut it off.

"This way is too easy," Soderstrom said softly. "Get up." He saw that Garth was not wearing a pistol. He backed off and leaned his rifle against a tie rail post. Garth floundered onto his feet, and then he did laugh.

Krag Soderstrom was big, but this man was like a young mountain. But Soderstrom's mood was jagged enough for him to shrug away any concern at all. He trusted his own reflexes, and he was light on his feet for a man of size.

Buckmaster was still making humorous noises as he shed his coat and, while his arms were locked in the sleeves, Soderstrom stepped easily into him. He drove his right hand into Garth's belly, rocked his jaw with a hard left, and stepped back out of reach.

Garth gave back a couple steps, more surprised than hurt. Blood sprang from his split lip; a slow fury kindled in his eyes. He dropped his coat. He shook his head like a bull and moved in with his great arms windmilling, and Soderstrom sidled away. He feinted low and darted in a hard high right that bounced off Garth's cheekbone. Garth bored in with a feral growl and caught Soderstrom under the ear with a full roundhouse. Earth and sky pinwheeled in pain; he was going down; he hit the dirt. But the impact seemed perversely to clear his head.

Soderstrom rolled up on his knees and onto his feet and the clean hot anger scouring his veins left no room for pain or doubt, only a dogged and wicked determination. Garth moved in swinging, and Soderstrom ducked under his arm and sidestepped him again, then fell into a circling backaway that drew Garth after him, awkwardly circling, too.

Soderstrom hooked a few tentative jabs at his thick sweating face to bring Garth's guard up and, mostly to feel out his defense, whipped a low punch into Garth's belly. He saw Garth's grimace of hurt, and then Garth tried a smothering attack to drive him backward. A glance over his shoulder told him that Garth meant to back him against a building, and he smiled and shifted away, letting Garth carry the attack, but forcing him always into a broad circle.

Garth was in bad condition. He had natural beef and maybe a rough-and-tumble background, but being a gentleman rancher had helped him go slack. His breathing was labored and whistling now, and there was a perceptible drag in his long, sledgehammer swings. Now that it was easier to evade his lumbering enemy, Soderstrom could feel the second strength of his own hard, durable life swaying a slow balance.

He watched Garth's face till a flicker of decision warned him. When Garth charged him suddenly, Soderstrom simply sank his head and let the blow slip off his shoulder and graze his jaw. He moved backward again, but not quickly now, landing a couple of light jabs and one hard hook, drawing Garth into a final furious rally. Garth's belly was not his strongest point, and Soderstrom concentrated on feinting him wide open.

When he saw his chance, he timed the low body smash exactly. It stopped Garth in his tracks and left him slightly bent, hands dropped to cover his belly. Soderstrom took enough time to set his stance and swung, putting his weight behind his arm and shoulder. The blow took Garth on the point of his shelving chin and snapped his head back; his legs buckled and he fell to his knees and pitched on his face in the dust.

Soderstrom stood a moment getting back his breath, then moved to his rifle and picked it up, raking the scattering of onlookers with his glance. Several of them looked pleased as Garth dragged himself up, hugging the tie rail.

"If I ever catch you on my land again," Soderstrom said then in a flint-hard voice, "I'll kill you, mister. Or any of your crowd."

Garth lifted his face, holding himself against the soreness of his belly, and he said sickly, "Jail him, Otis."

Soderstrom moved his gaze sidelong till he saw Sheriff Crashaw standing to his right. The old lawman coughed and came forward, and his eyes, Soderstrom saw without pity, were old and tired. When he had told his story, Crashaw said wearily, "You prove Wagontree did that?"

"No," Soderstrom said in a wicked and measured tone, shifting his grip on the rifle. "Ho, Sheriff, what now? You want to arrest me for assault on this citizen?"

Crashaw did not reply, and Soderstrom smiled. "Good. I guess Loftus Buckmaster and me are two make pretty big tracks, eh? You stick to what you do best. Dozing on your big fat star, mister."

He let the dregs of his anger out in cold contempt, then swung deliberately about and walked away. Crashaw said in a tired voice, "Hold on, you." Soderstrom did not even look back. Somebody laughed.

Soderstrom tramped into the hotel lobby, signed for the room Thera had reserved for him, and went upstairs. He paused in the murky corridor by her door which adjoined his, and knocked. She opened the door quickly, and he saw only the good warmth of relief in her expression, and was suddenly grateful that she had the gift of understanding much that went unspoken, he being no man of words. He said gruffly that later they would go down to supper together.

Inside the sweltering cubbyhole of his room he stripped down to the waist, then soaped and washed. The fight had spent his anger to deadness, and he felt a vast weariness as he dried himself on a strip of frayed toweling.

Beating Garth Buckmaster and facing down a sick old man had given him an arid satisfaction but had done nothing to solve his real problem. No matter what vengeful gestures he made now, he was through. Good God, he was supposed to be a practical Swede. More, he was a thirty-seven-year-old widower with a daughter to think of, not some wild buck who could follow up any whim that suited his fancy. Well, what now? He had come to town only to clear his conscience by telling the law what had happened, but maybe while he was about it, he should look for a buyer for the ranch.

This feeling of exhausted defeat had the power to frighten and arouse him; he rasped an angry hand over his whiskers, then got out his shaving kit and soaped his face, setting to with the razor before the lather could soften his beard, liking the keenness of raw steel along his jaw.

Someone tapped on the door and he growled, "Who is it?"

"Hannah Kingery."

Soderstrom told her to wait a minute and got into a clean shirt before opening the door. She stepped inside, and the slatted sunlight promptly brought out her freckles. She was wearing a starched blue dress and a pert straw hat and she looked very slim and supple; she brought a scrubbed freshness and radiance into the drab room, and somehow this disconcerted him. He swung back to the washbasin, muttering gruffly that he had to finish shaving.

"I don't mind." Hannah took the single straight-backed chair and met his eye in the mirror. "I overheard some talk of what happened and what you told Otis, so I quizzed my sterling brother a bit just before he left town. He had a good deal to say, mostly about your ancestry, and was occasionally lucid. Of course he denied dynamiting your herd."

"So, you have come for a story?"

"That can wait," she said calmly. "Now I am interested in hearing whether you can make a comeback. Well, frankly— how do you stand financially? That is none of my affair, but—"

"I am stone broke. I am busted flat." His savage stroke with the razor made a deep nick, and he swore feelingly. All his anger came flooding back. "Your old man thinks he knows what a dirty fight is. He ain't seen a fight, not till I have shown him one. And by God, I will!"

Hannah said calmly, "All right, don't listen."

"What?"

"I was about to tell you of a better way, but don't listen to me. By all means, fight him as you're planning to, and end up in jail or dead."

Soderstrom whittled grimly at his beard for a half-minute, then slowly lowered his razor, thinking, *Damn all your pride; ask her*. "What way is this?"

"The right way. As you were, standing up to him as an honest man on your own land, giving him back all he could give and better."

"Damn it, woman, understand one thing—"

"I know—money. I can loan you all that you need to restock your ranch on any terms that would be convenient."

239

Soderstrom stared at her quite impassively for some seconds. He concealed his astonishment, but not quite his instinctive suspicion. "Where does a woman who says she needs to work for a living get this kind of money?"

It was Hannah's turn to be disconcerted, and she flushed slightly. "In a way, it was true enough. My mother left me her jewelry ... I was still in my teens when she died. It was all I had as a remembrance of her, and I tried to retain the collection intact. I had to sell a couple of stones to keep my husband and me alive, and after his death, I gave up several more pieces to buy the *County Press*."

Soderstrom was already shaking his head. "No, keep your jewels. It would not be right—"

"Wait. Listen, please. Any bank in the territory outside of Mimbreno will give you a loan if I cosign and put up such collateral. The collection has been appraised at a value of fifty thousand dollars. We can take the stage to Salt City over east of here and arrange the loan with the bank there."

Soderstrom hesitated, watching her grave freckled face that was not pretty and not plain, and more than merely beautiful. The flat refusal on his lips came out as a temporizing growl. "That is splitting a mighty fine hair for any difference, missus."

"I know," she said quietly. "Look at it this way. Perhaps I am as desperate as you. This is something I must do."

"Against your father and brothers?" An insight came to him, and he said, "You hate your pa that much, eh?"

"I hate his ruthlessness and greed. Is that strange? So do a lot of people." She bit her lip and lowered her eyes, and murmured, "Very clever, Mr. Soderstrom, but it's none of your affair. Does it matter what my reasons are? My offer can save your ranch ... and there is your daughter's welfare to consider."

He nodded brusquely. "I have considered. I will take the offer of a loan; I will give ten per cent interest and not thank you, since I'm doing you a favor, too, eh?"

"Very well," she said crisply, and stood up. "I would like to make a suggestion ... and it is only that, a suggestion. You can never hope to rival my father in terms of land or size of herds; but for all his shrewdness, he's old and set in his ways, and the future will belong to those who act now." She hesitated. "You know of the shorthorn cattle that stockmen in New Mexico have been breeding successfully? They're a beef stock far superior to anything ever introduced in this country—"

"Look, I'm not so much of a fool. They are not built for this high country, and they won't weather here."

"That's what all the old-timers say, of course, but as a matter of fact the New Mexico cowmen have raised shorthorns successfully in country and climate much like this. That certainly warrants a try, and I hadn't thought of you as an old man—quite."

Women, Soderstrom thought dourly, had a knack for throwing up a proposal as a challenge seasoned with qualified insult. He held a skeptical silence, and she added sharply, "I was raised on a ranch, and I am not a fool, either. However, if you can't trust a mere woman's word, then ask Rafe Catron. You trust his judgment, don't you?"

"Yes," Soderstrom said stonily. He toweled the traces of lather from his stinging jaw, scowling at the mirror. "I would be on the trail a long time, bringing back this new herd. I would like to leave Thera with you, and I will pay for her keep."

"Why?" she demanded tartly. "I thought you disapproved of my possible influence on her."

"I do not deny it. But a trail drive is no place for a girl. Last night she could of got killed. I thought—" He checked himself. "Will you do this? Not for me—for her."

Hannah said that she would if Thera were willing. Soderstrom called his daughter in to secure her agreement; to his surprise, Thera was hesitant at first. But once convinced of her father's approval, there was a quiet glow in the way she agreed. However, she insisted on earning her keep at whatever work Hannah could assign her. *Newspaper work*, Soderstrom thought, and was not pleased.

After he and Hannah had agreed to take tomorrow's eastbound stage for Salt City to arrange his loan, Soderstrom got some much-needed sleep, and in the early evening, he and

Thera left the hotel for the café downstreet. The rough buildings were mellowed by the late sunlight; thick shadows barred the tawny dust of the street as they crossed. A man hailed Soderstrom and he turned, seeing with impatience that it was the sheriff.

But there was no nonsense about Crashaw as he halted before them. "I been thinking a good while, Soderstrom. There was a time when a man couldn't have spoke to me as you did and lived."

Soderstrom gibed, "That was a long time ago, eh?"

"It was. Maybe that's why what you said was true enough that I can swallow it now. But that ain't what I mean to tell you." The slow iron in Crashaw's voice took on an edge. "What I'm saying now, you make just one move against Wagontree on their patented land and you got a U.S. marshal to reckon with. I'll send for him."

Soderstrom said with a puzzled, mounting irritation, "Maybe you will have a time explaining to him how it is that Wagontree enjoys special favors in that regard, eh?"

"I don't reckon, after tonight. First thing tomorrow I'll head out to see Loftus Buckmaster. I'll tell him what I told you—there'll be no range war in this country while I wear the badge."

"Ho," Soderstrom said with a dry skepticism. "When did you decide to bite the hand that feeds you, Sheriff?"

Crashaw looked off into the growing twilight, and the saffron light was not kind to his seamed face. "I earned that, and expect I'll get more of it. And take it, too." His voice was distant and musing. "A while back I found my thinking getting slow and my hands shaky. A bad thing for a lawman any time, but worse when it makes him run scared. A man getting old is a man can forget when his reputation wasn't up for grabs to any bidder. When the badge meant something because the man behind it did. I ought to thank you, son."

Soderstrom was listening carefully now. The words came from a sick, aging husk of a man, but in them, for the first time, he felt the iron of what the man had been. And he said surlily, "Me, I never asked for the fight."

"You stuck your jaw out far as you could was all," Crashaw

said grimly. "But I'm minding that the trouble was deep before you come here. About your herd—there's no proof who dynamited it. Old Buckmaster will be on my back to serve a warrant on you for assaulting Garth. All I'm serving is a warning. From here on you better consider any score with the Buckmasters to be even. Because I mean to keep it that way. If a federal marshal ain't enough, I'll wire Fort Bowie to send troops and declare martial law. You mark me—this fight's done."

Ten

Thera selected a piece of ten-point type from the typecase dexterously enough, but, trying to slap the oily metal too quickly into the brass typestick, she dropped it. Bending to pick it up, she lifted a flushed face to see if Hannah were watching. Seeing that she was, Thera laughed, and so did the older girl.

"Didn't I say that you handle the type very well?" Hannah chided. "Don't worry about your speed; that will come with time and patience. Dan—my husband—used to say that all typesetters should be women, because they have small nimble fingers."

Soberly Thera spread her fingers out, studying them. "I want to be good. As good as you. There seems so little in the world that a woman can do better than a man." She sighed, and then smiled in an antic way. "I guess there's one thing no man can do, though."

Hannah laughed. "And what would you like to do most?"

"That, I guess." Her smile turned grave. "Be a good wife and mother like my mother was. I think there is nothing better, Hannah."

Hannah went thoughtfully back to her desk and tried

again to develop the germ of an editorial idea, but the approach still eluded her. The lesson she had absorbed from her quiet, quick-witted young helper in these few days still had a raw, rough-edged quality that needed to be shaped and smoothed by familiarity. Not that Thera had expressed any thoughts on the matter; she had simply shown, by her bright and active outlook, her eagerness to learn, that a woman could make a goal of home and husband and babies (as she had guessed of this girl long before Thera had said so) and still make of her life something more than mere drudgery.

This, Hannah had begun to suspect, was her real woman of the future, not the militant feminist who wanted to turn all of her sex into imitation males, thereby defeating her own avowed purpose: the emancipation of woman as woman, of that part of her which man had denied her expression of through the ages.

No doubt, Hannah thought, growing up in the house of an overbearing and lusty male like her father was responsible for her rebellion against male dominance. *By plunging into a bad marriage,* she reminded herself wryly. *So how much do you really know, my girl? About life or men or yourself?*

Impelled by boredom and restlessness, she threw down her pencil and walked back to the print shop to say that she was going out for a while, and could Thera hold things down? The girl nodded, an eager sparkle in her eyes. Obscurely, they reminded Hannah of Soderstrom's eyes, which prickled with the play of heat lightning on the horizon. And not a far horizon, with his temper.

She told herself resentfully that she did not want such a man invading her private feelings. But he was hard to ignore; like her father, he filled the sky wherever he stood, and it was unwise to measure such men impulsively.

Most of the county gossip, since Soderstrom and his three men had departed, had to do with the mild revolution of the shorthorn breed that Soderstrom meant to introduce, and what Loftus Buckmaster would do about it. Popular sentiment more-or-less swung behind the Swede as underdog, but favored her father as the long-run winner, even if this shorthorn thing were not a fool idea. The idea was sound, Hannah thought (with a wry smile since it was her own), but as a pioneer achievement in this part of the territory, it would be both miscredited and blown out of proportion. Krag Soderstrom was the kind of man around whom legend would naturally grow.

The town sprawled like a dozing, slat-ribbed cur in the morning sun as she rode east on a rented nag. The wind was brisk and silky on her face and carried the flavors of the country, and she rode against it with pleasure and forgot time. She came, as she often did, in a circuit of the hilly wilderness around Mimbreno, to the forking at the Wagontree boundary where a lone road switchbacked deep into Buckmaster land to the headquarters. It had been a long while since her last visit with Naomi, she remembered with a trace of guilt, and put her mount down the road.

Just east of the headquarters the road curved sedately around a high eminence of land. On whim, Hannah swung off from the road and climbed her horse to the summit of the giant rise. Here she halted, breathing in the matchless view this promontory had always afforded her. The shallow snake of water that was the lower Salt Creek made its crooked way around and below the hill on this side, and presently she took notice of two horses ground-hitched by a motte of cottonwoods that fringed the creekbank.

I know those horses, she thought idly, without particularly relating either animal to any person. Not until the two owners moved now out of the mottled shade of the trees—a man and a woman. Quite plainly, from the way they were standing together, she had surprised a moment of intimacy.

Hannah dropped quickly back across the brow of the hill, still unseen, and headed for the road. Even when the pair had stepped into view, she would have been hard put, at this distance, to identify them if not for the two distinctively marked horses. They belonged to Naomi and her brother Chad.

What she had seen did not greatly surprise Hannah, yet she was disturbed as she rode slowly on toward Wagontree headquarters.

She felt the familiar, quickening warmth at her first sight

of the old terraced house, and wondered a little, as she always did, that so many of the memories it brought back were good ones. She replied to the Mexican stableboy's pleased greeting, handed him her reins, and walked up to the house.

Loftus Buckmaster was sunning himself in a deep chair on the Spanish veranda, which was rare for him in these days of near-total confinement indoors. The chair gave a protesting creak as he leaned forward watching her sharply, resting his horny hands on his cane. "Good morning, sister."

Hannah nodded briefly, and said, in order not to betray what she had seen by the creek, "I want to see Naomi."

"She's out ridin'. You can wait for her inside, where it's cool. Come along and talk to your old man a spell." Laboriously he heaved to his feet; his great frame showed all the ravages of age and arthritis as he led the way unsteadily into the house, leaning heavily on his cane. He paused to rest halfway on the staired hallway to the parlor, letting his cane take his massive weight; his breathing was harsh and his legs unsteady, and Hannah reached for his arm. "Get your hands off me," the old man snarled, and stamped on to the parlor with massive slow strides, slumping into an armchair.

Hannah took the sofa, glancing about the parlor with its shabby heavy furnishings that had never, within her memory, been changed or even budged from their original arrangement. Unbidden, she had a sharp memory of a Christmas day when she was nine ... of her father sending out wagons to make the rounds of every poor family in the county, transporting all the children to Wagontree for a party, a turkey dinner and presents and pony rides. *How long ago that was,* Hannah thought, and turned her gaze on this giant, fierce-eyed old man who had fathered her, wondering a little sadly now, *Did you ever really know him?*

"Well," Loftus smiled grimly. "You look to see your friend Soderstrom back soon?"

"I see that your spies have been busy."

"The old man has a few friends here and there in the territory, sister."

"I wonder who," Hannah murmured. "The stage driver? A

246

clerk in the Salt City bank? But what's the difference—you know what to expect, then."

"Shorthorns," Loftus snorted. "Fat, stump-legged brutes. You think they can weather this territory long? No, I got a better question." He picked up a newspaper beside his chair and shook it in a veined hand. "And these damned editorials. What you reckon to accomplish by making a palsied god-damn spectacle of yourself, siding with the old man's enemies? A man's own daughter tearing him down in public is a miserable thing."

Hannah smiled. "Is that what bothers you? And I've been thinking it was my brilliant exposition."

Loftus sighed. " 'Land-devouring monster' . . . 'the modern-day Attila beneath whose galloping hooves of conquest the very grass dies' . . . 'Nineteenth-century Borgias.' That is damned bad writing, sister. You always was a sassy baggage, but it was almost a pleasure to hear, the way you twisted your tongue around words. Only take my advice for once, and break the pen."

Hannah found herself flushing defensively. "Well, that's journalism. And I'll tell you why, since you ask. I hope to get every man, woman and child in the county so inflamed, they'll flood the lawmakers with letters of—"

Loftus broke in softly, impatiently, "Not what I meant. No, I want to hear why you always have to fight the old man. Why you always had to do black when I said white. I'm just a crude old man, sister, but tell me."

"Whose fault was any of it? You pushed me, Pa, as you did all of us."

"Ah, is that the word? But your brothers took it. Seems you never could. Why run off with that printer fellow like you done? A sorry thing, if I reckoned right and you married that gutless boy just to spite me."

Hannah said coldly, "Well, you can always reckon."

"Sister, the old man is tired and he don't want to fight you no more. Quit acting like a bullheaded fool. Sell the damn paper and come back here to live. Things will be different."

Hannah turned her hand over and studied the faint, ineradicable ink stains on her fingers. "Different how, Pa? Can you admit you were wrong?"

Without raising her eyes she felt his slow stiffening, and he said, "I was never wrong. Sorry, yes, if the real mischief was that you took me amiss. But that was your wrong, not mine."

Hannah thought, *He will never change,* but she had already known this much, and she had no more to say. A spell of silence held for some minutes, broken to her relief by Naomi's arrival. She entered the parlor with a quick, eager step, obviously pleased to see Hannah.

"The stableboy told me you were here. Let's go to my room, Han. Will you excuse us, sir?"

At that moment Garth came in, the scowl on his bearded face deeper than usual. "I want to talk to you, Pa." He did not bother to greet Hannah, and she noticed a faint bluish welt on his cheekbone, a fading token of his thrashing at Soderstrom's hands. Garth turned the scowl on his wife. "Your rides is getting too damned long for my taste. You stay nearer the house hereafter."

Does he suspect? Hannah wondered, knowing that Garth's suspicion of an affair between Chad and Naomi, once confirmed, would result in no mild castigation. Naomi's head drooped, and the flushed brightness of her face drained away. Since her marriage to Garth, the life had gradually gone out of this once vivacious and bubbling girl. Thinking of that, Hannah found easy forgiveness for what she had seen by the creek. Remembering her mother, too, she thought then, *No woman can live under this roof and keep her soul intact.*

The two of them went to Naomi's room, which was terraced a half-level above the parlor. Here, once the door was closed and they were safely alone, the tension seemed to leave Naomi. With a vast sigh, she threw her hat at a chair and sank across the bed. Hannah, never one to mince words, thought, *Probably this is none of my business,* and then with a wry self-resignation, *When did that stop you? Get it over.*

"Naomi. What about you and Chad?"

Naomi sat bolt upright. Her whisper was tremulous and dreading. "You knew—Han?"

"It was hard to miss," Hannah said bitterly, and briefly

told how she had come on them by chance. "Dear, I'm not accusing you, or even lecturing you, but you're being very foolish."

"But we love each other, Han." Seeing Hannah's silent but unconcealed skepticism, she said with a kind of defensive desperation, "Chad *does* love me. You don't understand him."

"Just as I didn't understand Garth? I warned you what he was like, too, but you were finding gorillas attractive that season and wouldn't listen. You'd better listen now." Hannah moved across the room and, taking Naomi by the shoulders, shook her gently. "I know my brothers only too well. Don't deceive yourself about Chad. You're desperate and bored, and he's exactly the kind to use that fact."

"No," Naomi said sullenly. "You're wrong about Chad. That's all you see because you won't look any deeper."

Hannah sighed her exasperation. "Put him to the test, then."

"What do you mean?"

"Tell him to take you away from here, away from Garth and Wagontree. You should have left Garth long ago, anyway."

"Oh no!" A bright terror blazed in Naomi's face. "I'd be afraid. Garth would hunt us down if it took him forever."

"I would hazard," Hannah said dryly, "that you and Chadwick have discussed the matter, and that is what Chad said?"

Naomi flushed and said resentfully, "You're unfair to us both, Han."

"Not to Chad, not ever." Hannah pressed her shoulder gently. "All right, I'll say no more about it. But be more careful . . . if I could come on you so easily, so can Garth or somebody else."

Deliberately, Hannah turned the talk into other, lighter channels; but she had a disturbing conviction that the situation was drifting toward deep trouble. Chad would have private reasons for continuing the affair, and Naomi would be too weak-willed to cut it off.

It was a good two hours before Hannah took her leave. Each separate room in the terraced sprawl of the house had its own outside door, and, in order to avoid a second encounter with her father, Hannah left for the outside by Naomi's exit rather than through the parlor. She followed a flagstone path down the hillside, past the 'dobe main structure that enclosed the parlor and the dining room.

She paused by the wall to curiously watch a horseman who came loping into the yard, his mount's hide fouled with dust and lather. The young rider, as he dismounted by the stable, showed the signs of hard-driven exhaustion.

Leaving his horse with the boy, he headed immediately for the house, removing his dusty hat to beat it against his chaps. He had obviously come a long way in a hurry, and Hannah's first idle thought, that he had been dispatched home from a trail drive with some urgent message, was discarded. No Wagontree herd took the trail to Taskerville without at least one Buckmaster along; her father and brothers were on the ranch.

Standing as she was, partly hidden by a salt cedar that flanked the wall, Hannah escaped the rider's notice as he tramped onto the porch; she heard the door close behind him. With her curiosity fully aroused, Hannah looked furtively around before sidling over to the east wall window. It opened off the dining hall, and this room and the parlor beyond were connected by an open hallway. The voices from the parlor carried faintly to her ears.

"You sure of this, Sam?" her father was saying.

"Yes, sir," came the rider's drawling twang. "He is rolling up about ten miles a day, while keeping close to good water. Should bring him to the Baxley Peak country by tomorrow night, just about five miles north of the county line. That's what you wanted to know, ain't it?"

"That's it, Sam." Her father's voice boomed with a quiet exultance. "A fair job, watching his moves all this while. Sure you wasn't seen any time?"

"Nary once. I growed up with Injun kids, and I don't make no mistakes."

"What is this, Pa?" came Garth's gruff deep tones. "You got somewhat on the fire you ain't told of?"

"Somewhat, son." Loftus chuckled mildly. "I'm about set to nail Mr. Soderstrom's hide fast to an outhouse door. Don't

250

ever sell the old man short, boy. This goddamn arthritis may hold me down, but it don't put me out."

Hannah could picture Garth's baffled scowl as he growled, "Pa, Otis Crashaw is turned against us. First time you move against the Swede, he—"

"Not outside his own jurisdiction, he don't. Shut your mouth and hear the old man out. I have had Sam here watching the north trail over in Addison County for Soderstrom's herd. He was to follow the Swenska's outfit a couple days and size things, and then report back. You heard him. Soderstrom will make camp hard by Baxley's Peak tomorrow night. You'll be there with six or so men. You'll have to make your play on what you see, but that is rough and wild enough country that I wouldn't be surprised you could run this herd to death like his other one. . . ."

Hannah waited no longer. A sudden fear of discovery knotted in her throat, and she moved on at a fast walk. She forced a casual pace as she neared the stable. The boy, smiling his vast pleasure, went to saddle her mount, and as Hannah waited, she reviewed what she had heard to be sure she had the sense of it. There could be no doubt; Loftus was defying the sheriff's warning by striking a blow at Soderstrom outside the range of Crashaw's authority. Her father could afford to take an extralegal risk or two up in Addison County, where he had friends.

Baxley's Peak by tomorrow night, Hannah mused. And they were covering about ten miles a day, meaning the herd should be bedded at Blue Springs tonight. She stepped up to the sidesaddle and arranged her skirt, barely replying to the boy's happy, *"Buenas tardes."*

A good twenty miles of bad country lay between here and Blue Springs, but she knew most of it like her own hand. Well, why not? Her mount was fresh, and by starting now, she could reach the Springs before nightfall to give Soderstrom the warning he needed.

Eleven

It had been a long day on the trail, for Soderstrom wanted to make camp at Blue Springs. A sooty veil of dusk had fallen, softening the harshness of the land, before they achieved the moon-glimmering spring set in its deep natural saucer. Patiently, they let the herd water, then made camp and wolfed their supper, beans and biscuits. Afterward they sat on their heels by the fire and drank strong coffee and talked. The talk was idle, the sort of needless palaver men made when anything could break and they were keyed for it.

All four of them were honed to a quiet tension, but little of it stemmed from the long day on the trail. Soderstrom had held their progress to easy stages, wanting to wear as little tallow as possible off the heavy-bodied shorthorns. They had been bred for beef, not travel, he thought with satisfaction. Also, mindful of how skittishness from thirst had contributed to the fate of his other herd, he had timed each halt, where possible, close to good water.

It was really a knowlege of their adversary that had laid a shadow of tension over this drive. Tonight they were camped only eighteen miles or so from their home range, with four hundred head of prime whitefaces. And, because he read the man's mind as he would his own. Soderstrom was sure that Loftus Buckmaster would make his move before long. But would he, in the face of Crashaw's warning? *Yes,* Soderstrom thought decisively, *because that would not stop me, either.* Buckmaster could not afford not to act, for he had made his life a boast backed up, always, by his actions; because he was top dog, any man who successfully defied him would topple him: the only law by which such men could live. *We are dying out, me and Buckmaster,* Soderstrom thought with a fleck of grim humor, *but I think we will go down kicking damn hard.*

The move would come soon because once scattered on its home range the herd would be no target at all. Soderstrom hesitated to anticipate beyond this. *He is a sly old devil, so do not be too sure of anything.*

Out in the night Waco, on guard, crooned strangely to the herd. Rafe and McIver carried on an idle, joshing talk to which Soderstrom half-listened with a sleepy ear. In these last days he had been surprised to feel a growing sense of cohesion with these men; but he remembered from his younger days that it was always so with men who had lived and worked together for a good while. The rough edges of each man's character were filed down day by day until the early frictions disappeared and the men were in gear. They were an oddly assorted group, and finding a common level had taken time; by now the tolerations were fairly established.

This fact had enabled Soderstrom to see Dave McIver in a slow-changing light. Against his first dislike, he could not ignore the way the youth had taken what this land had to offer and paid its price in sweat and pain. At times only sheer will had kept him going, but he had won the biggest stake of his life. He had not coughed up blood in weeks; his appetite was hearty, and he no longer thought of liquor. What little excess flesh his ravaged body had carried was gone, replaced by hard spare muscle. The boyish lines of his face had tightened to the sun-blackened gauntness of an Indian's, and it still carried the faint scars of his beating. His young beard, bleached now to almost alkaline paleness, was in startling contrast, and did not quite conceal a new hint of iron around the chin and mouth. Soderstrom noted this, seeing in it the measure of a man finding himself. And, though McIver had education (which was perhaps not so bad a thing) he had never flaunted it. He spoke easily but seldom; he did not smile often either, but when he did, his thin serious face was fairly lighted by a boyish and self-chiding humor. He still wore the derby, discolored and sadly dilapidated now. It was no hat for holding off the sun; it had made him a butt for jeers and gibes since he had come West, yet he had refused to relinquish it. At first it had been a badge of defiance, finally of victory; and nothing could have impressed Soderstrom more.

Rafe got up and said good night, and walked away to his blankets. McIver rose too, then, and when Soderstrom said, "Dave," the college boy's glance held a pure astonishment. Soderstrom hadn't once called him by name.

"You have done pretty well this drive."

McIver eyed him a dubious moment, and finally said guardedly, "Thanks," before moving off. Soderstrom got out his pipe and packed it carefully. McIver was a lot better all right, but, he thought grimly, he would have to be very good to make the grade with Thera. Soderstrom was coming to a reluctant concession that someday Thera, having a mind of her own, would choose a man; and whatever or whoever he was, Krag Soderstrom would have to bow to the inevitable. So far McIver had come off well with her because his weakness had taken her sympathy. Now that he . . .

"Hello," said a woman's hushed voice out of the dark; and Soderstrom was on his feet, whipping up and levering his rifle in the same motion. "Who is that?"

"Well, there's no bounty. It's me, Hannah. Mind if I walk in?"

Soderstrom said gruffly, "Come in," concealing how astounded he was without much trouble because he was deeply nettled at being surprised this way.

After a moment, leading her horse, she entered the rim of firelight. She was wearing a very dirty and sweat-soiled riding habit; the skirt had several brush-tears, and her face was streaked with grime and sweat. The horse was limping, and Hannah promptly sat down, obviously footsore. "I misjudged my bearings and lost the trail, and when I found it again, he threw a shoe. That was just before it turned dark . . . walked ever since. I can smell the coffee. What's in that Dutch oven?"

By this time Catron and McIver were out of their blankets, and they listened intently as she told of her father's plan to waylay the shorthorn herd tomorrow night. Soderstrom asked all the questions he could think of, while she finished the beans and biscuits and had two cups of Rafe's caustic coffee. This was what he had needed to know about the trap he'd been positive would be sprung. All he needed now was a counterplan to meet it.

They talked it over a while, and Rafe and McIver returned to their soogans. Soderstrom said he would go on guard duty soon, and offered Hannah his blankets. "Rafe will fix your horse's shoe in the morning. We packed a few smith tools along with the grub and blankets on a couple horses, since we have no wagon now. How is Thera?"

"I was wondering when you'd ask." Hannah tempered her words with a smile. "She is fine."

"Let's walk a little," Soderstrom heard himself say, and then with embarrassment, "I am sorry. Your feet."

"Are not that sore. You might help me up, though."

They walked slowly down by the spring. The mirror-still blackness threw back the universe: countless white points of starfire. A meteor blazed a pale falling path, and died.

"How do you feel—" Soderstrom paused, scowling at his unlighted pipe. "Don't take this wrong, but I have wondered about your feeling for your pa."

"Oh—you think I'm betraying him now?"

"Not that. Just that the blood tie should mean something."

"It does." She bit the words off with a kind of snap. "Among other things, it meant seeing my mother die year by year because she was one who needed to be loved as a plant needs water. It wasn't even his indifference, bad as that was. He had chosen her as he would a mare he wanted bred. He was already forty, and hard clear through. She was only twenty, and for twenty years after that, she did nothing but die." Hannah was vehement. "Nobody who didn't have to live with it could understand. With his children, it was different, in the sense that he knew exactly what he wanted them to be. You've seen the results. Garth and Chad. Me."

Soderstrom struck a match and coaxed his pipe alight, remarking that he supposed Loftus had been less than pleased with his results.

"I didn't say he was pleased, did I? To escape from him, I did not marry the first man who came along. Just the most

255

spineless one, the most footloose and vacillating, an itinerant printer named Dan Kingery. He was at the other extreme from Pa, but I made Pa's own grand mistake. I would remold this sorry clay into exactly what I wanted.

"It didn't work out quite that way. Drinking is a second occupation with printers—that and traveling. A good compositor can get a job anywhere. And a bottle. That was one thing I couldn't control, and when he became stupefied, he couldn't work. We would have starved more than once if I hadn't sold several of Mother's jewels. At last, in one of his rational periods, I insisted that he show me how to set type. Afterward I was able to finish the jobs he couldn't."

Soderstrom took the pipe from his mouth. "What happened to him?"

"Fell over a stair railing one night, I needn't mention why, and broke his neck. So I came back to Buckmaster County—"

"Why?"

The blunt question made her frown in the starlight. "Why? Because this country is my home and I love it. Oh Lord, never mind. I know what you've wanted to hear me say. All right, I came back here and bought the newspaper less because I needed to make a living than because it offered the one way I could really fight him."

"Hurt him."

"Damn you," she whispered, dropping her face. "Yes, hurt him."

"And did you?"

"He admitted as much to me today," she said wearily. "There was no satisfaction in hearing him say so."

"Then it was all a waste." Soderstrom spoke gravely, and slowly puffed his pipe. "You have called me hard. But you, you set out to hurt your own pa, and it didn't even satisfy you."

"What about you, Mr. Soderstrom; are you satisfied? Having reduced my bright ideals to the cheapest shoddy, do you feel adequately revenged on me? Or on independent women?"

Soderstrom made a rough, impatient motion. "I don't care about that. I had something else in mind. I—"

"But you don't like independent women," Hannah persisted,

256

plainly antagonized now and unwilling to let the matter pass lightly.

"Their independence, no." He frowned, abruptly knocked out his pipe on the callused heel of his palm. "I will not pretend. A man has his place, a woman hers. The order is there for a reason in nature, and not to be lightly upset. Maybe it will happen just so, like you told me once, but I can see bad coming out of it."

"But only bad? That is part of any change—the pain—but only that?" Without waiting for a reply, she said quickly, wonderingly, "I hadn't expected any of this of you."

"What?"

"The—the depth. The understanding. You are not gentle about it, but it's there."

"I am a rough man. I live rough and talk rough. That is my way. Part of it, I never learned English too good. But more, I never talk much. To feel, to think, to be alive—this is the real sense of things for me. I am stubborn, though."

"Yes, you're stubborn. And you don't want people to see another side of you. But why? Even your daughter—"

"Thera knows me, and there is no need for talk. Listen." He paused; he did not want to speak of these things, but this once he would, extracting the memories like infected teeth—maybe this was needed. "In Sweden, in our district, my family was important. We had land and money. But I had an older brother. In the old country, the oldest son inherits all. The other children must depend on his good will. Well, when our *for* died, we quarreled, me and my brother Tomaas, and he turned me out. This is hard, to have much and then nothing at all. I came to America, maybe looking for something. I got married, built up my farm, and by thirty, was on my way to being a big man in the county. Then many things. Hedda died. Then the crops . . . the locusts . . . the hail . . . drought. Year after year. If a man is what he feels, then I could not have been brought any lower. There was mills, there was lumber camps to work in, but I could not. I needed to stand as a man on my own feet, on my own land. This, and the need to start over, brought me out here."

257

"Pride," Hannah said softly, "and the land. I can understand that."

"Loftus Buckmaster's daughter should."

To this, she seemed on the verge of saying something sharp, but did not. After a moment she said obliquely, "You said before that you were not baiting me about my father . . . that you had something else in mind. What was it?"

I don't know, Soderstrom thought, but all the same, as if the words were forming of their own accord, he said suddenly, "I was not trying to hurt you. I was shooting in the dark, trying to say things I felt were true about you. I wanted to know for sure."

"But why should you care to know my private thoughts? I don't—"

"A man should know such things about a woman if he asks her to marry him."

The thing was out now, the last words he had ever expected to say again, least of all to such a woman as Hannah Kingery. Yet now they were out, it became suddenly as clear as breaking sunlight that he had been leading up to this all along, and even the reason why. So that he was ready when she said almost timidly, "Why"—she cleared her throat—"why do you want to marry me?"

"Good reasons. You need a man, I need a woman. You are strong and healthy, as a woman should be."

"Getting a wife is not like buying a—a brood mare, Mr. Soderstrom! I might have expected—"

"You will let me finish, missus, eh?" Soderstrom half-smiled. "You have spirit and courage, a woman alone and unarmed coming to warn me across country you didn't know so well that you didn't get yourself lost. That was a brave thing to do. You have the good feeling for the land, too. I would not have a woman without it. There are many things I could say, but what is talk? Do you want to hear them?"

"That won't be necessary." There might have been a faint tremor in her voice. "Because I won't marry you."

"Will you say why? Maybe it's that I am rough?"

Hannah said quietly, "Do you think I mind that? I grew up in a family of men, and Pa and Garth have about four years of

258

schooling between them. Chad and I only six years apiece. As for hardship, I knew little else with Dan."

"Then what?"

"I'm afraid of you, I suppose. Of the things I see in you and what they might lead you to do. I made a mistake in marrying a man totally unlike my father, but that mistake could work in reverse. Thank you, but no."

Soderstrom's brows drew together. "A man is good to egg on, even give money to, when he stands up to your pa. But for the same reasons, he is not good enough to marry, eh?"

Hannah said in some confusion, "I don't mean—well, certainly—it doesn't follow that those qualities are what I want in a husband."

"Is that all?" he asked coldly.

"I'm not sure, since it hasn't been mentioned, but does love enter into your scheme of what a marriage should be?"

That brought him up short. There had been only one woman in his life, and in most ways she had been little like Hannah Kingery. There had been no sparring of complex thoughts and words with Hedda, only a good understanding, direct and simple and intense, that was unmistakably what men and women called love. "I know this much," he said finally, slowly. "I need a wife. Love I had once. Maybe it could be again, maybe in time. I can't say for sure. It could be good, even so." He paused. "If it were not for the other thing, I wonder . . . would you take the chance?"

"I—I can't answer that. I've had much of the romance knocked out of me, as I'm sure is the case with you. Perhaps to the good—perhaps people would be better off by being realistic. By hoping, at the most, to make a good life together." She looked away, then looked back at him as if on swift impulse. "Is there any gentleness in you? Will you ever show me that you can be gentle?"

"That is a hell of a question, woman."

"Your actions will answer it," she said quietly. "Please, let's don't talk any more about this. Can't we walk back now?"

259

Twelve

Chad Buckmaster tied his horse to the edge of the cottonwood motte after a careless glance at the circling hills, then strolled through the trees and down the creekbank. Halting by the water's edge, he dropped to his haunches beneath the mottling of leaf shadow and amused himself by breaking twigs in small pieces and tossing them at skittering waterbugs. While he waited for his brother's wife.

Almost idly, he wondered about that. Naomi was pretty enough, not very smart, docile and willing, with all the direct passion of a simple woman. This was pleasant frosting, but the cake itself, he supposed, was his big brother and the dominating shadow he had always cast across Chadwick's life.

Chad could not remember when it had been otherwise. Garth had been the firstborn son, the image of his father, and from the first, the old man had pinned his hopes for an earthly immortality (Loftus believed in no other sort) on Garth. When, as both boys grew older, it had become apparent that Garth was a dull-headed brute, the old man had stubbornly refused to relinquish that early hope, though it was equally clear that Chad was the heir to his father's wit and shrewdness.

At times Chad plunged with a will into the business of keeping the gears of Wagontree oiled and smooth-running; his Buckmaster's pride was deep and genuine, and not to be denied. But usually a growing bitter indifference was uppermost; the game did not seem worth the candle, and idleness and liquor and women were useful for dulling the knowledge.

There was nothing obscure about the satisfaction of dalliance with his brother's wife; it temporarily gave him a kind of rancid ascendancy over Garth, but did nothing to solve his larger dilemma.

Hearing a slow beat of hooves now, he rose off his haunches and peered through the trees with the lazy thought that perhaps he should be more careful. But it was Naomi, all right, and she stepped to the ground and left her horse, coming quickly to him. Her lips held a wild eagerness, and she trembled in his arms; he looked over her head with a wry and crooked grin.

"What's the matter?"

"It's all this . . . sneaking about, I guess. Hannah paid a visit yesterday."

"So Pa mentioned to me."

"But, Chad, she knows about us. She told me she saw us here together."

Chad scowled, but only shrugged after a moment. "So? If she was going to tell anyone else, she would have by now. What are you worried about?"

"If she could find out, so can others." She pressed tightly against his chest, shuddering. "I'm afraid. If we could only leave here. . . . Chad?"

"It's no good," he said patiently. "I told you before, once I leave Wagontree, I'm nothing."

She drew back slowly, looking at his face. "What are you here, Chad? What is either of us?"

Chad thumbed his hat back off his sweat-damp curls, thinking wryly. *Christ, every time she's been talking to Han, you see sudden courage. That will last about a week.* "Fed and sheltered, with every comfort. I don't aim to give that up. Neither do you, if you think a while."

"And Garth would follow us . . . of course?"

"That's right."

"Hannah thought that you'd told me that," Naomi murmured. "She said something else, too. That you were lying when you said you loved me."

Chad said feelingly, "Hell," with a wash of unfeigned irritation. "That damned meddler. Sure I love you. Who do you believe, anyway?"

"I told her I believed you."

261

"That answers it for everyone," Chad said softly. "Come here. Come here now." She whispered his name blindly and came against him, and her response was fierce and breathless.

A sharp crackle of brush high along the bank several yards down yanked Chad alert. He half-turned; he pushed Naomi away in the same instant that the huge, bullish form of his brother broke from a clot of thickets. Garth roared something inarticulate, and his gun came up.

There was no time to think. Chad's reaction was purely instinctive, letting reflex dip his hand down and up: his gunbutt slapped snug against his palm and the barrel came up in a lifting sideward arc. He had a glimpse of Garth's wide dark face before the roar of the two guns merged.

Garth was jolted back as if by a giant fist, and his knees folded. He fell over the cutbank and skidded down its crumbling slant till his face and one arm rested in the water.

Chad took two steps forward, dumbly holding his gun pointed out. Then he halted, letting his fist drop. There was an acid taste in his mouth as the brutal and inescapable fact of what had happened sank home.

Somehow Garth's suspicions had become aroused enough for him to follow one or the other of them today, but what did that matter? *Garth is dead. He's dead. Now what will you do? It was self-defense, wasn't it?* Quite abruptly, his mind was cold and clear. *Maybe that's good enough, but maybe not. A story is no better than it sounds. You killed your brother because he tried to kill you for stealing his wife. How will that sound to a cow country jury? But suppose you could satisfy the law; what about Pa? Garth was his pride and joy. He'll have your scalp one way or the other.*

His hand, as he rubbed it over his mouth, was shaking, and he held it out and halted his thoughts until it stopped shaking. He thought, *Now that's better,* and looked down at Naomi. She had dropped to her knees, hands flat to her cheeks, making small half-hysterical sounds. He could not tell whether she was trying to retch or moan.

"What will we do, Chad?" she whimpered, and without waiting for an answer, "I . . . I . . . I'm going to be sick."

Chad said, "All right, be sick," and climbed the bank in

lunging steps. He searched through the grove till he found Garth's big black, tied in a tangle of young willows.

Even as he reached for the animal's halter, the solution came with a hard, savage certainty. By now half the people in Buckmaster County knew that Garth and Krag Soderstrom had fought, and that Garth had taken the first whipping of his life while barely getting a hand on the Swede. Garth had not been shy about proclaiming his intent to somehow retaliate.

Chad thought with a quiet exultance, *It will work out fine*. And it would swing suspicion away from him beyond any doubt. He let the thought pause, backtracking: *What about Naomi?* Then he smiled, certain of his ability to handle her. He was still smiling as he pushed back through the grove toward the creekbank, leading Garth's black.

Today's drive had been held to an easy pace, and Soderstrom called an early halt not far from Baxley's Peak. He made his plan with deliberate care, consulting Rafe Catron's knowledge of the country. He had, Soderstrom said grimly, lost his other herd because the lay of the land had worked against him; this time it would fall to his advantage.

They made camp in a long valley enclosed by two well-timbered ridges, with a narrow pass at each end. To any watcher on the dark ridges above, the bedgrounds and firelight camp and scattered gear and small remuda picketed nearby would present the ordinary activity of any trail camp settled down for the night.

Soderstrom assigned Waco Millard, who was no hand with a gun and who would probably cut a sorry figure in any fight, to the first nighthawk shift. The herd was still behaving well, having been eased along as always, and the long valley contained a good spring and plenty of grass. If any commotion did spook them slightly, the ridges and Waco's guard should hold them all right.

Soderstrom yawned elaborately, tossed the dregs of his coffee into the fire, and reached for his bedroll. Rafe and McIver followed his example, not hurrying about it. Soderstrom stretched out and folded his arms under his head and looked at the stars, fighting the tug of drowsiness.

By tomorrow night, if all went well, the herd would be deep inside the county and Otis Crashaw's jurisdiction; and he would have won a victory that would at once begin to diminish the legend that was Loftus Buckmaster. For Loftus had cast his whole game on tonight's fall of the dice, and already his plan was betrayed, the game half-lost. *It is too bad,* Soderstrom thought, *but you asked for this, old man, and Soderstrom is obliging.*

Still, he felt a restlessness and discomfort, dispelling the temptation of sleep. Hannah Kingery had stayed over the night before at the Blue Springs camp, setting out early the next morning for Mimbreno. Their parting had been brief and unsatisfactory, and thinking back on this, and on her quiet and emphatic turndown of his proposal, words he had spoken to only one other woman in his life, Soderstrom felt angry and unhappy.

He could not salve his pride by deceiving himself, being a deep and stolid man who did not take such things lightly, that he had proposed on an impulse prompted by infatuation which he might well have regretted later. The thing had been slowly building all along, and had bided its time until the moment of realization. He had thought about it through the long day, and he could not give himself the lie; it had been this way only once before, with Hedda, and the fact that this time the knowledge had come with great reluctance, little by little, made it no less certain. *Be gentle* ... what did a woman expect of a man?

The fire had died to red coals, and their tawny glow began to fade. When he was sure that the presumed watcher above could no longer make out their blanketed forms, Soderstrom stirred upright in his blankets and reached an arm to shake McIver, who likewise roused Rafe.

Picking up their rifles, the three men moved with a stealthy care through the windless darkness toward the north end of the valley with its boulder-flanked pass. A sliver of moon shed the faintest light and whitened the boulders enough to silhouette any moving dark object.

They took their positions, Soderstrom on one side close to the outer mouth of the pass, McIver and Rafe stationed farther back on opposite flanks. With each man laid up behind a boulder, they had only to wait.

It seemed a long time. Soderstrom began to sweat at each fancied sound. Finally came the clop of muffled hooves, and he saw them ride slowly out of a black swatch of timber—three, five, six riders altogether. They would, he guessed, simply adapt their old tactic to the present circumstances. Beyond to the south of the valley lay a region of shattered volcanic rock, of which the herders had made a wide skirt today. There was no cliff to dynamite, but a sudden yelling charge might just as effectively stampede the cattle through the south pass and into death.

Soderstrom's heart pounded against the cool boulder. When he judged they were close enough, he drew in his breath, and rapped out: "Throw up your hands!"

The warning would give justification to what, he saw almost at once, could not be avoided. There was a hoarse shout as a rider spurred forward. Soderstrom shot the man from his saddle. Rafe and McIver fired together, and a second man tumbled from his horse and was dragged by a stirruped foot as it wheeled, bolting.

For Soderstrom, the rest was a pandemonium of wild yells, gunfire, and the stink of burned powder. The raiders dismounted and scattered for cover, and there was no certain target except illusive shadows and stabs of gunflame. Soderstrom became aware that he was levering an empty rifle, and the barrel was so hot he could hardly hold it. He shrank down against his rock and fumbled for fresh cartridges.

A sudden pound of hooves pulled his head up, and he had time only to see the rider, hanging low on his horse's side, veer recklessly down on him. He was not sure afterward whether the man leaped from his saddle or whether he dragged him off. He heard the man's pistol hammer fall on a spent shell, and then they were rolling and tussling across the stony ground.

His adversary was slight, but wiry as a weasel, and Soderstrom had his hands full. He saw faint light glance off a knifeblade and grabbed desperately for an unseen wrist and got it. For an instant, under the moonlight, he caught the grimacing face of Richie Sears. Then he recoiled from the pain of a knee close to his groin, and they broke apart.

The din of shots filled Soderstrom's ears as he scrambled to his knees. Sears was already on his feet and his dim form was weaving in low and fast, the knife poised. Coming up off his knees, not wholly on his feet, Soderstrom dove beneath the raised knife and butted Sears in the stomach. He heard a gush of breath and the deflected knifethrust ripped his shirt and grazed coldly along his ribs. Soderstrom gave a savage heave of his shoulder, his feet still driving, and Sears went down and Soderstrom fell on him and half-pinned him. Sears got an arm free and swung the knife back for another try. Soderstrom smashed his fist against the gunman's wrist and the knife clattered into the rocks.

His hold was poor, and Sears, writhing like a snake, broke away. Anticipating him, Soderstrom went after the knife on his hands and knees and got it and came around on his knees. He saw Sears almost on top of him, swinging a good-sized rock. Soderstrom thrust upward with the knife, a clumsy underhand stab. The point took Sears' raised arm at the elbow and tore upward through cloth and flesh.

The gunman pulled back and came to his feet, holding his arm. He made no sound, but Soderstrom knew the razor-edged steel had cut deeply. The gunfire had slackened off, and Soderstrom called hoarsely, "All right, quit."

"You better finish this, snork."

Soderstrom still palmed the bloody knife and breathing deeply now, he lowered it. He could not see Sears' face; his low, shaken words told enough. The shooting had stopped. Soderstrom saw in the thin moonlight that both Rafe and McIver were unhit, and were holding their guns on the three living raiders. One man was squatting down, cuddling a wounded arm. Two men lay dark and crumpled and still on the pale canyon floor. Soderstrom herded Sears over with the others, then retrieved his rifle. Methodically, he reloaded the magazine, and tramped over beside Rafe Catron.

"We got 'em tighter than a flea's ass," Rafe exulted with a wolfish satisfaction. "This time we can string up the lot."

Soderstrom shuttled a speculative glance at him. "That's a far tune from what you was singing, mister."

"Hell, this time we got 'em tight. No twelve men in cow country would give you one day for hanging the bastards."

Soderstrom smiled grimly. So much of your fine goodness in people boiled down to exactly this: Never cut a man's throat till it seems a safe thing to do. He said to Sears, "No Buckmaster is along?"

"Garth was supposed to lead this party," Sears husked. "He went somewhere this morning and wasn't about when we left. The old man sent Chad out with some men to find him. You better do it like that redneck said, snork, and finish this with a rope."

Unwillingly, Soderstrom was hearing Hannah's words again: *Show me that you can be gentle;* and now he said coldly, half-absently, "Why?"

"I think you ruint my arm for good." Sears' breathing was labored and broken. "You better finish this. You better, snork, or you're dead."

"Now I'm worried," Soderstrom said. "Anyway, this will be the third time for you, and they say that works the charm."

"Third time I what?"

"That you made a long walk home. If these others don't know how, you can show them."

Thirteen

Soderstrom made the two unhurt raiders bury their dead companions where they had fallen. They worked half the night, wresting huge chunks of rock out of two deep holes in the stony soil. A gunmetal hint of dawn had tinged the east when they finished piling up the cairns of heavy boulders over each grave. Afterward they, with Sears and the other wounded man, were turned loose, unarmed, to find their way back afoot to Wagontree where Loftus Buckmaster would be waiting word of their success. Soderstrom told Rafe Catron to drive their mounts away in the opposite direction and abandon them.

Rafe did as he was told and said nothing, but he was nursing a bitter anger. He had only to touch the ugly scar on his throat to remember, with shuddering clarity, that morning when Wagontree men had strung him up with no concern for his innocence or guilt. All right, he'd admittedly known that the steer was a Wagontree animal even before the hair had been clipped from the incriminating brand—a point he glossed over whenever he repeated the story—nor had that been the only strange beef to feel his butchering knife or branding iron over the last several years.

Still, just as his own guilt or innocence meant nothing to big augurs like the Buckmasters, so Rafe did not view any act committed against their kind as theft, but only simple justice. Rafe needed the taste of wild freedom as some men needed whiskey or women or good food, but times were mostly hard for any loner, and having no respect for society, he felt no scruples about easing his situation at society's expense. There was, particularly, a downright pleasure in taking from big, bloated augurs like the Buckmasters, who had built fortunes out of running roughshod over the little man.

Since the hanging that had failed, his hatred for them had deepened to a passion, but it went back a good deal further. . . .

After scattering the raiders' horses, Rafe returned to the camp, where Waco and McIver were huddled by the fire in the chill gray dawn, watching coffee come to a boil.

"Where's Soderstrom, Mac?"

"Out on nighthawk," McIver replied. "He says to get a couple hours' rest; we'll be moving out early."

Rafe squatted on his heels and rolled a twisted thin cigar between his teeth, reaching for a burning twig. "We shouldn't of let 'em off. I can't figure him."

"We're in Addison County," McIver pointed out. "The county

seat is two hundred miles away. We'd be days getting them there, even if we hadn't a herd on our hands."

Waco gave a shrill whistle of a laugh. "Youngster, Rafe wasn't meaning that just exactly. No, sir."

Rafe grunted, tossing the twig back in the fire. "My pappy used to say, always eat your bird in the hand."

"You must think a great deal of your father," McIver said.

"Thought. He's dead." Rafe stood abruptly, walking off a few steps. He watched the dawn grow and puffed his cigarette, feeling the chill pain of memory. It seemed closer and sharper on this cold morning than it had in years, and he knew this was because he was brooding about matters that couldn't be helped. Still, he found himself remembering.

Like hundreds of Texans returning to their homes after the War between the states, Sol Catron, Rafe's father, had found a broken, impoverished land with only one natural resource: countless thousands of longhorn cattle running wild in the brush. Sol had gradually built up his herd and, after a few trail drives to Galveston, had restored his family to a decent life. But fresh prosperity had attracted a loose confederation of rustler bands who moved stolen stock in night drives down to crooked buyers on the Gulf Coast. It was an "underground" operation, secret and well-organized. Inevitably, since a man's closest neighbor might be a cog in the crooked machinery, some innocent men fell under suspicion. A man like Sol Catron, taciturn and noted for his lonesome ways, made a natural suspect.

A semi-vigilante group headed by a blood-hungry sheriff in the pay of the big ranchers was drafted to deal with the situation. One night they had ridden up to Sol Catron's home and called his name. When he stepped into the yard, he was riddled by a score of bullets. Rafe and his mother were ordered out then, and every building on the place fired.

In Rafe Catron's mind, The Law was a powerful tool that wore the mask of justice and, in practice, was for sale to the top bidder. He hated The Law, but he feared it, too, and fear had bred a dim respect for its cold, malleable processes. Only a fool threw himself head-on against it, but by the same token only a fool did not get away with whatever he safely could when the opportunity afforded itself. . . .

The drive resumed at full dawn, though the night's broken pattern had meant little sleep for any of them. Soderstrom was impatient to see his herd safe across the county line. Rafe's spirits rose somewhat with the climbing sun. Last night's business had been, after all, a handy piece of work, and he felt vindicated in his decision of weeks ago to tie his star to Soderstrom's. The Swede was a fighter; he had brains and guts and tenacity, and these were paying off fat dividends on Rafe's old score with the Buckmasters. A contented grin cracked his dusty jaw; all that was lacking was a sight of old Loftus' face when he learned about last night.

Midday crept into deep afternoon, and they were perhaps five miles into Buckmaster County when a lone rider came up from the southeast, bearing directly for them. Soderstrom's keen eyes were the first to note the horseman, and he ordered a halt. The last stragglers were milling to a stop as Sheriff Crashaw rode up to Soderstrom and Rafe dropped over to that flank to catch the exchange between them.

"I want you to come in with me till this is cleared up," Crashaw was saying.

Soderstrom's face held a fierce bleakness, and he glanced at Rafe as he rode up. "Here's Catron. He'll tell you I have not been out of his sight in many days. So will McIver and Millard."

"What is this?" Rafe demanded.

"Garth Buckmaster is missing since early yesterday," Soderstrom said tersely. "It is remembered that I said I'd kill him if he ever set foot on my land. Now his horse has been found killed by a bullet, deep on our south range."

"Found by who?" Rafe's voice was parched and cracked. "When?"

"This noon," Crashaw said. "By Chad Buckmaster and three Wagontree hands who been on the search for Garth since yesterday."

Rafe turned a taut, furious glance on the sheriff. "But hellfire! You can't hang this on the boss. It's like he said, we

270

all been close to him every minute since we picked up this herd."

"Maybe," Soderstrom said gently, "the sheriff thinks you would all lie for the boss, eh?"

Crashaw shook his head. "No accusation. We don't even know what, if anything, happened to Garth. There's still some pointed facts here that can't be brushed away. One, you made a threat against Garth's life in front of witnesses. Two, you said if he ever set foot on your land, and that's where we found his horse. Three, the black was shot dead by someone, suggesting that Garth himself might of run into something similar."

Surprisingly, Soderstrom smiled. "How long was the horse dead?"

"Since early yesterday, Chad reckoned."

"Early yesterday, I was a good twenty miles from here. You think, then, I left my trail herd that I was driving short-handed to ride home and kill Garth Buckmaster because I knew—God knows how—I would find him on my land?" Soderstrom paused sardonically. "That would be quite a trick, Sheriff, even if my three men would all lie for me. Even if you had a body, which you admit you don't, except his horse's, eh?"

Crashaw was unruffled. "I'll find out the rest soon enough. All right, you have an alibi, and I don't even have a warrant. You're a hard-nosed citizen, Soderstrom, but I think you're an honest one. You'd want to abide by the law, even go off your way to help it if you could."

"I don't understand you, mister."

"After Chad told his pa about finding Garth's horse, the old man sent a hand to fetch me. I came fast, because I know Loftus Buckmaster as well as I do. He never had more ado with law or courts than he needed to, and a man his age has got deep habits. He minded what I told him and you, too, so he had me fetched, but what's holding him back from acting on his own makes a damn thin halter. He ain't going to bother with the sense of it: if something's happened to his boy, someone has got to pay, and that'll just naturally be the man who beat him up and threatened him. You."

Crashaw paused, then went on, "But here's the thing: he ain't sure yet, not without he knows what happened to Garth. When I asked him to give me time to find out what happened, he agreed, but on condition. He is afraid that if you done for Garth, you'll sneak away meantime. If I put you safely behind bars till I turn something up, I can keep Loftus simmered down. Otherwise he won't give his word to hold in. He made no bones about saying so.

"Now see where this has to lead? I can't hold him back alone, and men'll be killed. I don't want that, and I don't think you do."

Soderstrom considered for a moment, then nodded. "All right. I will go to Mimbreno and be locked up."

Rafe made a bitter objection, but Soderstrom said, "It must be this way. Right or wrong, I have respect for the law. And this is the best way to show my innocence. Now, we'll bed the cattle and eat, and the sheriff and me will ride to Mimbreno before dark."

"Good," Crashaw said. "Loftus warned he'd send a man into town tonight to check my lockup and make sure you was there."

Camp was made in a jag of cottonwoods bordering a sallow trickle of creek, and Soderstrom went over the sheriff's story with him several times, talking calmly and quietly. But Rafe had no stomach for food or talk; what had really happened was clear enough to him, and the conviction was balling like sour curd in his belly.

As soon as they had eaten, Soderstrom left with Crashaw, his parting order to Rafe being simply for Rafe to drive the shorthorns onto Ladder and scatter them, ending their potential as a target. For some minutes after he was gone, Rafe sat in silence, brooding sullenly at the fire. Only he and Waco Millard were in camp, McIver having taken the first nighthawk watch at the herd bedgrounds a quarter mile away. Waco sat cross-legged across the fire, watching Rafe suck cigarette after cigarette down to a stub, and his seamed face held a searching caution. Finally he said, tentatively, "If Garth turns up dead Soderstrom will be in real trouble, hunh?"

"Dead, hell!" Rafe's raw throat gave his voice a rasp, and he pitched his cigarette in the fire. "You jughead, don't you understand what that old devil Loftus has done? What he done was have Garth's horse hazed over onto Ladder and shot. Then Garth himself will lay low for a spell. Weeks maybe, or months. As long as the old man wants Soderstrom in jail and out of the way. Anyway it goes, Buckmaster has time to size up his next move."

Waco was utterly silent, unmoving on his haunches, as he digested this. Then he said in a voice of hate, "Looks like them bastards have taken the prize, Rafe."

Rafe looked blindly at the fire, unwilling to accept the situation. *Right or wrong,* Soderstrom had said, *I have respect for the law.* That was Soderstrom, but how could Rafe Catron, hating the law, swallow this savage injustice?

And then, as an idea took seed, he thought, *Maybe a frame-up can work two ways.* The details began crowding him thick and fast, so that he stood and paced back and forth in his excitement. Suddenly he swung to face Waco. "Last night the Buckmasters tried for us outside Crashaw's territory. What if they tried again tonight?"

Waco waggled his white head. "They won't, not and draw Crashaw's fire."

Rafe said softly, "Suppose they did, though. Suppose that twenty, thirty head of our shorthorns was killed by night riders and you or me could say positive that Chad Buckmaster was the leader?"

Waco's scarred face twitched as understanding came. "That would settle one Buckmaster's hash for certain-sure. Go a long way toward settling this child's old score, too."

Rafe nodded, knowing that he had a fast ally in Waco, whose hatred for the Buckmasters outmatched his own. "There's Natchez Canyon two miles over east of here. If a bunch of cattle hit that rim in a solid run, you could write them off to a critter."

"Only there's McIver." Waco's expression drained from his face and left it a blank mask. "I don't allow he'd go along, Rafe."

"No," Rafe said slowly. "The two of us can handle it, but we got to make it look right to Mac."

They talked the plan over for a half-hour, refining it here and there, until Rafe was satisfied that it rang about as true as human wit could contrive. When McIver's watch was ended, he would come in and wake Rafe for his stint. Rafe would ride out his two-hour watch, then Waco would join him and they would do the job quickly. The racket would wake McIver, but too late for him to suspect the truth. The story they would give him, and later Sheriff Crashaw, was that there had been a surprise attack by perhaps five or so night riders, who came down yelling and shooting and got behind an isolated bunch of shorthorns and ran it off. They had tried to make a stand, but were forced to retreat from superior numbers. However, they had identified the voice of the man calling the orders as Chad Buckmaster's. Then, having done their work, the raiders had vanished in the night.

Tonight, when McIver rode in off watch, both men were snoring in their blankets. Actually Rafe was awake and restless, but after McIver had shaken him awake, he made a show of stumbling groggily over to the picket line, lugging his saddle.

After two hours of watch, he was joined by Waco. Almost without words they went quickly to work, aided by the thin moonlight. The first part was the hardest, quietly cutting out twenty head from the flank of the herd. Afterward the two men hazed the smaller bunch off east, slowly so as not to alarm the herd.

A good half-mile from the main herd, Rafe pulled his gun and fired into the air. It was the signal, and now Waco joined him, firing, punctuating the shots with wild yells. The bunch shifted into a nervous trot, getting momentum. Shortly, lengthened into a loose wedge, they broke into a full stampede.

The bunch poured onto the east flat in a rumbling dark stream, and ahead now Rafe spotted the jagged form of dark boulders against the skyline. It marked the rim of the canyon, and he bawled at the top of his voice for Waco to stretch out and flank the running brutes. The bunch must be pointed into a shallow cleft which formed a natural trail to the very brink of the canyon.

Rafe and Waco pulled back off flank as the dark wedge hit the broad mouth of the cleft at a hurtling run. Then the lifting shoulders of rock, tapering inward, compressed it without slowing its doomed momentum.

The leaders neared the rim and tried to stop, and then the surging juggernaut behind them pushed them over. A slow milling began as the drag came up against the first resistance. The two men hoorawed the panicked animals relentlessly on, and Rafe could make out the dark bobbing humps skylined on the rim as they made the plunge.

Only a few head managed the last-minute turn and broke back past the men to safety. An almost invisible haze of dust made the night acrid as Rafe sidled his mount cautiously over to the rim and looked down. The bawling of crippled and dying cattle rose in a vast chorus of misery from the darkness below.

Rafe was a cowman born and raised, and all his instincts shriveled in protest against the total and savage wantonness of his own action. He said harshly, "Come on," and swung back from the rim. Waco followed him silently.

Before they had gone a dozen yards, Rafe had the shock of seeing a horse and rider lift suddenly out of the darkness. The horse was slowed to a trot, but it was winded and blowing, and his mind had barely registered this fact before McIver's flat question came.

"Night riders, Mac," Rafe fumbled. "Eh, we tried to stop 'em—"

"Both of you?"

"Well, I had just rousted Waco out for his watch when the two of us heard something out there. So we rode back together to see what, and got to the herd just as all hell busted loose."

McIver said with a cool, baffled anger, "That's a lie. Waco was restless, and that brought me awake. He was acting in a peculiar way, so I pretended to be still asleep. And I saw him ride out alone. I saddled up and followed him, but I was too far behind. But I know what you did, Rafe, and I can guess why."

A thick dread tightened Rafe's belly, and he said softly, "That 'why' ought to make a difference, Mac."

McIver shook his head curtly. "It doesn't. Don't waste your breath, Rafe. In the morning we'll ride in to see the sheriff. You'll tell him and Soderstrom exactly what you've done—or I will."

Rafe said sharply, "Mac, wait," as McIver turned his horse away, riding off. His shoulders and head made a faint outline as he topped a slant in the trail, and in that moment, Waco cocked his pistol. The sound washed against Rafe's brain like a dash of ice water, and he drove a heel into his horse's flank, lunging the animal sideward into Waco's mount as the gun roared.

He heard McIver's strained grunt of pain, and then McIver kicked his horse forward into a run, bowed across its mane, and in an instant was gone over the rise. Waco was fighting for control of his prancing horse, and he shrilled, "You crazy? Why he—"

Rafe cursed him, and heeled his horse into motion and went up over the rise and down its far side. The gully was banked with dense shadow, and he moved down it cautiously. Then he saw McIver's riderless horse.

Rafe stepped down and stooped low and struck a match. The washback of light showed dark wet stains on the rocks. He followed them up the stony bank to where they faded out in a vast litter of boulders. McIver must have been jolted from his saddle, but he had had enough left to push off on foot. The match burned Rafe's fingers and he struck another and studied the ground, feeling the hammerbeat of his pulse. There was nothing, and now he listened for a sound. There was none. McIver had faded into the forest of rock, and there would be no finding him in the dark. He was hard-hit, perhaps dying, but he might still stay on his feet a long while.

Rafe dropped the match, his mouth dry. Suddenly things had gotten out of hand in a way he had not foreseen, and he was in far above his head. A suffocating fear came over him, and on its heels the cold alternatives—*run or bluff it through?* McIver might live to talk, but alone and losing blood, he might be dead before morning. Rafe reached for a blind courage now, and, beyond that, did not allow himself to think. He climbed heavily down the bank to get his horse, and already he was revising his story for the sheriff and Soderstrom.

Fourteen

After the set fashion of an aging man, Otis Crashaw greeted each day according to a strict and unvarying ritual. He rose directly at 6:00, went into the kitchen, started his fire, filled the coffeepot, and laid strips of bacon in the frying pan. He washed up and honed his ancient razor, paused to turn over the bacon, then shaved with short, careful strokes. At 6:20 he broke two eggs into the spitting bacon grease, then dressed himself. He ate unhurriedly and fired up his pipe. He locked his front door at exactly 6:54 and made a leisurely stroll uptown to his office and the day's duties.

Crashaw liked the comfortable routine of his life of the last several years. He had often congratulated himself on buying his little house on the edge of town. It was a refuge where a man could enjoy a quiet pipe after a long day and muse on the past. Being sheriff of a finely populated county in a backwater of a dying frontier placed few demands on his waning energies. Loftus Buckmaster had brought him here, but the little people had voted him in, proud that a great marshal of the boomtown days had chosen to cap a turbulent life by making his home among them.

Lately Otis Crashaw had given much thought to what he owed these people. Too many years in a line of work that was brutal and often dirty had blunted his conscience to a dry cynicism. As his eye and hand had slowed down, he had become satisfied to take with both hands whatever past-earned glory might get him and ask few questions. But the recent choice he'd made had sharpened his blunted tools and tempered them with a new outlook. At sixty-three he had begun to find meaning in work he had always followed because it suited him.

As always, he found the street deserted at this early hour. The sky, he noticed, had a faint bleak overcast, and he sniffed the air and decided that a heller of a storm would hit before long. He might have to postpone the search for Garth Buckmaster for a while, no bad prospect if the Swede were a good checkers player.

Nearing the office he felt a nudge of curiosity at the sight of a rider coming into town from the north, moving briskly. Recognizing Rafe Catron then, Crashaw quickened his steps and reached the tie rail by his office as Rafe stepped down. Catron was usually a loafer and ne'er-do-well and, Crashaw was reasonably sure, a petty cow thief of long standing, but too trifling and easy-going to take very seriously. So Crashaw's greeting was neutral and mildly curious.

"It'll take some telling," Rafe said soberly, and tilted his head toward the jail. "Reckon the boss had better hear this, too, if he's in there."

Crashaw unlocked his office. The jail comprised two large cells with steel-barred doors at the rear of the room. In one of these, Krag Soderstrom was stretched out on the bunk, wide awake, hands folded behind his neck. He came to his feet in one complete motion, reminding Crashaw of a large, powerful cat.

"Bunk hard enough for you?"

"I slept on groundsheets softer," Soderstrom said, walking to the barred door. "Well, Catron, you moved the herd home already?"

"Not yet." Rafe removed his hat, cuffing the dust from it. "There was trouble last night. Wagontree raided again. Reckon they want to take advantage of the herd being still bunched."

Crashaw glanced at Soderstrom, and the Swede's eyes seemed to burn deeply as he said, "Go on."

"They was at least ten. If we hadn't made a game fight, they would of got off with the whole herd. As it was, they managed to drive a good twenty or more head off the edge of

Natchez Canyon. We looked down there this morning." Catron shook his head, dropping his gaze to his hat. "Worst of it, Mac is missing. He was shot and his horse bolted. After it was over, I looked for him. Couldn't make out in the dark. Searched awhile after it turned light enough, and kept Waco looking while I come in to tell you and the sheriff. Figured you'd want to know at once."

"All right," Crashaw said with a weary bafflement. "You know they was Wagontree men?"

"Sure. Both me and Waco recognized Chad Buckmaster's voice. He give the orders. Don't offhand know of any other outfit he rides with, do you?"

Soderstrom spoke now, with a contained and wicked anger. "All right, Sheriff, I'm taking you at your word. Is your jail big enough to hold Chad Buckmaster?"

Crashaw was troubled. There was much in this situation that did not tongue-and-groove cleanly, and he did not like it. He had made his own position clear to Loftus Buckmaster, and was sure that he had left Buckmaster with no doubts of the consequences of any move against the Swede in this county. He said slowly, "It makes no sense. Loftus knows when not to spit in a man's eye."

Soderstrom said flatly, "A man can get desperate, being kingpin so long and watching it slip away."

"Maybe. I'll tell you this: Catron and Millard better be sure."

Rafe shifted his feet. "Would swear to it on my pappy's grave. Waco, too."

Crashaw nodded tiredly. "I'll get a warrant and ride out to Wagontree. The warrant will only get Chad."

Soderstrom frowned, chewing his mustache. "Maybe you should take along a pair of special deputies. Catron and me."

"No." Crashaw shook his head. "That would make trouble for sure. I don't understand all that's going on, but one thing for sure about old Loftus: he coppers all bets. If Chad was with that bunch last night, any number of lying witnesses have been primed with his alibi. Chad was playing cards with the boys in the bunkhouse half the night, or he was pulling taffy with his daddy. He'll have no reason not to come peaceably."

"Wait." Soderstrom gripped the bars in both hands. "Handle Buckmaster any way you want, but let me out now."

Crashaw had started for the door, and now he halted. "Why?"

"You heard Catron. McIver is bad hurt, maybe dying, somewhere out there. He is my man, and seeing after him is my job. I got to look for him."

"If he's dead," Crashaw said dryly, "it don't matter. If he was hurt bad, he didn't get far and your men can look for him in a tight area. If he still ain't found, then it becomes my job. Anyhow I want you right where you are, Soderstrom. I'll have enough of a time holding Buckmaster down without worrying about you, too."

A vein of temper swelled and beat in Soderstrom's temple, but he held his voice low. "You are wrong. I want to look after a man of mine. Not get revenge for those cattle. If it was otherwise, I would say so. That is my word."

"I won't take the chance." Crashaw's tone was hard with a growing irritation, and he thumbed Catron toward the door. "Outside, so I can lock up the place. I'm taking no chance with you, either."

Catron went silently out ahead of him, then stood watching Crashaw lock the door. "You worried I might try to bust him out?"

"Yes. There's your horse. Fork him and ride."

He waited till Catron had ridden out of sight, then went to the livery and ordered his horse saddled. Moments later, as he was jogging down the street, he saw Hannah Kingery and Soderstrom's daughter leave the newspaper building. Both girls were carrying covered trays, which meant they were heading for his office. Last night, when he had brought Soderstrom in, he had granted the Swede's request to see his daughter before being locked up. It had been agreed then that Hannah and Thera would prepare all of Soderstrom's meals.

Reining over to them now, Crashaw touched his hat. "Sorry, but the office is locked up." He explained why, uneasy under the cold resentment of Hannah Kingery's stare. Beneath the professional disdain he had cultivated toward them, women always made him uneasy. But the response of mingled shock and distress in the Soderstrom girl's face was harder to endure, and then he realized that worry for young McIver was the case. After a hesitation, he said gruffly, "Look, Missy. Window of your pa's cell opens off behind the building. You can talk to him back there, and pass his food through the bars."

Thera thanked him, but Hannah's silent and icy stare did not relax. *The hell with her,* Crashaw thought, as he rode toward the courthouse. After rousing the clerk who slept in a back room, he left with a warrant in his pocket.

It was early forenoon when he put his horse up the long west slope of the hill beyond which Wagontree headquarters sprawled. The place always put him in mind of the old-time monarchies he had read about. Bad thing about a monarchy was the hereditary part; a strong man assembled power in his lifetime, but like as not the blood ran thin in his heirs.

That thought was trivial. His mind had always veered to triviality when there was a danger that the real issue might impel fear. Crashaw, not being a fool, knew that gaunt specter of old. He wiped his hand along his pants to dry the perspiration, then looked at it. It was trembling. It always trembled now, even when he was not afraid. *Too old,* he thought bleakly; you could fight fear and even sickness, but not that.

Coming off the wagon road into the layout, Crashaw loosened his gun in its holster. His muscles were too tight for comfort, and he forced a slackness to them as he threaded through the outbuildings. The blacksmith shop was deserted as he passed it, but from the house, still out of sight, came a dog's excited barking, as if something were up. Crashaw rode unhurriedly to face whatever it was; the baffling events of the last few days, coupled by the strange disappearance of Garth Buckmaster, had left him wearily ready for anything.

Most of the Wagontree crew, he saw as he came into view of the house, was gathered in the yard. They were armed to a man, sitting their horses in a kind of deadly hush. Chad was one of them; he had reined in close to the veranda where his father stood, leaning heavily on a pair of crutches, as if the slightest movement cost him infinite agony. Crashaw's glance flicked to Naomi Buckmaster, who was leaning in the doorway looking on. Her face was deathly pale, he saw, and suddenly sensed the probable reason for this assembly of force.

Loftus had been speaking, and now he was letting his words sink in. Crashaw ranged up to the veranda steps, saying mildly, "What's this, Loftus?"

Loftus did not even look at him, and it was Chad who spoke. "Me and the boys found Garth's body on Ladder ground. It was buried on a ridge back of Soderstrom's house."

"You and the boys, huh? You knew directly where to look?"

"In a way," Chad said soberly. "We knew enough to look for a place where the soil was freshly turned. We found it."

Richie Sears gently sidled his horse closer, watching Crashaw. Sears' right arm was muffled to the elbow in a thick bandage, and he wore a sling around it. In the seamed mask of his face his eyes were ugly with pain. Soderstrom had made little detail of his fight with the gunman, and Crashaw thought, *So his gun arm was busted,* but this was a thin solace in a situation that was, he knew, as dangerous as any he had faced. He made his voice mild and purposeful:

"Loftus, it's clear enough. You're aiming to send your boys to take Soderstrom out of jail. Listen. If he's guilty, then—"

Old Buckmaster spoke for the first time, in a dead, exhausted voice. "Who'll stop me?"

"I will."

Buckmaster faintly jerked his head sideward, a gesture flecked with contempt. Crashaw slowly slipped his gun from its holster, cocking it deliberately. "I will," he repeated. "I'll stop you, even if every gun here is turned on me."

The old man's eyes squinted nearly shut under his brows. "What's your business, Crashaw? What d'you want here?"

Crashaw watched his face carefully. "You had your warning, Loftus. I told you I'm through taking sides."

"I know, I know. Get on with it." Under the heavy dullness of wrath, the old man's tone was irritated and puzzled.

"When a man kills a bunch of someone's cattle by pushing them off a canyon rim, he goes to jail. That plain enough?"

"It don't mean a goddamn thing, and I don't bluff a goddamn jot, Crashaw. Spell it out."

"Last night twenty to thirty head of Soderstrom's shorthorn beefs was pushed into Natchez Canyon. Your boy Chad led the party. Want to see the warrant?"

A slow, amazed anger flooded Chad Buckmaster's face. "That's a lie!"

"You were identified by Rafe Catron and old Waco."

"Then they're a pair of liars. Hell, I never stirred off the place last night, and I can prove it."

"You'll get that chance. Meantime you'll ride in with me." Crashaw paused, then said with a quiet irony, "Your pa observes the law, and the law says so."

"I will, like hell—"

"Steady down," Loftus declared heavily. "Crashaw, you're walking on Indian territory, and you better pull in your horns. No Buckmaster is going to spend one night in your fleabit lockup, so just pull in your horns."

There it was, the unequivocal challenge which, if Crashaw let it pass, would end forever any voice of authority he might have. "You pull in," he said flatly. "One thing you're not is a fool. Maybe there's more here than meets the eye. But Chad is coming with me."

Loftus gave Crashaw an unblinking, heavy-lidded stare intended to disconcert him. When it did not, he said with a massive impatience, "Don't be a damn fool, Otis. Come back into line, man. It can be the way it was all over."

"No," Crashaw said. "It'll never be that way again." And turned his gun on Chad as the younger Buckmaster's hand brushed back the skirt of his coat. "Don't," Crashaw said sharply, even as the dead-weary taste of hopelessness filled his mouth and his hand tensed for the moment when Chad's gun came up.

In that moment, his hot pained eyes glinting, Richie Sears whipped his left hand around to his right side and flipped up his gun with incredible speed. He fired twice.

For a fleeting instant Crashaw felt the hammerblows of

the bullets in his chest, and as he fell forward, heard Loftus
roar belatedly, "Sears—no!" That sound was already fading,
along with Naomi's scream and the dying light in his eyes,
and it was all gone before his body hit the ground.

Fifteen

Soderstrom was pacing the narrow floor of his cell in a quiet
rage when Thera's voice brought him to the barred window.
He pulled up the sash. Hannah was there too, and he knew
from the troubled anger in her face, and the shock close to
tears in Thera's, that they had talked with Crashaw.

"Papa, we must help David if he—"

"I know, I know." Soderstrom ran a hand through his pale
shaggy mane. "I must get out of here. You'll have to help
me."

Thera bit her lip in dismay, for she had been reared to a
strict respect for the law. "That is wrong, but . . . but there is
David. You must find him, Papa. Maybe it's not too late."

Soderstrom glanced at Hannah, seeing no hesitancy at all.
She said matter-of-factly, "There is probably a spare set of
keys in Crashaw's desk. But his office door is locked."

Soderstrom growled under his breath, swinging restlessly
away, then back again. "The lock of the outside door would
not be hard to break, but how can you do it without attracting
a lot of people?"

"It's still quite early for town folk," Hannah pointed out.
"Haven't seen a soul on the street outside of us and Otis."

"It is too quiet this hour. The noise would bring somebody."

Thera's face brightened; she fumbled in the pale corona of
her hair, and brought out a pin. With an intent care she
pressed the tip against the jail wall, bending it back at an

acute angle. Soderstrom scowled. "What are you doing there, girl?"

"I am going to open the front door with this little pin."

"Where the devil," Soderstrom began to roar, then caught himself. "Where did you learn such a trick, eh?"

She colored a little, but her eyes were very clear. "It's just something I picked up . . . oh, when I was small."

"Who taught you? Tell me that!"

"Uncle Haakon, Papa."

Soderstrom muttered, "Ahh—Haakon!" His wife's brother, a scamp and reprobate if ever there was one, dropping in from nowhere at odd times and departing just as suddenly. Well, it was no surprise. He glanced with brief embarrassment at Hannah, but she seemed only amused.

"I won't be but a moment," Thera promised, and hurried away. Hannah bent and lifted the white cloths that covered the two trays they had set on the ground. "Here . . . you must eat something." She began passing food through the bars, and Soderstrom ate quickly, washing it down with gulps of hot coffee.

Hannah smiled. "I like to see a man eat as though he means it. You flatter the cook, too."

"Thera. I know her cooking."

"Hm. I should be indignant, but if you can't tell which things which of us prepared, I guess that's a compliment."

"It's all good. So you cook?"

"Do you object to that, too?"

Soderstrom grinned, glancing over his shoulder as the office doorlatch made a gentle rattle. "A man can change his mind. Maybe it's good if a woman knows some things besides cooking and keeping house. I would be in a fix if my daughter had never learned to pick a lock."

Hannah laughed, and now he said soberly, "Nobody can say what may happen next. So now I will ask again, while there's time."

"I'd rather you didn't." She shook her head with a frowning indecision. "Yesterday you told me about sparing my father's men who raided your herd, when you had them at your mercy."

"I did not mean to use that on you," he said forcefully. "I was only telling what happened. Now are you asking why?"

"Yes."

"Then I'll tell you. Those men are alive because of what you said. That my actions would prove something."

"If that's true, I'm glad, But does it really mean a change? That would be a big one for you, and how can you be sure?"

"It was a change. I know, because I found it easy to do. If it was not a change, I would not be asking the question again."

"I wish you hadn't asked . . . so soon. I wish I could feel as sure as you do."

Again the latch rattled, and Thera swung the door gently inward, then stepped inside and quickly closed it. In a few seconds she found a spare ring of keys in the litter of a desk drawer. After an experimental minute or two the right key was fitted in the lock, and Soderstrom opened the cell door and went to the gunrack where Crashaw had placed his rifle. With the familiar assurance of the weapon against his palm, he moved to the office door to inspect the deserted street, then stepped outside with Thera. They slipped into the areaway between the jail and the adjacent building, where Hannah waited now. Soderstrom talked quickly.

"When I find McIver, I'll bring him to the ranch. It is a lot closer than the town to last night's bedground, and if he's hurt bad, those miles could make much difference. Go to the ranch and wait for us, Thera. Have everything ready to treat a gunshot wound."

"But what will you do then?" Hannah asked.

Soderstrom shrugged stolidly. "Give myself up. But no time to lose. Go back to your newspaper now."

"Can't I do something?"

"Yes. Stay in town and keep your eyes open." He hesitated. "If anything happens I should know, bring word to the ranch. Now, Thera, wait five minutes after I ride out, then get your horse."

Soderstrom expected no difficulty from the half-witted lad who was night hostler at the livery barn, and he got none. Smiling stupidly around his yawns, the boy saddled Soderstrom's horse. Soderstrom paid him and rode out at an easy pace, not lifting to a quick lope till he was beyond the last building.

Riding steadily northeast, he studied the metallic gloom that was thickening the sky, and thought glumly, *What a time for a storm.*

Inside of three miles, he saw a rider on the flats ahead, and knew it was Catron. He was not rushing himself, Soderstrom thought with a grim displeasure. He overtook Catron shortly. While explaining his escape, he did not miss a puzzling hint of sullenness behind the redheaded puncher's surprise.

As they rode on, Rafe glanced at the sky and shook his head. "If that's a bad one coming, we'll have a time finding him. He was hurt bad, or he should of controlled his horse when it bolted—least he would of found his way back. Of course we got to try, against any chance at all."

"The storm may hold off till tonight," Soderstrom said, knowing this was a thin hope.

Back at camp they found Waco Millard hunkered by the fire watching the coffee come to a boil. They squatted by the fire, and Waco asked why Soderstrom was out of jail, then remarked diffidently, "Well, I couldn't find nothing."

"So I see," Soderstrom said curtly. He poured some of the scalding brew and drank, letting it jar his thoughts to the need for organizing his next move. "Catron, you saw which way he was headed?"

"Directly west," Rafe said, and pointed. "We was about there when the raiders struck. Several of 'em engaged us while the others went after the herd. Of course it was dark and we was shooting blind, but Mac was hit right away. I left off the fight and went after him, but his horse was running hard, and I lost him. By the time I got back, the night riders was gone with them cattle."

Soderstrom was silent, studying the rugged dark lift of the badlands to the west. They would have their work cut out, trying to find a lone man in all that. Beyond lay the vast northern sweep of Wagontree graze, but it was unlikely that McIver had gotten that far.

He drank half his coffee and tossed the rest out and swung back to his horse. "Let's get to it."

Rafe said, "What about the shorthorns, Mr. Soderstrom? They'll get straying."

"Let them. Finding McIver comes first."

When they were in saddle, Soderstrom gave his orders. The three of them would separate and work out toward the west, each confining his search to a general area and covering it thoroughly. The man who found McIver would signal the others with two quick shots.

For hours Soderstrom drove himself with a relentless fury, pushing his horse through brush, over jagged abutments, down cramped and winding gorges. Where his horse could not go, he dismounted and reconnoitered on foot. When hunger pangs came, he dug out jerky and cold biscuits and ate without leaving his saddle.

Later, exhausted and discouraged, he rode back toward camp. He had explored to the edge of the west foothills where they shouldered against the peaks. A lone searcher could not cover every pocket of ground in a large area where a wounded man might lie up. Even his horse would not be easily spotted amid this rugged upheaval. Still, if alive, McIver could fire his rifle. If he were not dead, he must be close to it. Soderstrom's hopes had threaded fine.

And now the storm broke at last. The rain fell in blinding cascades, and a high wind lashed it against his slickered body. Soderstrom was half-drenched when he reached camp. The gear and provisions were gone, and the fire was a sodden heap of ashes.

Pulling up, he heard a voice hail him, and Rafe, his yellow slicker flapping formlessly in the wind, stepped from the nearby stand of trees. Waco was there too; they had toted the gear into the semi-shelter of the trees. Here, the force of rain and wind were broken, but the water seeped steadily down through the soaked branches, and the three men could only squat in unwarmed misery and wait it out. The sky writhed with white veins of lightning; thunder cannonaded deafeningly, and softened to a sullen mutter as the storm's first fury ebbed. The wind died off and the rain rattled on the leaves and sobbed on the drenched ground.

Rafe ended the long silence, and his tone was surly: "Well?"

"I don't know." Soderstrom rubbed a hand over his wet face, a gray and hopeless conviction in him.

Rafe said, "We looked all over, and not a sign. Anyhow a man can't track in this miserable rain, even if the sign wasn't wiped out."

"That sure shines to me," Waco shrilled softly. "I hanker for some hot grub and a warm blanket."

Soderstrom eyed the pair of them narrowly, positive without knowing why that they were concealing something behind this sullen, uneasy reluctance to pursue the search. Still, there was some meat to their argument. It looked increasingly hopeless, and this was not a thing to which a man should be forced against his will.

For himself, he would not quit until McIver was found, dead or alive. He said so, adding curtly, "When the storm stops, you two will get the herd on to Ladder. The north range is only a few miles. Scatter it there, then do what you like." At this moment, he did not give a particular damn what either man did.

Shortly the rain thinned to a faint drizzle. A smoky mist curled off the ground as the men rose from their cramped squat, wet and chilled to the bone. Soderstrom and Waco rubbed down the steaming, shivering horses, while Rafe found a rotted deadfall and kicked it apart. It yielded enough tinder-dry wood for a fire, and they had kept their food, gear and spare clothes dry by rolling them in their ground tarps.

With dry clothes on their backs and warm food in their bellies, they separated, Rafe and Waco moving the herd out while Soderstrom prepared to take up the hunt still farther west. There was the possibility, however slight, that McIver had stayed on his horse while it strayed that far.

Soderstrom buttoned his jumper to his neck against a raw rising wind, then followed a canyon trail west. The clouds were shredding before the brisk wind, turning the sky a neutral gray. He swung north and south in slow zigzags, occasionally firing off his pistol.

This time, when he returned to the deserted camp, his discouragement was total. He sank down on his haunches, rubbing his bent head between his hands. Maybe it was only the miserable weather coupled with his crowding weariness, but for the first time he felt his iron control slipping, a feel of defeated misery seeping through him. He was fed up with burned-out hopes, tired of fighting, sick of his own part in a deadlocked conflict. What would it mean, getting the short-horns through safely, if he had to return to the ranch without McIver and face his daughter's eyes? And it was this, the thought of Thera, that drove him back to his feet. There were still a few hours of daylight, and he would use them. He would pack up the remaining provisions and comb over a limited area, stopping wherever the need for meals or sleep dictated.

Making up a sack of grub, he tied it on his saddle and rode out of the cottonwoods. He had gone a short way when he saw the plodding horse coming up from the northwest. The rider was slumped across the pommel, and seeing only this much, Soderstrom savagely roweled his animal around and headed back.

McIver's head was bowed against his chest, and he lifted it with a drowsy effort. His face was almost colorless, but the ghost of a grin flickered there. "Still a hell of an adventure, Mr. Soderstrom . . . working for you."

Sixteen

After the rain wetted down the deep dust of Mimbreno's street, hooves, boots, and wheels chopped it to a chocolate mire. Hannah, carrying a sack of groceries, picked her way over the oozing islands between glassy-puddled ruts, and paused on the opposite walk to scrape the mud off her shoes. "Uncle Bill" Goodrich, standing in the doorway of his store, said good-naturedly, "You're too old for puddle-hopping, Hannah. Where are all the young Raleighs in this town?"

Hannah made a wry face. "Lord knows. Isn't there a cloak or two in your stock, Uncle Bill?"

The old man chuckled. "And I'm too old to do myself any good by getting chivalrous, worse luck." His glance passed down the street where a body of riders was swinging into town. He said briefly, "Your clan, looks like," and spat carefully in the street, then wheeled ponderously into his store.

There were an even dozen of them, and Chad was heading them. Riding close to his stirrup was Richie Sears, his arm heavily bandaged. Her brother did not look at her as they rode past. All of these men were new hands, except three who lagged somewhat behind the others, as if ashamed.

Impulsively Hannah hailed one of them, a man who had punched Wagontree cattle when she was a child. She felt a vague reluctance in his manner as he reined over to the sidewalk. She said bluntly, "Red, what is this? And where's Otis Crashaw? I know he went out to Wagontree."

"Yes, ma'am. You can see for yourself what we're about." Red motioned with a horny hand, and she saw that the Wagontree men had halted by the sheriff's office. Chad dropped off his mount, tossing his reins to a crewman, and tramped into the building.

Hannah felt a coldness of premonition. "Red. What about Otis? What happened?"

"Dead, Miss Hannah." Red rubbed a finger vaguely along the rusty droop of his mustache, and shook his head. "That Sears. Crashaw, he wanted to take Chad in for stampedin' some of this Swedish fella's cattle off a cliff, he said, and Chad said he hadn't done it. Then Sears pulled on Crashaw. He was a tough old dog, but he didn't have no chance."

Hannah said slowly, "No," feeling a qualm of sickness. "But I still don't see what you're doing here—"

At that moment Chad emerged from the jail; he rapped orders at the men, who dismounted. They began fanning out in pairs and threes, heading for different buildings.

"Your brother's been found, Miss Hannah," Red said, watching the others. "Now don't tell me that Swedish fella has got away."

"Garth found? Found . . . how?"

"Shot to death, ma'am. I don't know. This don't seem like the way to handle it, but your pa is plenty upset."

Hannah simply watched him in stunned silence, and he went on lamely, "Well, he sent us to fetch Soderstrom out to Wagontree."

Hannah found her voice. "For what?"

"Now you know your pappy better than to ask, Miss Hannah." Red seemed embarrassed, and touching his hat, he rode on to the jail.

For a few blank moments Hannah stood watching the Wagontree men disperse into the buildings, searching for the missing prisoner, and then she turned slowly into the newspaper office. She set her groceries on the littered desk, knowing with a deep-reaching fear that the finding of Garth's body meant that no Wagontree men would be permitted to rest until Soderstrom was dead or captured.

Hannah kneaded her knuckles against her palms. She had to do something. Soderstrom would take his wounded man to Ladder if he found him, and he had said to bring any word there. He had to be warned—if only she could find him before any Wagontree man did. With that thought, she was tearing off her paper cuffs and ink-soiled apron. She started toward her quarters at the rear, but somebody's quick, urgent rapping on the office door brought her impatiently hurrying back to open it.

Naomi stood there in her riding habit, hatless, and seeing the bright cold terror in her face, Hannah let her first words die unsaid. She beckoned her inside, and closed the door behind her. "Naomi, good Lord. What is it?"

"Oh God," her sister-in-law moaned. "I wish I were dead. First Garth, then Crashaw, now Soder—oh my God, Han! I want to die!"

Angrily, Hannah caught her by the shoulders and shook her. "What *is* the matter with you? Control yourself!" Naomi only wailed.

Hannah thought, *All right then,* and slapped her, hard. Naomi stepped back, blinking in shock; her mouth fell open.

"There's been enough dying," Hannah said matter-of-factly.

"Soderstrom is out of jail. He's still alive—for a while at least."

"Oh, thank God for that!"

"Hurry now, tell me what this is all about."

Within a few minutes she knew all that could be gotten out of Naomi, and she said bitterly, "You knew the truth? You even saw it happen—and you didn't say a word? Do you realize—"

"Yes, yes! But I didn't before, Han. I swear! All that Chad told me was not to worry, he'd arrange things so that nobody could ever find out how Garth had met his death. He didn't tell me he was going to fix the blame on Soderstrom. I didn't know what he'd really done until he brought in Garth's body and told your father about finding him by Soderstrom's place."

"I can believe that. You're foolish enough to be bamboozled in exactly that way." Hannah's tone was hard and accusing; for once her easy, charitable nature could find no pity for this girl whose acquiescence and weakness had finally pulled others besides herself into deep trouble. "But once you knew what Chad had done, you could have told my father. I needn't ask—I know you couldn't find the courage."

Naomi walked aimlessly back and forth, sobbing like a small girl. "I c-couldn't, Han, I'm a-f-fraid of h-h-him."

"Of who?" Hannah demanded acidly. "Chad or Pa?"

The door opened quietly, and Hannah turned her head. Chad stood in the doorway with his scuffed muddy boots planted apart, and his bulk seemed to fill the room. His eyes were abnormally bright, and there was a hint of wicked violence in his thin smile. "Hello, girls."

"Hello, goodbye," Hannah snapped, hiding the cold alarm she felt.

"Don't get pleasant, sister. Soderstrom around here?"

"Why should he be?"

"He's not in the jail, for one thing." Chad moved idly past them into the room and paused, hands on hips, eyeing the typestand thoughtfully. "For another, you kind of shine to that big Swenska, don't you? I just wondered."

Hannah said with a forced mockery, "Why, do you believe all you hear?"

Chad continued to stare curiously at the typestand, letting one shoulder lift and settle lazily. "I dunno. Point is, if he didn't make tracks out of town, he's hid out somewhere around here. What do you think?"

"I really couldn't say."

"Uh huh." Chad sauntered back to the doorway that opened on Hannah's quarters and looked inside. Watching him, she had the uneasy realization that Chad would only have had to question the night hostler at the stable to know that Soderstrom had gotten a horse and ridden out. If he knew that, then he had come here because he had seen Naomi enter the office, and was wondering whether she had come to Hannah, her friend, to relieve her burdened conscience. He might even have caught a little of what they'd been saying.

Chad came back to the typestand and leaned his shoulder against it, folding his arms. "Well, you can't always go by what folks say." He gave Naomi a negligent glance. Her face was bloodless; she was, Hannah saw, actually petrified with fear. "What's the matter with her?"

"She doesn't see her husband's dead body brought in every day of the week," Hannah said coldly. "It's also quite an occasion in a girl's life when the sheriff gets killed trying to arrest her brother-in-law."

"That could be," Chad said agreeably, then gave a powerful heave of his shoulder. The typestand tilted and then crashed over on the stone composing table, the upper and lower case trays banging down and littering the floor with hundreds of pieces of type.

Hannah could only stare in stunned, appalled silence as he strolled over to her desk then, remarking, "On the other hand, we know how our sister-in-law here is kind of prone to imagine things, if you can guess what I mean." He picked up the desk chair and smashed it down on the desk. A rung and a leg broke. "And when she gets imagining, she gets to running off at the mouth, too." He clubbed the chair down three times more, splintering it to kindling. He picked up the only other chair and swung it against the wooden railing. "I sure don't believe all I hear, and I hope you don't, Han. Furniture's cheap, if you can guess what I mean. A body's life, now, that's another case." He proceeded to carefully smash the chair and railing to fragments.

The spell that held Naomi broke, and she ran forward, crying, "No, Chad—"

He did not even look at her as he swung his arm sideways, his hand still closed around a heavy piece of the chair. His fist caught her backhanded across the mouth. She screamed and fell, and lay face down moaning in the litter of metal slugs.

Hannah looked on helplessly, in shocked disbelief, as Chad went about systematically wrecking the office. He could do little damage to the heavy press, but he broke the filled forms to pieces on it, types and quadrats flying everywhere. He finished up by dumping all the paper stock on the floor, pouring ink over it, and stamping it to a black soggy pulp. He did all this with a child's destructive pleasure contained by a man's cold ferocity.

Afterward he walked over to Naomi. She still lay where she had fallen, motionless with terror, and he prodded her with his toe. "You want to be careful what you go telling people after this, honey. Otherwise I'll just naturally have to do something drastic."

He looked slowly at Hannah now, and something chill and repellent was in his eyes. She had not been really afraid until this moment. He raised his arm, pointing his finger at her like a gun. "You mind what I tell you. Don't say a word. Don't print a word. Your life wouldn't be worth it." He went out the door, closing it softly behind him.

Why, Hannah thought with a peculiar detachment, *why he is crazy*. The dark coldness of the conviction felt strange in the harsh gray reality of this midday. Only a madman could pledge raw murder in a tone of calm indifference and still leave you unshakably convinced of his sincerity. Pure desperation, she supposed, could do that to someone.

Recovering, she went to Naomi and helped her to her feet and into the living quarters. Hannah settled her on a chair and got a cold wet towel. Naomi held it to her split, bleeding lip, whimpering softly, eyes still blank with shock.

It made little difference whether something he'd overheard or only a brooding suspicion had led Chad to this open, brutal act of intimidation, Hannah thought bleakly. If he dared to do this much, in town and in broad daylight, there was an excellent chance that he'd try to silence for good the one witness to his brother's killing, and at the first opportunity. Not only Naomi, but herself as well, now.

She drew up a chair in front of Naomi and sat so the other girl had to face her. "Listen to me. You must go to Pa and tell him the truth."

Naomi roused with a jerk, and her eyes seemed to withdraw into a recess of fear. "I can't . . . Han. I'm more afraid of him than of Chad."

"He'd do nothing to you," Hannah said with asperity. "That's part of his code; treat a woman like a stick of household furniture, but never abuse her physically. Anyway, your only wrong was in covering up for Chad. You've got to make it right now, or Pa won't stop till Krag Soderstrom is dead. If he knows the truth, he'll call off his men. Are your tender fears worth a man's life?" And quietly, pointedly, she added, "Don't delude yourself any further about Chad, or what he's capable of. Don't forget, you're the only witness to the killing."

Naomi burst out, "But it was self-defense, Han! I'd testify that Chad had to shoot. I don't see why he . . ."

"He framed Soderstrom for the killing, and he'd draw a prison term for that. But even that's a small part of his thinking. Pa would disinherit him if he knew the truth, and especially how the situation came about, if he didn't shoot him like a dog. I know my dear father."

Still doubtfully, Naomi murmured, "But Chad wouldn't . . ."

"He would," Hannah snapped. "If you doubt that after what you just saw, you're an idiot. Neither of our lives will be safe as long as you keep Chad's secret. Can't you get that through your head?"

Naomi was still plainly afraid, but Hannah knew she was scoring; and with only a little more persuasion, was able to

296

secure Naomi's reluctant agreement. The two of them went up front to the office, and peering out the window, Hannah saw that Chad, a short distance down the street, had gathered the Wagontree men around him, issuing orders.

"Go out and get on your horse," she told Naomi, "and ride out past them slowly. If you're asked, you're going home, that's all. Chad thinks he's thrown the fear of God into you. See that you look like it." She added dryly, "You shouldn't have a lot of trouble there."

"What will you do, Han?"

"Soderstrom couldn't know that the Wagontree crew is looking for him; he has to be warned. He'll probably be bringing a wounded crewman of his to Ladder, so I'll go there. At least his daughter will be there, and—but never mind. Get going now."

Hannah watched, holding her breath, as Naomi mounted and rode slowly toward the end of town. Chad gave her a fleeting glance as she passed, then ignored her. Nobody spoke to her, and in a minute she was out of sight.

Hannah released her breath, but caught it again with her realization that Soderstrom's ranch would be one of the first places to which Chad would dispatch searchers, and she had no time to lose.

She hurried back through the building and let herself out the rear door; there was no time to change to her riding costume. She swiftly skirted the rear of the buildings till she reached the livery barn, entering it through the runway entrance at the back.

The day hostler, three-quarters drunk and blinking owlishly, was forking hay into a stall. He grinned, "Hallo there, Miss Han."

"I want a horse, Lex. No, no sidesaddle. Give me a man's."

Lex gave her a long look of rheumy disapproval as he moved to the saddle pole. Hannah fretted with impatience as he laboriously saddled a jughead paint. She snatched the reins from him and bunched her skirts in one hand, drawing a deep breath as she toed into stirrup and swung awkwardly up.

"Miss Hannah, that's—"

"Oh, shut up!"

Hannah reined along a few gingerly paces till she had her seat, then swung out through the back archway. She rode slowly till she was past the last of the houses, then urged the paint onto a road fetlock-deep in mud, gratful only that she wasn't contending with a sidesaddle while trying to get a little speed. The man who had decided that women had limbs and not legs was merely a fool; the one who thought up the sidesaddle had a streak of downright cruelty, she thought, trying furiously to straighten her wadded skirt and petticoats.

Then she realized, with a sinking fear, that she could not have chosen a poorer mount for the purpose. No matter how she drummed his flanks or talked to him, the jughead could be stirred barely beyond his stolid, plodding pace. It was too late to undo the mistake, and she could only hold to a dwindling hope that Soderstrom would for some reason not come to his ranch. Something like a sob broke in her throat, and she hated to think why.

A faint rain was still falling, wetting her slowly. She shivered miserably, wondering what her father would do if he ran down and killed Soderstrom. Probably buy enough alibis and lying witnesses to cover himself; he might even make it appear that it was Soderstrom, not Chad, whom Otis Crashaw had gone to arrest, and that Soderstrom, not Sears, had killed the sheriff. In that event, he could make the claim that Soderstrom had later resisted citizen's arrest by her father's men, and they had been forced to shoot. *Yes,* Hannah thought dully, *he would think of something like that.*

Perhaps five minutes later, as she had expected, a half-dozen riders came into sight on the muddy switchbacks behind her. Shortly, without speaking, the body of men had ranged their mounts up beside and around her, quietly but effectively surrounding her. Resignedly, Hannah brought the sluggish jughead to a halt.

Richie Sears appeared to be in charge. He touched his hat and said with soft courtesy, "What you doing out here, ma'am?"

"Enjoying the weather," Hannah said in a wintry voice. "Where is Little Chadwick?"

"He cut out for north of here, in case the Swede headed for his last trail camp. He sent me to Ladder, seeing that our man might go there, too." Sears' temper, no longer masked by his dead cynicism, lay plain and wicked in his pain-drawn face and murky eyes. "Chad knows I would fancy doing a job on that snork, even if your pa wants him alive. Well, ma'am, seeing as you're heading our way, we'll just give you some company."

Seventeen

When Soderstrom had spread a fairly dry pack tarp on the ground and eased McIver onto it, he found that the bullet had passed clean through, low on the left side. He said quietly, "It could be worse, boy. Thera can tend you good as any sawbones. I'll do what I can now."

McIver's face was slick and sickly in the gray wet light, and his teeth were set against the pain. "Maybe you should raise my pay," he said faintly, "for getting shot at."

Soderstrom remembered, with a sudden mixture of feelings, that McIver was still working for nothing but his food and a bunk. "Anytime you don't like it, you can quit," he growled.

McIver smiled around his pain. Soderstrom applied a bandage of sorts. "Now rest a while, and we'll be going home. Maybe you can sleep a little, eh?"

But McIver, despite a distant and drowsy look now, was not ready for sleep. He wanted to talk, and he had enough left to tell what he knew, though he was rambling almost incoherently toward the end. After eluding Rafe and Waco last night, he had simply staggered and crawled through a forest of rock until his wound had sapped his strength completely. Afterward he had been unconscious or delirious for hours,

299

finally coming to his senses to find his horse nuzzling him where he'd fallen. He had not fired his rifle, for fear the shots would bring Rafe or Waco. After a dozen tries, he had made it into the saddle and given the animal its head. He remembered little more until the horse had plodded into the old camp and Soderstrom had found him.

Soderstrom, not an easily affected man, felt a little sick. He had not considered that Catron's and Millard's hatred for Buckmaster might carry them this far. Lord knew what would come of it.

He let McIver have an hour's sleep under the misting sky, then reluctantly aroused him. The boy had gotten some sleep, but his eyes were glazed, his breathing labored, as Soderstrom dragged him upright. He muttered, "Don't think I'll make it, sir."

"Good," Soderstrom said. "It will be good to have Thera learn what a yellowbelly you are."

McIver's eyes seemed to burn away the fever; but as if he saw behind Soderstrom's words, he made a show of vitality then, his whole body tensed against the pain as Soderstrom gave him a lift into the saddle.

They rode south at an inching pace, McIver rocking loosely in the saddle to minimize the pain, Soderstrom making aimless talk to divert him. But McIver was dully silent, his chin sagging on his chest. Soderstrom watched him with a deepening worry, and he was ready when the boy began to cant sideways in his saddle.

He reined over and halted McIver's horse and spoke sharply. No answer, and Soderstrom dismounted and worked swiftly, tying the boy's feet together beneath his horse's barrel, then lashing his wrists to the saddle horn. It was crude and unpleasant, but it would have to do. The bandage was bloody, which could not be helped, either.

Again in the saddle, leading McIver's horse, he rode on. The rain had ceased entirely, but weariness added to the aches of his body, fast dulling his senses.

He snapped alert, realizing that he was dozing off. He had passed through a skimpy motte of mostly dead trees, with a rank undergrowth of heavy brush, and in this moment as he reached the end of the motte, he picked up the bunch of slickered riders heading north through the misty drizzle, swinging past the motte at perhaps fifty yards' distance.

Instinctively Soderstrom pulled back into the brush, watching them till they were lost in the mizzling veil of rain. Then he rode on, his eyes and thoughts totally alert. He could not have told exactly why he had avoided contact with those men ... but why in this lonely country and miserable weather was a sizable group of horsemen heading north, away from any settlement, and in the direction from which he had just come?

An interminable time passed, it seemed to Soderstrom, before he achieved the rim of drab low hills behind Ladder headquarters. The dampness was deep in his bones now, numbing them, so that he felt only a meaningless drift of sensations. He was barely hanging onto wakefulness as he crossed the hills, and then by a wrenching effort, dragged himself alert once more.

Thinking of the riders he had seen made him wary; he swung in a watchful half-circle of the place before approaching it finally. He was still careful then, holding off a ways as he rode along back of the outsheds and corrals, sizing them up. If there were men here, there would be horses too. There was no sign of either. The buildings lay solid and still in the moist twilight, and the windows of the house shed cheery squares of light. So Thera was there, waiting his arrival.

McIver startled him by saying suddenly, weakly, "We're home?"

"Yes, home." The boy's strong rally was a heartening thing, Soderstrom thought as he dismounted by the corral. He opened the gate and led both animals inside. Rafe's and Waco's saddle mounts, along with the two pack horses, were here, he noticed; they had arrived all right, and the clinging tension washed out of him.

His own rawboned roan, which had carried a brutal load of work for many days, was on its last legs. After he had gotten McIver into the house he would see to proper care for both mounts. Now he could spare the time to remove the galling saddles. He uncinched and swung off his own hull, and was coming around on his heel when a voice saluted him softly.

"Hello, snork."

Soderstrom carefully finished his turn. Richie Sears leaned in the doorway of the stable only yards away, his gun loosely trained in his left hand. "Arm hurts to beat hell, snork. Will for a long time. Now," he brought the gun up steadily, "where do you reckon a man will die slowest from a bullet?"

Soderstrom said, "Think you can handle this all by yourself?"

Sears' chuckle was a thin and whispery sound. "There's others. You was covered from the time you rode off them hills. Others is laid up around the place where I told 'em to. Horses are hid, too. That's just insurance. I want you all to myself, snork, so I stationed myself where there wouldn't be no question of it. Old Man Buckmaster wants you brought to him alive, but I don't see letting him have the pleasure."

Soderstrom had supposed that this was Sears' personal vendetta, his alone, and he said in puzzlement, "Buckmaster? Why? He gave Crashaw his word—"

"Garth's been found. Up on that ridge yonder. Shot dead. You wasn't fooling, was you snork?"

Soderstrom felt clammy sweat form between his palms and the smooth saddle. "The sheriff will still not like this, Sears."

Sears' laugh made his spine crawl. "He won't mind. He took sick all at once out at Wagontree. It was fatal as hell."

"You, Sears?"

Sears laughed again.

"So, you mean to cheat your boss of his pleasure. You better have a good story, then."

"I got one already." Sears' cartwheel spurs jingled softly as he walked forward. He halted a couple of yards away. "Nobody can see us from here, and I give the others an order not to close in till I call 'em. Said no sense in being messy if one man could take you prisoner. My story, you made a break just as I sung out to bring 'em. Understand? I had to kill you."

He thumbed the hammer to full cock, then half-turned his head to summon his men. And Soderstrom, with nothing to lose now, made his move. The saddle was hugged chest-high to his body, and he flung it out with the heels of his hands and took a long step sideways. A strained grunt left Sears as the heavy rig hit his body and arm, bearing down his gun so that the bullet exploded into the mud.

Soderstrom made a swift long lunge; his fist meeting Sears' neck in a savage chop. The gunman went down, and Soderstrom wheeled for McIver's horse, snatching up the reins. He could hear running steps across the yard, and there was no time to lose. He yanked his rifle from its scabbard, then pulled McIver's horse along with him into the stable, hauling the door shut after him. He stood in the dim runway and listened, his rifle ready. From outside came a flurry of excited voices as his men found Sears. Quite abruptly the voices broke apart as the men scattered off.

They had a fair certainty of where he was, Soderstrom grimly guessed, but none were foolhardy enough to make a head-on entry into the stable. In a very few moments, things would get too hot for comfort. Working swifly, he untied McIver from the saddle and carried him into the deep shelter of a stall. "Give me a gun," the youth whispered as Soderstrom lowered him onto a heap of straw.

"No. You stay here and keep yourself down." Straightening then, Soderstrom froze as a rasp of strained breathing reached him in the dim musty stillness.

Somebody else was in the stable, and Soderstrom catfooted swiftly to where he had left his rifle. Training it on a dark corner, he said softly, "All right, whoever that is. Come out now."

"Don't know as I can make it that far, Mr. Soderstrom," Rafe Catron husked weakly. In a moment Soderstrom was kneeling in the corner, striking a match. He found Rafe tied hand and foot on the floor, his shirt caked with dried blood. Beside him, wide-eyed and sightless in the grotesque sprawl of death, was the body of Waco Millard. He had been shot through the head.

As Soderstrom pulled out his claspknife and freed Rafe, the redhead whispered, "We scattered the cattle like you ordered and come directly on to the place. They was laid up waiting. When that guntipper Sears ordered us to stand fast, we made

303

a break instead. They dropped me off my horse and done for poor old Waco."

"No talk now. Can you handle a gun?"

"Give me a hand over to that front wall. There's a few choice knotholes there."

Soderstrom assisted him over to the wall and fetched McIver's rifle from the scabbard on his horse. It struck him that things were too quiet out in the yard, and he put his eye to a knothole. A man was coming stealthily toward the building at a half-crouching trot. Soderstrom nudged his rifle muzzle to the knothole and fired above the man's head, and watched his wild retreat.

This must have been only a hopeful maneuver to take him by surprise, for now that it had failed, they opened up a concerted fire at the thin stable walls. Soderstrom and Catron hugged the dirt floor while the rain of slugs through the wall above showered their prone bodies with rotted splinters.

Almost as suddenly, the shooting slacked off. Soderstrom eased onto his haunches and peered out the knothole, as a body of riders thundered into the yard. He heard one of the new-comers shout a question, and recognized the voice as Chad Buckmaster's. It came to him that the Wagontree force must have been split, with Sears heading up the group dispatched to Ladder, while the others, led by Chad, had headed for his recent trail camp. That would be the bunch that had passed him earlier and now, finding nothing, had come to join Sears' men at Wagontree. If there was one thing they had not needed, Soderstrom thought dourly, it was reinforcements.

Now there was a long respite in the shooting, apparently ordered by Chad so he could size things up. Soderstrom sank down against the wall, a gray hopelessness in him. Loftus Buckmaster wanted his blood, and with all pretense of law in Buckmaster County wiped out by Crashaw's death, what could stop him? What chance did Soderstrom and two wounded men stand against Buckmaster's whole crew? This lawless vacuum was a temporary thing: the U.S. marshal, and prob- ably the Army, would step in before long—but too late to do Krag Soderstrom any good. He could only wait in the hot breathing gloom of the stable, wait for a fighting death.

Soderstrom was a fatalist, therefore not a praying man. Still he came close to praying that, whatever happened now, Thera would not come to harm. He felt a weary sadness that he had never found the right words with Hannah, but then that had been his trouble in most things, and his own fault. He had always prized actions, not words. *So much to say, and now there is no time.*

He was, he realized, afraid as he had been only twice before in his life. Once when Hedda had lain dying, and he could do nothing. And again during those twenty agonizing seconds when he had believed that his daughter's body lay crushed beneath tons of dynamited rock. Now, for the first time, he was afraid for himself. And he thought of the old Vikings, the berserkers who in the lust of battle, shouting above their shields, would "run to meet their fates." *They were something, those old boys,* he thought; a smile straightened his lips at the thought of his kinship with those mad fighters, and the fear ran out of him.

He became aware that Rafe Catron, weakened by loss of blood, was speaking faintly. ". . . Better tell you while there's time. Don't fancy going out with it on my soul."

"I know," Soderstrom said stonily. "Don't waste your breath."

"Mac told you, huh? Jesus, I was sorry about that. We looked for him come daylight, before I rode in to tell the sheriff. Not finding him, I concluded he had laid up in cover somewheres and died there. So I carried through the plan." Rafe sighed. "Poor crazy old Waco. He shot Mac, you know, but I don't blame him none. It was my idea, so really my doing. Couldn't stop myself."

"What about Crashaw? You couldn't help that, either, eh?"

"Crashaw?"

"He went to arrest Chad Buckmaster on your lie, that you already know. Sears killed him. No—I think you and Waco done that."

"Lord God," Rafe whispered.

Soderstrom thought, *There is one thing I can do,* and raised himself to his knees, placing his mouth to the knothole. "Buckmaster! Chad Buckmaster!"

"Want to give up, Swede?"

"No. But listen. There are two wounded men with me, Catron and McIver. Let them be taken out before—"

A fusillade of blistering fire cut short his words. Again Soderstrom flattened along the dank floor as slugs hammered the old walls. He moved along the knotholed wall, firing at the gunflashes, then shifting along quickly before they had his position. He saw a dim form sprint across the yard in the slow dusk; he hesitated, but this was war. He sighted carefully in the bad light, then pulled the trigger. The man stumbled and went down, then started crawling back to cover, dragging a broken leg.

The shooting was too heavy, and Soderstrom dived back to the floor. Next, he thought, his sweating face against the dirt, somebody would think of firing the stable, and it would be all up. This was no good. *Give up, then. Maybe these two will be saved anyway—maybe they will not kill two wounded men in cold blood. Give up now.*

He was about to get his feet under him to call out, when, dimly above the shots, he heard a deep voice roaring an order. All at once the shooting died, and Soderstrom came to his knees and set his eye to the hole. He saw that a buckboard with two people had pulled into the yard, coming to a stop squarely between the Wagontree men and the stable.

"What's happening?" Rafe murmured.

"I don't know. But old Loftus himself has come. Now we'll see. . . ."

A faint creak of rusty hinged metal warned Soderstrom. He came pivoting around on his haunches. Someone had stealthily pushed open the door. It was easy to identify the whip-lean silhouette in the doorway as Richie Sears. The gunman's vision must have been momentarily baffled by the gloom, but the gritty sound of Soderstrom's heels as he turned gave a target. Gunflame erupted from the level of Sears' hip. The bullet hammered into the wall close by Soderstrom's head, and frantically he levered his rifle.

A shot roared almost in his ear. Rafe was on his knees, rifle in hands, his dim shape half bent in an agony of effort, as he shot once, twice, and then again, with a clean and deliberate care. Sears fired twice at Rafe's gunflashes, and then he swayed and shuddered. His last shot angled into the floor, and he caught at the doorframe as he plunged downward. His hand slipped, and he pitched down on his face. His outflung hand twitched in the fading light, and was motionless.

Soderstrom gathered his shaky legs under him and rose, walking over to Sears. A reek of powdersmoke filled the stable. He bent briefly, and straightened. "You got him good, Catron. You—"

He paused, catching an odd, broken note in Catron's breathing. By the time Soderstrom reached him, he had toppled over on his side. Swiftly Soderstrom struck a match and held it low where Rafe's denim jacket fell open from his shirt. Both of Sears' bullets had found the mark. Even as he saw this, the last of Rafe's breath sighed away.

Eighteen

Soderstrom groped to the doorway and stood there, cupping his hands to his mouth. "Buckmaster! You hear me? I want to give up. I'll throw out my gun. I ask only that you not hurt this boy with me. He's hurt bad enough."

There was momentary silence before Loftus Buckmaster rumbled back, "I hear you, Swenska. You can come out any time. Throw your gun away or keep it, makes no difference. Been all the shooting there's going to be. What was that racket in there just now?"

Surprise held Soderstrom mute for a moment, and then he called, "Rafe Catron. And your man Sears. They have killed each other, mister."

"That's a fair exchange," said old Loftus. "All right, come along out. Need any help with that wounded what's-his-name?"

"McIver. I'll carry him out."

Gently Soderstrom lifted the feverish boy and carried him from the stable to the house. He stepped into the lamplit parlor and halted, taking in the room with a glance. Thera was seated on the leather sofa, and seeing Hannah beside her, he felt a wash of surprise. A Wagontree tough was also present in the room, evidently stationed to watch the girls. Both of them had a pale and shaken look, but were well enough otherwise, he saw with an intense relief.

Thera came to her feet with a soft cry, and he sternly told her, as he carried McIver into his own room, that this was no time for nonsense. Thera steadied at once; she had the proper dressings laid out and ready by the bed, and she said quietly, "Keep those people out of here, Papa," and went to work.

Soderstrom returned to the parlor. Several more toughs had entered the room, and they all eyed him guardedly. "You wait here, mister," one of them said curtly, and Soderstrom, bone-weary again, slacked onto the vacated sofa. Hannah had left the house, and now from the yard he heard old Buckmaster say, "Lend me your shoulder, sister, will you? Chadwick, I want to see you inside. Naomi, too. The rest of you stay out here."

There were heavy slow steps on the porch. Loftus entered, his arm around Hannah's shoulders, and with considerable difficulty she supported him across the room to a battered armchair. Naomi Buckmaster followed them closely, a white, pinched expression on her face. Chad stepped inside, too, looking angry and baffled. The old man planted his cane firmly, trembling a little as he eased his great weight into the chair. Drops of sweat glistened on his furrowed face; he shut his pain-dulled eyes for a few seconds. When they opened again, they were as bright and sharp as a hawk's.

"Red," he said quietly.

A staid-faced puncher, older than the others, drawled, "Boss?"

"Give me your gun."

Soderstrom's muscles grew tense, his hands tightening around the rifle across his knees. One of the toughs murmured, "Mister, don't move about like that."

"Shut up, Macklin," old Loftus said flatly. "Red, I want your gun."

The middle-aged puncher palmed it out of his belt and, crossing the room, slipped it into Loftus' outheld hand. The old man painfully adjusted his thick, arthritic fingers around the grip and, slowly, thumbed back the hammer. He swung the muzzle till it was fixed squarely on the broad chest of his son.

"Now, Chadwick. I trust you now. You bat a winker and I'll blow you apart where you stand."

The color drained from Chad's wide face. He faintly lifted and settled one shoulder. "Pa, I hate to spoil a good joke, but ain't you putting a gun on the wrong man?"

"I wish to hell I was. Now, Red, you take his gun. Mind you don't get between us, and go slow about it."

Red stepped carefully behind Chad and lifted his pistol from its holster. Old Loftus flicked a flinty glance at his daughter-in-law. "Now, you say in front of these witnesses just what you told me. Don't leave out a word, you hear?"

Naomi's glance slid to Chad, and her eyes held a stark fright, Soderstrom saw. She started to talk, her voice low and thin. Loftus broke in growling, "Now, damn it, girl, you speak out so everyone can hear. Talk up!"

And one by one, as Naomi spoke, the gazes in the room turned on Chad Buckmaster. But Soderstrom watched the face of old Loftus and his hand that was rock-steady now, and he thought, *When she has finished, the old man will kill him.*

Chad's eyes were hot and brilliant; his fleshily handsome face told nothing. Suddenly he laughed with a shattering mockery, throwing back his head and letting the laughter spill from him.

All he intended was to throw everyone off guard; this was clear an instant later when he wheeled with a spring-muscled grace for the doorway two feet away. He plunged out the door as the gun in Loftus' fist roared, the bullet chewing splinters from the door casing.

As swiftly as Chad had moved, Soderstrom was on his feet diving across the room and out the door. As his heel touched the porch, he veered in a quarter-turn, in time for a glimpse of Chad's bulky form vanishing around the house.

Soderstrom vaulted across the porch and off it, skirting around the corner in pursuit. The dusk had deepened almost to full dark, and he hauled up, briefly losing Chad in the shadows. Then he caught the thud of running feet and followed the sound. All of it had happened so quickly that the men lounging back in the yard only now broke a stunned quiet in an aimless chorus of curses and questions.

Soderstrom did not pause again. He knew from Chad's line of flight that he was heading for a stand of cottonwood a short distance upcreek. A moment later he caught a wild crashing of brush as Chad flailed his way along the thicket-choked bank. Soderstrom plunged after him, and soon saw the dark ragged silhouette of the grove ahead.

He had nearly reached the trees when a horse's whinny lifted out of the darkness, then Chad's savage curse. A moment later came the crackling passage of a heavy body through the trees. Soderstrom hauled up with the thought that when Sears, in laying his trap earlier, had had his men hide their mounts, at least one man had concealed his horse in this grove, where Chad had stumbled on it.

Soderstrom gave a long sidelong step into a thicket, hugging its shadow just as the horse broke clear of the trees. The rider lay flat to the mane, urging the animal into a reckless dash back along the creekbank, as Soderstrom had known he would. For the upstream country was boxed for several miles by ridges that made it impassable by horseback; a mounted man on the run would choose the open flats to the south.

When the horse was almost abreast of him, Soderstrom sprang from cover, sweeping back his clubbed rifle. Chad jerked upright in his saddle with a hoarse and startled cry. The sound snarled off in a breath-torn grunt as Soderstrom swung his rifle in a full-armed arc that just cleared the horse's head: the barrel caught Chad in a smashing blow at an angle across his belly and chest and shoulder. Soderstrom felt the solid ache of impact through his body, as the weapon was nearly ripped from his grasp. The horse thundered on past him.

Chad held his saddle, reeling, for perhaps six more yards, and then he toppled sidelong, the horse bolting on through the brush. Chad's body hit the bank and plunged down it into the shallow water. He was still conscious, making sobbing, half-retching noises. Soderstrom lowered his rifle, wearily supposing that he had crushed several of Chad's ribs. He slogged down the bank toward the downed man, guided by the roiling sparkle of water where he was thrashing feebly.

When a couple of the men had carried Chad back to the house, the sight of his son's condition had a considerable dampening effect on old Loftus' murderous fury. That, and Hannah's remonstrations: all other things aside, it remained that Chad had shot his brother in self-defense. Could Loftus shoot his son in cold blood—his one remaining son? Hannah, knowing her father, stressed this last part with some emphasis; nothing would finally gall a man like Loftus more than dying without a male heir. She was right. The thought put a sober punctuation to the old man's pawing and bellowing.

When Chad's four broken ribs had been securely taped, Loftus ordered his men to lay him in the wagonbed. Then, slowly and painfully, he heaved his massive frame up onto the seat.

Naomi sat beside him, her head down. She had, in a final burst of courage, declared her intention of leaving Wagontree and moving to town. Loftus was plainly not concerned one way or the other.

Sears' body had been tied across his horse, and the other men, already mounted, flanked the wagon, waiting to move out, but Loftus motioned them to get going. He had something to say, and he peered testily at Soderstrom who stood on the porch against the outflowing parlor light. He said, "You ain't won the pot yet, Swenska."

Soderstrom shook his head. "I won all I need, mister. It's you who wants to own the earth. No man can do that, Buckmaster. It will outlast even you. I think that's the big difference between us. I have felt for the earth as a man feels maybe for his woman, or for his kids. But you, to you it is like a big spread of food, and you have got to swallow it all."

"The hell with you," Loftus said, but a weary flatness had overtaken the granite rumble. "All right. I can't take on you and the government both. The U.S. marshal will be on my back for Crashaw's killing, I suppose, even if it was Sears done it. I never wanted that, but I've taken on the federal boys over land and water rights in my day, and I don't mind taking 'em on again." He tilted his head toward the back of the wagon. "And I got to get this thing I sired back on his feet and try to get him a short sentence. He ain't much, but he's all there is to carry on. I expect the devil will grant me the time I need to straighten some things out."

"I'd say you got enough trouble to keep you busy for all the time you got left," Soderstrom observed. "It is ended, then? The fight?"

"Our fight is." Loftus' iron-eyed glance shuttled to Hannah, who was leaning in the doorway, her arms folded. "I don't know about the one with her. I asked her to come see me now and then. What do you say, sister?"

"My opinion of you hasn't changed," Hannah said calmly.

"All right."

"I think you're a hard-hearted, bullying old tyrant, and I intend to continue saying so. But I'll visit you on one condition. Your door has to be open to Mr. Soderstrom, too, if you can resist making ultimatums—"

"The hell you say! Why should I let this goddamn squarehead set one foot across my line?"

"Because I'm going to marry him."

Soderstrom turned his head to look at her. His mustache stirred to his faint smile, and he glanced back at Buckmaster.

"Well," old Loftus said at last, dourly, "leastways you ain't spiting me this time. Are you?"

"Not a bit of it," Hannah said gravely. "This time I'm picking a rough, tough, honest-to-God shoot-out-their-liver-and-lights man like my daddy because I knew it would please you."

Loftus glared at her bitterly, and took up his reins. "Well," he said, "I don't like him, but finally I got a mote of hope for your good sense."

He shook the reins and clucked the team into motion, and

wheeled away into the shallow darkness. Soderstrom looked at Hannah again, and discovered that he could not say anything. There was a strange fullness in his throat. She said lightly, "Shall we go inside?"

They found McIver awake, weak and colorless. Thera had pulled a chair close to his bedside, and he was holding her hand.

"Only think of it," he was saying exultantly. "A few months ago, the wound alone would probably have killed me. Now, after being wounded, lying for hours in the rain, no dressing of any sort—why, I may be on my feet by tomorrow."

"Do not be foolish," Thera said contentedly. "Please stop talking now, David, and go to sleep."

Soderstrom stood in the doorway. He coughed abruptly, and they looked at him. McIver flushed, but did not let go of Thera's hand. "Perhaps you'd tell me something of what's happened, sir. I'm not clear on a good deal."

Soderstrom talked briefly for everyone's benefit, and his words left a sobering effect on them. The bodies of two men they all knew well lay out in the stable. "I'm sorry," McIver murmured, "for both of them. Waco was strange, and you couldn't really become close to him—but I liked Rafe."

"So did I," Soderstrom said brusquely. "But he had a mistake to pay for, and he paid."

"That was too big a price," McIver said shortly, and his hand tightened around Thera's. He met the older man's eyes defiantly. "I imagine you'll care no more for some of my judgments than I do for many of yours, sir. But you may have to get used to them, and I won't apologize for them."

"That's the least of our troubles, sonny," Soderstrom said with a grim satisfaction. "It ain't me you have to make the grade with. It happens my daughter likes caring for helpless things like you are now. But you wait, boy. You got farther to go yet than you know."

Hannah said good-naturedly, "Oh, come on, leave them alone, can't you?" She took his arm, and they went to the kitchen. "Sit down and watch, and I'll prove I can make a good cup of coffee."

"It better be good. A Swede can tell." He sat down, watching her movements as she laid a fire and set out the coffee-grinder. And he said quietly, "Why did you change your mind?"

Her busy hands paused, and she turned slowly from the stove. "I didn't, really. I knew what I wanted the first time you asked, just as I do now."

"You didn't see what you wanted before?"

"Oh, a lot of it. A woman wants marriage and a nice home and children and a husband who is clean and upright and a good provider. But first she wants a man, and she wants all of him. That's what you were withholding from me. That's why you couldn't speak of love. That's why I asked for gentleness. You've been living with too many ghosts, Krag, and they'd all but smothered the man I needed. With the gentleness, anything is possible—without it, nothing. The second time you asked, I still wasn't sure of it. But now . . ."

He got to his feet and came slowly to her, watching her face. "I am a rough man. Don't look for too much of it."

"I won't," Hannah smiled. "Just enough for a lifetime."

ABOUT THE AUTHOR

T.V. Olsen was born in Rhinelander, Wisconsin. "My childhood was unremarkable except for an inordinate preoccupation with Zane Grey and Edgar Rice Burroughs." He had originally planned to be a comic-strip artist, but the stories he came up with proved far more interesting to him than any desire to illustrate them. Having read such accomplished Western authors as Les Savage Jr., Luke Short, and Elmore Leonard, he began writing his first Western novel while a junior in high school. He couldn't find a publisher for it until he rewrote it after graduating from college with a bachelor's degree from the University of Wisconsin at Stevens Point in 1955 and sent it to an agent. It was accepted by Ace Books and was published in 1956 as *Haven Of The Hunted.*

Olsen went on to become one of the most widely respected and widely read authors of Western fiction in the second half of the twentieth century. Even early works such as *High Lawless* and *Gunswift* are brilliantly plotted with involving characters and situations and a simple, powerfully evocative style. Olsen went on to write such important Western novels as *The Stalking Moon* and *Arrow In The Sun,* which were made into classic Western films as well, the former starring Gregory Peck and the latter under the title *Soldier Blue* starring Candice Bergen. His novels have been translated into numerous European languages, including French, Spanish, Italian, Swedish, Serbo-Croatian, and Czech.

The second edition of *Twentieth Century Western Writers* concluded that "with the right press Olsen could command the position currently enjoyed by the late Louis L'Amour as America's most popular and foremost author of traditional Western novels." His novel *The Golden Chance* won the Golden Spur Award from the Western Writers of America in 1993.

Suddenly and unexpectedly, death claimed him in his sleep on the afternoon of July 13, 1993. His work, however, will surely abide. Any Olsen novel is guaranteed to combine drama and memorable characters with an authentic background of historical fact and an accurate portrayal of Western terrain.